Praise for R.B. Egan

'Pace, action, intrigue, mystery, dark secrets, relatable characters and an intricately woven plot. I devoured it in one weekend. A fantastic debut!'
ANDREA MARA

'Engrossing, fast-paced and relentlessly tense – kicks off with a brilliant moral dilemma and never lets up.'
T.M. LOGAN

'I raced through all the unexpected twists and turns, right through to the riveting ending. This is a great read that hits the spot . . . highly recommended!'
K.L. SLATER

'R.B. Egan is an exciting new voice in Irish crime fiction . . . With twist after twist that keeps you turning the pages. Brilliant, twisty fun!'
EDEL COFFEY

'An intense and twisting mystery that ——— at every turn. Thrilling stuff!'
C.M. EWAN

'A tense, taut, pacy r
ANE CORRY

'A suburban nightma ——— twists.'
CATHERINE KIRWAN

'Immediately hooks its readers into a merciless moral decision. Brilliantly paced with high stakes and tension ramping with every turn of the page – I flew through it.'
L.V. MATTHEWS

'Thrilling read . . . I absolutely tore through this book. You won't see the twist coming!'
LEAH PITT

'Terrifyingly tense, a thriller to read in one sitting . . . the story is peppered with breathtaking twists and white-knuckle moments. I didn't come up for air.'
HEATHER CRITCHLOW

Copyright © Mark Nixon Studio

Dubliner R.B. Egan started out as an actor. He worked in London in theatre, film and television before moving to Tanzania where he developed a safari hotel and tourism business with his wife. Now based in Dublin with his family, he writes fiction.

For Isolde and Laragh, and all the joy you bring

I

CATHY

Blood. It bubbles from his nose. Thick, dark and steaming in the night air. I want to scream. To hide. But I can't take my eyes from his face. Now the blood spouts from his ear, a long arc splashing across the grass.

Christ. How did it come to this?

I look at the shovel. It's red and dripping. This was not how it was supposed to end. But it isn't over. Before night turns to day there will be more blood.

Lots more blood.

2

Lunch break from rehearsals. I release a tortured groan as I slip away. Shakespeare isn't my bag, not even close, but I'm hanging in there, giving it my best. Right now my career depends on it. I see Justin's on the phone. Head-turning, fast-talking, piss-taker that is my boyfriend. His dry laugh rattles hard down the line.

'How long did you say the director made you practise the speech?'

'Nearly two hours.' I grit my teeth as I say the words.

'All alone in the corridor, away from the rehearsal space?'

'Yes.' My reply hisses out. 'Because I forgot two lines in our opening scene this morning and Andy said top professional productions deserve better.' I exhale, watching the knuckles bulge on my clenched fist. 'The way he said it you'd think I hadn't been working professionally the past ten years.'

'Jayz, that *is* a bit grim, Cath. Maybe you should cut and run?'

I close my eyes, imagining it. Our director Andy's livid beetroot face getting the news. 'You know I can't. It's the first work I've got in ages, a lifeline, Justin.'

'A shitty, crappy one, Cath?'

I blow out my cheeks. 'God, don't I know.' For a second I stop, my mind casting back to this time last year and how smoothly everything was running, getting my break in TV, bagging a slew of voice-overs and even squeezing in a cinema commercial. It had all looked so rosy. 'You're the girl next door,' my agent Melissa had cheered gleefully, signing me up while complimenting me on my average height and build. 'You've got that perfect sweet-but-familiar face with emeralds for eyes and mid-length brown hair that we can style six different ways as and when we need to.' Unfortunately, the need to change it from straight and tapping gently off my collar bone hadn't materialised as planned. 'I'm skint, Justin. I can't stomach another three months temping just to get by again. I have to get my career back on track. Whatever it takes.' Sometimes I don't think my boyfriend fully understands what it means to have no family to fall back on, and no property to call your own. How it can be only you and your career, so when it's floundering, the sky feels so close it could collapse on your head.

'Oh dear,' he offers pitifully. 'Let's talk about something else. How 'bout that course you took last month. Weren't you mad keen on that?'

'I was. The woman in the employment office said it would help me find my strong points, so I could then get extra skills for when I was out of work. Then I wouldn't be stuck doing min wage stuff in between my acting jobs.'

There's a snort. 'Cath, you make me laugh.'

I know I do. I also know it's probably why we're still together. 'Why?'

Justin laughs some more. My shoulders lift as I picture his handsome face with his sharp cheekbones and wavy hair, and to my annoyance I find I'm laughing too. 'Well didn't you say that course found that your judgement of character was one of your best points?'

'I wasn't going to put it quite like that, but I guess, yeah.' It sounds self-important when Justin says it but it's not inaccurate. I wait for his reply. There's none. Just hoarse rasping. 'Why are *you* laughing?'

'I'm just remembering the story about the time you picked that guy to go to your Debs?'

'Which guy?'

'You know, the quiet bloke who turned out to like boys more than girls.'

'So?'

The Landlord

'Then that time, when we were in Italy getting that ferry and you insisted we get those discount tickets from the guy who legged it with our cash.'

I really enjoyed that trip but that always seems to be the only bit Justin ever recalls. 'Yes, I haven't forgotten.' I feel the words tighten inside my throat.

'And then ...'

I pre-empt him. We've done this before. 'I know, the flatmate, right?' Justin's laughter peels out of the phone. 'Not exactly *that* funny, Justin?'

'Oh, come on, Cath, it was you who told me the story. You have to admit it *was* funny.'

Sometimes when I thought about it, maybe it was. But I've never claimed to be some sort of mastermind, I'm just explaining what the course assessment gave me. And now I'm annoyed, because I was hoping this course, which I happened to really like, would give me something that would help me. Because it's like the play has opened up so many invisible holes inside me, I don't even know where to begin to put it right.

'I'm a bit brassed off at the minute,' I say, my voice low and beaten.

'The play, right?' Justin's kind voice whispers down the line, the one that always makes me never want to hang up.

'Yeah. That and ... I don't know ...'

'You'll be alright.'

'How's your mum?' I ask, changing the subject. Justin should have something to tell me about Angela since he's been shacked up in her house the past three days instead of our apartment. Hauling over his clothes to wash, his music system to tune up, and just about everything else in between. All for seventy-two hours of getaway time.

'Oh, same old.' Justin doesn't like his mum, which is why I'm surprised he's been gone so long. 'Where there's life there's hope, Cath.'

The sadness in his voice tugs at my heart and suddenly I feel the need to see him. To patch him up. 'Listen,' I say, thinking of how I might surprise him, 'what are you doing later?'

'A bit of mixing on my decks, nothing too hectic. Why?'

'Come over for eight. And make sure you're hungry.'

He hesitates for a second. 'Sure.' His voice is louder now, cocky again. Justin once more. 'I was planning to swing over anyway. See my girl in the flesh. Maybe scantily clad?'

'Just bring a bottle of wine.' A grin rises to my lips and spreads across my face. 'Red and posh.' From the corner of my eye I see Malia winking at me as the other actors start shuffling back into rehearsals. 'Just the two of us. It'll be nice. I promise.'

Waiting alone in the apartment, I scroll through the pictures on my phone. There's one of Babs, from the music festival last summer. She's jumping around in a skimpy white dress, her clear skin and bright eyes radiating health and beauty. The next one is me and Justin. Justin hugs me around the shoulders with both arms, white teeth gleaming, the sun bouncing off his Armani shades underneath a sweep of carefully tousled hair. I'm smiling too, just a lot less certainly.

The time has just gone past half eight which makes him late. I open my banking app and see I've got barely enough left to cover next month's rent and no more. The food, candles and wine have eaten all the rest but I cling to the hope that it's worth it. I've been meaning to sit down with Justin for so long, so we can talk about where we're going. Our relationship was never the most passionate, more of a pragmatic drifting together when I moved from the sofa to Justin's bed after his other flatmate Gary moved on, graduating from non-paying couch-surfer to fully paid-up co-signatory on the lease. But now we're suddenly into year three and I'm getting that awkward feeling like we need to start talking about things instead of just talking.

Just as I'm having this thought I hear a click. The door opens and Justin enters the apartment. 'Hey,' he says, his slim athletic

The Landlord

frame turning away from me momentarily as he closes the door softly behind him. When he faces me again I look at his hands. I'm expecting to see a bottle. Maybe even flowers. But he's just holding a big empty bag. One of the long sports ones tennis players often keep for their rackets and shoes. But Justin doesn't play any sports.

'Hey,' I reply, my voice shaky all of a sudden. I note his clothes. Justin rarely overdresses but tonight he's wearing scratched shoes and grey pants with a stain on one leg. His T-shirt has sweat patches.

'What's this?' He stares at the candles like they're gargoyles.

'A surprise.' The words come out like a question.

He shakes his head. 'Oh, Cath.'

Tiny hairs on the back of my neck are standing up and I hear the air sifting through my nose. 'What?'

'Us.' His voice is pitiful though his face betrays no emotion.

I swallow, reaching for the wine glass in front of me, 'What about us?'

3

'You alright Cathy?' I look up and see Malia, her gentle face with its silken sheen of smooth black skin. She's the prettiest Cordelia I've ever seen. A great actress, and a great ally in this snake pit production of *King Lear*. We've all just come out to break from rehearsals. The director, AA, being short for Awkward Andy, walks past me giving me a look that tells me he's not impressed with my morning's work.

'Yeah. Just got to make a call here,' I say, working hard to keep my voice steady.

'I'm scooting up to grab a coffee at the corner. Want one?'

I throw her a weak smile. 'I'm OK, honestly. I'll follow you soon as I'm done. But thanks for offering.'

With a gentle pat on my elbow, she leaves. We don't get long on break and the timekeeping is strict so I use it to call Babs.

She answers after one ring. 'Cathy, he is so, *so* out of order. What an absolute *twat*.' Babs's outrage is fever pitch. 'He really said that?'

'Yeah. 'We're done, Cath. And that was that. He even had his bag with him to collect everything so he could go back to his mum's place.'

'But can't you just find somebody else to share it?'

'No. He told the landlord we're vacating and he's got other people coming to take it in two days.'

'Jesus.' Babs vents, not hiding her outrage. 'You could fight it. Refuse to leave. You'd be within your rights.'

'The landlord has been good to us, Babs. I'd have to start a case and everything. It wouldn't feel right.' I try to sound upbeat. I have to cope with this and move on. What else can I do? But thoughts of how bad the rental market is have been flitting through my mind all morning. Everybody knows it's next to impossible to get something at short notice and there's no chance of getting anything affordable. It seems almost ridiculous that a day ago my biggest problems were my relationship with Justin and my part in the faltering production of *King Lear*.

Babs groans softly. 'Oh, God, Cathy.' I inhale, feeling my stomach lurch as I rub a knuckle against my right eye which is forming an unwanted tear. Then Babs comes back. 'Wait!' Her tone is surprisingly upbeat. 'I think I remember hearing about a place. It might have been Heather's friend Joan who mentioned it. She's the professor at Heather's university.'

'Really? Where?'

'Look, I'm not sure. I better check it out because I don't want to be telling you something that turns out to be wrong. Give me an hour and I'll call you back. Deal?'

'Sure.'

Malia links her arm in mine as we shuffle back in. 'Everything OK?'

'Sort of. Not really.' I shrug, glad we don't have time to get into it.

Soon as rehearsals wrap, I rush out and down the street. It's early evening and I'm aware that my time to find the miracle solution to my accommodation crisis is frittering away with each lost second. I switch my phone on as I make my way to the bus stop and find another message from Babs.

Call me. Now!

Heart pounding, I tap in her number and ring.

'Cathy, you are not going to believe it,' she says, her voice high and excited.

'What?' I press two hands together as if in prayer. I need good news. Too desperately.

'Turns out I was right. Joan texted me the guy's number and address. Seems she knows a nurse called Linda – and her son knows his son or something like that, but the thing is, he's expecting you. It's a room in his house.'

'Oh?' I wasn't really expecting a room in a shared house but I don't want to say that.

Babs continues almost breathless. 'I gave the landlord a call, explained who I was, mentioned you, and asked is it available.'

'And what did he say?' I frown, a weird mix of gratitude and worry pooling in my stomach.

'He said he just had a call about it earlier but is waiting for the woman to get back. But then he said if you want to go and look right now, you're very welcome.'

'No way!'

'Yes way.'

'Where?'

'This is the best bit, Cathy. Belleview Road and he said the rent isn't much.'

I love Belleview Road. It's one of my favourite streets. A street where my father designed a handful of renovations back when I was a child, even taking me to see a few so I could marvel at the architecture. The memories of my dad come flooding back, how he used to be so kind to me and my brother Desmond when we were small. 'Follow your dreams, kids,' he'd urge, hugging us with his big arms, 'that's all that matters in this world.' Then his sudden departure from our lives when he died of a heart attack. I had thought I'd be inured to grief after that but I was wrong; when mum died years later and then Desmond, also in an accident shortly after, it was like my world shattered again each time. Taking a moment, I bury down the memories of my lost family and refocus on the brilliant news my good friend is telling me. 'Get lost.'

'Serious.'

'Shit.' Babs knows I love Belleview Road. The wide streets and Georgian facades with their sash windows and climbing ivy, the granite steps and brightly painted doors. 'So now what?' I ask, the words tripping excitedly out of my mouth.

'Hurry over. I've already told him to expect you.'

The Landlord

The bus is delayed so I don't waste precious time but order an Uber. I get the cab driver to drop me off a few doors down so I can admire some of the houses on the way to number 762. The light breeze is balmy and smells of flowers. Birds flit in and out of the trees which are a mix of oaks and sycamores. Everywhere I look, people of all stripes mill about in soft cottons and pastel summer colours. The entrance to the park is close by and I can spot the people inside licking ice pops, pushing strollers, swapping kisses, working up a sweat. A hip-looking couple zip by on matching electric scooters as a bare-chested man glides up the opposite side of the street on a motorised skateboard, weaving between cars. I can't get enough of it. Picking up my pace, I hurry ahead, remembering not to dawdle. Babs did warn me that another woman had called about the place already.

Seconds later, standing outside number 762, blowing the hair off my sticky forehead, I reach for the brass knocker when the heavy wooden door opens inwards.

4

There's an unusually tall and strikingly handsome man in the doorway. He's what my dad would have called bull-shouldered. I reckon him to be somewhere north of forty but he looks fit and could easily pass for younger. His hair is thick and dark, his skin smooth and fair, his jaw strong. He's very still. And just a little unsettling. I wipe the sweat off my brow when he speaks.

'Hi.' The outlines of a smile appear at the corner of his lips. He looks me up and down, casually assessing me. I clasp my hands behind my back, a strange urge to step back and away from this man's gaze fighting another impulse to move towards him, as if pulled by an unseen magnet. 'Cathy?' he asks in a husky bass voice.

'Yes.'

'Wonderful.' He turns, stretching a long arm towards the hall. 'You're right on time. I was almost on my way out but it's great I've caught you. Please.' Seeing me hesitate he shoots a playful glance inside.

'Oh, right, thanks.' I step inside and linger a little stiffly next to him, not sure whether to go into the front room or remain in the corridor.

'Your friend Babs was singing your praises earlier.' He closes the heavy door and turns back to face me.

'She was?' Standing there in the huge Georgian hallway I try to figure out where to look. My gaze rests on his mouth when he steps forward down the hall, tapping the big white door to the front room with a knuckle.

'Have a look around, Cathy.' Casually he steers us through the living room and across to the adjoining dining room. I note the high ceilings with ornate cornices, the double fireplace, the tall sash windows, heritage rugs, antique dressers and mahogany dining chairs. We circle back to the front room and he points to a brown leather settee as he sits on another. 'Take a seat and we'll chat.'

I squash down and the smell of ancient leather whooshes up around us, reminding me of the old sofas my mother used to cherish, picking them up at auction houses so she could painstakingly restore them and sell them on again.

'So, I explained to Babs,' he continues, 'the whole plan is pretty last minute really. I live here on my own with my son, Jamie, but he surprised me by moving to Aberdeen earlier than expected. He's going to uni there in September. Now suddenly this place feels empty – so I got the slightly madcap idea to share it with somebody.'

'Right.' I grip my knees and nod, wishing the desperation would stop oozing from my pores, praying it isn't as blatant as it feels.

'I suppose strictly speaking it's not really a rental.' He stops, his cheeks dimpling. 'I mean, I'm not too bothered about the money side of things. I guess with my architecture work I'm comfortable enough without really needing that to be honest.' For a second he looks embarrassed. 'I'd just like to have somebody around, if that makes any sense?'

'Of course.' I can't really get my head around wanting to share a giant Georgian pile this big without the pressure of paying the bills but I want to try. A lost look flickers across his face when he stares at me, but he breaks eye contact suddenly to look out through the window in the adjoining room. I follow his glance to the back garden beyond, momentarily mystified by his pained expression. In a second, his frown vanishes and his smile returns.

'That makes sense,' I offer gently, trying to reignite the conversation.

'So, all in, there's four bedrooms. Three up on the top floor with two to the front and one to the back' he continues, almost as if he hasn't heard me. 'Jamie's stuff is in one, and I keep that for him. I use the last room at the back on the split level landing but either of the other two are completely free for you to choose from.'

I nod and the soft leather seat squeaks when I adjust my position. The way he's talking it sounds like he's simply giving me the place. A nervous jolt of excitement shoots through my body. 'OK.'

'So we have ground floor, split level and top,' he continues, pointing to the high ceiling. There's a tiny crack in the plaster and I see it meets the ornate coving around the central lampshade which hangs above us. His gaze switches to the floor and he taps it with his foot. 'Then underneath we've got the basement. It's laid out as flats so there is no route down there except through the door out front – but I leave a key on a hook in the hall, just in case there's an emergency or anything. There's nobody using them for now, since I need to do a bit of a job on them. Well, probably a lot of work really.'

He waits and I cross my legs, working hard to think of an intelligent question, the kind a desirable tenant might pose. 'Is there anybody else looking?' I finally say.

He nods. 'There was a lady who called me earlier.' I sink into the sofa, my hope faltering as his dark eyes hold mine. 'But we've yet to arrange her visit.'

Breathing again, I sit back up.

'Do you like it?'

'Yes. You have a beautiful house, erm ...?' I clear my throat, stalling.

'Ian. Ian Fitzsimmons.'

'Ian Fitzsimmons,' I repeat.

His rugged features blossom into a broad smile. 'Just Ian is fine, Cathy.' A strange tingle of pleasure laced with surprise slithers through me because the way he says my name is like we've known each other for years. 'Were you hoping to move in straight away?' I'm about to say no when I suddenly rethink. I need a place.

The Landlord

Desperately, right now, without delay. And I don't have the luxury of looking gift horses in the mouth, as my mum used to tell us growing up.

'I guess?'

'Crap.' He slaps his knee. 'I'm tied up tonight. I've committed to dinner with a friend who's over visiting so I won't be able to help.'

'That's OK. You'll need to think about it anyway.' Silently, I try to make sense of how quickly things are moving. He's not asked for references from work or my old landlord. Or even a deposit. It's strange and yet I know already there's another woman waiting to come and view if I back away. Surely she'll take it without even blinking? Ian's openness and generosity are disarming and I know if I decline, the chances are I'll end up sharing a house with a bunch of strangers but it won't be half as nice as this one.

The next second, he's off the couch and on his feet. 'Well, look, Cathy. If you're happy, I'm happy. Why not just go for it?' He plonks a set of keys on the table. 'Now, I must apologise but I've got to dash. I won't be back till late. Kitchen's all yours and anything edible you can find in there just be my guest.' He puts his hand on his heart playfully. 'And forgive me because I didn't get the cleaning done yet today.'

I get up and follow him into the hall where he plucks a Panama hat with a navy ribbon from the coat stand.

'This is exciting,' he says, spinning round and putting his hat on. For the first time I notice his clothes. A blue linen suit, a white cotton shirt, casual shoes. It's a good look.

Opening the front door, he steps out onto the imposing granite steps and surveys the street beneath us. In the space of five minutes, it's like we've swapped roles. I hold the hefty door ajar as he lets it go, lost for words at this largesse.

'Mr Fitzsimmons,' I say, unable to contain the question that's been screaming inside my mind since he dropped the keys on the table. 'This feels a little sudden. Are you certain you're happy with me coming to stay with you? I mean, I'm a stranger, with no references, and you know nothing about me.'

He listens, hands clasped in front of him loosely, as he looks at the ground. Then he tips his chin up, glancing at me side-on. 'True. Only just remember, Cathy, you don't know anything about me either.' I hold the edge of the huge door as he adjusts his shirt cuffs, pulling them clear of his jacket sleeves. 'I'm happy to take a chance if you are.' A beaming smile lights up his face. 'And anyway, your friend Babs sounded way too sweet to be feeding me tales.'

He walks down two steps and I think he's gone when he suddenly stops and turns. 'Oh, listen, Cathy, almost forgot to mention. The only way in to the garden is through the basement and the keys are hanging there by the front door like I mentioned, but please, I have to ask you to avoid going in there. It's all very overgrown and I need to get it sorted. I prefer to keep it off limits until I have it in order. Is that OK?'

'Certainly.'

'Lovely.' He tips his hat. Underneath its brim, he regards me hungrily. 'I look forward to seeing you again soon and if there's anything at all you have my number. We'll have a proper talk soon as we're both free and I'm really hoping it works out for you. Or for *us*, I should say.'

Babs calls up an old ex-boyfriend called Dave to help me out with his van and two hours later I'm back in Belleview Road with all my hastily boxed possessions. I waste no time and get busy unpacking and before too long I've got it all out of the way. The back bedroom I've taken is vast so the space to fit everything is more than enough. When I'm done, I sit down on the bed, take a moment to breathe and walk down into the living room.

The long summer day has finally ended and the city outside the front sash window looks pretty in the fading twilight. A quietness has descended on the street and it seems almost empty when I notice a lone figure lingering on the corner. He's on the opposite

The Landlord

side of the street, a distance away, but he seems to be looking over. It's almost dark so he's little more than a spectre. Abruptly he turns and disappears into the shadows. Gone like he was never even there.

Realising I'm holding my breath I let it out. I step back, a strange tension in my legs as I move, but I remind myself it's the middle of the city and a main street, so I shouldn't be alarmed at people hanging about on corners late at night. Stepping forward again, I pull the curtains. Retreating from the living room, I move to the hall and start up the huge wide staircase to my new bedroom, the only sound in the old house the creep of my feet on the thick wool carpet beneath them.

I yawn when I climb into bed, my body a weird mix of nervous energy and total exhaustion. The mattress feels feather soft beneath my body, which now craves rest so I can be ready for rehearsals tomorrow. Switching off the light, I pull the duvet tight and snuggle up when my phone rings. With a groan I reach for it, knowing it will keep going all night if I don't mute it. I squint and see it's Justin.

My teeth grit as my thumb hovers above the cancel icon. Perhaps I could simply cut the call and send him a message with a picture of my new accommodation, followed by a picture of my two fingers? I know it's what he deserves. This disappointing boyfriend. Or ex-boyfriend I silently correct myself as I give in and pick up.

'Cathy?' he says, his voice unusually serious.

'What?'

'Where the fuck are you?'

Wide-eyed, I prop myself onto my elbow. '*Excuse* me?'

'Tell me you're not staying at 762 Belleview Road?'

'What's it to you where I'm staying?'

'Look, I'm not even going to get into it right now because it's far too late,' he snaps loudly. 'Just lock the fucking door, put your head down, and get out bright and early. I'll explain tomorrow.'

I push myself up off the bed, as blood flushes my cheeks. Before I can reply the line goes dead. I slam the phone down on the mattress but snatch it back up seconds later so I can call him back. But it goes straight to message and I hang up.

With nervous fingers I power the phone down, shivering at the sudden draught that has entered the room. Slowly I walk to the bedroom door and lock it, then retreat to the warmth of the bed and get under the heavy covers.

Justin's words keep coming back to me, replaying over and over. '*Lock the fucking door, put your head down, and get out bright and early.*' I decide not to turn off the light but bunch the covers around me and shut my eyes tight, furious at the tension which now grips my body, alarmed at the fear one stupid phone call from my ex can still hold over me. But why did he say that and what could it mean?

5

Rehearsals are a bit better today. Just a bit. Last night I hardly slept. Whenever I'd think I'd nodded off, I'd find myself waking up, bristling with an urge to call up Justin. My teeth grind as I realise he's invaded my thoughts again; if it wasn't enough for him to shaft me on the flat we'd been sharing for the past two and a half years, dump me over a candlelit dinner I had personally cooked, he has to add insult to injury by scaring the shit out of me with some weird message about evacuating my new-found accommodation. I know he doesn't warrant another thought and seethe that I can't get him out of my head.

I do my best to focus but I'm struggling. I'm still preoccupied and just treading water, acting badly through each stilted scene. Nobody else says anything, and even AA manages to desist from commenting, but I can feel a gentle undercurrent of curiosity. What the hell is *wrong* with Cathy Quinn? She's either stiff as a board or lost at sea, trying to make something of the character of the evil sister Goneril. I plough on until we're finally released once again into the summer evening. Then I bolt straight to the Waterside pub where Heather and Babs are waiting, drinks in hand. Fair-skinned, slim and effortlessly pretty, Heather looks smart in a white shirt and bright blue suit jacket. Next to her, Babs's honeyed skin and shapely figure radiates health and vitality in a light peach summer blouse.

My black T-shirt sticks to my back and my heavy denims cling to my legs as I take my place next to them. I'm not sitting five minutes when I notice half my bottle of beer is gone. 'What a prick,' Heather says with a frown after listening to my story.

'Capital P on that one,' Babs agrees, clinking my bottle. I let out a dejected sigh and rub the sweat off my brow.

Heather looks rested and calm after her weekend in Paris. She adjusts her specs and smooths her fringe of black hair with two fingers, a thing she often does when trying to figure out complex questions. 'OK, so first Justin does a premeditated runner on you from your apartment. Then he drops the break-up bomb, and follows it by swearing at you to get you out of your new place?' She looks across to Babs, as if waiting to be told it's a joke.

'That's it,' I say, relieved but also devastated in equal parts. 'I mean, I think it's been heading that way for a long time but we hadn't really got into it.'

'Surely he could have flipping talked to you about it?' Babs replies, her chestnut brown eyes showing their horror. 'I mean conversation isn't that difficult for men, is it?'

Heather taps her chin. 'For a lot, sadly, it is.' As a lecturer in psychology, I know Heather is speaking from professional experience.

'He's still an arse.' Babs makes a face and even I manage to join in the laughter.

When it subsides, I lean back in my seat. 'I so badly want to blank Justin and simply forget about him but I can't until I understand what his message was about.'

Heather gives me a concerned look. 'Have you tried calling him?'

'Three times. Midmorning, lunch time and on my way over here.'

'The asshole's got his phone off now?' Babs puffs out her chest, her ample bust making her look even more seductive than usual. Two men sneak a glance at her from a far-off table.

'Looks like it.'

'You could go to his mum's,' Heather suggests.

'Thought about it ... but ...' I trail off. I like Justin's mum, Angela. She's funny and kind just like my mum Jean used to be, but I'm not ready to talk to her, especially about Justin. 'I don't have the appetite for it tonight.'

'Don't worry.' Babs pats my arm, teasing a long lock of golden highlighted hair behind her ear. 'It's probably a classic bloke thing. Justin thinks he's checkmated you and you land a swish pad the next day, right off your own bat. He's probably just trying to get back at you by scaring you with this lock the door, get out now crap.' She glances over to Heather.

'Yes, Babs is probably right.' She nods.

'So, tell us about this Ian fellow then?' Babs swirls the wine in her glass as her eyes widen. I know she's been waiting to ask. 'What's he like? It's all a bit *mysterious*.'

'Well …' I perk up, relieved to be off the subject of Justin and onto something far more uplifting, '… he's pretty … drop dead fucking *gorgeous*!' They both laugh.

'Go on,' Babs urges.

'Broad, rugged, probably late forties. Very intense, though softly spoken, and very polite. A bit old-school with his manners but …'

'Yes?'

I take a second, trying to think of the best way to describe my new landlord. 'Charming.'

'Interesting,' Babs coos. Heather cocks her head and Babs makes a circle with her lips.

'And weirdly generous. Because it seems like he doesn't even care about how much I pay him for rent.'

Heather's eyebrows raise.

'Not that I'm taking advantage. I'll suggest what I was paying in our last place.'

'Nothing odd about him?' Heather then asks.

I look off towards the busy street, thinking for a second before replying, 'Not immediately, though I get the feeling he's not just your regular guy. He comes across as quite individual, but let's face it, I've only just met him the once.' As I say this, I recall one of the last things he said to me. 'He did say something about avoiding the basement and was quite specific about not going into the back garden.' The girls look at each other, puzzled expressions evident. 'It's wild and overgrown, and the basement needs a refurb apparently.'

Heather taps me on the wrist. 'Put Justin out of your mind. We don't know what he's playing at. I'll get on to Linda and try and get a little bit more info about Ian. If there's anything unusual at all give me or Babs a call. Yeah?'

'Yeah.' I give the girls a hug and let them go. Then I make my way back to what I still can't quite believe is my new home.

It's a beautiful evening. Warm, balmy, busy. It's Dublin at its loveliest and liveliest. Everybody on the move. Smiles. Sunshine. Acres of pink and tanning skin on display. Cold drinks and picnics in the park. I'd love to ring the girls up and go straight back to the pub but know I can't because I have lines to learn.

I'm making my way back when I suddenly remember the man I saw at the corner in the darkness last night. A shiver runs down my spine as I recall catching sight of him, if it was a man that is, because I couldn't really tell for sure. I chase the thought away but it slithers back unwanted and I find my senses heightening like a sort of animal instinct. Suddenly I'm looking round and checking each time I turn a corner and I know it's over the top but I can't seem to help myself.

I don't see anybody, yet at the same time I get the sense that somebody might be following me. It's paranoia but I still can't shake it. I shrug as I stop before the front gate. I'm about to open it when a hand lands on my shoulder.

'Shit!' The word gasps from my mouth as I turn. Justin stands behind me, a smug smile on his face. 'Fuck's *sake*, Justin. You frightened the life out of me.'

He grins as I shove him away. 'Where the *hell* did you appear from and what do you want?'

'Calm down, Cath,' he replies softly. 'I'm sorry. I shouldn't have had a go at you last night. It was out of order.'

The Landlord

I groan. 'Yes, it was. Your whole scheming, flipping escape and evacuation to your mum's house is out of order too.'

He sighs, nodding – Justin's way of silently acknowledging his fault. It's as close as he usually ever gets. 'I know I've been stupid about this, Cath, and I went about it all wrong. I'm kind of shit at the whole taking a break thing.'

I pause, remembering his late-night message followed by him switching off his phone, 'Justin, what do you want? And how did you even know I had moved here?'

He holds out his phone and I see Snapchat Map with my avatar on it. 'You've got your location on', he says innocently.

I huff, annoyed with myself that I had forgotten to hide this from him and making mental note to do it later. 'Well, why were you telling me to lock my door and get out of this house?'

He steps back warily, glancing about. 'I don't want to freak you out. But I don't think this place is a good option for you. That's all.'

'Why?'

'Come with me.' He drops his voice almost to a hush. 'We'll grab a beer and I can explain a bit. It's better than standing here outside this gate.' I open it and walk inside, expecting him to follow but he doesn't. Instead he stalls. In the distance I see Ian approaching.

Justin frowns when he spots him too, instantly releasing the gate. 'I've got to go,' he announces, his body jerking away. 'I don't want to interfere, Cath, but I *really* want to talk with you.' I'm about to reply when he steps back. 'Check your messages in the morning, OK? I'll be in touch.' The words trail behind him as he hurries down the street.

I walk down the long footpath next to the dividing hedge, up towards the bright red door. Moments later Ian appears, nimbly making his way up the steps and extending a wine bottle to me as we both stand on the raised granite platform outside the front door. 'Something cool for these warm summer nights,' he says, handing it to me with a broad smile.

I take the bottle, feeling its cold chill inside my fingers. 'Sorry, I'd love to but I've got a backlog of lines to learn tonight so I won't.'

'Lines?' Ian stares at me in surprise. 'You're an actress?'

'Yeah.' I get a tiny knot in my gut as I think about rehearsals and the tension with Andy and the cast. From the get-go, I had always told my agent I didn't do period drama because I was no good at it and it wasn't for me. My ability was in contemporary drama and screen acting, an opinion and ambition she agreed with without so much as blinking an eye when she poached me from another agency three years back. And yet here I am, clinging to this production with my fingernails like I'm grabbing on to a life raft.

'Sounds like fun?'

'For the most part.'

Smiling, he stands beside me and we both peer down at the bustling street. 'Somebody drop by?'

I flinch, not wanting to mention Justin, not even clear what my relationship is to him anymore. 'No. Just somebody selling stuff door to door. Solar equipment. I told him the owner wasn't in.' I curse myself for lying but know it's too late to take it back.

He looks in the direction where Justin disappeared and laughs. 'Good move, those door-to-door guys can be hard to shake.' I'm expecting him to go inside but he drops back down a step. 'This is really bad of me,' he says, his voice soft and contrite, 'but I've been called away again to catch up with an old friend. He only buzzed me as I was on the way home with that for you.' He points to the bottle. 'I'd invite you to join us but if you're learning lines, I'll not tempt you.'

'Probably for the best.' I tap the chilled glass, resisting the urge to suggest I go with him.

Ian looks up at the sky. 'Sleep OK last night?'

I hesitate, trying to imagine how he'd react if I told him the truth. But I won't do that because I'd sound ungrateful and I still don't know what Justin is playing at. 'Yes.'

'Great. Well, soon as our timetables allow, I'll make us both dinner and we can sit down and chat like civilised people. In the meantime, make yourself at home, Cathy.'

I skip dinner and spend the rest of the evening learning my scenes for tomorrow. Before long I begin to tire. Dragging myself to my feet, I haul myself clear of the couch and trudge up the huge wooden staircase to my new bedroom. Once I'm in bed, I drop off instantly and fall into a deep sleep but it doesn't last.

An agonised shriek tears through the darkness, reverberating off the walls of the room. I startle, bolting upright in the bed, hands clutching empty space where normally Justin's body might be. My mouth is dry as I fumble for the switch by the bedside table when the noise happens again. Piercing and shrill, I detect it's coming from the garden.

I clamber out of bed, my heart thumping as I hurry to the window. Drawing aside the curtains, I peer out tentatively. But all I see is darkness. Nothing moves. The sound doesn't return. Cold air seeps through the window pane, raising goose pimples on my arms. Barefoot and trembling, I wait, but there isn't anything more. Just an ink-black gloom and a draught, so I hurry back to bed.

Lying there, I scrunch the quilt between my fingers and hug it tight. I want to think I imagined it, but the scream was real. Sharp with pain, eerie. Justin comes back into my mind and a ripple of fear washes through me. Sitting up, I drop my feet to the ground and slip quietly to the bedroom door, locking it fast, then double-checking it to make sure.

There's something badly wrong. And I can't wait any longer to find out what.

6

I wake up earlier than expected. Justin's cryptic messages are churning through my mind. The carpet flattens and the boards beneath creak when I stand. With stiff fingers I reach for my clothes and hurriedly get dressed, trying my best not to remember the scream from last night, but thinking of it immediately. *Christ, what the hell was it? And did it really come from the garden?*

I switch on my phone to see if Justin's message has arrived but there's nothing new.

'For God's sake,' I groan, hurriedly messaging him. **What's this shit about?** In a rush I get showered and brush my teeth, ducking back to my room to slap on some make-up. There are dark shadows beneath my eyes and I don't want them to show. Today was supposed to be my recovery day at rehearsals, to get AA and the other doubters off my back. But my mind is far from work.

The bus comes. I have my lines all printed out and use the time to run over them as I sit upstairs, pressed against the window. I want to give Babs a call and tell her about the scream from last night but the bus is the wrong place for it. I keep checking my messages but there's still nothing.

When I get off at my stop, Malia is up ahead of me and beckoning me over. I wave back mechanically when my phone pings. 'Finally,' I snap, stopping for a second to read Justin's text which has eventually arrived.

Cathy get out of that house now. Your landlord Ian Fitzsimmons is a killer.

7

The remainder of the morning is a fog. I'm a thousand miles away, going through the motions of talking and listening while I think about Justin's message. *Your landlord Ian Fitzsimmons is a killer.* Each time I have the thought I see Ian's face: twisted, demonic, bloodthirsty.

At lunch I go for a salad with Malia and tell her about what's been going on with Justin, then about what happened last night. She listens attentively, asking me if I thought about calling the police, and I'm surprised how it hadn't even occurred to me. She tells me not to worry and I agree. But I can't help myself, and as soon as we're let go that evening I'm straight out the door and on the phone to Babs.

'You heard a scream in the night?' she gasps. I can barely make her voice out because of the chatter in the background. 'Oh, dear, not good. I'm sorry but I'm down in Galway on a department get-together thing so we're all out in the hotel bar and staying over for the night.'

A deep frown stretches across my forehead. 'It's worse, Babs,' I explain, so wishing she was here. 'Then Justin texts me this morning saying the landlord Ian is a fucking killer.

There's a stunned silence. Then a loud gasp. '*What?* That's insane. What's that about?'

'I've got no idea.'

'OK, listen. You have a key to my place. Stay there, alright. When I'm back tomorrow we'll meet and sort this out.'

'Thanks, Babs.' For a brief moment I'm so relieved I could lie down on the grass and refuse to get up.

By the edge of the canal I sit alone. There's a good throng of people chatting and hanging out and enjoying the summer weather.

One of the bar boys is out collecting empty glasses and I signal to him but he peels away before I can catch him. Frustrated, I open the web browser on my phone and google *Ian Fitzsimmons Belleview Road*.

Instantly the story appears.

I scroll through it. *Murder suspect Ian Fitzsimmons arrested in connection with the disappearance of Ms Anna Cunningham, February 2023.* I'm suddenly shivering. There's no mistake. Same man, the same address. I place the phone down on the grass and look away anxiously when it rings.

'What are you doing right now?' I recognise Heather's voice.

'Sitting alone outside a pub reading a story about how my landlord is a wife killer.' A shudder passes through me as I say the words.

'Shut it down before you read any more and I'll give you what I know.'

'Why?'

'Because reading all the online stuff about Ian Fitzsimmons is just going to upset you and probably half of it is nonsense. Just stuff they spit out to sell papers.'

'Right.' Obediently I close the browser. 'Done.'

'I have to apologise, Cathy. I had no flipping *idea* about your landlord.'

'It's not your fault.'

'Linda thought his name was familiar and I'm sure we both must have heard about the story but somehow forgot it. I completely messed up.'

'Heather, you did me a huge favour, honestly it's alright.' I mean what I say. She was only trying to help, as she always does. 'So what *is* the story?'

'It's not entirely clear. His wife disappeared about eighteen months ago. She was some high-flyer in the corporate world. Then it was the classic scenario; the husband who claims total innocence comes under scrutiny and ends up chief suspect.'

'Justin texted me earlier to say he's a killer.'

'Well, the press did pretty much hang him out to dry. There were a few stories about him getting into trouble before and it sounds like his alibis were a bit all over the place but the thing is, Cathy, they didn't have the evidence. So it could be innocent until proven guilty or guilty but got away with it. I don't know.'

'What should I do?'

Heather sighs. 'Perhaps it's a case of trusting your gut?'

'Yeah,' I say weakly.

'But …'

'What?'

'Sometimes if it looks too good to be true …'

'It's because it is?'

Heather groans. 'Oh Cathy, this is just so shit and I'm so sorry. Look, you don't have to make your mind up right now. Sleep on it. If you're uncomfortable around him then leave instantly, and if you're stuck at all just come stay with us. It's no problem.'

I immediately imagine Peter getting this news but he doesn't have to worry. I can't accept the offer. I'm too old to be couch-surfing in friends' houses while I try to sort out my life. 'Thanks Heather,' I say. 'I'll think it over.'

'Where are you staying tonight?'

'At Babs's. She's out of town on a work thing. Don't worry. I'll be fine.' Silently I pray my words sound more convincing than I feel. A thought occurs to me then. 'Hey, before you go, you wouldn't happen to have that nurse Linda's phone number, the woman that passed the place to Babs.'

'I do, my friend Joan sent it to me. Her name's Linda O'Leary and she lives over in Castleknock. Do you want me to forward it on to you?'

'If you could. I might have a chat with her and keep you posted.'

After three short rings, Linda O'Leary picks up.

'Linda?'

'Speaking.'

'I'm sorry to be bothering you. My name's Cathy Quinn. My friend Babs passed me your number.' I hesitate, realising I've rushed into this call without properly preparing. 'I'm sorry, it's about a house let she got from you.'

'Oh, yes, Ian Fitzsimmons's place. His son Jamie used to play football with my son Conal. Do you need his contact?'

A little awkward now, I start to explain. 'Well, no. You see I've actually already taken the room and moved in.'

'Oh?'

'And the thing is ...' I pause, racking my brain how to even address this, how to put it out there without sounding ungrateful for the favour. 'Well, I've just learned that he's the main suspect for murdering his wife.' There's a long, pregnant pause on the other end of the phone.

'Oh dear, you hadn't heard?'

'No.'

Linda makes an apologetic groan. 'Well, that must be one hell of a shock so I'm sorry to hear that. But you see the thing is, Cathy, I'm not sure the coverage on him was entirely fair. A friend of mine used to live on that street a few years back before she moved to Chicago and she maintained he was the loveliest guy, so I really don't know. And Conal's been in the house a few times too and said the same. Perhaps I'm being biased but I got the impression the media made him a bit of a target.' She stops and I hear the sound of her lips smacking. 'But again, listen, I do understand that in your position that might be little reassurance so I'm sorry for that misunderstanding.' I'm suddenly not sure what else to ask. How can I expect poor Linda to solve this dilemma for me. 'Listen, if you're unsure, and I can appreciate you might be, it might be better for you to find something else. I think you'd only stress yourself out staying there.'

I pause, remembering how I ended up there in the first place. Linda doesn't know that I lost my flat, that I'm almost broke, that I don't have options I can pick and choose from, or the time and space to do that. And who am I to be bothering her with my problems when she doesn't even know me? She's only generously offered to help and given an honest opinion.

'I won't keep you, Linda. I guess I'll have to give it more thought. Thanks for taking my call.'

'Any time.'

As soon as Linda is off the line, I open the web browser on my phone and start digging for info on Ian again. I know Heather has just warned me away from this literally minutes ago but I want to check again, to see if there's something in what Linda has mentioned, some redeeming evidence that counters Justin's claim that Ian's a wife killer.

The articles appear. *Wife Slayer. Chief Suspect. Murdered or Disappeared? Police Believe Fitzsimmons is Guilty.* Then a different one. *Ian Fitzsimmons's Grief.*

Nervously I click into it and start reading. I scan furiously. There's a question from the interviewer. '*And how have you coped since your wife Anna's disappearance? Has it been hard living with the suspicion of being a cold-blooded murderer?*' Then Ian's reply. '*The days since Anna's disappearance have felt like a dark and inexplicable dream to me to be honest. The world has been a cruel and unforgiving place, wherever I walk, like into a shop to buy some milk, or wherever I sit, if I'm grabbing a coffee or a beer maybe, there's somebody looking, whispering, pointing – not even caring that I notice. Other times they simply walk straight up to me and call me a murdering bastard. One guy even threw his tea at me as I walked down the street,*' Fitzsimmons offers glumly. '*And it's hard, because all I feel is sadness. Disbelief that Anna is gone and I don't know why. And there's days I don't want to carry on, because I don't think I can, but then I remember…*' '*What do you remember Ian?*' '*That I have a son, Jamie, and he needs his father.*'

I click out. My stomach is clenching. Linda didn't believe Ian sounded guilty and the words I've just read sound like a man in pain, not in denial. Yet what do I really know? The one thing that seems clear is that Heather is right. I need to avoid getting sucked into this online.

It's a short walk back up to Babs's place and I get there quickly enough. I'm just making myself comfortable when my phone rings. *Justin.* Again.

'*What?*' I snap, annoyed I'm picking up but desperate to give him a piece of my mind.

'I'm sorry.'

'About?'

'About everything, Cathy. I probably shouldn't have sent you the text today but I just didn't know how to put it.' I press the phone to my ear with an exasperated sigh. 'Please tell me you're not in that house, Cath.'

'I'm at Babs's.'

'Have you left then?'

'I haven't decided.' I wait for him to come back but he's quiet. 'What makes you sure Ian Fitzsimmons killed his wife, Justin?'

There's a loud gasp. 'God, Cath! Have you not read up on him yet?'

I feel suddenly foolish. 'Heather advised me not to.'

He sniffs. 'She's smart, Heather. Yeah, probably for the best. But from what I've read he looks a dead cert for topping his wife, so honestly, Cath, I'd give it a miss if I was you.' I'd like to laugh if I wasn't so angry. Justin never came across as the most honest type so I don't know why he's sounding so hand on heart. Maybe it's guilt. 'Look, I've been thinking,' he starts again. 'I might have made a mistake.'

'I'm not following you?'

'About the whole flat thing.' He lets out a tired moan and I feel my resistance melt a little. 'So I wanted to make a suggestion. Why don't you come and live with me at my mum's?'

I press my fingers to my cheek and lean forward, both elbows on my knees. I blink as confusion and rage spiral inside. 'Justin? What on earth are you talking about?'

The Landlord

'I'm in the mews at the end of the garden. It's small but it's cosy. The old girl won't mind and we need to save money.'

Old girl. I wince as I hear the words. I hate it when he calls his mother that but he has a point about the money. But he's also casually forgotten that I had no say in any of this. It's not my plan, it's his. And while I love his mum dearly, I don't want to be living under her feet because I'm too broke to pay my rent.

'Sorry, Justin,' I say, finding a new resolve, 'but no fucking way. I'm thirty bloody two and it simply does not make any sense to me to do that. It's moving backwards.'

I hear a familiar grunt of disapproval. Then he's back again. 'OK, look, don't worry because I've got a bit of good news.'

'What news?'

'My aunt Beth died.'

I try to remember an aunt Beth but can't recall one. 'Why is that good news?'

'Well, I hardly knew her and she's gone and left me ten grand, Cath. Which means I've got some money for another apartment.' I stand up and pace across the polished floorboards of the spacious living room. 'I've found another one that might suit us too. Please just have a look at it at least?'

I come to a stop, kneading my eyes with my fingers. I want to pour beer on Justin's head and tell him to fuck off, but to my huge annoyance, I also want him to call over so we can snuggle up and forget all about the last forty-eight hours.

'No.'

'Oh, come on, Cath! This could be perfect. It's an opportunity.'

'Justin! This relationship …' I squeeze the words from the back of my throat, annoyed by the tearful sound of my voice. I don't want Justin to hear it. 'Only days ago you were saying we're done.'

'I'm a fool sometimes, Cath, I just talk shit, you know that. We can sweep it under the carpet.'

'And why should I believe you?'

'Because,' he comes back, exasperated. 'Because,' he repeats, softer this time, with a more caring voice, the one he always uses when it really counts. 'I wouldn't make this call if it didn't matter. I know I'm my own worst enemy sometimes and I've got to sort that out.' He lets out a sigh. 'We're good together, Cath. Everybody has these moments.'

I place my phone on the mantlepiece and rub my hands over my face, keeping them there for a second before picking it back up again. 'Listen, I need to figure out what I'm doing,' I say, trying not to sound as weary as I feel.

'Of course.'

If I suspect that Ian Fitzsimmons really is a killer, I don't want to be under the same roof as him. But until I know that I could simply be acting on the fears that Justin has planted. I know that's what Justin wants. I don't want to do what Justin wants. I decide to stay strong.

I hold my bottom lip between my thumb and forefinger. *Why was Ian Fitzsimmons so open and generous if he's a murderer? Because a murderer is anybody*, the voice that won't quieten cautions – and I know what it's telling me makes sense.

'Justin …'

'What?'

'We'll talk in the morning.'

8

Lunch break from rehearsals and Justin's just collected me. I try not to catch Malia's eye as I get into the passenger seat of his mum's little Fiat 500. Instead I press my hands down on my knees and stare straight ahead.

Justin spins the steering wheel and we screech away at speed. He's a fast driver and I often have to tell him to calm down when he gets too carried away. Today he looks all fresh and bright-eyed. Clean-shaven, the hair neatly messy, sky-blue jeans. I notice he's got a lovely pair of new Converse trainers and a pair of Hilfiger shades. His shirt is pressed and he smells of aftershave. It's Armani Code. I know because I bought it for him.

'Been shopping?'

He guns away from the lights and grins. 'Just a few essentials.' He taps the dial on the wheel and increases the volume of the music. 'I love this track. Listen to it.' It's a dance tune. Justin knows I hate dance music. But I'm actually happy he's got the volume up. In the silence he'd sense me bristling at his extravagance after claiming that we were broke. I zone out, trying to guess where to begin with my ex and his shapeless plans which keep changing from hour to hour.

Before long we're at the apartment. Justin parks up. He does it super quick, one hand on the steering wheel like he's rubbing a cloth one way and suddenly the next. It's all very slick and fast, and the Mini squeaks into the kerb, fitting like a glove in the tiny space between the two parked cars.

Justin points to the estate agent who is waiting as he fob locks the car. It clunks, the shining lights flashing twice as I walk up the steps and meet the agent's smile with an uncertain glance.

'William,' the agent says politely.

'Cathy.' He shakes my hand vigorously.

'Alright, Bill.' Justin gives him a pat on the arm and lets him usher us inside.

'Good timing.' The agent opens the apartment door, inviting us to walk past him. 'It's just come on the market and you're first to view.'

I peer into the space. The place is bright, clean and spacious. I take it in, working hard to hide my surprise. 'It's an old period building that's been subdivided into four very spacious apartments. It's a really neat job and they've been very generous with the layout.'

What he says is true. The living room is enormous and feels even bigger because of the high ceiling. We follow him into a tidy tiled kitchen.

'Nice finishing,' Justin remarks, trailing a finger across the smooth plasterwork like some savvy tradesman.

'And it's a first let,' the agent adds. 'So all furnishings are new. Come, I can show you the bedroom.'

I try to remember the last time I slept in a new bed. Probably the time Mum bought me one when I was ten, after the previous one collapsed when my friend Clare jumped on it during a sleepover.

'No need. This is right up our street,' Justin says, turning to me and winking. Then he spins round to the agent again. 'We'll take her, Bill. You've got all our refs already so I'll just get you the deposit and first month's cash later this afternoon if that's OK with you.'

The agent beams. 'You don't want to inspect the rest of it?'

Justin gives him a disinterested shrug and waits for me to say something.

'I'll have a quick look,' I mutter, hurrying down a long corridor, past a newly painted bathroom to the double bedroom. It's clearly perfect, which Justin obviously knows too, but it bothers me badly that he's assumed I agree with him. It also feels odd that Justin couldn't care enough even to inspect properly.

The Landlord

'Right then,' Justin says, tipping his shades further up into his messy hair when he sees me return and silently nod to him. 'Better get you off and back to rehearsals, Cath.' Drawing an arm around me, he ushers me to the door. 'I'll bell you later, Bill. I might pick up the keys when I'm dropping the deposit over. That good with you?'

The agent smiles, extending a thumbs up. 'Bye Cathy.'

'Bye,' I say, but see Justin has already shut the door behind us.

'Was that Justin?' Malia asks in a hushed voice as we shuffle out into the warm evening, the feeling of it on my skin a release from the stuffiness inside the rehearsal space.

'Oh, Malia,' I groan. 'It's such a long story.' She grins. I want to invite her for a drink so I can explain but remember I still have to tell Ian about my new plan to move out and back in with Justin. 'I've got to run. I'll tell you all when I see you Monday.'

'Learn those lines, Cathy Quinn.' She waves me away joking in AA's sniffiest voice. 'We can't carry anyone in this production.'

With heavy steps I make my way back to Belleview Road, stopping every few minutes to take in the gently swaying trees, the wrought-iron railings and neatly laid out front gardens, all of it a backdrop to the buzzing hum of happy summer people. In the blink of an eye all my hopes for this unexpected house-share have crashed and burned. Forty-eight hours ago, I was all done with Justin – but now we're starting again and I've got to pass Ian the news, literally before we've even talked properly. Dejected, I trudge on when I'm suddenly stopped by the unexpected sight of a small dog standing in the middle of the busy street.

There's a large white delivery van bearing down on it and worse still, the driver is on his mobile and can't see it. Scanning the pavements I search for its owner but find no one.

'Shit,' I mutter, impulsively dashing out, scooping him up just as the driver looks up and honks at me furiously. I give him the finger as his van trundles forwards, and I rush to the safety of the pavement.

'Christ.' I heave, as the tiny dog licks my hands and wags its tail. I'm a little dizzy and trying to make sense of what's happened when a voice from across the street gets my attention.

'Put. The dog. Down.' I turn to see a middle-aged woman pointing an accusing finger in my direction. She's got a bottle-blonde bob with dark roots and is dressed in expensive pink jogging pants. Aggressively, she strides towards me, hands out stopping the oncoming cars like they shouldn't be in her way. There's a phone in her outstretched hand. 'You heard me.' She points it at me like a weapon. 'I have you on video, there's no point in running away. If you try, the police will find you.'

I glance around for bystanders but see none. 'I'm sorry?'

'Last warning,' she snarls. When she's close enough she snatches the dog back.

'He went onto the road,' I explain, my voice tight but calm. 'If I hadn't picked him up, he would have been run over.' In a flutter of hands, she snatches him from me before I can offer him.

'I saw what you were doing. Every thief has a story.' Clutching him close to her chest, she steps back. Then she holds him out with straight arms, admiring him and making loud baby noises.

I'm about to reply when I notice a turd pushing out of the dog's bum, angling towards the woman's chest.

'Ugh.' She drops him like a hot coal and the dog continues its business on the pavement while she scrabbles for the leash. Lost for words, I hurry past her and walk home. I could laugh out loud if I wasn't feeling so thoroughly miserable.

At the top of the granite steps I pause to prepare myself but find the front door already open.

9

'Cathy!' Ian stands in the doorway, his friendly smile greeting me. He's wearing a navy cotton short-sleeve shirt with a patterned collar. It's a tailored fit and looks nice. 'I was hoping to catch you.'

'Yes,' I reply meekly.

'Everything alright?'

'Fine. How are *you*?'

He pulls the door back. 'Great.' He looks at me, sensing something's off, waiting for me to say something. Awkwardly, I stand there, hands inside my pockets when his gaze switches down towards the street. The wound-up woman with the small dog is pacing past, eyeballing us both. Ian grins, returning the stare. The woman throws a final dismissive glance in my direction before trotting away imperiously.

'My charming neighbours,' he murmurs, now looking across the road to a house on the other side of the street. There's a fleeting snap of curtains and Ian turns to me. 'You know, Cathy, I'd love to take you for that glass of wine if you're free. Or perhaps a bite to eat? We've hardly had a chance to talk since you moved in and I know it's overdue.'

'I'm sorry,' I mumble. 'I'm afraid I won't make it. There's been a change of plan.'

He steps back. 'There has?'

'I'm moving out.' Ian sags against the door frame. I hesitate for a second before continuing. 'I've patched things up with my boyfriend, you see, and we found a new place. Sorry. I hope to be gone tomorrow.'

'Oh ...' I hear the wounded note in his voice. 'Didn't even know you had a boyfriend?' The edges of his mouth turn down. 'But of course you do.' His chest puffs up and he regards me sternly. 'Naturally it would have been nice if you had figured all this out *before* moving in with me, you know, Cathy.'

I tense at the sudden edge in his voice, the new deep lines scored across his brow. 'Of course. I'm very sorry.'

His eyes flash as he shoves away from the door frame. Then he reaches his fingers to the bridge of his nose and pinches it. Nervously I wait, unsure if I should speak. Seconds later he looks back at me. The dark cloud of anger is gone and he brightens.

'It's fine, Cathy. Sorry for overreacting, but you caught me off guard there.' He raises a smile. 'I had this wonderful summer night plan about grabbing a glass of wine with you and getting to know you a little when boom!' He smacks his fist loudly into the open palm of his other hand and I jolt backwards. Unaware, he looks to the sky, throwing his arms wide, the palms of his hands now facing upwards. 'You're off and away.'

'I know.' My shoulders bunch. *But you're the chief suspect in your wife's disappearance*, I desperately want to add. So at least it's out there. So he can defend himself. Or not.

'Listen,' he comes back, holding each of my shoulders lightly. 'My fault. These things happen all the time. You've got to do what's right for you. So if patching it up with your ex is the way to go, then the last thing we need is me in the way.' He laughs, letting me go, and just for a fleeting second I wish he hadn't. When he smiles it's easy and relaxed again. 'Right then.' He steps aside to let me in when his phone rings. 'Yes Charlie?' He answers holding the door till I've taken it from him, before stepping back out onto the wide stone step. 'Love to join you. Twenty minutes?' He turns. 'Wait, hang on. I'm sorry, Cathy but would you like me to help you with your stuff?'

I shake my head. 'It's fine.'

'I'll see you in the morning I hope?'

I nod. Not sure if he will. Not sure if I want him to.

After Ian leaves I expect to feel calm. But I don't. I feel ungrateful. I'm confused and a bit torn.

The Landlord

In the living room I drop onto the couch in a heap, using the last of my time here to memorise lines for the night. But my mind is restless and I keep wondering what I might have learned if I had gone for a drink with Ian, told him what I'd heard and let him answer my questions. For a second I think of googling him and reading all about his wife's disappearance, but then I remember Heather's advice and hold back.

Eventually, tired out, I walk to the window and look down to the street. I check for the man I thought I saw out there the other night but he's not around. Annoyed, I grip the curtains and snap them closed.

Head bowed, I troop wearily up the stairs to the bedroom to call it a night when a shiver runs down my spine. Could the scream I heard in the night be connected to the man I saw lurking on the corner?

10

Much to my surprise, I sleep well and am fresh when I get out of bed. In the kitchen I find an envelope on the table. It's got my name on it.

I pick it up, slide my finger inside the seam and tear it open.

Dear Cathy,
Charlie invited a few of us over to his seaside bolthole for the weekend so I'm out of town till Monday evening. Sorry I didn't get to see more of you and I really hope the new place works out for you and your boyfriend. It was a pleasure to meet you and I wish you the best with everything.
Ian

My arm feels heavy when I place the paper back down on the table. Did I really call Justin my boyfriend? Isn't he more accurately my ex-boyfriend? Trying not to feel too downhearted, I mope back up the stairs. The sunlight is streaming through the windows and I have to get out.

I arrive at Leno's Café, the pretty little spot round the corner from Ian's house I've been aching to visit. I pull out my earbuds and wipe the sweat from my forehead, trying to guess what kind of juice I'd like best after my jog. Outside there's a pile of bikes parked up, helmets glinting in a bunched heap on top of the handlebars. I walk into the bright, airy space full of scrubbed wood, industrial lighting and metallic windows, but the bicycle group is sauntering out so I make space to let them pass. There's

The Landlord

about half a dozen of them, a mix of men and women, most of them around Ian's age.

'Next week then, JJ,' a plummy voice booms to the handsome man at the till. 'Same time, same spot if you can.' A jowly, high-hipped man wrapped in Lycra swaggers past.

'Righto, Gerry,' JJ replies in what sounds like an Aussie drawl. In one push the group follows Gerry, and I recognise a fraught blonde-haired woman. It's the woman who accused me of stealing her dog and I exhale silently when she passes me without looking up. When I get to the till there's another woman in cycling gear chatting to JJ. She too has blonde hair, which looks freshly shampooed as it bounces off her shoulders.

'Where do I put the tips?' she asks, delicate hands fluttering to her hair, eyelids blinking. My guess is she might be in her early forties but she looks like a woman who takes care of herself. With a pretty and inviting smile she's flirting with the man at the counter, who I have to admit, is making my own pulse race a little faster.

'You don't have to,' JJ says.

'I insist.' Her head tilts, eyes fixing him like laser beams.

JJ points to the glass jar with a few tossed coins inside. Slowly and deliberately, she places a ten euro note in. 'The salmon was gorgeous.'

'Glad you liked it,' JJ says politely, but not making any effort to return the flirtation. I'm guessing it's a skill he's had to fine-tune over time. When his attention turns to me, I hear a gasp.

'You're the new girl living in 762 with Ian Fitzsimmons?' The woman who was flirting with JJ is gripping my forearm excitedly. I nod, perplexed by her excitement but trying not to show it. Then she lets go of my arm, placing her hand on her heart. 'I'm sorry. Forgot to say I'm Anthea.' With a breathless, girlish giggle she extends a delicate-looking hand which I shake.

'Cathy.'

'Settled in yet?'

'I was just staying a few days.'

A sparkling fingernail lands on her bottom lip. 'What a shame! I was going to invite you to join us for brunch here next weekend. That's our mob.' She points to the departing cyclists. 'We all live local and get together a couple of times a week but call ourselves the Sunday Club, since that's our main bike ride. But it looks like they've forgotten all about me.'

JJ smiles and Anthea claps her hands, quickly skipping after the others before they depart. 'Well, nice to meet you all the same, Cathy.' Turning one last time she throws a warm-hearted wave and hurries out the exit.

JJ watches them all file out, his relief clear. 'What'll I get you, Cathy?'

'Juice. Please.'

He beams and I take in his mid-length sun-bleached hair, his golden skin and ivory teeth which flash briefly beneath starry blue eyes. Immediately I forgive Anthea. 'Just made some fresh this morning. Orange juice if that's good?'

'Perfect.'

JJ keys it through and turns the card machine but when I tap it beeps and declines.

'Thing's a bit temperamental,' he says, chewing his lip, and waiting for me to try again, but the second attempt gives the same result. I check my pocket for cash and realise I don't have any.

'This is embarrassing. I've no change.'

JJ waves it away. 'On me. Till I see you next time.'

'I don't know if there is a next time.'

'Then it's just on me, Cathy.'

A family of four appears behind me and JJ's attention turns to them. He smiles one last time as I whisper a grateful thank you, taking the juice he has poured and finding myself hanging on his every word just like Anthea before me. In the blink of an eye, I seem to have accidentally joined JJ's list of admirers.

Late in the evening I text Justin, surprised that he hasn't been in touch. **Let me know what time you're collecting me.** I hit send and carry on with my packing up. Anthea is on my mind. I imagine she might be familiar but I can't think from where. And JJ too. The café was so bright and he was so handsome and friendly. And like Ian, I probably won't see him again, because I'll have no reason to come back.

When my packing is finished, I take my stuff downstairs and sit on one of the big comfortable couches, irritated now that I haven't heard from Justin. When I check my phone again there's nothing so I call him but it goes to message. What's going on Justin? I was expecting you here an hour ago? Call me. Please! I hang up, annoyed that I've said please, almost like I'm pleading, begging him to come and get me.

I scroll through some options on Netflix but don't find anything that hooks me and then restless, I do the one thing I've promised myself I would avoid. I google Ian Fitzsimmons again.

It pitches up on the screen almost instantly. More pictures of what look like classic tabloid horror. I pick the coverage from *The Sun* and dive right in.

'Wife Killer' is the title.

Chief suspect in the disappearance and murder of Anna Cunningham, husband Ian Fitzsimmons was remanded in police custody today. Despite assuring police that he knows nothing of his wife's disappearance, Ian Fitzsimmons is now under investigation for her murder. Anna Cunningham of Belleview Road, a highly regarded management consultant who worked with big brands including Nestlé and Siemens at home and internationally, has not been found. Neighbours claimed that the couple's relationship was stormy and that Ian Fitzsimmons's drinking had led to heated arguments, one in particular at a restaurant called Caprice where Fitzsimmons openly threatened his wife's life. Sources also suggest that CCTV footage placed Fitzsimmons at the scene of his wife's disappearance on the night she went missing. Fitzsimmons stands to inherit substantial wealth should his wife die. Fitzsimmons denies any wrongdoing and says he is committed to assisting the police and bringing the culprit to justice.

Underneath the article is a picture of Ian looking dishevelled, baggy-eyed and hungover. He seethes, glowering at the camera as a police officer presses him into the back of a car. I almost don't recognise him.

I push the laptop away. Heather was right. There's a twisting in the pit of my stomach. I open my mouth to breathe but feel nausea rising. The article has done nothing to help my understanding of the truth, but it's fed my imagination with dark thoughts of violence and bloodshed, all pointing to Ian Fitzsimmons.

Rising wearily from the couch I go to the window, remembering that Justin hasn't called. That he most likely won't call, and he probably won't arrive. I look out onto the street and my heart jumps when I spot the strange man again on the corner. Once more, just like last time, he's lurking like a phantom. Instantly he turns, disappearing into the shadows. Warily I step back. Could it be a drug dealer? I have no idea, but now, in this moment, I seem to imagine he was staring at my window.

Hastily I shut the curtains, a tension balling in the pit of my stomach. I rush past my packed belongings and scamper upstairs into the bedroom, locking the door behind me.

This is not the plan Justin promised.

It's the worst possible start to our new beginning.

I clench my jaw and fling myself on the bed, annoyed that I did the one thing Heather advised me not to. Because now I don't trust Ian Fitzsimmons, I don't trust Justin, and I don't even trust myself.

I want the morning to come so I can make a decision. But I only hope the man on the corner hasn't returned, and that I only imagined he was staring up at me.

11

I'm five minutes from rehearsals when my phone rings.

'Babe?'

'Justin, is that you?' The tension in my voice is audible.

'Babe! I finally got through to you.'

I look out the window of the bus and try to make more space for the large woman sitting next to me. She smiles appreciatively as I huddle over. 'Justin, where are you?' I whisper, straining to contain my irritation.

'Oh, babe, I'm in Madrid. Change of plan.'

'What are you talking about?'

'I had to pull the plug on the new apartment.'

The bell chimes for my stop and I bolt from my seat, squeezing past the turned knees of the woman beside me who looks at me with concern. The urge to scream is so strong but I hold it down, scrunching my eyes shut, waiting till the bus doors open before rushing off.

'Justin?' The word almost bursts out from me. 'What the *fuck* are you talking about?'

'Hon, I bought myself a new set of wheels.' He sighs, almost surprised himself. 'I'm sorry, it wasn't planned. Just my mate Alex had a Subaru Impreza he was letting go and I couldn't pass on it. You know I've been looking for one for ages.' I'm shaking as the words singe my ears. He keeps going. 'It's got the silver metallic paint and everything, Cath. You'll love it.'

'Justin?'

'Yeah?'

'I don't care about your new car's paintwork.' There's a pause as I let him digest my anger. 'You told me we were starting afresh in a new apartment. Yesterday! Have you forgotten?'

'I know, I'm sorry, Cath.'

'And what are you doing in Madrid?'

'It's just a thing Benny organised for a few of the lads I had forgotten about. I'm home soon. Look I've already organised for Benny's mate Al to drop over with his minivan and he can collect all your gear. You can still stay at my mum's till we sort ourselves out.'

I'm ten paces from the front door to rehearsals. In a couple of minutes I'll have to forget all about this so I can concentrate on my work. The pressure inside my head surges.

'Justin?'

'Yeah?'

'Fuck off.'

I get through the morning but it's hard. My hands sweat, my neck strains and I move like I'm made from bolted metal. I'm *furious* with Justin. But I'm more furious with myself for ever agreeing to his plan. Once again, I'm hanging on in my scenes rather than showing what I can do. And I know it's putting me on thin ice.

During the morning break, AA calls me over. His small, ferret-like eyes peer down his pointed nose. 'You OK, Cathy? You seem a little distracted.'

I trudge over to him, too drained to lie. 'Sorry, Andy. I've got all this stuff going on with my landlord at the minute and I don't know if I have a place to stay right now. I thought I had it sorted but it's not.'

AA listens, swiping thin wisps of oily hair. He's not mad, which is good, but I can't make out what he's thinking. It's like he's trying to make up his mind about something. 'Alright, if it's any use to you, my couch is free. My girlfriend is away for a fortnight so it's just me and the cat. If you're stuck.'

'Right,' I reply slowly, clearly not expecting this. I struggle to think of a response. Offending the director is the last thing I need right now. 'I appreciate that ... erm ... I'll see where I'm at and let you know.'

The Landlord

'Good. Just make sure it doesn't interfere with your work. It can happen too easily you know. Yeah?'

'Of course.' There's some kind of warning in AA's offering. It worries me but I know he's justified. 'Thanks.'

During lunch I tell Malia what's happened with Justin. I don't mention that Ian is supposed to be a wife killer, I just say I wasn't relaxed there after hearing the scream in the garden. Then I tell her about AA's surprise offer of his couch.

'No bloody way!' Malia's nose almost hits the table she finds it so funny.

'What?'

'You're not going to believe this, Cathy.'

'Tell me, Malia, I'm hanging here.'

'The creep offered me his couch too. Before we started the production. I was in the process of moving flat and he just threw it out, casual as you like, his dirty nails scratching his scrawny chest as he was looking at me up and down, like I was something on sale at the butcher's.'

'Fuck's *sake*.' I pretend to wretch and we both laugh. 'No free lunches?'

She polishes off the remainder of her wrap and nods. 'Not a bloody chance.'

I'm all at sea when I get back to the house that evening. I'm not even supposed to be there but I don't know my next move. I considered leaning on Babs but hate the idea and I'm not going to speak to Justin. I walk in wearily when Ian appears from the kitchen.

He's straightening out his jacket sleeves like he's leaving to go somewhere. 'Cathy? This is a surprise.' He greets me warmly. 'Everything OK? I had thought you'd be gone.'

'Sorry,' I mumble in a contrite voice, gripping my hands together. 'I think I've made a terrible mistake.'

'Oh?' His voice softens. 'Come in and take a seat.' I follow him to the living room and we sit. 'Apologies because I'm rushing off again,' he explains, 'but at least this time I can say it's for work. What's happened?'

'I've changed my mind. I'm not moving in with my boyfriend anymore. We're not even going out. I wanted to ask if you'd mind if I stayed on. And if you do, I fully understand. I've been a complete idiot about this.'

'Not at all, no harm done.' He stands up and gives me a reassuring smile. 'Really. Consider it forgotten and you can invite your friends around if you feel you need company or anything. I'm not exactly clear when I'm back yet and I can see you need company.'

'I'm fine. Honestly,' I gabble, almost completely disarmed.

Seconds later he's gone again.

Lying in bed I run through what's happened. Justin's plan for our new apartment. Then his call from another country, telling me he's bought a car instead, like I should be happy for him. I can almost taste the disgust in my mouth and yet I also feel relieved, because it means my houseshare with Ian isn't over yet. And even though I know what I've read online, I can't bring myself to believe it. Not fully. I need to know more before I write off this man who's been nothing but a fountain of generosity to me.

The memory of the first time I saw him comes back. His rugged looks, his calm, his effortless ease; and his mesmerising openness. The whole effect is like a magnet on me. Drawing me closer. Making me want to understand him. And even though he's older, I can't help but find him attractive. I can't deny it.

I remember that Babs and Heather are both back in town and make a plan to contact them in the morning. With their advice I might be able to figure things out.

As I'm thinking this I drift off to sleep, dreaming about a wild, overgrown garden when suddenly there's a loud cracking noise and the sound of a voice. I shoot upright in the bed, the blood rushing to my head. There's more noise coming from inside the house. Shuffling, clanking and banging down in the hall; and the

The Landlord

sound of a young man's voice talking to himself, not drunk, but certainly not sober.

I'm a little edgy when I put on my coat but I ease the bedroom door open and peer out and down to the hall. 'Where the hell has it gone?' the man says to nobody. I expect I'll be terrified but I'm not. The man looks very young and fumbles about on the floor as if searching for something under the hall table. Suddenly tired and defeated he sits on the floor, only then noticing me.

I can make out his delicate, almost feminine features. He looks like a college student. With a loud cough he clears his throat and speaks. 'Hello.'

'Hi.'

'Are you staying here?' he asks, looking confused.

'Yes. I live here.'

'Oh, sorry, I didn't realise.' Confident he's not a burglar I come down a couple of steps so I'm close enough to make him out clearly. Medium to slight build, just above average height, chestnut brown hair, bright blue eyes, very pretty in a boyish way. More harmless than terrifying. 'I had a few drinks and dropped my key under the hall table. Then I couldn't find it.' He displays it proudly. 'Got it at last.' He clambers to his feet with a small stagger. 'I'm *so* sorry I woke you. I had no idea anybody was even here.'

'You're staying here?'

'No. I was,' he hiccups loudly, then grins sheepishly, 'but I won't.' He does a playful salute to me from beneath the stairs. 'I'm Jamie. Ian's son.'

'Ah.' The picture before suddenly begins to make sense. Bashful and awkward, he's not at all like Ian. But it's endearing.

Confident now, I come down the stairs. 'Cathy.'

He looks at me for a second as if unsure what to do next. 'Right, well.' He walks to the door. 'Please forgive me because I had no idea you were here. Dad never mentioned anything.' He opens the door quickly. 'But that's my dad for you.'

'Where are you going?' I ask, guilt rising inside me.

'Back to my friend's place. I wanted to collect some stuff from my room but I'll do it in the morning. I know I've freaked you out.'

My shoulders relax but I don't want to turn him away from his own home. 'I hope you're not putting yourself out on my account. This is *your* house.'

Jamie is already out the door and down the steps, waving back as he looks out to the street. 'Sorry if I scared you. We'll chat another time.'

Without another word he runs into the night.

12

I tap the switch down on the kettle, wait for the familiar blue light to show and then turn round and read the text again on my mobile phone.

Come in for two Cathy. Take the morning off.

The message from our director AA surprises me because he doesn't give mornings off. But I decide not to waste it, so I go upstairs, change into my joggers and nip out for a run in the park.

When I get home half an hour later, I stop at the gate, a little shocked to see Jamie is back and sitting outside on the broad stone steps. He's holding two takeaway cups. Shyly, he greets me as I walk towards him.

'Hi,' he says, smiling. In the bright sunshine, with his Nike sneakers, peach tie-dye T-shirt and ripped jeans he looks relaxed, and a lot more put together than last night. 'I spotted you jogging as I was coming up and guessed you might like a coffee after.' He holds out a cup. 'They're still warm.'

'That's so kind.' I take it, thinking how it's like father, like son with his generosity.

'There's a new Aussie guy running the local café and he makes great coffee.'

I take a sip, inhaling the freshly ground smell. 'Yes. I met him the other day. JJ, I think?'

'That's him.' I sit next to Jamie on the step and we both drink from our cups. 'Hope I amn't delaying you?' I swallow the coffee, waving the idea away. 'I just wanted to say sorry again about last night.'

'Don't be.' He brightens a little. 'Ian had said you'd moved to Aberdeen, to get ready for uni?'

He nods. 'I have. I just popped back last night for a short visit. I'm staying with a friend but was hoping to grab a few bits from my room if it's OK with you?'

'Of course.'

Instantly he jumps to his feet. 'Great. Should take me two minutes tops.' Before I can reply he skips away, letting himself inside and closing the door behind him. I wait on the step and drink the coffee which is as good as Jamie suggests and within moments he returns. But this time he doesn't sit and I can sense he wants to be off.

'Right,' he says, a little breathless and holding a small plastic bag tightly in his fist. 'Got what I needed.'

I stand up too, realising that the question that kept surfacing all morning as I jogged around the park needs to be asked, because if I don't take this opportunity I don't when it'll come round again. Bracing myself I begin. 'Jamie, listen, you don't know me, and I don't know you or Ian. And I've landed up in your dad's house almost entirely by accident since I split up with my boyfriend; my situation is that I can't afford another place at the minute so I know I probably look like a pathetic gold digger to you.'

His cute face breaks into an apologetic grin. 'If I was stuck and my dad offered me this,' he points to the house, 'I'm sure I wouldn't think twice either.'

'Well, that's very kind of you,' I say, my stomach tightening. 'But look, I also wanted to say that I heard about your mother.'

A muscle in his cheek twitches. 'My mother?'

'Yes,' I reply as softly as I can, feeling the prickle of irritation spreading out from him like an aura. 'And I know it's absolutely none of my business but I just wanted to say that I can imagine how tough it is, having a parent go missing.'

Jamie takes a gulp of his coffee and stares back at me solemnly. Then he glances away down the street, a forlorn look replacing his sunny expression. 'It is.'

I think about leaving it there for now but get the tiniest sense he might help me more. 'Did the police ever …?' He watches me closely as I search for the right words. '... offer any hope of understanding as to what might have happened?'

He steps back, breathing out heavily, looking suddenly glum. I think he's about to walk away in silence when he turns and speaks. 'What do you know about the story, Cathy?'

I shrug sheepishly, worried now that I've pushed too hard, that I've gone and lost him. 'Next to nothing really.'

'But you read the headlines, about my dad, right?' His voice is a little defensive. I nod, guessing the less I say now perhaps the better. 'Cathy, my dad is many things and not all of them are pleasant. We don't see eye to eye, and a lot of the time I find myself hating him, especially since Mum disappeared. He's a Jekyll and Hyde character and I'd advise you to be careful with him. Right now, he's probably sweetness and light, but there's sides to him he doesn't reveal to strangers. But I know him through and through.' My neck stiffens and I wait for him to continue. 'But the thing is, the police couldn't solve Mum's disappearance, and my dad made a nice story for the press so they nailed it on him.' He pauses, looks at his coffee but decides not to drink it. 'Is he capable of it?' He inhales, his agitation growing. 'I'd say certainly.'

I clutch for the railing to steady myself, anxiety crawling across my skin.

'But what you want to know is *did* he kill Mum?' He looks down the road for a second considering the idea, then makes a doubtful face. 'I don't believe so for a minute.' He stops, like he's too dejected to go on.

'What is it, Jamie?'

'As long as we don't know what really happened, this family will never be at peace.' He walks down the steps, almost shrinking away.

'I'm sorry Jamie ...'

'You needed to know. Now you do.' He waves and throws me a broken smile. Then he turns and walks out through the gate to the street. 'Hope you liked the coffee.'

13

In the living room I try to get busy walking through some of the scenes for the play but it's pointless. The image of Jamie slouching away as he walked down the street keeps haunting me. Was I right to ask him about Ian? Was it too blunt and crude? He looked so broken when he left. But I had to know what he truly believed about his father. *A Jekyll and Hyde character with countless shades. A person capable of killing his wife for certain?* My stomach lurches as I remember his words. Why did he think Ian capable of killing Anna and yet remain so sure he could never have actually done it?

I recall his anguished expression when he said the family will never have peace until they know the truth. But by family he could only have meant him and Ian? And how can I really stay here if I don't know the truth either?

Suddenly I understand how awful it all is. How unfair it is that Jamie has to merely carry on in limbo, not knowing what really happened to his mother. Not knowing whether Ian is hiding a dark secret from him too.

I bite down on my lip, resolving that if nobody else can bring his family peace then perhaps I could. And the only way to do it is to find out what really became of Anna.

With a weary groan I throw down my script and hurry off to take a shower.

On the way to rehearsals, I call my agent. Melissa hasn't answered my last two messages.

'Melissa?'

The Landlord

'Yes, Cathy,' she says formally, picking up. 'What can I do for you?' From her clipped voice I can tell it's not the greatest of starts.

'How are you keeping?'

'Fine. Busy. Tell me?'

'We haven't spoken in a while.'

'Yes. How's the play going?'

'OK.' Melissa knows I didn't want to do it in the first place but only agreed after she twisted my arm, despite us both agreeing clearly on ruling out period drama. 'I was wondering if there's anything in the pipeline?'

'Nothing I'm afraid.'

'Was there anything back from the clothes commercial I tried out for?'

A deep sigh. 'They went for another girl.'

I deflate. 'And the American TV series you mentioned, you thought I might be suitable for it?'

'They're only taking actors from two agencies. We missed the cut.' A lump wells in my throat because I know she's lying. I met Rebecca White last week who told me Melissa was sending her in for it. 'Look, Cathy, try and make an impression with Andy, at the moment he's the only director of note who's expressed any interest, and a bit of Shakespeare could broaden your range and give you some technique.' The barb in her tone stings. And I remember how differently she used to talk with me when I first signed after getting cast in the TV pilot. 'Got another actor on the line here, Cathy, we'll catch up soon, OK?'

'Sure.' She ends the call and I fight back a rising tide of dejection. Then I take a moment to compose myself and start to text Ian.

Are you free for dinner tonight at 8? I'd like to invite two friends over and get takeout.

The text sends. Seconds later he replies.

Sure. C u then.

Relieved I immediately text Babs and Heather.

Girls, please come for dinner at 8. I need you both to meet Ian so I can decide what I'm doing. We'll get takeout.

Three minutes later I have two more pings. They both say yes. I swallow heavily, tense, excited but fearful at the same time. Tonight will be the test.

The afternoon doesn't start as planned.

'Sorry, Cathy, won't need you till three. Grab some sunshine,' AA says as soon as I walk in the door.

Malia appears behind me and loops her arm in mine.

'Let's go feed the ducks, Cathy. I've brought some bread.'

'OK,' I agree, slightly stunned, letting her lead me outside where we find a bench. Malia has a finger to her lips, indicating the need for silence, but when we sit she finally talks. 'You're not going to believe what happened Cathy?'

I stare at her, a ripple of fear spreading through me. Is this the moment where my only ally, Malia, tells me she's just been cast alongside Matt Damon in his next blockbuster and is quitting the show this evening. Feeling a little tearful I get my hands ready to clap.

'What?'

'Old John,' she says with a sick look.

I nod, strangely relieved as Matt Damon evaporates to be replaced by our lead actor who plays King Lear himself, an arrogant, tetchy man, and part of the reason the whole production is so gruelling.

'What's he done?'

'He pinched my fucking ass, Cathy.'

'No?' The blood drains from my cheeks. I feel ill.

'I'm telling you. During costume this morning, the girls were in doing some quick checks on the gear and he pinched me as I got past him.'

'What happened then?'

'I said "what are you doing?" and he said, "you're in my space" and laughed.'

'Did you tell AA?'

She nods. 'Immediately, Cathy. But he just said Old John does it all the time.'

'Pinching?'

'No, pressing other actors' buttons. He said it often works to enhance the character interplay.'

I grind my teeth. 'So in your case it gets you pissed off at him just like it is in the play between Cordelia and Lear?'

'Something like that, yeah. He said all great actors do it.'

I feel like puking. 'You can't stand for that shit, Malia. It's wrong.'

'I know. But I haven't made any decisions about it yet, OK?'

I nod. My stomach knots but I accept it's her choice.

'I just wanted to tell you, so you know. Be careful with them, Cathy. They're pretty rotten.'

14

The girls arrive first. It gives us the chance to do a quick sprint around the house and I show them everything. Once that's out of the way, we retreat to the living room to ogle the chandeliers and plasterwork.

'It's heavenly.' Heather beams, easing her fringe away from her eyes to view it better.

'Isn't it just,' Babs laughs. 'Cathy Quinn! How did you bag this?'

'I didn't. You did. Remember?'

'Must be fate.'

My friends both look captivating, Heather in slick black trouser suit and Babs in a short but vibrant red cotton dress. Heather's black hair is freshly cut and shining under the light and Babs is sporting two glittering new earrings, framed by dangling tresses. They've brought wine which we put out on the table beside the glasses. For a second I want to change out of my simple blue jeans and white blouse and put on something glamorous but then I remember; this night isn't about having fun, it's about learning something. 'Girls, I really need you to help me here. I've got to figure out Ian and come to a decision about whether I'm staying or not. And I'm done with Justin.'

'Thank bloody God,' Babs cheers. Heather gives me a sorry look.

'It's fine, Heather, trust me. Now I want you both to enjoy yourselves but later you've got to give me your opinions. Alright? We all know I can't live with a wife killer.'

Suddenly the front door closes and we freeze.

The Landlord

'Hello,' Ian calls. 'You there, Cathy?' A second later he breezes in. 'Oh, I'm the last one home. Hope I haven't been keeping everybody waiting.' He's wearing a light short-sleeve shirt that hangs casually over his cream cotton trousers. His aftershave is spicy and the scent of it fills the room. Unfreezing, we chorus a stiff hello while Ian excuses himself to get something from the kitchen.

'Did he hear us?' Babs whispers but I don't get to reply because Ian appears again with four champagne glasses and a bottle of Dom Pérignon. 'That looks tempting,' Babs coos.

'Should I pour one for each of us?' Ian jiggles the bottle.

'Please,' I say, nervously passing out the glasses, a terrible thirst taking hold of me.

'The house is stunning,' Babs begins.

'Very elegant,' Heather adds.

Ian nods. 'These Georgian beauties are a bit special alright. Until you start heating them in winter.'

The girls respond with a loud laugh. Then Ian clinks our glasses and we all drink. 'So, tell me all about yourselves,' he says, as we get comfortable on the aged leather sofas. 'I've been dying to get a chance to sit down with Cathy and suddenly there's four of us. What a treat.'

The conversation gets going and flows without a hiccup as the champagne disappears and the wine gets poured. Ian recommends a Malaysian restaurant and orders it despite my protests that it's my treat. When it arrives, he tips the delivery guy a twenty and we eat straightaway. The food is delicious and I can only shrug silently as Heather slurps her noodles wide-eyed and Babs winks at me.

Ian asks about our jobs. I tell him about my acting work, Babs about her job as product manager and buyer with Brown Thomas and Heather about her lecturing at the university. Ian is fascinated by it all and interested in everything, even surprising Babs by knowing some of the products she sells.

'You see I only know, Babs, because my wife, Anna, used to be very fond of that particular serum Shiro Tamanu, and BT was the only place she could find it. She explained to me that its hyaluronic qualities made it unique and the only products that came close were Lift from Clinique and Vital from Kiehl's.'

At the mention of Ian's wife, I grip the stem of my wine glass hard between my fingers. 'I love Kiehl's,' I blurt tensely.

Heather looks at him in surprise. 'I've never met a man who'd heard of hyaluronic acid.'

Ian arches an eyebrow. 'Neither have I.' There's a second of silence but then it breaks with the sound of Babs laughing loudly.

'I didn't know you were married, Ian,' she lies with ice-smooth coolness.

'Yes,' he says, the brightness in his face fading. 'Although my wife hasn't been in the picture for some time.'

'How so?' Heather asks.

'Oh,' he waves his hand as if swatting a fly, 'a god-awful long story I won't bore you with.'

'No, tell us,' I plead, aware suddenly that everybody is watching him keenly. Suddenly nobody is moving. Nobody is making any sound at all.

'Well, I'm surprised you haven't heard already to be honest. It seems like the whole world has.' He sighs, looking momentarily wretched as he glugs a mouthful of white wine before placing his glass down on the table. 'You see, around eighteen months ago, my wife Anna disappeared without a trace. I went to the police immediately but within a week I became their chief suspect as they were convinced I had murdered her.'

We sit like statues and listen. The word 'murdered' seems to echo in the silence that follows. 'Yes,' he says then, breaking it. 'I know it's awful but there you go. Our relationship had been rocky over the last six months and I had been behaving badly for reasons I won't go into, so I sort of teed myself up to be suspect number one.' Suddenly his voice is choking in his throat. He folds his lips nervously and rubs the corner of his eye. Babs stares at him sadly but I notice Heather is observing him keenly. I don't know what to think. I sit and watch on, mute with confusion.

'Their evidence never stacked up, of course, so eventually they threw in the towel, but by that stage my reputation was shredded and my life in tatters.'

'That's terrible,' Babs offers.

Ian shakes himself out and tries to perk up. 'Look, I know this must be a terrible shock to you all, especially you, Cathy, so if you feel too uncomfortable being here after learning about it, I understand one hundred per cent. I mean, I'm being ridiculous even thinking that I can tell you this and expect that you'd want to stay.'

'It's OK,' I mutter, almost immediately wishing I hadn't opened my mouth.

Ian smiles weakly. 'At least now it doesn't have to be this bloody awful elephant in the room business.'

'It is better,' Heather agrees, without sounding too sympathetic.

He heaves out a dejected groan. Then he snatches the wine bottle and does the refills as we all look on glumly. 'I guess it's just been bubbling away inside me for so long and then accidentally sometimes it just comes out.' He raises a glass and we all do the same. 'But please, no pity. Now I just want to put it all behind me.' We nod acquiescently. 'Let's give this toast to Cathy and hope her stay here is a happy one.'

'To Cathy,' everybody agrees, but I can't help noticing that there's something in Heather's demeanour that tells me she isn't feeling quite so celebratory.

Minutes later the girls announce their plan to order an Uber.

'Please feel free to stay if it's easier,' Ian suggests kindly. 'It's really no trouble. There's lots of extra beds.'

'Thanks, Ian, but I wouldn't impose.' Heather shoos the suggestion away and slips out the door followed swiftly by Babs. The edges of Ian's mouth turn down all of a sudden but when he catches me glancing over, he swiftly resurrects his smile. Everybody waves and for a fleeting minute I have the odd sensation of imagining being a married couple saying goodnight to friends.

It must have been exactly what Ian's wife Anna did before she mysteriously disappeared.

When the front door shuts, I go straight to the kitchen to clean up but am stopped short.

'*No.*' The force of Ian's command is so striking it makes me flinch. I remain still as a stone, my heart hammering inside my chest. His vexed expression vaults into a grin. 'I won't have you lift a finger, Cathy. I'll take care of all of that and you get your rest. You've got rehearsals in the morning.'

'Sure,' I say, fidgeting with my neck as I move towards the stairs, keen now to get to bed, wishing I had somehow invented an excuse to leave with my friends. 'That was a lovely night.'

'Overdue,' he simply replies, giving me a glazed smile and turning back to do the dishes.

As soon as I'm upstairs in my bedroom I text both the girls.
Well?

Babs is back first. **Weird night. Fun though?**

Next comes Heather. **Get some rest and we'll chat tomorrow.**

15

Lunch is a conference call. Babs, Heather, me.

'Drop-dead gorgeous,' Babs laughs.

'Definitely,' Heather agrees.

'I enjoyed it. Mostly anyway,' I say.

'The food was fab,' Babs trills.

'And the *champagne*,' Heather adds.

'And wine,' I add.

'And *more* wine,' Babs chirps.

'God yeah,' Heather sighs. 'Anybody else feeling hungover?'

There's a collective groan. Then I wait, trying not to feel on tenterhooks. '*So then*, what's the verdict?'

'God, Cathy,' Heather says and I watch her frown deeply. 'I just don't know. Gorgeous house. And Ian's charming as hell, but the whole set-up of you being there alone with him, well, I'm not sure.' She pauses. 'And I'm sorry. Because who knows what happened to his wife really?'

'Fair point,' Babs acknowledges, refusing to concede entirely. 'But *still*.'

I deflate a little. 'Still what, Babs?'

'He's funny, loaded, kind?'

'He is,' Heather agrees.

'So?'

'So it's hard to know what to advise. Because he seemed to be happy to talk all about his wife at one point. But then when I got home and thought about it, I realised it doesn't mean anything. Other than that he knows we know.'

'So you're not sure, Heather?'

'I'm not sure I want to advise you to stay or to leave. I don't think it's my decision to make.'

When I get back to the house that evening, Ian isn't around but there's a note on the table again.

> Cathy, last night was a treat and your friends are wonderful. I'm happy we got time to finally sit and chat. Am away once more on business but back in a few days. Hope you get settled and comfortable.
> Ian

I drop the note on the table and go to the kitchen. There's a half bottle of wine left in the fridge so I pour a glass and return to the living room. As I drop down on the couch I feel my spirits begin to wane. The girls were honest with me, just as I asked them to be and I'm still no wiser; no closer to a decision on what I should do next.

I sit and slowly drink the wine. I try to unwind. But my mind keeps wrestling with the big question. What am I going to do? It's clear now that Heather is right. This is my own decision and I have to figure it out without delay.

I get up and walk to the back window in the dining room and look out to the garden. It's wide and deep and I think I can see some kind of building at the end of it. Perhaps a cabin of some sort. I wonder why Ian is so reticent about letting me in there. I wonder too about the blood-curdling scream which woke me the first night I slept in the house, though I've never heard anything since. Was it from the garden like I thought?

My mind switches to Jamie. Part of me regrets probing him for information about his mum. I know it was certainly a bit crude and unfair and yet still he answered me clearly, saying that although he believed Ian could be capable of the crime, he was still certain his dad wasn't the one who made Anna disappear.

The Landlord

It hits me like a hammer blow. If Jamie is right and Ian isn't responsible for Anna's disappearance, *then somebody else is*. Somebody has murdered an innocent boy's mother, tarnished his father's reputation, shattered their family. Jamie's words repeat like a silent echo ... *as long as we don't know what happened this family will never be at peace.*

I decide then. I want his family to have peace, to get closure. If Ian really killed Anna, then justice must be served. But if Jamie is right, then somebody is hiding secrets. Secrets I'm making it my business to find out.

16

Buoyed with a new resolve I return to Belleview Road after rehearsals to find an elderly woman coming out through the front door. She wears a long old-fashioned raincoat, carries a small black leather handbag and has her white hair meticulously arranged. I haven't seen her before and I'm surprised by how tall she is.

'You must be Cathy?' She stops at the edge of the high granite steps and peers down.

'That's me.'

'Cathy …?' She waits, stiff-backed and po-faced.

'Quinn.'

'I see.' She looks underwhelmed as she runs two slightly glassy eyes over me.

'And you are?' I ask, suddenly a bit irritated by the bluntness of the interrogation.

'Regina Bastible. I'm Mr Fitzsimmons's housekeeper.'

'I see,' I say, mimicking her and immediately feeling very childish. But my curiosity races into overdrive. Ian never mentioned a housekeeper. How long has she worked for them? What might she know about Anna? About what happened.

'Nice to meet you, Mrs Bastible. Fancy a quick cup of tea?'

'No.' I'm sure I hear a Scottish lilt in her accent. Walking down the steps she stops when she reaches my level. 'Mr Fitzsimmons said you will be staying indefinitely. Is that correct?'

I shrug. 'I haven't decided.'

'Well, if you do, I'm sure we'll have time to get acquainted. I come once or twice a week, depending upon Mr Fitzsimmons's schedule.'

The Landlord

'I'll look forward to that.' I'm about to stick out my hand, to claw back some hope of connection with this hostile woman, when she steps down and past me.

'Goodbye Ms Quinn.'

Mercifully, Leno's is open when I get there and I smile when I see the golden Aussie behind the till.

'Evening, Cathy.'

'JJ.' I make a determined effort not to gush this time. 'Hi. Didn't expect you'd be open.'

'Two nights a week, just a thing I'm trying out at the minute. We'll see how it goes. Anthea and her gang were keen on it.' The way he says it I get the feeling his keenness may not have matched hers.

I remember Anthea, the stylish and friendly woman I judged too quickly for flirting with JJ only to find myself doing the same a few minutes later.

Craning my neck, I spot her cycling group huddled together in the same spot as last time, with Anthea at the centre. Now she looks my way. 'Cathy, you're back.' Both her arms wave excitedly.

JJ grins as I return the greeting a little weaker than intended.

'Come on over.' Anthea makes a beckoning gesture and the group stare at me in unison. I don't want to join them but can see now I don't have an option, not unless I wish to be openly unfriendly, which I don't. 'Gerald, grab Cathy a chair,' Anthea says to the jowly man with the plummy voice. Gerald fusses with a nearby chair, squeezing it amongst the group, and everybody shifts for me to take a space beside Anthea.

Silently I sit, feeling part captured fish, part new girl at school.

Gerald waves at JJ. 'What'll you have, Cathy?'

'Orange juice would be great, thanks.' He relays it officiously as Anthea places a hand on my knee. 'Everybody,' she announces, 'this is Cathy who was living in 762 with Ian Fitzsimmons.'

Shocked gasps ricochet across the table. Somebody laughs and I hear a garbled *'no'*.

'You're still *alive?*' a pale man quips. He has wispy ginger hair with a side parting.

'Stewie, would you stop.' Anthea wags a playful finger in his direction. 'Cathy, let me introduce you. This is Gerald – hedge fund guru and so loaded we're all envious.' Gerald turns sideways and juts out his chin, his large breasts jiggling inside his Lycra as the group laugh heartily. He grips his hands together and sighs dolefully. 'Guilty as charged.'

Anthea points to a bald man with small eyes. 'Clive, our legal whizz.' He taps his long nose by way of introducing himself. 'Jemima, who looks after our chakras.' A birdlike, ethereal woman breathlessly says 'hello'. 'Computer Stewie, who finds it impossible to say what he really means.' The ginger haired man, confused to discover me still alive, snorts the word 'not'. 'And Carol, our health and well-being expert.' A stretched-looking woman nods back, her dyed blonde hair peeled back from a perma-tanned forehead into a coiled bun. I flinch when I recognise the woman who accused me of stealing her dog. I wait for her to spot me but her attention remains on her phone.

'Hope I can remember all that.'

'No rush,' Clive says dryly, his whisker-thin eyebrows arching.

'Were you passing?' Anthea asks.

The juice arrives and I gulp down a mouthful. 'Not exactly. I might actually stay on in Belleview Road for a while.'

The collective sigh is instant. 'You do *know* about Ian Fitzsimmons,' Stewie says, a puzzled frown lining his forehead. 'I mean about his wife?'

'Yes, I understand she disappeared.'

'*Got disappeared* more like.' Carol eyeballs me, and I can't tell if she recognises me as she tucks her phone back inside her pocket. 'Surely you know that much?'

'It's still a mystery, Carol,' Jemima whispers.

'Not in the slightest.' Gerald dismisses the idea with a wave. 'Fitzsimmons knocked her off. The dogs in the street could tell you that.'

The Landlord

'Wait now.' Anthea holds up two ringed hands. 'None of us really know what happened. They were always an unusual couple.' The others nod, happy with Anthea's gentle admonishment. 'I prefer to think the best of people. It's perfectly possible Ian is blameless. You shouldn't listen to this lot.' She rolls her eyes to soften the telling-off and the rest smile.

Gerald, who had detached himself briefly from the group, returns and taps the table with his knuckles. 'Got the bill so we're good to go.' The group stands as if to command. 'Right, we've one hour before Stewie has to put on his pyjamas so I think that gives us enough time to do the rest of the park. Hopefully that'll have us all in shape for Saturday week.' He starts to walk out and the others file after him.

Anthea stalls, turning to me quickly. 'I'm delighted to see you back, Cathy. You'll be a breath of fresh air here,' she whispers. 'Don't mind this crowd, we like to joke but they're a great gang. Now I better get back on my bike before they leave me behind.' She presses my forearm gently. 'Hope we'll bump into each other soon.'

The tension eases from my shoulders as Anthea skips away and out the door. I finish my drink but find myself standing at a large empty table full of dirty plates. I'm about to turn and leave when JJ appears. 'Juice alright?'

'Gorgeous.' He starts clearing. 'Here, let me help.' When I look around, I see only one other girl working.

'Naw, you're alright.'

I gather them with him anyway, not ready to go home yet. 'It's for my free coffee. Remember, I owe you.'

He grins. 'Fair enough.'

'But I still have to pay you for today.'

He shakes his head. 'Boss man Gerald got that.'

I laugh. 'Is he the boss?'

'Naw, that's Anthea. Or maybe Carol.'

I shuffle after him gathering up the empty glasses as he makes his way back to the washing station with his tray. 'An interesting bunch.'

JJ puts his tray down. 'You'll get to know them soon enough, Cathy. But what is it the Romans used to say?'

I shrug, clueless. He grins, spotting a stray customer wandering in. 'Make haste slowly. Hope to see you around then.'

17

Malia doesn't bring up the issue of Old John again and even though I'd like to talk to her about it, I get the feeling she doesn't want to. So I let it lie. I've been watching him and he's not doing anything out of the ordinary bar the usual stuff, explaining other people's lines to them, advising where they should stand in relation to his position, and what their attitude to his character ought to be at any given moment. AA does a lot of nodding, rubbing his pointy nose and flattening his wispy hair across his scalp while teasing out the wisdom of Old John's suggestions.

Once or twice I question the blocking AA and Old John come up with, but each time it galvanises their determination to stand together and keep me in my place. Taking Malia's advice, I follow her lead, and keep my battles occasional. But quietly it gets me how blindly the rest of the cast accept everything AA and Old John tell them, like serfs before their imperial masters.

The play no longer preoccupies me, though. I only want to get through it so I can get home. Ian's still away. His last text suggested he would be delayed. Tonight is my chance to go into the garden.

The key to the basement is where Ian left it, hanging on a brass hook by the door in the hallway. I take it down, place it carefully inside my pocket, when suddenly there's a loud knock and I step back. Fumbling, I return the key to the hook, gather myself and open up.

Justin stands there grinning. 'Hey, Cath.' Nonchalantly he hangs there, dressed in his Rolling Stones T-shirt and blue jeans, chewing gum and looking at me with his sunglasses stuck up in his hair. 'Going to invite me in?'

I frown, close the door, retrieve the key and open it again. 'What are you doing here, Justin? What do you want?'

He chews noisily, flashing his shiny white top teeth in a cocky smile. 'I could explain, Cath, if you'd let me in to talk.'

I'm about to tell him I don't want to talk to him right now, or any time, that he's not worth another second of my life. Then I get a better idea.

'OK.' I step out onto the granite step closing the heavy front door behind me.

'What are you doing?' His cool calm morphs to confusion.

'What did you want to talk to me about, Justin?'

'Us.' He says, his voice rising. '*This*.' He points to the house. 'Everything.'

I walk down the steps. 'I've got to go down to the basement so you can talk to me as I'm working.'

He follows. 'Working?' His eyebrows raise. 'What are you working on in the basement?'

'You'll see.' I put the key in the door but it doesn't budge. 'Shit.' The door is worn with its clouded glass and peeling paint. I take a step back and try and get a look in the window but the curtains are pulled so there's nothing to see.

'Cathy, what are you doing? You don't even have the right key. Are you sure you're supposed to be going in there?'

I ignore Justin and keep trying. But cautiously. I know if the key snaps the plan is doomed. There'll be no way of explaining it to Ian other than coming up with some tall story and then he'll be watching me.

I keep fidgeting as Justin smirks. I'm about to give up when there's a click, followed by a twist and the noisy pop of the door releasing. I stand back.

The Landlord

'There,' I say, 'we're going in.'

'What for?'

'Just move, Justin.'

He steps forward, pushing the shades deeper into his tousled hair and I nudge him inside, pulling the door fast behind me. Suddenly it's pitch black.

'What are you doing?' he bleats.

'We're not supposed to be in here and Ian's away so I can't risk him coming home and discovering me. Flick the switch.'

He clicks it but nothing happens. 'It's dead.'

The place smells of damp and mould. I touch the wall but it feels wet and I pull away quickly. I don't like touching things I cannot see, especially wet things.

'Now what's your plan?'

I search my pocket for my phone but find I've forgotten it. 'Put your torch on. I left my phone in the house.'

He pulls it out and gets it lit. 'Battery's almost out,' he explains, rolling it over the walls and across the stairs leading back up to the house. I see peeling wallpaper stained black in places. A battered staircase with no carpet. Scratched, dirty walls. 'What is this, Cathy? A fucking dungeon?'

I lift a foot but it unpeels noisily from the ground. 'Shine it on the floor.' He points it down and I can see it's covered in a thin film of mud.

'Aw, fuck's sake, that's on my trainers now,' he whines.

'Light that door to the first room.'

He does as I ask and I try the old worn knob. It twists but doesn't open.

'Probably rotted,' Justin snipes. 'I mean smell this fucking place, Cath.'

The dusty odour clings to my nostrils. The old staircase that should lead into the ground floor has been boarded off with plywood, preventing the whole area getting any proper ventilation. A musty stench of abandoned bedding and unopened cupboards hangs in the clammy air.

'What are you doing down here?' he demands.

'Just keep going.' I poke him again and he shuffles reluctantly down the corridor. 'There's two more rooms and the garden. I want to check them all.'

'Why?'

'Just *move*, Justin.'

We're shuffling quietly towards the door to the second room as Justin sprays the light from side to side when a pair of eyes light up on top of an old dresser. Something jumps and knocks the phone from his grasp. Justin reels, slamming me into the wall.

'Fuck.' Cursing, he drops down to search for his phone. 'Oh, you are *kidding* me.' He finds it, cracked and caked in wet mud. 'The screen is ruined now.' A trickle of light escapes from it, barely enough to make out bits of a broken vase on the floor but there's no sign of the animal. 'What the hell was that?'

The doorbell rings before I can reply. I clutch Justin's arm. The muscles beneath his skin pull tight and hard.

'He's bloody back, isn't he?' he hisses.

'Shush.'

He snorts and the bell rings again.

'Why would he ring his own bell? He's got a flipping key, Justin.' He moves to leave but I block him. 'Wait,' I whisper. 'Just give them a minute.' Breathing heavily, he stands next to me, his annoyance oozing from him in waves. I hear what sound like footsteps departing. Then nothing.

Satisfied they've left, he brushes past me, opening the door like an escaping prisoner.

Outside in the light, he grimaces at his muddy sneakers. His swagger's all evaporated, leaving him pinched and petulant. 'Well?'

'What?'

'What are you going to *do*, Cathy?'

'I haven't decided.' I think he's about to leave when he leans into my face.

'Cathy, stop playing *fucking* games. You know this guy's killed his bloody wife. I've already told you. You're playing with fire and you're going to get burned. It's madness. Get as far away from here as you can and do it quickly. I can't believe I even agreed to come down to this dump with you.'

Open-mouthed I stare back at him. The bitterness of his outburst catches me off guard. The anger and naked aggression as he leaned towards me.

'Justin,' I blurt, but he turns and hurries out through the front garden and across the street. With a huff I step out, locking the door to the basement and scurrying back up the steps to the main front entrance. I hate Justin right now. What I hate even more is that he might be a hundred per cent correct.

18

Work improves. Today I'm nailing every scene and forcing Old John to keep up. My timing, movement and delivery are finally coming together and I can feel the muted judgement losing its traction.

At lunchtime AA calls me over, tapping his chin with a bony finger.

'Cathy.'

'Yeah.'

'How're you feeling?'

'Great.'

'I mean about the play.'

'Oh ... great. I think I've got on top of it a bit better now.'

AA nods, the faintest trace of a thin smile appearing. 'Yeah, you were struggling a bit in the beginning.' He pauses to sniff noisily. 'How're you getting along with the rest of the cast?' AA knows the rest of the cast are hostile to both Malia and me. They all worked together recently on another show and are tighter than a fist. What's more, AA has almost been happy about it and egging Old John on so I don't get why he's asking this. 'Fine,' I say, not taking the bait, 'and I love watching Malia.'

'Holding her own, isn't she?' he replies with a sniff. It's like he's skirting around things. 'So, the couch? Think you'll be needing it?'

Suddenly I remember his offer. 'Oh, sorry, yes, no! Sorry but I got a place.'

'You did?' He looks at me suspiciously, scratching the stubble on his neck.

'Yeah.'

'When?'

'Some days ago.' His eyes narrow. 'Just got confirmed last night, though,' I mumble.

'Good for you, Cathy.' His small mouth smiles tightly. 'Just needed to know in case somebody wanted it.'

As I walk home that evening I think about Justin. I'm not surprised he showed up at the house. It's exactly what he would do. Trying to worm his way back with me. Switching on his caring side like he's putting on a coat. But I'm past buying any of it now. I know he doesn't care, and probably never really did. What I can't understand is why he wanted me out of the house so badly. He ran the other day at the first sight of Ian. He got so nervous when he thought somebody had caught us in the basement. I could feel his body tense and quiver. And then when he leaned over me, snarling and insisting that what I was doing was stupid and reckless ... Why?

I choose not to think about him but then find myself remembering the housekeeper, Regina Bastible. 'Cathy who?' Another person whose hostility is difficult to understand. Her withering stare, the questions, her refusal to answer mine directly. She made no secret of her contempt for me, despite having never met me. I can only guess she assumes I'm a gold digger or some kind of leech she needs to sweep out of the house. I have no doubt it's what she intends to do, but I know she must know things about Ian and Anna that very few others would. So when I see her again, I'm going to have to figure out a way to get her to help me.

I walk through the front gate, wrestling with the idea of how to make it work, when there's a ping on my phone. It's a message from Ian saying he's left a casserole dish in the next door neighbour's front garden for their dog, and could I please collect it. 'Sure' I reply, making a mental note not to forget. Then I look up and see Babs. She is sitting on the top step, grinning behind yellow rimmed sunglasses, her long golden hair up in a messy bun, her arms spread wide. 'Hello there.' She greets me warmly. We hug and I inhale her gorgeous perfume. 'Thought I'd pay you a visit at your manor.' We both gaze down at the joggers and cyclists drifting by. 'People-watchers' paradise this!'

'Isn't it?' I smile, delighted to see my friend.

'Big bad wolf away?' Babs jokes and I frown. 'Sorry, bad joke!' I lighten up. 'He is in fact.'

'I know. I rang three times.' Babs laughs and I throw my arm around her. 'So, what did you decide?' She swivels and looks up and down the imposing red brick facade. 'I mean, am I jealous or what?'

I glance up at it too, wondering if my friend has already figured out my answer, sensing she has. 'I'm staying.'

Babs doesn't seem surprised. 'Ian?'

We both laugh. 'Actually, I met his son, Jamie.'

'Jesus, you move fast,' she elbows me playfully.

'Be serious for a minute.'

'OK.' Babs makes a contrite face. 'Tell me then.'

'He's back from Scotland, where he's recently moved. He's lovely. Kind, like Ian, but different. Bashful. Anyway, to cut to it, I just straight out sort of probed him about his missing mum.'

'What?'

'Yeah ...'

Babs's face drops. 'Please tell me you're joking?'

'I know it's bad. But I just wanted to know about her. He was there and I didn't know when I'd get another chance.'

'But what did you say?'

'I said I knew his mum was missing and it must be hard living with that.'

She looks worried. 'So what did he say?'

'That he knew I wanted to know if his dad was responsible.'

'Shit!' Babs makes an icky grimace. 'Well, does he think he was?'

'He said he didn't believe for a second that Ian did it.'

'OK.' Babs pauses to digest this for a second. 'Well, isn't that good?' I think of telling her the rest. Of how he also said he believed it was something Ian was capable of. But I won't. Not yet.

'Yes, but it made me realise that if it isn't Ian then I want to know what really did happen to Anna. Because then what's happened to Ian, what's happened to Jamie, is brutal. And plain wrong, Babs.'

Babs sees the bulge of a tear in my eye and pulls me towards her. I feel the soft press of her lips on my forehead as she draws me close.

'It's OK,' she says.

I stay like that for a second. Just happy to be held. To have a friend understand what I've been feeling alone. 'Babs, do you remember I told you he has this thing about not going into the basement and the garden.'

Babs draws back, spooked. 'You're not? You want to go down and check it out?' I nod. 'Oh, *shit*. You want *me* to come with you?'

'Would you?'

Babs glances over the edge of the steps, worry lines on her brow. 'If you need me to.'

The tension lifts from my chest and I jump to my feet. 'Wait here. I'm getting the key.' I open the front door, dash inside and grab the key from its holder, and return. But when I get outside Babs is standing, sucking her teeth and looking at her phone.

'What?'

'Oh, Cathy, it's work I'm afraid.'

'You have to go?'

She nods, her mouth turning down. 'They've just texted to say they need me to do a trade show in the morning and want me to make a big presentation. I'll have to prep it.' She gives me a kiss. 'Another time. OK?'

19

The key works today. Like the rust or stiffness of the lock has shifted. This time it clicks smoothly, releasing with a pop like the lid coming off a well-sealed jar, and the door eases inwards. My hand reaches to my neck and I fidget with the top of my dress. I keep the door open for a second, staring into the dank corridor. *I'm alone but it's going to be OK. I have nothing to be afraid of* I tell myself silently. Then I step inside, close the door and seal myself in from the world outside.

The smell hits me first. Rich, soupy and heavy with the dust which shimmers in the crack of light that edges through the door glass. With my torch on I make out the peeling walls, the scuffed staircase, the streaked filthy floor. The vase is where we left it. I step forwards and over the broken pieces, spotting cat prints in the layer of caked dust.

There's a chest of drawers against the corridor wall which also has the paw prints, revealing what must have happened.

I try the drawers but they barely budge. It's an old solid wood thing and the damp has stuck them. Tugging them hard, I get them to inch out a fraction but there's nothing inside so I leave it. Along the corridor there are three doors; one at the front, another at the middle and the last at the back. I go to the middle one. It's fitted with a standard issue exterior door lock. I expect it's locked but when I push it gently it eases open. The inside switch isn't working so I use the phone to light up the space. There's nothing of note. A disused, stained mattress on a bed and some old clothes tossed on the floor. I keep shining the light around and see the kitchenette and toilet. It must have been a studio apartment that has been abandoned.

The Landlord

I get out and down to the last room. Again it's unlocked. It squeaks when the door opens. It's the same set-up, another compact studio apartment, similar to the middle one but slightly smaller. The bed is twisted on its side and old black bags with clothes tumbling out of them litter the floor. It's almost like somebody was packing up to leave and got bored and gave up.

I don't waste time but get out so I can try the back door at the far end of the corridor, which leads to the garden. I'm about to try the handle when I spot footprints on the floor. Large fresh prints twist inwards to a door behind me under the staircase. I pull the handle expecting a cloud of dust but there isn't any. The door opens easily to reveal a storage room. Inside I make out different tools and a pair of navy-blue overalls hanging off a nail on the back of the door.

I venture deeper in; against the back panel are old leather boots, wellies, an ancient lawnmower, and a toolbox. Then a big spade, its handle worn smooth, leaning into the corner. It has an angled tip, like the ones builders use to mix cement. Kneeling closer I inspect it.

It's bloodstained. A broad patch of it at the sharp end, and as I look closer, I notice more streaks up the shaft. My heart thumps and I swallow. I turn the shovel round to find something sticking out from the edge of it. Touching it, I discover a knotted clump of hair.

Staggering backwards, I scrabble to my feet, the air suddenly too thick to breathe. I stumble to the corridor, bumping into the chest of drawers, winding myself. I reach for the wall to steady myself when the doorbell chimes.

'Hello?' It's a woman's voice. She is outside. 'Cathy?'

'Crap.' The word escapes through my clenched teeth.

'I think the doorbell is broken.' The basement door pushes inwards. A gust blows down the corridor. I wait but nobody comes in. 'Cathy?' This time I can place the voice. It's coming from above on the steps. I hurry up the corridor and peek out to find

Anthea leaning over the railing. Closing the door quickly behind me I rush up to her. 'Did I disturb you?'

'No.' I shape my mouth into a smile and command myself to act.

Anthea looks me up and down, then reaches over and brushes something on my arm.

'What's that?' She inspects her fingertip which is covered in black dust.

'Sorry, I was doing some housekeeping and didn't expect I'd get so dirty.' I rub at it but it smudges my dress. 'How are things?'

'I thought Ian had a housekeeper?'

'Yes, he does. It's just I had some stuff I wanted to store and Ian guessed the basement might be best.'

Anthea smiles but shakes her head. 'That's so strange.'

'What?'

'He always said to me it was a no-go zone till he got it refurbished.' She holds my gaze, her smile rock steady.

For a second I freeze then I remember that I'm a trained actress. I must appear unruffled, affect a casual demeanour, pretend I have not seen a blood-soaked spade. 'He must have had a rethink. Like to come in?' I offer the suggestion as nonchalantly as I can, slipping into acting mode. Before she can answer I about turn, opening the front door wide.

'No.' Anthea's hand lands on my shoulder. I swallow but keep steady. 'I was just collecting a casserole dish I had dropped over to Ian.'

I spot it inside on the hall table. It's the one Ian asked me to collect from next door earlier. The uneaten dish he gave to the neighbour's new dog.

I pick it up and Anthea takes it from my hands.

'Sorry. It hasn't been cleaned I'm afraid. I wasn't expecting you.'

Anthea crinkles her nose as she inspects it. Then she runs a hand through her hair and I watch it shimmer. 'It's just what the dishwasher does, Cathy.' She points at the caked remains round the edges. 'It bakes it in with the heat. Poor Ian, he's too busy to notice but the main thing is he ate it. That's all I'm concerned about.' I try to think of something to say. Some words to explain. But I don't have any. 'I must get you over whenever you're free, Cathy. One of the gang will be doing something soon so I'll let you know. We'd love to have you. Would you come?'

'Course,' I say, meaning it. I'd like to get to know Anthea a little better, maybe get her thoughts on what happened between Anna and Ian, or if she might care to share what the rest of her gang think about it, even though I already know most of them are convinced of Ian's guilt. And now that I've found this spade, can I say I really blame them?

'Fab.' Anthea slips across the road. I watch her weave through the cars and make her way back up the steps to her front door. Before going in she turns and waves. My mind returns to the bloodied spade and I wave back weakly.

20

'I've given it a lot of thought, Cathy,' AA says, as if already bored with the conversation which has only just begun. I rub the sleeve of my blouse, feeling my bracelet snag the fabric. When I unpick it and get it loose, I notice AA is shrugging. 'I've even discussed it with John and we're all of the same opinion. It would be for the best.'

My chest heaves. 'Sorry, Andy,' I reply, my voice straining with the effort to remain polite. 'But why would you discuss my part with John?'

Another weary groan. 'Because John has been at this game a long time, Cathy.'

'This game?' A knot balls deep in the pit of my stomach.

'Yes, he's got a wealth of experience. We're both on the same wavelength here. That comes with experience.'

'Sorry, when did you decide this exactly?'

'We've been reviewing it for a while. I just thought last night was time to execute the decision.' I blink, my head shaking side to side, confusion and disgust erupting within me. 'While there's still time and you can get to grips with playing Regan instead of Goneril. I really think it's the character in the play most suited to you.'

'Well who's going to play Goneril now?'

'Ellie.'

'So Ellie and me, after three weeks of rehearsals, are switching from playing one sister to another sister?'

'Cathy,' he says very deliberately, 'it's *my* mistake. Ellie was miscast, she *is* Goneril and you'll make a *fine* Regan.'

The rest of the cast troop back in from coffee break. Old John's first in and Andy swaps his 'deed done' nod with him.

The Landlord

Malia comes in too, followed by Ellie. Neither of them meets my eye. I'm getting that 'last one to know' feeling and I want to scream.

'Do what you can with the lines for today, Cathy. I imagine you'll have a lot of them by heart through osmosis at this point and then you can just keep working on them in the evenings and weekends. I'm sure it'll be fine. We still have a whole fortnight.' Andy beams a smile so fake at his cast I'm surprised it doesn't slide straight off his face. 'OK everybody,' he announces importantly, 'let's get down to business.'

My legs are heavy when I lope across to Babs's flat. She doesn't answer. When I text her, I learn she's away with work.

Stay over. Will catch up when I get back.

With a despondent groan I let myself in, then instantly drop onto the couch in the living room where I hold my face in my hands. The spade is all I can think of. Each time I close my eyes I see the dark stain of blood at its tip. The tangle of knotted hair on its edge. All day long I've been fighting the urge to go to the police because I had the idea of telling Babs, of getting her advice. I didn't want to tell her over the phone. But now she's not here I don't know what to do.

I toss my sheets with my new part underlined on the floor, trying just to focus on absorbing lines. If I can turn on to autopilot and try and learn them, I can block out all the worries which are starting to overwhelm me. *Evidence. You have the evidence of what Ian must have done.* I keep telling myself silently, *Justin was right. You're acting crazy.*

I blow out and lean back, releasing a tired groan. I can't jump to conclusions. I have to work through this. Things can be explained. I have to trust Jamie's judgement.

When I look down my phone is ringing. Almost listless, I answer.
'Cathy?'
'Yes.' The number isn't familiar.
'Anthea.'

'Oh.' I try to remember exchanging contacts but can't recall it. 'Is now a bad time?'

I rub the back of my neck and clear my throat. 'No. It's fine.'

'I was wondering if you'd like to hook up for a drink tonight?'

My gaze switches to the wall of Babs's apartment then back at the pages splayed on the floor and I sit up. 'Sure.'

'Great. Chez Jack on Elgin Street in half an hour. Would that work?'

'I can't wait,' I say, surprised I actually really mean it.

Anthea smiles as we clink white wine spritzers. Chez Jack is busy and bouncing. A pocket-sized wine bar, it's a crisp mix of exposed red brick, polished wooden floors and elegantly displayed bottles on steel racks. Anthea is dressed in a light blue linen shirt, with several buttons open at the chest, and I notice a gold chain on her neck with a small locket. Her make up is fresh, her lipstick bright red and her hair shines. I'm regretting having skipped my shower and wondering if I might have chosen something more appealing than my simple white shirt and blue jeans but if Anthea has noticed she isn't letting on. 'You're looking so well as always,' she says, 'and I'm so happy you could make it with such short notice.' I shrug and take a long drink, content to listen to her earnest compliments. The alcohol tastes just right as I swallow it gratefully. 'So, I have to ask, what is it you do, Cathy?'

I place my glass back on the table. A sudden burst of indignation bubbles up when I think of the play. 'I'm an actress.'

Anthea lights up, big blue eyes gazing at me warmly and a wide smile flashing a row of neat, polished teeth. It's so radiant it makes me smile back, but I feel relaxed because this meeting is helping to keep me sane. 'I used to *love* acting.'

'Yeah?'

She nods, sweeping a strand of expensively coloured blonde hair from her eyes. 'But I don't think I was any good at it. You either have it or you don't, isn't that what they say?'

I shrug. 'I'm not sure.'

'What kind of stuff?' Anthea wiggles in her seat, excitement exuding from her in waves. 'Box office gold, I'll bet?'

'Anything I can get,' I say flatly.

This makes Anthea shriek with laughter and she covers he mouth. 'Cathy! I think I just got alcohol up my nose.' She wipes a tear from the corner of her eye. 'We need more people with a sense of humour around here. You'd be surprised at how rare it can be.'

I think of Old John and AA. 'No, I wouldn't,' I say laughing also, pleased to find myself warming to my new chatty neighbour. Anthea clinks my glass once more and I sense some invisible soft core inside her itching to free itself. Something gentle but bruised, hidden deep down under layers of expensive body lotions, blow-dried hair and polished nails.

'And you?' I ask.

'Oh,' she rests her chin on the heel of her hand, 'I was an executive assistant for years but then you know the story … kids came along and all the rest of it. We've the three boys and my husband, Harold, has his own insurance company so we agreed it was best we let him focus on that so I let it go.'

'You miss it?' I ask, not entirely sure what the role is.

She twists one of the rings on her finger. 'Not really, the work wasn't that exciting. More like something to keep me busy, but sometimes I suppose I do, if that makes any sense.' I heed the raw note in her voice and don't pursue it. She gulps down some spritzer and makes a happy face. I know she's switching tack and wonder where to. 'I wanted to talk to you about Ian.'

'OK.'

'How are you getting on?'

The tension returns to my shoulders and my carefree mood wobbles. *I found the spade he used to slay his wife*, I want to say. *It had blood and hair on it and I can take you right over and show it to you. Because I need someone to tell me what to do right now. Whether I'm crazy to still be there.* 'OK,' I say breathing out heavily. 'It's kind of an unusual set-up for both of us so it'll probably take a bit of getting used to for everyone but I think we're getting there. Slowly.'

Anthea nods, giving me a concerned look before speaking again. 'You probably already know this but a lot of the gang were shocked that a beautiful young girl like you would even think about taking a room in a house with a man suspected of murdering his wife, Cathy.'

'Guess it makes sense.'

'In a way certainly,' Anthea agrees. 'But I also reminded them you're a grown woman. And a smart one too.' She sips her drink. 'So it's not like you don't know what you're doing.'

'Not sure I'm that smart, Anthea.'

This makes her smile and she taps the table. 'Only a smart girl would say such a thing.' She leans back and sighs. I beam, pleased to finally meet somebody who I can relate to, who I can talk to about everything. 'I don't think Ian is a bad guy. I couldn't even imagine him laying a finger on poor Anna and it pisses me off the way the others are all so quick to jump on him. I mean, yes, OK, some elements of his character were a bit off. But—'

'How do you mean "off"?'

Anthea drops her voice. 'Well, Ian did have a bit of a temper and sometimes liked a drink or two, if you get me. But I don't think that's a hanging offence, is it?'

'Probably not.'

'Exactly. And it was one of those cases that never made sense and we just don't know.' For a second, she sounds almost exasperated. 'And his wife, Anna, well, she wasn't an angel either.'

I twirl the wine glass. It's the first time I've heard anybody tell me something about Ian's disappeared wife. It dawns on me that I know nothing about her. 'What do you mean?'

Anthea looks around cautiously. Once satisfied nobody's paying us any attention, she leans forward. 'We were friends, Anna and I. I mean, not super tight friends but still, you know. Our boys, Eric and Jamie, were the same age so we had that and the usual stuff with husbands with one deaf ear and that kind of thing.

The Landlord

And she could be really sweet, Anna. I mean sometimes just as good as gold.'

'OK.' I nod, prompting her gently to continue.

'But she could be hard too. And I think she was hard on Ian. It put a strain on them.'

'In what way hard?'

She sighs. 'Anna was an alpha female and Ian's no slouch but I guess it might have been hard for him to keep up and she was very, how should I put it? Flamboyant. I'm not sure Ian liked that.'

'What do you think happened to her, Anthea?'

'God, Cathy! I think I ask myself that question almost every day. That's the problem. I have simply no idea, and nobody else does either except for laying it on Ian.' Her phone buzzes then and she picks up. 'Gerald, hi, I'll be right out.' She returns her focus to me. 'Cathy, it's been a pleasure getting to know you and I'm sorry I've got to run but I'm chairing a committee meeting in fifteen minutes at Gerald's house.'

'What's the committee?' I ask, watching her rise to her feet.

'Keep Belleview Clean, something I've been running the past three years. It's really helped address the litter problem.'

'Sounds great.'

'I've already got the bill.' Gently she rests her hand on my forearm. 'Now, if you need somebody to talk to at any time, don't hesitate to drop in. I'm right across the road.'

'Sure,' I reply, thrilled to have made my first real friend on the street.

'Take no notice of all the gossip about Ian,' she whispers, dropping her voice, 'but if you ever feel uneasy, don't hesitate to let me know. That's what neighbours are for. Right?' Her face brightens and the edges of her red lips lift into a smile. Then she leaves.

When I return to 762 I let out a jaded sigh, flatten my back against the big hardwood front door and stare up at the corniced hallway ceiling. Ian isn't about and I'm so relieved; I don't know what small talk I could muster with the image of the bloodied spade still fresh in my mind. I eat a microwave curry and polish it off quickly. Then I disappear up to my room and pull out the new scripts AA handed me. I try to busy myself with the new part but it's hard. My mind drifts, thinking of calling up my agent Melissa to complain but knowing it will fall on deaf ears. And I don't want Melissa's pity or scorn. I resolve to fight. To give it my best shot. Not to allow AA any more reasons to throw the book at me.

I keep working, eventually dropping the sheets to the floor, exhausted. Somehow, I keep the discovery of the bloodied spade out of my mind and manage to think about my evening with Anthea instead. It was a pleasant introductory drink and I found her kind and generous. She's the only one from the group with any sympathy for Ian, even taking the trouble to drop him meals he refuses to eat.

I think Anthea is going to be helpful to me, and if not, at least she's someone I can talk to. But before I see her again there's something I need to know. What is it that Ian is really hiding in the garden?

21

Under AA's watchful eye and Old John's sneer I bulldoze through the day, making a good go of the new part which has been thrust on me. It isn't easy but I keep up and I'm surprised how much I recall. I manage a little small talk with Ellie, telling her she's doing a great job and she'll be perfect.

At lunch I hook my arm inside Malia's, taking her across the road to the bench we often sit on. She's squirming when I begin.

'So did you know?'

Malia presses her lips together. 'No. I mean, look, Cathy, there was a lot of whispering going on. But this cast never bloody stops. You know what I mean? I could tell AA and Old John were up to something and when AA was giving you time off, I was pretty certain it wasn't good but I just hadn't figured it out.'

'I see.' I can tell she's holding back.

'OK,' she concedes. 'I did hear Ellie was fishing for your part and at the start you were a bit wobbly, if I'm honest.'

'I was,' I admit. 'But you know why.'

'I know, I know, Cathy. People don't appreciate how much personal shit we have to park just to do our bloody job.' She frowns, looking straight at me with her kind face, 'But I reasoned it out and thought if I go to you and tell you then I was sure you wouldn't let it go.'

I nod. 'Maybe.'

'You would have given it to AA. And then I thought if it all turned out to be just smoke, you'd be up the creek. See what I'm saying?'

I don't reply but silently concede my friend could have a point. I don't want to be mad at Malia. I can't afford to lose the only ally I have in this production.

'You were fucking brilliant today, you know. I don't think I'd be ever so cool. You even had cheeky Ellie looking in awe of you.'

'Thanks,' I say and decide not to talk anymore about it.

The basement door closes behind me. The damp earthy smell rises up and I put a hand to my mouth as I breathe it in, double-checking the lock to make sure it won't give this time. I've brought a real torch which I turn on as I make my way through the ink-black gloom to the storage shed. I need photos of the spade. Then I'm going to the garden. I have to get in and out before Ian gets home. I know there's something there and today I want to find it.

I reach for the bolt lock to the storage door to pull it back but am surprised to see it's already pulled. The door hangs loose, releasing a faint draft from within. The thump inside my chest makes me gasp. *Somebody has been here.* Drawing the door back I search inside with the flashlight, over the floor and across the walls.

The vein at my temple throbs. Same space, same boots, same lawnmower, overalls hanging off the nail on the back of the door. *But when I look for the spade, it's gone.*

There's only one conclusion I can make. Ian has been here. He has come down and removed it. Did he hide it or possibly dump it? Why would he do that?

With shaking hands, I close the door but don't bolt it. All my carefully laid plans to go into the garden evaporate. My pulse races and I suck at the air which I can suddenly taste in my mouth. I have to leave, to get away from this foul underground place.

In the living room I chug the glass of water I have just poured. I try to calm but pricks of sweat open on my scalp and when I run my fingers through my hair it's damp. I need to call someone so I can explain. Heather will know how to advise me. I put the glass down and it lands on the table with a bang. She'll advise me to face up to what I'm avoiding – to leave this house and never look back. But I still can't bring myself to do it. Pacing, I move up and down in front of the window, walking from the fireplace to the couch, across to the dining room. Then the front door opens.

'Good evening.' Ian appears, his hands holding heavy plastic bags.

'Hi.' I grab the water glass.

'All good?' I nod, gulping nervously. 'Learning lines?'

I swallow too much and liquid dribbles down my chin. I wipe it away. 'Yes.'

Ian gives me a relaxed smile. 'I grabbed a bite from a lovely Nepalese restaurant just around the corner. I thought I'd include you, just in case you were home. Hope you're hungry?' I nod mutely. 'Great. Sit.' He points to the big mahogany table in the dining room. 'I'm bringing everything.' In seconds he's back. He hands me a plate of steaming food with a glass of white wine and then fetches himself the same. I drink and start to eat, swallowing nervously yet relieved not to have to talk. Once again, the food tastes good.

'I love this white wine,' Ian says, raising his glass, his mood visibly upbeat. He starts to explain about a job he's working on. The difficult builders he has to handle, the tricky engineers, wily estate agents and over-demanding customers. He keeps topping us both up and before long I unwind. Ian hasn't noticed my unease; hasn't noticed anything about me at all, because he's too busy topping up my glass, replacing dips, bringing extra helpings of rice and making sure I have enough of everything. The food, drink and Ian's stories work some kind of calming spell on me. It seems like he's been aching to unload his days on whoever might lend an ear. Eventually I begin to talk, telling him about the play and what's been going on with AA. He's indignant on my behalf and says it's people like AA that prevent flowers from blossoming.

'Hate those types,' he fumes, and I feel an outpouring of gratitude towards him. When I look at him now his expression is peaceful and gentle. Then the talk turns and weaves in another direction. 'You know it's a funny thing, Cathy. But I think sometimes it's true the way the old cliché goes.'

'Which?'

'The one that says out of darkness comes the light.'

'Why?'

'Well, take this,' he makes a sweeping gesture with his outstretched hand, 'us two sitting here, having a lovely old time, talking, dining, enjoying each other's company. It's really quite special.'

'It is.'

'And yet it's arisen out of a state of total darkness, after the disaster with my wife Anna.' Slowly I place down my wine glass, the mention of Anna pricking me back to reality. Instantly my mind leaps to the spade in the basement. The spade Ian most certainly found and removed. But I have been busy forgetting. 'Then, of course, there's my son Jamie.'

'Ah Jamie, yes.'

Ian chuckles. 'God, Cathy, you say that like you know the boy.'

I prop myself onto my elbow. 'Actually, I did meet him.'

'What?' His brow furrows, a dark look clouding his expression. 'What are you talking about?'

'Sorry, I forgot all about it. I should have told you.'

'Told me what?' Straightening up, he exhales, his chest suddenly bulking and his frame elongating, like some creature rising out of the sea. 'Exactly?'

My throat is strangely dry. 'He came back. One night you were away. He woke me up.' Ian glowers in the shadow of the light from the ancient chandelier above our heads. 'It was an accident. He never knew I was here so he dropped over in the middle of the night.' I watch as Ian folds his arms across his chest. I swallow, my body now tensing and alert. 'But he didn't stay. He went to a friend's house and came back the following morning to fetch some things from his room.'

The warmth leaches from Ian's face, which now looks hard as flint. 'Really, Cathy?' He says, almost growling. 'You didn't think to tell me this?' I gulp, the iciness of his tone catching me off guard. 'I would have hoped you could have at least *mentioned* it in passing.' He rises abruptly and I shrink back, perplexed at this sudden drastic change in his mood.

'Sorry, I just assumed you knew.'

I think he's about to move towards me but he goes to the door. 'I'm off to bed,' he announces solemnly, not looking back. 'Goodnight.'

Heavy footsteps plod up the stairs and his bedroom door shuts hard. I hear the sound of his shoes landing on the floor followed by silence.

Agitated, I get to my feet, walk to the front living room window and look out. There's a figure again by the corner, just a dim shadow of a man barely visible in the faint light. I watch him as he lingers, his hands in his pockets, his neck stretched as he peers up and down the street. Once more he turns and disappears from view. I shiver, hugging my arms tightly across my body.

I'm no longer certain what I'm playing at.

I'm starting to feel out of my depth.

22

Downstairs in my dressing gown I read the message from AA telling me to take another morning off. I think about texting him back but decide against it. I hardly slept last night. I yawn and rub at the dark bags beneath my tired eyes.

I go to the kitchen to make coffee when I see the housekeeper at the sink, her apron on, and bright yellow rubber gloves on her hands.

'Not working today, Cathy?' she asks by way of greeting.

'Good morning, Mrs Bastible. Sometimes our hours get a little irregular.'

'Of course. An actress,' she replies, opening the water tap and rinsing her hands.

'How's your day going?' I offer, steadfastly refusing to rise to the hostility exuding from her. She doesn't reply but turns and looks at me. It's like she's peering through me, the way you do when you catch somebody being dishonest and are waiting for them to own up. But I'm not sure what I'm supposed to be owning up to exactly?

'I had best get to *work*.' The housekeeper rubs her hands with a tea towel, then smoothes them down her dull, grey apron, 'As you can see, it's a big house Mr Fitzsimmons has here. Isn't it?' The trace of a cruel smile appears at the edge of her flat mouth. The wrinkles on her cheeks pull, stretching away like claw marks on her skin. It's clear she's waiting for me to give her space to begin.

'It is.' I turn, deciding to skip the coffee and retreat to the living room where I sit on one of the couches and start reading my scripts. I hear the light tap of Mrs Bastible's old feet

The Landlord

shuffling about on the wooden boards as she goes about her business but I pay it no attention. The minutes slip by and bit by bit she draws ever closer, now directly behind me in the dining room, tapping with her duster and wiping afterwards with a wet grey cloth. Next, she's in the living room over by the mantlepiece, quietly and earnestly seeing to every speck and spot that challenges her gaze. She's ignoring me and I oblige her by doing the same but then change my mind. I've been waiting to speak with her and this is my chance, even if she's keen to knock me back.

I clear my throat noisily. 'Mrs Bastible?'

With her back to me she carries on cleaning. The rubber gloves squeak as she rubs a gold mirror. 'Yes?'

I observe her in the glass but her expression reveals nothing. 'Did you know Ian's wife Anna a long time?'

The yellow gloves stop moving and I notice her mouth tightening. 'Five years,' she replies, as if it's a question she's been asked many times before.

'Can I ask what kind of person she was?'

She straightens up, considering the question. 'Anna? I'd say demanding but fair ... intelligent too, and ambitious. Very ambitious.'

'She sounds very dynamic.' She doesn't reply to this but simply blinks. I keep going. 'It must have been a shock to hear she had gone missing?'

The housekeeper folds her arms, locking the duster underneath one of her armpits and it sticks out like some odd appendage. 'Of course,' she says tersely.

With my friendly smile in place, I will this frozen woman to thaw, to give me some clues to the mystery I need to solve. 'Did you ever wonder what might have happened?'

Her chest pushes her bony shoulders upwards as it fills, then they fall down as she lets the air out, fixing me with a frosty glare. 'I did. And then I stopped. I find it helps me sleep better.'

'Do you think—'

'Well,' she interjects briskly, cutting me off, her steely features creasing into an imitation of a smile, 'now, Cathy, if you'll excuse me, I'm going to make myself a cup of tea.'

The evening is pleasant and warm. I smell the flowers as I walk up Belleview Road but I can't enjoy them as I want to. I check my phone again. Nobody has answered my texts.

There's a discarded crisp wrapper on the ground and I snatch it up, depositing it in a nearby bin when I hear the phone ringing.

I jolt as Ian's name appears.

'Cathy?'

'Yes.'

'I'm ringing to apologise.'

'About what?' I pretend ignorance.

'No, there's no need to do that,' he insists formally. 'We both know my behaviour last night was bad. Unforgiveable really.'

I frown but feel the tension ease from my throat. 'You were upset, Ian. I upset you.'

'Don't apologise, Cathy,' he says, his voice a little softer, 'you're a guest in my house and I should do better.' He exhales. 'I have certain triggers, you see, and as you can tell by now, Jamie is one of them.'

'I could tell it was a sore subject.'

'There's history obviously,' he continues, 'but we're a work in progress. I shouldn't get wound up so easily about him. And the worst thing is, I know all this but I still do.'

'It happens.'

'It shouldn't,' he growls. 'I mean,' he softens his voice again, 'I have to do better. And I want you to know that my anger wasn't with you, it was with him. He knew you were staying, so I'm annoyed he even suggested otherwise.'

'He could have forgotten.'

'Well, he probably frightened the life out of you. I mean what was he thinking popping up at all hours in the morning?'

'I think he had a few drinks. And he's young, Ian. Very young.'

The Landlord

'I know.' He groans. 'God, Cathy, I really appreciate you being so understanding. I don't deserve as much.'

Twenty minutes later I'm barely in the door when I spot the flowers on the porch table. It's not just a small bunch, more something you might see for a wedding display. A giant peacock tail spread of blooms, an explosion of summer colour and a riot of fragrance, perfuming the entire house. I pick it up and bring it into the living room, placing them on the mantlepiece above the massive fireplace. Even there, against the big wall and raised ceiling they look immense, but spectacular too.

I pick up the note that has fallen on the floor, feeling soft inside. Any residue of anger I had towards Ian has evaporated.

> Just a token Cathy. I had to grab them in a rush so I hope they're to your liking. I know they say never to trust a man who apologises with flowers but I'm hoping I'll buck the trend! On a more serious note, sorry again.
> Ian

I ease back into the couch, a burst of gratitude welling within. Ian's kindness is too much. I look up at the ceiling, breathing in the sweet floral scents, a giant wave of pity for him washing over me. He's a man fighting a war with himself, one he can never figure out how to win, like a disturbed dog biting its own tail.

With a groan I stretch out, enjoying the feel of the soft aged leather, marvelling at the elegance of the house, relishing the extravagance of the flowers and the unexpected kindness. I want to stay there, savouring the moment but something has suddenly dawned on me. I sit up as if snapping awake.

I am being deflected. Lulled into a sense of security that doesn't exist. *I found the bloodied spade. Somebody came soon after and took it away.* That somebody can only have been Ian.

And right then I have another thought. Did I really see a spade covered in blood? The basement was dark and gloomy, I was so tense as I walked to check the storage room, is it possible I saw something else? I know I have a vivid imagination. 'Nobody comes up with the stuff you dream,' my favourite drama teacher once said to me, way back when I was taking my first youth theatre course. 'It's like you find the imaginary waterfall of inspiration, Cathy.' She had meant it as the best of compliments and I had been gleeful to hear it, but what if it's my imagination that is now playing tricks on me? That the evidence I thought was beyond any doubt only a short time ago, is simply a figment of my own mind?

I pick up the phone, find Heather's number and hit dial.

'Cathy!' Heather answers chirpily. 'How are you getting along?'

'OK.' I try to match her upbeat mood. I don't want to alarm her. 'How have you been?'

'Fine. Just working. Busy, you know how it is.'

'Busy's good, isn't it?' I stall, not sure how to bring up the issue I'm so desperate to discuss with my friend.

'It is.' Heather can sense my hesitation. 'Tell me, what's up?' she kindly offers.

'I wanted to ask, seeing as you're a psychologist and all that …'

'Yes?'

'Well, might there be a list of clues or signs in the personality of somebody who knocked off his wife?'

Heather bursts out laughing. '*What?* Are you *serious*, Cathy?'

'Kind of, yes.'

'Oh shit, what's happened?' All trace of humour disappears from Heather's voice. 'Tell me, Cathy, honestly now. If there is something you need to let me know.'

I rub where my temple is starting to throb. 'Nothing specific, Heather. I just thought there might be general things. You know, within the personality. Things I should look for.'

Heather pauses and I imagine her blowing out her cheeks. Silently I curse that I've missed the chance to be honest. To tell her plainly what I know. 'Gosh, big question, Cathy. I mean I don't know where to start. The field is so broad. It's not even my specialty but I mean I could ask you the obvious.'

'Go ahead.'

'What? Now?' she says, clearly puzzled.

'You might as well since I have you on the phone.'

'Right, OK.' She clears her throat. 'I have to think for a second. Well, for example, does he have mood swings?'

'Yes.'

'Are those switches very sudden?'

'Yes.'

'Is he extremely charming?'

'Yes.'

'Does he make grand gestures? For example, if apologising?'

I look at the flowers on the mantlepiece. 'Yes.'

'Does he make you feel for him in an emotional way?'

I swallow. 'Yes.'

There's a long pause on the end of the line. I think I hear her groan. 'Cathy?'

'Yes?'

'I'm not sure what to say. You've just given me a bunch of affirmations which all point in one direction.'

'What does it mean?'

'That's the problem. It doesn't necessarily mean anything. Other than that it would highly advisable to proceed with extreme caution in relation to Ian Fitzsimmons. But I think you already know this. Don't you?'

This time I groan. 'I do.'

There's a pause when Heather comes back. 'Cathy?'

'Yes.'

'What do you *feel*?'

I pause for a moment, not sure what to say. 'I feel I need to *know*, Heather.' I brush a tear away. 'I need to know if Jamie Fitzsimmons's father really killed his mother. I need to know what truly happened to make her disappear. It's like she's been completely forgotten but nobody seems to give a shit anymore.

The police don't look like they're doing anything. When I spoke with Jamie it's like he's already accepted his mum is gone without a trace. Even Ian seems to have just given in. And the neighbours here, Heather?' My chest rises and my eyes mist as I battle a surge of indignation. 'They have all agreed it's Ian even though he was never convicted. Why doesn't anybody want to know what really happened anymore? If nobody's going to do a damn thing about it then maybe I can at least be the one who tries not to let her disappear without a word being said? I want to know the truth about Anna Cunningham and I don't think I can remain here much longer without knowing for sure if Ian Fitzsimmons is who I think he is or if I'm sad and deluded.'

'Oh Cathy,' Heather commiserates. 'I can feel you're stressed. Do you want me to come over?'

'No.' I sniff, rubbing the tracks of the tears that have tumbled down my cheeks out of nowhere. 'It's not necessary. I don't want to trouble you.' I fear if she does, I'll tell her everything. Then, like the good friend she's always been, she'll make me come with her.

'Promise me you won't do anything silly. Take any risks?'

'Promise.' I hold back a sniffle as I hang up, wishing I hadn't lied to my good friend, knowing what I have to do next is a risk I'm certain I must take.

23

Work is bumpy. It's like being on one of those small planes and the captain suddenly buzzes on his intercom to tell you to fasten up, there's a bit of turbulence. And the next thing you feel the whole cabin tilting and reeling. Everyone's brave-facing, flattening out the peak of the worry with calming faces but nobody will be relaxing until it's over and done with.

That's today. Not uncommon and every production has days like this. Little tetchy push and pull days. We're well past halfway in; we're supposed to have turned a corner, to feel the home stretch in sight. And yet somehow, in a way nobody quite understands, we're back like it's only one week in. The timing's off; the dialogue too slow; the emotion forced and the drama all rushed. Lines are getting bashed and sliced, giving a stop-start grind to every scene instead of its natural rhythm.

At the centre of the brewing storm is old John. Spluttering and frothing, he's almost bursting at the seams to pull together a performance and the strain is showing. It's common knowledge he drinks and I'm guessing he may have hit it hard and overdone it. Ellie once told me over coffee that Old John had actually told her that the harder you drink, the more creative you become, like it's some sort of magical petrol for your own personal bonfire. It was so ridiculous I couldn't tell if she was joking. Today Old John's theory is haemorrhaging badly, smoking like a plane being shot out of the sky.

In contrast, Malia's work is pitch-perfect, and Ellie and myself are making a go of it, but it's all a little hopeless. Every twenty minutes, Old John breaks everything up to carp to AA. We're too huddled, there's not enough fire in Goneril's belly, Cordelia has the wrong attitude to Lear, and we must all redo the scene so he can have it to his liking. Out of the blue he starts making barbed comments about Malia too. But it's absurd; Malia's miles ahead of him and he knows it. And worst of all AA is indulging the old fool.

'Jesus, Cathy, heavy going in there or what?' Malia grins over her coffee during break.

'I know. It's all over the place. And old John is a mess.'

Malia laughs. 'A beetroot red, frothing dragon.'

'Can't believe he's daring to have a go at *you*.'

She frowns. 'Yeah, felt like telling him where to get off once or twice.'

'Why don't you? You'd be well within your rights. You shouldn't be putting up with it. He's out of line.'

Malia looks worried for a moment but then her frown breaks into a grin. 'Cathy, don't even tempt me. Seriously. I just want to get through today and go home.'

Break ends and we all troop back in. I resolve to follow Malia's suggestion and simply have it over with and go.

But Old John isn't done complaining and won't let up. We're all in the middle of a lumbering scene *again*. Me, him, Malia and a few of the others, AA staring on like everything's fine, when Old John stands up and flings his script to the floor.

'For fuck's sake,' he fumes at Malia, 'can't you get the rhythm to your words? This is Elizabethan English not bloody street slang.'

For a second there is silence. Shocked and frozen we stare at him. Then I glance at Malia, noticing her pained expression. Silently scowls back at him.

But he's not finished. And he's *not* joking. His cheeks have turned puce and drawn tight in a snarl as he turns in my direction. 'And as for you,' he spits with derision, 'you might as well be auditioning for a children's pop music video.' He whips round, glancing to AA who watches on without saying a word, 'but if you

The Landlord

don't know your arse from your elbow, girl, then you're just using up space. And you don't warrant your place in this production.'

Next AA is up wagging his finger and grinning inanely, trying to grease some humour into the situation, but it's well past that now. Malia glares at Old John, indignant but dignified in her silence. Nobody else speaks or even moves. Like they're zombies who've had their batteries taken out. The muscles along my spine tense. I try to speak but find my mouth clamped shut.

'And we had hoped,' Old John continues barking in a snide voice, 'that since Goneril was beyond your limited gifts, you might at least rise to the opportunity of Regan. But sadly it seems even that is too much for you, Cathy Quinn.' He harrumphs out a harsh snort as he finishes, tipping his chin at me, daring me to defy him.

I grip my script so hard the pages twist and bend.

'You pig,' I spit.

Old John wheels on me. 'Excuse me?'

'You heard me,' I say, finally finding the voice that was stuck down in my stomach. I'm so angry, not just for myself, but for Malia and all the people in this production who have to suffer this man's rude excesses. For a second I imagine leaping over, shoving him to the floor and clawing at his face. 'You sorry, ignorant pig.'

'How dare you?' he snarls.

'Cathy,' Andy entreats feebly, 'John was joking, calm down. Let's not make a big thing out of this.'

'*No*,' I spit. 'Don't try and fob me off. And don't protect him.' I step towards John, the muscles straining in my neck. 'He's an ignorant, conceited arsehole. And nothing you say is going to change that, Andy.' I point at Old John and he puts his lumpy hands on his hips, planting his feet wide, glaring back at me. 'And yes, John, I also know you're a dirty old man who gropes female cast members when others aren't watching.'

Old John's mouth hangs. He juts his thick fists into his pockets, his mouth twisting but not making any words. Then finally he finds some.

'I'm not standing for this, Andy.' He throws his hands up like some angry ape.

Malia steps in front of me. 'Cathy,' she whispers, her voice tight, 'leave it.'

Trembling, I look at her.

'I'm leaving,' Old John announces, storming off.

Malia fixes me with a stare, wide eyes pleading. 'It's not worth it,' she says in a hushed voice. I know she has my best interests at heart but it's too late for this now. I've already spoken. I need support, but everywhere I look I see nothing but mute blinking faces. I want to shake Malia, to beg her to roar in outrage with me, but she's already stepped away.

AA frowns and sighs. The obedient others watch on from the wings. I want to scream at all of them but my voice is trapped in my throat.

'Go home, Cathy,' Andy says quietly.

On the way home I ring Malia three times but she doesn't pick up. I think about texting her but decide against it. We need to speak. She was with me during the scene. She understands what happened. Surely she can vouch that I was within my rights to say what I did. Didn't she feel the sting of Old John's poisonous tongue too? Hadn't she even been groped by him, as she told me in private?

I decide to let it wait. I need to calm down and expect she'll need to do the same. I didn't know I had so much rage inside me, didn't know I could get so furious. I recall Old John's insult again and immediately my stomach knots. I could have attacked him and still know if I met him here and now, I'd feel the same. If Old John had even laid a finger on me, I could have readily murdered him without a second thought. As I consider this it worries me. *Is that how easy it is to kill somebody?* In the wrong moment, when the wrong button is pressed and you're primed to respond? But what had me primed? Of course AA and Old John have been a thorn in my side since the get-go and I've been struggling to make the best of a play I never wanted to be part of, but merely undertook to placate my agent and show her how willing I was to do anything to help my career, and yet something *else* was coiling inside me. Deep down I know it's not merely about the play.

Spent and hollowed out, I fall onto the couch in the living room. Within minutes I'm in a deep sleep and when I wake up it's already started to turn dark outside. Somebody is knocking loudly on the door. It comes again. An impatient flurry of harsh slaps with the knocker. I heave myself up. When I open the door, I discover Carol standing in front of me.

'Hello,' she says flatly.

'Hello, Carol,' I reply sleepily.

'I remember you now,' she says.

'From where?' I know the answer but ask anyway.

'You're the woman who tried to snatch my dog.'

I look down at her feet and see she's left him at home. 'No.' I yawn. 'That's not correct, Carol. You were mistaken.'

'I'm pretty sure I know what I saw,' she says, a grim smile pulling sharply across her cheekbones. I listen, wondering if changing Carol's mind will be like trying to lift the ocean over my head. 'Anyhow, that's neither here nor there.'

'OK,' I say calmly, wondering what she wants.

'I'm simply here to warn you.'

'About?'

'Ian Fitzsimmons.'

'What about Ian?'

She sneers. 'Don't be a fool, girl. I saw him with my own eyes.'

'Saw him do what?'

She leans forward conspiratorially. 'I saw him threaten his wife outside Leno's. He shoved his big nasty face right up into hers when they were standing outside and said, "Push me too far, Anna, and you'll see what you'll get". Then he smashed his wine glass at her feet and stormed off. Like a big, menacing bear he was, in the cold light of day.'

I tense, gripping the door. I don't want to let this wound-up woman under my skin but I'm thrown. 'Did anybody else witness it?'

She lets out a derisive grunt. 'Just me. But I know what I saw and heard. I told the police too. We all know it's him that made Anna disappear. She was too good for him and he always knew it so it drove him crazy.' She leans back, pausing for a second. 'Don't mind what Anthea tells you. She's soft on the man and always was. But just think.'

'About?'

'You.' She smirks. 'He's got you right where he wants you. Anna gone. Younger model moved in. Sympathetic. A little clueless.' She groans. 'Don't be *that* girl, Cathy. I wouldn't think it's worth it.'

My fingers move to my arm and I rub it nervously.

She takes a step down, sensing she has me rattled. 'Well, there we are. I've said my piece and that's all I wanted to do.' Her voice lightens but there's no warmth in her expression. 'I'm merely telling you what the rest of the neighbourhood already knows. I don't want to stand by and watch it happen all over again without saying I tried.'

'You did,' I reply coolly, wishing her far, far away.

'I'll look forward to seeing you at one of our committee meetings soon,' she says by way of departure. 'No doubt Anthea will keep you posted.'

She doesn't turn. Doesn't wave, or even say goodbye. She just retreats quickly and marches away like we never even met.

In the kitchen I pour myself a glass of white wine from a bottle I find in the fridge. I take it back with me to the living room and sit and drink it slowly. From the comfort of the couch I stare out the front window watching the light turn to darkness when I feel tears dropping on my cheeks. It's been a hard day but I don't know who or what the crying is for. Is it my job? Which now looks on the rocks. Or what happened with my only friend in

The Landlord

the production, Malia? Is it Carol and her spiteful stories about Ian which I didn't want to know but now do? Or am I pitying myself?

I finish the last of the wine and get to my feet. Turning round, I move through the dining room and go to the window at the back of the house.

It's pitch black outside now. There's no sign of Ian.

It's time to go into the garden.

24

Slowly I walk down the steps into the basement, my flashlight flicking across the damp grimy walls. The 'dungeon' Justin called it, and I know it's not far wrong. The scent of something foul from its depths reaches my nostrils, clawing its way inside my nose. I twist my neck, trying to avoid inhaling the lingering rot, shuffling quickly forward as quietly as I can. I open the back door lock, push, and then I'm in the garden.

Where I'm not supposed to be.

It's pitch dark. I still have no idea when Ian will return. If he comes home, I have no back-up plan – but I don't want to think about that now. I have to keep going. To explore it. To see if it has secrets about Anna Cunningham's disappearance.

My torch is switched to its lowest mode. It emits a dull, muted light, just enough to show me where the paving meets the grass. I follow it and make my way deeper in.

Either side of the perimeter wall the flower beds have pushed out. The shrubs are shapeless, wild things, and untamed trees overhang in places. Some are covered with brambles, and what I imagine might be blackberries, though it's too dark to see. The grass is long, rising above my knees, and clearly gone to seed, but I make out a trampled section which looks like a path and I take it. It's flat underfoot, suggesting somebody has walked on it not long ago.

I stare down at it and the beating inside my chest grows louder. Ian had told me the garden was abandoned so why is there freshly trampled grass? Cautiously I walk on, the only sound the soft brushing of grass beneath my feet. Thick-stemmed nettles protrude every few paces and one catches my arm. The sting burns into my flesh and I muffle a curse.

The Landlord

Further along the path I have to duck and pull away some briars which have collapsed sideways overhead, almost forming a tumbledown roof. A thorn catches my finger and draws blood. The track keeps going, snaking in bends like a river till it meets a clump of trees. They are low-hanging, with thick trunks covered in a grey moss and as I shine the beam over the branches I see red apples.

I press on, deeper into the darkness, marvelling at how such a vast overgrown jungle can exist in the centre of the city. I scan the ground in front of me, stopping every few steps to look around, searching it with the torch beam, desperately trying to glean any signs of disturbance. But nothing reveals itself. Sighing I continue, determined to remain optimistic, wondering how far back the garden goes before it reaches its end. Silently I remind myself of what I saw. The bloodied spade with hair on its edge. *The same kind of spade a murderer might use to bury a body.*

In the gloom, not far in front of me I make out the trace of a small wooden cabin. I move towards it, noting how a portion of grass in front of it has been cut. I kneel down to inspect it and discover soil mixed in with the grass, overlaying it like it's been tossed. Tentatively I touch it, and I prod gently, finding grooves in the soil. I shine the torch closer to see cut sods. They've been put back into the soil but haven't gelled correctly. Recoiling, I push to my feet, now making out the pattern of where they've been knitted together. It's a rectangle.

It's the shape of a *grave*.

My mouth clamps shut, trapping the air inside my lungs. Blood thumps in my ears. I rub the soil off my hands, sweat now dripping down my back. But I don't feel hot. A strange chill has entered my body. My stomach is churning, telling me to leave, to get away.

How long will it take me to reach the house? Minutes? Seconds?

I start back towards the main house when I hear the sound of a heavy breath. With a gasp, I twist round, now discovering a silhouette. A man towers over me.

'Cathy.' The voice is angry and cold, but also familiar.

'Ian?' I flick the torch and it illuminates his joyless face.

He breathes noisily. 'Why are you here?'

I hesitate. 'I ...'

'You know what time it is?'

'Late,' I stammer.

'Very late. What could possibly make you want to come down here at this time of night?' He stands very still, his hands in his pockets, and I let the torch hang by my side.

'I thought ...' my voice trails away faintly. He walks over and takes the torch, shining it on my hands then down at the cut sods by my feet.

'I'm disappointed, Cathy.' He says in a grim voice, tapping the torch against his knuckles. I can see he's angry but tonight it's different, contained and squeezed down tight like the steam inside a pressure cooker.

He looms like a dark silhouette in front of me. 'Ian ...' I begin to speak, my voice low and quivering despite my best efforts to keep it still, 'what are you doing here?'

'I was in my garden office. It's where I go to think when I'm stuck on a project. It's my private space. Like the garden.'

'And this?' I point to the ground and we both look at the sods near my feet.

'Something I need to explain.' He says more softly now. 'Something I didn't want you to see, which is why I expressly asked you to not come out here. He returns the torch to me. 'I'll let you know about it in the morning.'

'Ian, please tell me this is not what I think it is.'

'What do you think it is?'

'A grave?'

He frowns. 'Oh, Cathy. Please let's not do this now. It's late and I'm angry. You've come to the one place I asked you to stay away from. I know you're anxious. And I know Anna's disappearance is preying on your mind. How could it not be?' His voice becomes pleading. 'But you have to trust me when I tell you, this isn't the time or the place to discuss that right now. Please go to bed and we can talk about it all when we're fresh.'

Confused by this sudden change I can't think. 'OK,' I hear myself reply.

'Would you like me to go and stay somewhere else tonight?' He sighs, looking apologetic. 'In a hotel, maybe? I can see you're shaken and I don't want to put you through anymore upset.'

'I'm fine.'

'Good then.' Hastily he turns away. 'I'm going back to my office for a few more hours. You won't see any lights on down there because the electrics have been tripping due to some water getting on a switch but I find it suits me fine as I get much better ideas in the dark. I'll try and be quiet as I can coming in so I don't wake you.' Silently he paces away, opens the door to the cabin without a sound and disappears, closing it behind him.

Instantly I turn, my heart thumping, a bead of sweat trickling between my shoulder blades. I'm about to run but realise if I do, I won't hear anything moving behind me. So I walk, keeping the torchlight on, whispering to myself to stay calm.

But as I move through the garden, retracing my steps, the fear slips away. Ian isn't following me. He didn't panic when he met me, despite me doing the one thing he asked me not to. He was calm, even polite.

When I get back inside the house, I don't order the cab like I thought I would. I don't take a drink from the fridge but have a glass of water instead. Then I go upstairs and lay down on the bed, too tired to take off my clothes.

It's only when the sunlight pours through my window that I see I'm still wearing my jeans.

25

You're off AA's text simply says. **I need to straighten this out with John and Malia.**

Fine I write back. I'm tempted to add more but think better of it. The day off is a relief because this morning my head is a million miles away from Shakespeare and his world of kings and warring daughters. I don't care for Old John, AA and all the gossip they have to say about me. Malia's the only one I care about. It still bothers me that she didn't side with me publicly and yet I know she was probably only being fair, because I've no right to tell her what she has to do when it comes to her professional career. What I desperately want to do now is phone my agent Melissa, but I won't. I can't face her jaded voice groaning down the line.

When I get up, Ian is gone. There's another one of his notes on the porch table so I pick it up and take it with me into the living room. Sunlight slants gently through the window and I look out to the bright blue sky. The petals have started to fall from the flowers above the fireplace already and I can tell it's going to be a hot day. Warily, I open it up.

Cathy,
I know I have a lot of explaining to do. And it's long overdue. I'm not angry with you going into the garden. Not anymore. You are right. There are questions I need to answer and I'd like to do just that if you'd give me the opportunity. I can be back by nine tonight if suits you to meet then. Just let me know.
Kind regards,
Ian

The Landlord

The tightness in my chest eases. I want answers so desperately. I text him.

9 is good

He replies, **Brilliant. Will I bring food?**

Yes.

I know the food will make both of us relaxed. I need Ian to be relaxed so he can give the explanations I've been craving.

I walk into the kitchen to make some coffee but change my mind. Instead I decide to go to Leno's, hoping I might catch up with JJ. I think of his bright smile and the calm ease with which he handles Anthea and all her bunch, like Gerald with his wagging fingers and the sarcastic Stewie, and feel a wave of sympathy for him.

When I walk out through the front gate, I see a man across the street. He wears a V-neck white T-shirt with skinny jeans rolled up his shins. *Justin*, I think and my pulse spikes, but when I look again, I see it's a stranger with only a passing resemblance. Calming, I breathe out, wondering why my mind jumped so quickly to my ex and why Justin has gone so quiet. It's not like him to give up and disappear, or to lie low. I won't call him. I don't want anything to do with him, but I know it's unusual and it makes me suspicious.

That evening Ian is waiting in the living room when I arrive back to Belleview Road. I'm not sure when he got in but it must have been a while ago because he has the dining room all set out as if he's expecting the Queen. Neatly arranged food holders all on their own particular mats in the centre of the table, wine glasses for each of us, a bottle of red wine and also a bottle of white in a bucket with ice, two shining plates, stacked with cutlery on top.

'I hope you don't mind,' he says. I raise a smile, pleased. Then I remember last night, seeing him appear like a ghoul in the darkness of the overgrown garden. A shudder passes through me. 'I just had this urge to do something this evening. I feel I frightened you last night and I'd like to set things straight between us.'

Ian's dressed in a bright peach shirt. He's clean-shaven, his hair is combed and he smells of aftershave. 'Will I have time to shower?'

'Of course.' He grins. 'We're in no rush.'

I go up, shower and find a nice light summer dress. Throw on some make-up with some jewellery and go back down.

'Gorgeous, Cathy,' Ian says, walking in from the kitchen. I blush, pleased, then stop and take a second, remembering it's not a date. He points to the wine.

'White or red?'

'White please.'

'Great choice.' He pours a glass, handing it to me. Then he pours his own and we toast. 'What do you think?'

I try it. 'It's lovely.'

He starts lifting all the lids off the food and hands me my plate. 'Now, self-service and ladies first. It's Keralan cuisine, from southern India. Hope that's good with you?'

I nod and get busy.

He grins. 'Super.' Dutifully he waits for me to finish serving myself and then takes his own modest portion. With his glass and plate in hand, Ian saunters back to the living room, plonks down on the leather sofa, and waits until I come and join him. When we're sitting comfortably, he starts the conversation. 'So last night, Cathy, you asked me if I had a grave at the end of my garden and the answer is I do.'

My wine glass bangs into the side of my plate with a clang but fortunately doesn't break. 'What?' I have to steady my plate which almost slides off my lap to the floor.

'I'm sorry but I want to be up front tonight.' Casual and relaxed, Ian sips his wine. 'Was there any other reason you guessed it might be a grave other than the soil you saw?'

I place the plate of food on the coffee table, gripping the stem of the wine glass tightly. 'Yes.'

'OK?' he says, waiting.

'A spade I saw.' I gulp as my stomach twists. 'One covered in blood and hair.'

The Landlord

'Ahh.' He exhales calmly. 'I had suspected as much.' He eats a little more. 'You were in the basement, I think?'

'Yes.' Bewildered, I stare at him. Why isn't he acting guilty? Or even pretending to be concerned. It's like he isn't fazed at all. *Like a psychopath* I hear the unwanted silent voice chime. 'I saw it in the store.'

'Right.' He nods, like it all makes perfect sense. 'I went down to take it away but see now I was too late. I didn't want you to witness that, Cathy, but now you have, I'll explain everything.'

I wait, my back stiffening, not sure I want to hear this but knowing I have to. It's the reason I'm sitting here, the whole reason we're doing this, whatever this is.

'I've been under so much pressure this past year I really can't describe it. My relationship with my son has fallen badly by the wayside, my professional reputation, which I worked so hard to build, was decimated, but worse than all of that ...' He chews his lip, hesitating for a second. 'I've been deemed guilty of murdering my wife, a woman whom I love very dearly.'

I drink from the wine glass, swallowing a mouthful nervously.

'Can you imagine how that feels, Cathy?' I shake my head. 'To know the police, the neighbours, your colleagues, even people you've never even met have pegged you for killing the person that mattered to you most.' His voice trembles but he holds it together.

'I can only try.'

'Well.' He collects himself. 'It's been very rough and I haven't handled it so well. I've always been partial to a drink,' he holds up his glass, sunken eyes giving him a hollowed look, 'as you've probably figured out by now. But I've been overindulging, thinking it would diminish the stress when all it really does is enhance it.' He puts his glass down. 'I was always brittle but of late I've become even more so, the slightest thing just setting me off.'

'But?' I say, unsure how to pin this conversation down, feeling it ebbing away.

He raises a hand. 'I know, the explanation.' He nods. 'So, I liked to keep birds at the end of the garden. Anna was always very fond of wild spaces and she always talked of turning this giant space at the back into a kind of meadow. Since she disappeared, I let it go wilder than before, almost like a shrine to her in some ways.' His eyes glisten. 'So, these birds, they were pigeons, homing ones a fellow had sold me and I had grown quite attached to them. Six of them in all there were, and I used to keep them in a netted coop at night.'

'What happened?'

'It was the night you moved in. I was woken up by the sound of the flapping wings. I'm such a light sleeper these days even that will do it for me. I suspected it was a thief and grabbed the shovel for protection. Then I went to see what the commotion was.'

'What was it?'

'A fox. It had already pulled them all out, killed four and was trying to savage the last pair.'

'What did you do?'

'I tried to shoo it with the spade but it was no use. I had heard things about foxes developing bloodlust during killing but I wasn't prepared for what came next. It got hold of my leg and sank its teeth in my calf. I pushed it off but it came again and got hold of the other leg. I tried to pull it free but I couldn't dislodge it.'

He stops abruptly, as I swallow. 'And that's when I hit it with the spade. I had to hit it three times before it let go. Then I saw I had gone too far. It was staggering and bleeding from its mouth, clearly in severe distress. So I brought it down a final time and put it out of its misery.'

'Jesus, Ian.'

'I know but it's the truth.' He returns my glum look. 'I buried it there and then along with all the birds, since the last pair never survived. It was five a.m. by the time I got to bed and I went to the airport an hour later.' He sighs. 'I had meant to get rid of the spade or wash it or something but I just couldn't face even thinking about it. I'm so sorry you had to find out about all this. It should never have happened.'

The Landlord

He holds his big hands either side of his jaw and peers down at me guiltily. The story is so brutal but so honest I'm unsure what to say.

'There was a scream the second night I slept here. It sounded like a woman in terror, coming from the back garden.'

He nods as if he remembers it also. 'The fox's mate. It's so human it's caught me out a few times too.'

Neither of us speak for a moment. Then Ian reaches across, picks up my plate and hands it back to me. 'Let's not waste this. It's too good,' he says. Uncertainly I start to eat and he does the same.

'Carol called by.'

'Oh, yes?' He looks surprised by this.

Struggling to chew, I squeeze down a mouthful, deciding to tell him plainly. 'She told me to get some sense and get as far away from you as I can. She said she saw you threaten your wife outside Leno's and is certain you're the one that made her disappear.' I expect him to react but he doesn't. He simply nods. It's like he's heard it all before a thousand times.

'I did give Carol good reason to have me pegged and what she's told you is true. Unfortunately, I let it happen a couple of times so I've only myself to blame I suppose.' He tops up my wine glass, then empties the remainder of his down his throat.

'Anthea seems a little more reasoned,' I say. 'She doesn't seem so quick to put the blame on you.'

Ian smiles in agreement. 'That's kind of her.' He refills his glass, banging the bottle when he brings it back down on the table. 'She's nice, Anthea. Anna liked her, even though it surprised me.'

'In what way?'

'Well, the two of them were so unalike. Anna a high flyer, rarely taking the time to shoot the breeze with anyone, and she would have rather hung herself than join one of these community committees Anthea devotes her time to.'

'Could it have been opposites attracting?'

He sips his wine, eats another mouthful of food, then pushes his plate away. 'I don't think so. I think it was something to do with Anna's personality. She was so strong, so unstoppable, that she could beguile even the most unlikely admirers.'

'Well, I returned her casserole dish and kept quiet about the dog enjoying it.'

Ian lets out a guilty laugh, breaking the tension. 'Oh God, Cathy, please don't ever let her know but I can't abide her food. I know she means well. The only way I'm letting myself feel better about it is by telling myself the dog next door is a Saint Bernard so he needs the calories.'

I laugh too. Then suddenly the room goes silent and we sit without saying a word. Finally, I stand up.

'I'm off to bed.'

Ian's already started to doze and snaps awake. 'Of course,' he stands ceremoniously, 'and thanks, Cathy. For listening. You've no idea how much that means.'

I'm too spent to reply. So I just smile and walk upstairs. But I'm troubled; worried that Ian could inflict so much violence on an animal; relieved the grave isn't what I truly believed it might be; grateful that Ian had an explanation, that it all made sense somehow. In so many ways I believe Ian Fitzsimmons is a wonderful, sweet and deeply misunderstood man in a very bad place.

But I also believe there's a bit missing to his story. A bit he isn't yet ready to tell me. A bit that I have to figure out if I'm really going to learn the truth about what happened to Anna.

26

I fall asleep but it's fitful. I keep thinking about the man I spotted on the street corner across the road from the house. I imagine him lurking there after dark watching me, but whenever I look back he disappears into the shadows. I'm annoyed I didn't mention it to Ian because I had meant to but it just went out of my mind after he told me the story of killing the fox with the spade, the gruesomeness of the revelation shocking me so badly that I plain forgot all about it. It's clear I've been too easy-going about this. The next time I see Ian I'll have to tell him. I just have to find the right moment.

It surprises me that Ian was so up front about what happened with the fox. He didn't need cajoling; he was happy to tell me, almost seeming relieved to get it off his chest. I could imagine most people not wanting to admit to committing such an act. He also knew I had gone into the basement against his wishes, and to the end of garden in the dead of night to snoop, and though he was angry at first, he was eventually more apologetic than anything else. Despite this, the irritating suspicion keeps nagging me, like an invisible finger nudging me, with a whisper saying there's more.

I twist in the bed, trying to banish the thoughts from my mind when the flash of orange light comes through my bedroom window. I get up, hurrying over to look outside, trying to make sense of the fiery glow in the garden.

When I draw back the curtain I shudder.

Outside, at the very end of the back garden, a blaze burns. It's generating so much flame I can make out the figure of Ian standing beside it. He's not moving, just looking at it, like a frozen statue, hands on hips, as if it's a puzzle that's beaten him and all he can do is admit defeat. I check the alarm clock to see what time it is and find its five past three in the morning. What could Ian be doing? The only thing that makes sense is that he's disposing of something, but what?

I step back, my breathing heavy, my head pounding. Without thinking, I throw on some tracksuit bottoms with a hoodie and hurry down the stairs. The key is gone from the hook by the door so I run out and down and keep the front door on the latch. But when I get to the entrance door to the basement, it's locked. Cursing, I run back into the house. There is second door to the basement, I know – the one from inside just next to the kitchen, where he's boarded it off from the ground level with plywood. He keeps it locked at all times but it's worth a try so I run to it and give it a go but have no luck.

No. I run back upstairs to the bedroom, heaving the sash window loose and up. I'm about to yell out when I stop. I don't want to wake the neighbours. I don't know who's watching. Who's seeing what I see now. When I look again, I see the fire has died down. Gone are the giant flames and in their place occasional flickers of orange light. The doors to Ian's cabin, which were hanging wide open, have closed, and Ian is gone, like he was never even there.

I shut the window, slumping back down on the bed. The adrenaline has fizzled out of my system. I don't want to confront Ian in the garden. Not now. Not until I've figured out exactly what I need to say to him. I don't want to blindly accept any old explanation he cares to give me.

Moving to my door, I lock it and get back into bed. Beneath the blankets my body shivers. I don't want to sleep but it comes anyway.

27

Back in rehearsals the atmosphere is cold enough to cut with a knife. Everybody's tight smiles, fleeting eye contact and too busy to chat. I ignore the tension and carry on with the grimly formal facade of politeness, doing my scenes with Old John like nothing happened, AA pretending nothing's changed, saying he's too busy to sit down and talk about things but that by the end of the week he should have time. But I'm indifferent, my only concern being my relationship with Malia who says 'we'll chat, Cathy, but not today it's too soon'. I nod, leaving it lie, and take my lunch alone, too preoccupied by what happened last night at the house to spare it another thought. In the evening, I hook up with Babs at the Waterside pub.

'Wow.' Babs makes big eyes and drinks her gin and tonic. We sit side by side in a tucked away corner. I pluck an ice cube from mine and crunch it noisily. I've just given her the whole story about everything that's happened since we last spoke. The bloodied shovel, the trip to the garden in the night, the discovery of the grave, Ian's appearance out of the darkness, and then his long story about the fox. Then finally, the bonfire in the early hours of this morning. 'I mean, I have heard about foxes doing that to chickens alright but it's certainly unusual for one to attack a human.'

I nod. 'It is, isn't it?'

'That's not to say it doesn't happen,' she adds hastily. 'I'm sure it can.' I can see she's doing her best not to make me feel gullible. 'But the bonfire during the night, that *is* very strange. What would he even be doing out there at that hour?'

I shrug. 'He said he likes to go to the garden office to think. That it helps him when he's mulling over issues at work.'

'Well, that makes sense.'

'And the fire, Babs?'

She taps a finger to her lips. 'Yeah, guess you'll just have to ask him?' I slump and she wraps an arm around my shoulder. 'Oh Cathy, is everything OK?'

I lean into her, a low groan escaping from me. 'Not really. I had this whole debacle at work with this stupid play.'

'AA or Old John?'

'Both. Well, Old John mostly. You remember my friend Malia, the girl playing Cordelia whose parents come from Ghana.' Babs nods. 'Well, we'd been getting on great. Watching each other's backs because the cast are a handful. But then something happened.'

'What?'

'Old John pinched her ass, she told me in confidence.'

'*Shit.*'

'Yeah, and then the other day he had a go at her.'

'And what did she do?'

'Nothing.'

Babs looks confused. 'So?'

'Well, that was the problem. I felt so bad for her. And then suddenly he turns and starts laying into me, telling me I'm just some lame-ass who should be doing pop videos and not serious theatre like some big fucking thesp like him.' The words catch in my throat.

'But he can't get away with that. What did the director do?'

'He ignored it. Tried to pretend it was a joke.' Babs's brow furrows. 'I know. So I just lost it and gave it to the old bastard, telling it to him straight that I knew he groped girls in the cast.'

Babs hugs me tighter. 'Oh shit. You meant Malia, right?'

I nod, suddenly comprehending how much I must have offended her by spewing this out to everyone, how the cast must be a haven of gossip as we speak. 'Well, you showed guts, Cathy, so screw them all,' she says proudly letting me go and looking into my face.

The Landlord

'It went down a bomb. The rest of the cast all tried to say it was a joke and I think Malia might not be talking to me.'

'For God's sake. That is *so* bloody unfair.' Babs sighs. 'Listen, why don't you come stay with me. To cheer you up a little, till you're back feeling yourself.'

I think about the offer for a second but know I don't really need to. 'Thanks, Babs, but I'm OK where I am. I made a decision about it some time back.'

'Oh?'

I nod. 'Yeah, I decided I'm not leaving till I find out what really happened to Anna Cunningham.'

Babs doesn't reply. I can feel she's waiting for me to explain and I want to. I'm just unsure how. She draws closer to me. 'It's not just about Anna though, is it?' she asks quietly. I shake my head. 'You like him, don't you? Ian?' I nod. 'And you can't fit him to the crime so it's getting under your skin because you want him to be innocent?'

I flatten my hands on my jaws. 'I just can't put him and that together, Babs. And I believe what he's told me. Well ...' I pause. 'I did believe him, I mean. Until the bloody bonfire. Now I'm pissed off because I feel like a fool.'

Babs counters, 'You're *not* a fool, Cathy. You're smart, you're sweet, and you might well be right.' She clinks my glass. 'Listen, I've an idea. As soon as Ian shows up, we'll both confront him together. OK? I think he needs to come clean about whatever it is he's concealing.'

'Thanks, Babs.' Her phone beeps and she picks it up. 'Your date?' She smiles a yes. 'Is he hot?'

She nods. 'But not like your Ian.'

When I get to Leno's my heart lifts. JJ's there, just as I'd hoped. But unfortunately, he's wrapping up.

'Sorry,' I say, walking inside as he gathers dirty glasses. 'Got my days wrong and thought this was one of your late evenings.'

He beams a warm smile. 'Don't worry, Cathy. You can still sit down. I haven't closed up yet.' He grabs two upturned chairs off a table and places them back onto the floor. 'What'll you have?'

'G&T?' I ask, hoping I'm not imposing.

'Gimme two minutes.' He goes behind the counter to fix it and I sit, chuffed that he's being so nice. The place is empty bar the pair of us. 'Will I join you?' he says, slicing lemon and dropping it on top of the ice inside the glass.

I ease into the chair, my mood brightening. 'God, JJ, would you? I think it would be just too sad to sit here drinking on my own.'

He laughs. 'You're not on your own. We're here together.' He plonks a second glass next to the first and adds ice and lemon. A minute later we sit opposite each other raising glasses and mirroring smiles. There's beautiful new artwork all over the walls and I point at the pictures.

'The artwork's stunning. Where'd it all come from?'

'Yeah.' He nods, pleased, 'I had it in storage and mentioned it to my mate, the guy who owns the place. It was costing me a lot to keep it there since I don't have space in my flat for it. So he said, since I'm doing him a favour minding his operation while he's back home, I should put it in here.'

'It's gorgeous.'

'Thanks.' We both look at the walls. 'It's indigenous and each one tells a story. So it's sort of personal for me.' He looks wistful for a moment.

'I think they're beautiful. And it changes the place completely.'

'Hope so.' The corners of his mouth lift into a grateful smile.

'So, is this what you do? The café business.'

'Naw.' There's a tea towel draped over his back and he dries his hands on it. 'I'm a product designer. I took leave from my job, trying to develop my own thing. So I came over here just for a change.'

'Are you going back soon?' I ask, taken aback at the worry I hear in my own voice. I hardly know him and yet the thought of him instantly disappearing hurts.

He shrugs. 'Dunno. Haven't been here long.'

'What are you developing?'

'It's a technical innovation for surfboards, which makes them lighter on the water by changing the tail shape. It crosses over to snowboards and windsurf boards too. I've got a crowd interested in it but I've got to keep working on it to get it right for a bit yet.' He pulls out his phone. 'Suppose I fit under the label of entrepreneur, though I don't really call myself that. Seems a bit much, you know?' He swipes the pictures and I look at them, nodding, remembering the really mean guy I once dated who had a burger van but labelled himself an entrepreneur. I can't help agreeing with JJ as he keeps scrolling. 'I like doing the artwork side too so I put a lot of indigenous art in with the design.' The pictures are stunning sports shots and the close-ups of the designs are amazing.

'Those are incredible.'

'You reckon?'

'I do.'

'Thanks, Cathy.' His voice inflects upwards on my name. 'I haven't actually shown them to anybody here yet. I only took this job to get to know people but I'm mostly chasing my tail rather than socialising.' He puts the phone away. 'Sorry, I know, here's you trying to relax and I'm bombarding you with my photos.' I stare at him, gobsmacked at how stupidly handsome he is but without a trace of vanity – the polar opposite of Justin, with his sculpted hair and designer outfits. His blue eyes shine and the sunbaked edges near his temples crinkle. I remember Anthea gushing the first day I came to the café and find I'm doing the same. Again.

'This is the nicest moment of my day.'

'Good,' he says. 'Mine too.' He laughs then and I find the tension easing from my tired body.

'Can I ask you a question?'

'Shoot.'

'What do you make of the cycling gang?'

'Well, they like to talk, and some of them do like to throw their money around, acting a bit like they own the place and all that, but they're OK most of the time. They're a little older than me and you so they've got different things going on I suppose.' He offers this generously as he sips his drink, his gaze shifting to one of the artworks on the wall before returning to look at me. 'How about you? I was worried you were gone so it's good to see you're back. Settled in yet?'

I twist the cold glass between my fingertips before replying. 'I don't know, JJ. I love the house, the neighbourhood, and Ian is really welcoming and generous. But …'

JJ sees my hesitation. 'Yeah, I know, Cathy, because if I'm honest I hear all about it from Carol and her friends. When they come in here they'll often have a go at him. Seems like they all have Ian nailed for doing away with his missus.'

'Does Ian ever drop in?'

He nods. 'Very early, or late afternoon when the place is quiet. Think he likes the solitude.'

'What do you think of him?'

'Nice bloke for sure.' JJ says this with confidence, like he's already given it some thought. 'But I guess I don't really know him. Probably not the first nice bloke to top his missus either. So it's a hard one.' He drinks some more gin. 'What's it like house-sharing with him?'

'He's very generous.' I swallow hard, feeling my cheeks flushing. If JJ notices he pretends not to. 'Ian confuses me, though, and I'm not sure he's totally honest with me. I was going to leave, but then after I met his son Jamie, I decided to find out what really happened to Anna.'

'Fair enough.' JJ puts his empty glass down. 'Well, if you need help I'm here. Or if there's anything I can do, let me know.'

I lean forward, an urge to tell him everything swelling inside, but also knowing he's done for the day and must want to clean up. Then I remember. 'Actually, there is one small thing.'

'What's that?'

'A guy. I keep seeing him standing across the road from the house. Not every night. But often, when I look out, he's there in

The Landlord

the same spot, watching me. Then soon as he sees I've noticed him, he slinks away.' JJ rubs the stubble on his jaw, a bit concerned now. I finish my drink and put the glass down. 'I'd love to know who he is and why he's watching me.'

JJ searches for something in the pocket of his apron, then lifts a pen and paper from it. 'Next time you spot him, call me.' He scribbles out his phone number and slides it across. 'It's only two minutes on my bike up to your corner. I'll go and check him out for you.'

I take out my card to pay but he places his hand on mine. I feel his rough skin as he presses lightly. 'No need, Cathy.'

I go and catch a movie and when I get back to Belleview Road it's dark. I'm a little drowsy, still feeling the effects from the alcohol. There's no sign of Ian and no note either.

I pace through the living room, the tension in my body growing. All the way home I'd prepared to meet with him, thinking exactly how I would ask him about his bonfire last night, anticipating it; hoping I could finally get him to come clean and be honest, because I know, now, he's disposed of something. With a huff, I decide to text him.

When are you back?

Instantly there's a reply.

Called away. Sorry. Not sure. Not tonight.

I sit down on the couch and text back, my thumbs jabbing the keys. **I saw you last night. Making the fire in the garden.**

I expect a reply or maybe even for the phone to ring but there's nothing. Only silence. I think of ringing him but know my mood is all wrong. I throw my head back and stare at the white ceiling. Gone is the calm I enjoyed listening to JJ a short while ago down in Leno's. Now I think of the play, Old John and the way they so glibly glossed over what he had done. Then Malia's silence. Lastly, I think of Ian; the weirdness of his latest action, followed by his immediate disappearance.

It's got to be deliberate. It must be. He knows I'll have questions. Questions maybe he isn't prepared to answer. Why?

I get up and cross to the window. I look out for the man standing on the corner. I want him to be there so I can instantly ring JJ. I know he'd come because I trust him and he wouldn't lie to me. Then I could find out who it is and why they're stalking me.

'Christ,' I hear myself whisper into the empty room. Is that what it is, a stalker? Because that's what it feels like.

But tonight, there's nobody. Only a ghostly light casting a hollow glow onto the footpath and the swaying leaves of the tree above it.

I think about going upstairs to my bedroom to take an early night when there's a loud knock on the door.

28

Outside on the raised granite steps there's a man standing with his back to me. He turns round suddenly and I clamp my hand over my mouth.

'Hey Cathy.'

'Justin!' I muffle a gasp, my irritation surging. 'What are you *doing* here?'

He grins, amused at how he's spooked me. 'Am I getting invited in?'

'No.' I hold the door tightly, refusing to open it fully. 'It's late. Do you know what time it is?' I smell alcohol off him.

'It's eleven. So what?'

I don't answer. My mind is busy trying to make sense of his sudden appearance. He's trying to act like it's normal and reasonable but he looks awkward, almost mechanical in his forced ease. I also note he's managed to drop by when Ian is out. I don't think that's a coincidence.

'Justin, are you spying on me?'

He recoils. 'What?' His voice carries down into the quiet street.

'You are spying on me, aren't you?'

'Cathy, what are you talking about?'

'So why are you here?' I don't want to offer him an olive branch. I don't even want to talk to Justin again. And he knows because I've told him this clearly.

His face puckers. 'God, Cathy. Not this again. You know.' He points at me and I see he's holding something. It looks like a roll of newspaper. 'I spelled it out last time you made me go down to that underground dump with you. What are you playing at?'

'I'm not playing at anything but you're acting strange.'

'Well did you find anything in your dungeon?' he says sarcastically. But I can tell he's deflecting the question, shifting my focus, like he used to do whenever I'd ask him a question he'd prefer to avoid.

'Maybe you should go back down for another look?' I say dryly. 'Though I expect Ian might be back any minute.' He steps back, tapping his knuckles with the rolled-up paper, the mention of Ian visibly unsettling him.

His gaze switches to the street. I watch him searching for words to throw at me but he can't find the right ones. Something cutting enough, something to knock me back. 'This will end badly for you, Cathy.'

'Does that bother you? You seem worried about Ian?'

'Ian means nothing to me. It's you I'm worried about.' He glares at me, no trace of concern in his flashing eyes.

'Justin, if I see you spying on me again, I'm calling the police. Goodnight.' I shut the door.

'You'll regret not listening to me, Cathy,' I hear him spit from outside. 'I tried to help you but you wouldn't listen.' His voice sounds desperate as he grapples with a failure he most certainly hadn't expected. 'Well, I'm leaving you some bedtime reading to chew over.' I hear a grunt then see the rolled wad of newspaper pushing through the letterbox and dropping to the floor. Then nothing but his angry, flustered footsteps disappearing into the night.

The following evening there's still no sign of Ian. Just another brief text. **Away, will call.** I don't reply. I have nothing to say to him until he appears so we can talk face to face.

I have removed Justin's roll of newspapers from where they fell through the letterbox. Initially I wanted to bin them but I changed my mind and now I flick through them, curious to know what Justin believes is so important that he must visit me late in the night and try to frighten me with.

There are printouts of various articles from a short time after Anna's disappearance. I scan down through the paragraphs to see what's there but it's mostly just a rehash of the few snippets

The Landlord

I've already read, despite all my promises to Heather to stay away from searching for the story online. I put them aside when I notice a large colour piece. It's a picture of Anna, and Justin's taken some trouble both with colour printing it, and also with blowing up Anna's picture so it dominates the page. Her appearance is striking. She has the same jet-black hair I've seen in other photos, cut in that angular shape, straight across the brow just a fraction above each eyebrow, giving her doll-like bangs, then the sides framing her features with symmetrical precision as they drop down to her collarbone. It's a hard haircut to pull off but it works, the ink-black locks contrasting with her chalk-white skin, scarlet lips, and glass-green eyes. She wears a smart white shirt under a gunmetal business suit and radiates confidence.

I read the caption underneath. *Beauty, brains, power. Anna Cunningham, corporate raider and management guru, disappears into thin air. Police say husband Ian Fitzsimmons stands to inherit a fortune.* The word fortune is looped in red pen and an arrow swings down to a word Justin has scrawled at the end of the page. *Motive.* The theory isn't news and means little. From what I already understand, Ian was also independently wealthy, a successful architect in his own right, diminishing its relevance.

I put it aside, trying to figure out Justin's intentions which are clearly nothing like what he's suggesting. Anna's face stares back at me, a look of steel in her gaze, the look only a woman with pure self-belief can give, the kind I imagine you might earn when you break through glass ceilings, because you're tougher than any of the men standing on top of them trying to keep you down. I keep staring at it, and bit by bit, note the likeness to Jamie. A hidden gentleness beneath the armour. I can sense she wasn't a woman to give in easily or without a fight. I imagine whatever happened must have caught her unaware, or swept her away with brutal force.

I'm about to stand up when I see another page has fallen to the ground. An old article dated from eleven years ago. It has a picture of Ian with a black eye and a cut over his left cheek, looking badly dishevelled. He's in handcuffs and quarrelling with a policeman who is trying to wrestle him into a car. Underneath it says **Violent Fracas at Rugby Social**. I frown, agitated at Justin's determination to vilify Ian, but I read it anyway. *Two senior rugby team members were taken to hospital after an altercation involving Mr Ian Fitzsimmons. The club said there will be no charges pressed as it is resolving the matter internally. Mr Fitzsimmons was unavailable for comment but eyewitnesses claim they saw the altercation develop after a heated argument between Mr Fitzsimmons and the players.* Ian's name is circled in red this time and another red line leads down the page to where Justin has scrawled *previous form*.

The picture of Ian looks bad. The story worse. I grit my teeth, placing it on top of the pile, silent disgust stirring inside. It's true what Justin has pointed out. It isn't the first time Ian has been in trouble; not the first time he's come to the attention of the police for violence. I recollect the night we argued about Jamie, how his mood changed so suddenly, one minute a picture of calm, the next hulking over me, his eyes dark and menacing.

My stomach begins to twist when the doorbell rings. I jump, pressing a hand to my chest which feels like it could explode. I move quietly to the door, open it carefully and see Anthea outside. Her hair is in a high blonde ponytail and she is walking on the spot in her sports gear.

'Cathy.' Glancing down I see her bike parked on its stand at the base of the steps. 'Just finished doing our ride around with the gang and thought I'd drop in.' Anthea stops moving her legs and rests her hands above her hips. 'Sorry, that was my cool-down. A must according to our resident training expert Gerald, I'm afraid. Don't suppose Ian's about, is he?'

'No, he's away.' I try to rouse from my daze.

'Really? Where?'

'I'm not sure. Something work-related.'

'Right,' Anthea agrees, as if I've just said the secret code. 'Mind if I pop in?' She eases the door back and I watch as she slips into the living room. Bouncing past the coffee table she spots the

The Landlord

newspaper cuttings. She stops, staring aghast at the picture of Ian with his black eye and handcuffs.

'What is *this*, Cathy?' She holds it away from her like something toxic.

'Papers somebody stuffed in the door.'

'Who would want to send you stuff about Ian?' I bite my lip and shrug. I don't want to talk about Justin. Not now. He's not worth it. 'I never knew this about Ian.' She points to it with a bewildered expression. '*A violent fracas at the rugby club?*' She places it down gently. 'I'm sorry. I hadn't meant to pry but it was just sitting there.'

'It's fine.'

'Is somebody trying to frighten you away?'

I nod. 'Seems like it.'

She drops onto the couch, exasperated. 'What is *with* people? Have they nothing better to do?' She drums the armrest with her fingers. I think about offering her something to drink when she speaks again. 'Look, I dropped by to tell you something.' She waits to see she has my full attention before continuing. 'There was a thing with the gang this evening about something that happened the other night.'

'The other night?' The muscles around my ribcage tighten.

Anthea sighs. 'Yes, one of your neighbours, Lorraine, saw Ian out during the night burning things in his garden and told Carol. And now Carol's calling a meeting about alerting the police.' She blows out her cheeks.

'I see.'

'Were you aware?'

'About the fire?'

Anthea nods but I shake my head and look blank. 'God, this relentless hounding annoys me, Cathy, but I thought at least if we let Ian know he could ...' She breaks off.

'What?'

'He has to *stop doing* these things. Giving people reasons to point the finger. Digging a hole for himself.' She glances towards the papers on the couch. 'There's too many people out there who want to keep this whole nightmare going and I'd dread to think what Carol would say if she read that one.' She points a finger at the picture of Ian. He looks so haggard I have to glance away.

'I agree.'

She wrings her hands. 'I mean, I miss Anna, Cathy, probably more than most of them who never really cared for her that much when she was actually around.'

'Ian mentioned she was fond of you.'

She stops, surprised. 'He said that?'

'Yes, that you were friends.'

Anthea frowns, wrinkling the edges of her eyes and making her look older. 'In her own way I think she did like me but she was a complicated woman, Anna. Even more of a mystery than Ian I sometimes think.' She bounces to her feet and her sad look vanishes. 'Cathy, I want you to come along to this meeting they're having in Leno's. As soon as I get the time and date I'll be straight back with it. Then we can calm the whole thing down a little. Would you do that for me?

Stalling, I try to think of an excuse. 'I ...'

'The lovely JJ will be there so you'll get to see him again.' She grins, noticing my surprise. How does she know I met him recently? 'Don't worry, if you think JJ's easy on the eye you're not alone. There's not one of us who isn't weak at the knees for him, myself included.' She winks, slipping out to the corridor and opening the front door. 'It's a crying shame he's engaged.'

'He is?' The words hiss from my lips like a puncture.

'So my friend Harriet claims anyway.' Jogging down the steps, Anthea then takes her bike and starts to wheel it off. 'I'm still planning our get-together so I haven't forgotten you, OK?' I nod. 'And make sure you get rid of those papers of Ian. God knows the man is troubled enough. Some people just can't let bygones be bygones round here.' She throws a final wave and departs.

I traipse back inside. The fallout from Ian's fire hasn't fizzled out yet. The certainty of his guilt still burns brightly for too many on this street.

29

Work is dull and joyless. I grind through on autopilot, doing my level best to block out everything that's happening with Old John and the director, Andy. But I refuse to dwell on it; it only makes me more aware of how hard it must be for Ian, losing his soulmate Anna, only to find the whole world set against him too.

Ian hasn't returned or texted. I want to call him but choose not to. I can't hound him. I have to be patient.

In his absence, I fall into a pattern of ruminating. I think about Anna, her arresting beauty and steely confidence; Ian and his bruised eye, guilty and bound as they arrest him for assault; and Jamie, lost between them like some sad deer not sure which way to run so it stands paralysed and still. The more I think of Jamie, the more it strengthens my resolve. Though he doesn't know it, I will find out the truth about his mother. I will not give up until I bring him the peace of knowing what really happened the night she disappeared.

Justin doesn't return. I'm not surprised. I spent so many of our last few months together tolerating his excesses, suffering his excuses as he used me as his doormat, taking me for granted like somebody that would be there for him no matter how badly he behaved. I could see his confusion the last time he called by, like he couldn't recognise the woman shutting the door in his face, threatening him with the police. I remember his flustered movements, his features contorting into a grimace, the defeat in his voice as he shoved the papers through the door and his angry footsteps as he stomped into the darkness. But I'm still unclear why he went to so much trouble. Why print out all these clippings of Ian and Anna and stuff them through the letterbox? Justin was never as smart as he liked to believe but even he must know I'm not going to believe it's all for my good.

I'm grateful to Anthea that she dropped by to let me know about the meeting. She didn't have to do that, especially since I suspected many of the people attending would probably be from her own cycling group. Her concern for Ian feels real and balanced, and it gives me some hope that I'm not the only one in the whole neighbourhood who wants to stop the lynch mob mentality. I wonder about the woman she mentioned, Lorraine. I imagine her looking cross, twitching her curtains, judging Ian with gusto, her two thumbs busy on her phone, telling her WhatsApp groups all about his bonfire. Then I picture Carol when she got the news, like some kind of early morning jackpot for her breakfast. Was it Carol who suggested getting the police involved? It would seem to fit, though I know it could be anyone because sympathy for Ian is in short supply if what I heard down at Leno's is anything to go by.

Hungry, I lumber down to the kitchen. It bothers me that Ian hasn't returned. I won't get my chance to question him about the bonfire, to make him explain what he knows he must. Justin's carefully circled words snake around inside my mind. *Motive, previous form.* I fold my arms as I lean back against the counter, riled that Justin's succeeded in doing exactly what he intended; planting the seed of doubt that Ian Fitzsimmons can be anything other than a murderer.

When I go upstairs, I lie on the bed. The time has passed midnight and I start to sleep. But soon, in the pitch darkness of my bedroom, I hear the front door open downstairs.

Heavy footsteps thud across the floor. I get up instantly and throw on some clothes.

'Ian?' I call out softly, padding gently down the stairs and into the living room which, like the hall is in complete darkness.

A figure slumps on the couch, motionless in the gloom. The only sound is the person's laboured breathing. My chest tightens and I remain still. What if it's not Ian? The other night Jamie appeared out of nowhere. What if it's someone else? How secure is this house really?

The person drapes two long arms across the back of the couch. The hair on my bare arms stands up and I clutch my dressing gown tight around my body, noticing a sudden cold draught. My head pounds. I look back to the corridor when the person speaks.

'Don't turn on the light.' The voice is weary and deep. But familiar.

'Ian?' I can't tell if it's him. I'm too distracted.

'Cathy,' he replies heavily. 'Yes, I *have* been drinking. Too much, as you can tell.' Recognising his voice, finally I move towards him tentatively. He doesn't sit up or turn around so I walk over. Now I see his head almost lolling. His usual poise is gone. When he flicks on a side lamp his eyes look glazed.

He points to the seat across from him. 'Take a chair.' Quietly I sit and he glances over squinting.

'Where have you been, Ian?' I ask, the anxiety in my voice clear. I've never seen him like this. So hollowed out by booze.

'Busy,' he replies flatly. 'Let's cut the small talk, shall we?'

I bristle at the hostility. Then I shiver. If Ian is drunk, he may also be volatile. Too volatile.

'Fine,' I say as calmly as I can.

'You want to know about my bonfire? Well, I had things to burn. So I burnt them.'

'At three in the morning, Ian? At the end of the garden?'

'It was personal. OK? Just stuff I can't put it in the green bins. Not with my neighbours. And I'm not spending three days standing in front of a shredder. What do you want me to do?'

'What things did you burn?'

He slaps the seat. 'All the things that burnt a hole in my heart from the years with Anna.' Leaning forward, he tries to steady. Then he looks at me again. 'A *lot*, Cathy.'

I shift uneasily. I don't want him to see my pity as I watch his handsome proud face twisted with alcohol, trying to explain how he's reduced to burning his life away in the darkness. All for the sake of privacy. Who am I to demand he explain? And yet I need to push him. If he can't explain it to me, then there's nobody else, and I won't give in until I understand what he's really doing. What really happened to bring him to this point?

'God, Ian,' I groan. 'You know this makes you look guilty about Anna's disappearance.'

He grunts. 'More guilty you mean.' The words slur from his mouth. 'I'm already guilty, remember? They've all decided.' He trails off, his eyes closing over.

'Anthea called round earlier to say one of the neighbours saw you.' I don't say anything about the police and how they're thinking about contacting them. I don't know how he might react. 'She wants you to stop giving people reasons to doubt you.'

'Ah,' he sneers. 'Anthea. Worried about me? Thought she was telling Anna to be shot of me when she could bend her ear.' He snorts. 'She bring a casserole?' I've never seen him like this. So bitter. So sad. I frown but try to hide my disappointment. Am I finally witnessing the flip from Jekyll to Hyde Jamie warned me about? It feels too like it, and I've seen glimmers of it before already.

Ignoring his outburst, I change the subject. 'Ian, why is your relationship with Jamie so fraught?'

'Ah, Jamie. I thought you might ask about him. Oedipal complex. All boys have it. Had it with my own father.' He glances over, assessing my reaction, but I stare back, waiting for a proper explanation. 'Oh, trust me, Cathy, it happens. Add in threatening his mum's life a few times which I happened to do, directly to her face, mind, and that'll do the trick.'

'Why did you threaten her?'

I notice his mouth twitch and he gives me a dark look. 'Because fucking relationships are so damn complicated, Cathy.' Suddenly he's snarling. 'And when mine was falling apart I couldn't handle it so I lashed out in the weakest way possible.' His arms flail in the darkness. 'Big, ugly, useless threats.' Stopping abruptly, he looks at me sadly, his eyes glistening.

The Landlord

'Why was your relationship with Anna falling apart?'

He doesn't reply but rubs his hand back and forth along the arm rest. Then he pauses and looks at the floor. 'Perhaps I should just accept that Jamie is right. Accept that I've fought long enough. Admit to myself what I've always known.'

'What's that?'

'That I'm a monster, Cathy.' He swallows noisily. 'That my wife disappeared because of me.'

'Did she?'

He shrugs, attempts a feeble smile but it quickly fades, then his eyes cast about and his mouth turns down. Next his head is in his hands and I hear sobs. His hulking body judders as the sobs become deeper and louder. I wince, my heart so heavy then, but I don't interfere. I don't know what Ian is going to do next and I'm afraid. When he stops, I get up and take the papers from the hall table. I pluck the picture of Ian in handcuffs being arrested by the police. I look at his haunted, swollen face and give it to him.

'Somebody sent me this. Somebody who thinks my life is in danger living here. Can you explain this to me?'

He takes it in his hands and stares at it, the memory reawakening. 'Yes, I remember. Two big, ugly rugby players at the bar beside me and my friend Alan; Alan was gay and small, but loved the game, so he enquired if his son could sign up to start training.'

'What happened?'

'Nothing surprising. They said the club didn't accept faggots and certainly not baby faggots.' He places the paper down on the couch. 'I asked them to apologise, they told me to fuck off, so I sent two of them to hospital. Understandably, I was told to not come back.' He shrugs, as if unsure what else to add. 'Afterwards I was livid with myself for losing it so easily, but that wasn't the thing that bothered me, Cathy.'

'What was?'

'My friend, Alan, decided never to speak to me again.' He staggers to his feet. 'OK, I've got to go to bed.' All the hostility has left him. He sounds empty, defeated. 'I've a client meeting in the morning and I've badly overdone it.' Waving sadly, he shuffles away. I rise and follow him out to the hall, waiting there to watch and make sure he gets up the steps.

'Ian?'

He turns wearily. 'Yes?'

'There's a man who's been watching me from across the road, near the corner. I've seen him quite a few times. Do you have any idea who it could be and what he wants?'

He stops for a second, considering the question. 'No, but we should try to find out.'

'I'd appreciate that.'

He smiles weakly, takes two uncertain steps and turns back again. 'Cathy?'

'Yes?'

'Sorry.'

'About what?'

He rubs a hand through his hair, heaving out deeply. 'Everything.'

30

The planned café meeting finally comes round. I check my watch and see it's in ten minutes.

When I get there I discover Anthea chatting to JJ inside. She's gesticulating at the walls, an astonished look on her.

'Aren't these fabulous, Cathy? All these gorgeous little pieces JJ's stuck up to decorate the place and it's all done by the native population, isn't that right, JJ? What do they call them again? The aboriginals, isn't that it?'

'Hey, Cathy,' JJ greets me, not hiding his relief. 'Come on in.' He turns back to Anthea. 'We call them the indigenous people, you know. It's part of the respect for their culture we're trying to give back to them after all the years of taking it away.'

'Yes, of course,' Anthea agrees, a little too volubly. JJ throws me a sideways glance and a very subtle roll of his sparkling blue eyes. 'Aren't they so wonderful the way they can find things to eat under stones and all these places you'd never even think to look. I even saw a documentary where they showed one guy make a homemade straw from grass so he could catch ants. Amazing.'

'Genius,' JJ agrees, his polite discretion speaking volumes as he pats me gently on the arm. 'Hey Cathy. All good with you?'

'Fine, thanks,' I say a little stiffly, my heart feeling for him, wondering how he stays so relaxed and calm when people must be getting up his nose all day long. I know Anthea means well, but even listening to her from a distance my skin is prickling. Can't she just admire the art without patronising the man? Now I'm suddenly here I'm not so sure it was such a good idea to come to this meeting. Who's even coming?

Anthea keeps ogling the walls. 'I remember travelling there years ago. We only did a week in Sydney so just got to see a few of the nearby towns, but Harry couldn't stop joking about how they were all called Woolymagong and Boorawoora and the like.' She laughs to herself at the memory. JJ listens to her attentively but his eyes get a faraway look, like Anthea is something distant on the horizon, a shout in the breeze he happily cannot hear. I want to reach out and touch him, just to let him know that if he'd like to tell her to fuck off that I'd be right with him all the way. I want to grab Anthea by the wrist and say stop making these jokes. They're not funny, not even close. But I can't cause another scene. I can't do in Leno's what I just did at rehearsals. I can't lose these people before I've got to know them. And I want to get to know JJ because somewhere deep down I just know he's worth it.

The same group I remember from their Sunday club meeting are all there, muddling around in their corner, like a flock of resident parrots. I see one new face, who I'm guessing must be Lorraine. She's gesticulating as she chats to the woman standing beside her, and appears flushed and animated. If she was a dog, I'd say she's straining at the leash. JJ peels away, helping to get them all seated.

Gerald remains standing, gesturing to everybody at the big table. 'Shall we make it simple and just say coffee and juice for all? That way we don't waste too much time and can get down to business?' As usual, he sounds officious. Everybody agrees and Gerald does a circular thing with his fingers, with a commanding nod to JJ who just says 'righto'. I imagine Gerald in some conference room on a slow Monday morning, when he's not squished into his Lycra gear, pumping his fist on the table and telling his staff he expects better if they want a Christmas bonus. I silently agonise that any moment he might ask JJ to 'fetch' him something.

Anthea pats the seat next to her. 'You're sitting next to me, Cathy.' I produce a smile on cue, not sure if it's an invitation or a command.

The Landlord

'Just running to the loo,' I reply. 'Back in a sec.' When I get to the counter, JJ is lining up cups. 'Need a hand? I'll gladly help. I've probably done enough waitressing to have a gold star at this point.'

'Naw, I'm good but thanks for asking, Cathy.'

'Kind of quiet?' I say, wishing I wasn't alone with Anthea's cycling group, as if some random strangers might screen me from their interrogations.

'Gerald threw down a wad to book it out for the hour.' He starts grinding some beans and the noise drowns out the chatter of the group. 'I didn't want to agree to it to be honest, thought it was unfair to our regulars,' he says, raising his voice above the noise, 'but my mate Ben, the owner, said to take it. So had to be done.'

'Hopefully it won't last too long.' I throw him a look of sincere apology as I slip away to the toilet. When I get back, JJ has already delivered the entire order by himself. Like a one-man machine.

Carol is making a pained expression and pointing at something on the wall. 'Is that one of those didgeridoos or whatever they're called?'

Everybody laughs as I grit my teeth.

'They're hilarious,' Stewie quips. 'Aren't they? Like a giant penis.' It's the sarcastic guy I remember. His mean ferret eyes dart across the table towards the others, waiting for the laughs which they offer willingly. I suspect Stewie might be the office comedian, the one that plies himself with booze for the Christmas party, making most of the female staff decide to leave early.

'I wouldn't call that giant,' Gerald says, doing something suggestive with his eyebrows. More laughter.

'It's supposed to be a musical instrument,' Clive joins in, 'but has anybody ever heard one?'

'I have,' Carol replies. 'It goes burr, and then burr burr again.' As the group throw their heads back laughing, I sneak a glance at JJ. He nods, a picture of serenity and calm, and I give him the tiniest nod to let him know I understand. If he came over to empty the coffee on the floor, I feel I could forgive him. I take a long drink of juice, suppressing the urge to step across to Carol and pour it into her lap, suddenly wishing I was a million miles from this meeting. Now I think about her dog, imagining commiserating with it. How must she treat it behind closed doors?

'OK, everybody, joking aside now. It's time to be serious,' Anthea announces.

'Bloody right it is,' Carol agrees and several heads nod either side of the table.

Anthea looks at the new woman. 'Would you like to start us off, Lorraine?'

Lorraine thrusts forward, almost quivering, like she's about to explode with anticipation. I brace myself and without needing further prompting, Lorraine gets going, launching into a breathless story of what she saw that night. How she woke up to a fireball a few houses down and her first thought was that a building had caught fire; how she thought she was going to have to call the fire brigade but couldn't find her phone. Then, when she did find it, it was out of charge, so she had to get it powered up first. But finally, when she checked the fire again, it had dwindled right down and she guessed she was too late.

'The thing is,' she says licking two dry chapped lips, stabbing her finger into the table, 'it's plain as daylight that Fitzsimmons is disposing of evidence because he's responsible for his wife's murder.'

Wincing at the words, I reach for my juice again and take another mouthful. Everybody joins in and throws in their opinions. About how it's crazy stuff to be going on in a respectable neighbourhood; about how it could have been far worse and set the entire street on fire or swept into the trees and gone all the way to the park. How nobody goes out in the middle of the night to burn things unless they are deeply suspect. How it's illegal to burn things and a criminal offence, not to mention what it does to the environment – like giving people all sorts of breathing problems with smoke and chemicals.

The conversation thrums with a heated outcry about how Ian Fitzsimmons has got away with murder.

The Landlord

Stewie slurps his coffee noisily and puts down his cup. 'Even if the police have chucked in the towel, they cannot ignore what is certainly sufficient evidence to resurrect the case. It's clear, like Lorraine is saying, the man is guilty and that's the only logical reason he'd be doing something so bloody daft.'

'Exactly,' Carol agrees. I try to guess what she might do for a living. A school teacher maybe? Maybe in one those prim posh schools where she gets to drum in her mantras of obedience and discipline, barking from some astroturf sideline, that she expects better, never relenting even when the kids are reduced to tears. Clive snorts a laugh, more amused than anything at how excited everybody has become. The only one of them who hasn't said anything yet is the ethereal Jemima. Jemima looks like she might be performing a civic duty listening to the others, that she'd be happier in a quiet park doing stretches on her mat. I wonder who corralled her into making an appearance and hope it wasn't Carol. If there's any hope of balance around the table, she might be it.

Gerald puffs himself up, readying himself to speak, like he's summarising for the jury. 'Yes, well. I'm in complete agreement with you,' he then throws in. 'But, and here's the big but folks, I really can't see how getting the hapless pigs back on the job is going to help things. I mean they were incompetent first time round and I wouldn't have any faith in them doing any better second time out either. And remember, reigniting the whole thing will put a serious dent in our property values. That's the thing I'm worried about.' I muffle a gasp. *A woman he knows personally has disappeared and all he can worry about is the value of his house?* For a second I almost get to my feet but I fight back the urge and stay where I am, digging deep for my acting skills, forcing a look of casual indifference.

'Good point, Ger,' Clive agrees.

Carol lets out a disgruntled groan. 'Flip's sake. We can't win with this killer on the loose on our own road. Why do we have to put up with it?' The venom in Carol's tongue seeps across the table like some invisible toxic cloud between us. I'd like to wave it away but I sit tight as Anthea, who has been strangely quiet, assumes control. 'Jemima? Would you have any thoughts?' she asks calmly.

Languidly, Jemima puts her glass down and breathes a deep, yogic breath. 'I feel all this disturbance is bad for the spiritual health of the community. It's like a trapped nerve to the chakra.' She waggles her head sadly. 'But inviting police will only add to this disturbance so I wouldn't recommend it.' I release an inaudible groan of relief.

The others grin, like they've already anticipated what Jemima would say.

'OK,' Anthea, says soothingly. 'Well, everybody, I'm inclined to see a lot of sense in what both Gerald and Jemima have to say on this. While it might pain us to let it go, it could be for the best, and God forbid, if anyone should consider selling on down the line and their home is devalued.' She raises her eyebrows and I hear mumblings of acknowledgement. I nod my agreement, swallowing my distaste again for Anthea's jokes, but allowing that she's doing her best, wooing this group with the words she probably knows will work best. And it seems to be working so I'm grateful to her. 'But what about you, Cathy? Would you like to leave us with the last word on this? I'd love to hear your thoughts.'

Anthea's question catches me off guard. I've been too busy listening, pondering this random mix of self-appointed judges, to think clearly about my own position. Necks crane and the collective gaze latches on to me, waiting. In a split second, I make up my mind. I don't want the police to be alerted, even if it does make sense, even if I still don't know what Ian was truly doing, because though he's explained, he still hasn't really. Not satisfactorily. Or maybe it's me baulking at the excited faces I see all around the table, so eager to point the finger at Ian, so sure without concrete evidence.

I sit up, readying myself to go out on a limb. One I hadn't prepared. Not even a bit. I silently command myself to act, to improvise. 'I have something to confess,' I announce, my voice

The Landlord

low and quiet. Faces lean in. Anthea is so close I can feel her hair brushing my arm. Suddenly I'm like a character in one of the many plays I've performed in and I know what to do to carry these people along with me some way, the way I've done before with a live audience. 'The bonfire was mine.'

I hear gasps. There's a hushed silence. Confused faces become stone-still. Arched eyebrows await, the outrage palpable.

'Would you like to tell us why?' Anthea suggests softly. In the corner of my eye, I can see Gerald huffing and Stewie sneering. Carol's face has screwed into a tight pinch but there's no hostility in Anthea's, just curiosity.

'Ian had asked me to get rid of stuff from his shed while he was away. I was out that evening with my friends for a few drinks and had a few more than I should. So I decided to go down and see what needed to be done that night when I got home.' Beyond the table, in the distance at the counter, I see JJ listening too. He's watching on, relaxed and attentive. 'When I found out how heavy the bag of rubbish was, I decided I wasn't going to do my back in carrying it, so I decided I would burn it there and then, thinking at night the smoke wouldn't be such an issue.'

'But it was like a bomb blast,' Lorraine protests, her neck extending as if she wants to bite me.

I nod. 'I accidentally dropped the bottle of lighter fluid into the fire and the whole thing went up in one go. It was an accident. I then got it under control and it just smouldered on for another half an hour till I could stamp it out and go to bed. I'm sorry. I had hoped nobody noticed.'

Carol's eyebrows raise and her lips twist scornfully. 'Madness.'

Gerald folds his arms across his chest. 'Mm,' he says like a judge weighing evidence, then he raps his knuckles on the table. 'Didn't see that one coming. Well, that settles that then. But a word of advice to you, Cathy, best not to try that again in a hurry or we'll have to call the fire brigade.' He heaves his big frame up to stand, his interest evaporating abruptly. 'Right, still time for one more lap of the park. Shall we?'

Slowly they all rise, stunned into silence, snatching wary sideways glances at me. Once more I'm a stranger, watching on as they shuffle out whispering into one another's ears.

Only Anthea remains. 'That was brave, Cathy.' She gives me an approving look, her voice full of appreciation. 'I'm not saying I agree with what you did but you had the guts to admit it.' She throws her arms around me, hugging me so quickly I forget to hug her back. 'I better rush before the gang take off.' She runs after them, waving hurriedly to JJ on her way past.

I think they're gone but then I see Carol turning around and walking back over. Next thing she's extending her neck out whispering into my ear.

'I don't believe you,' she says. 'Not a single word of it.' Before I can reply she turns and leaves.

After they've all gone, I just want to go and talk with JJ, but unfortunately another small group come in and he's suddenly busy so instead I go for a walk in the park. I want to try to process what's happened. I had no plan to tell them that I lit the fire. I've invented a far-fetched lie which has implicated me in an act I never committed. I can't give a good rationale, other than it seemed like the right thing to do at the time. I'm acting like somebody with something to cover up, even though I haven't done anything wrong. I'm acting in ways that don't feel familiar anymore, that don't feel like me.

Suddenly I understand how Ian must feel, because if it is true, and he has done nothing wrong, then the only difference is that his case is so much worse in every way.

31

The doorbell rings and I go out to open it. Anthea's outside. She's changed out of her cycling clothes. Powder-blue jeans, white lacy top revealing her shoulders, white tennis shoes, no socks. One hand flicks to her hair and the other holds a baking tray.

'Heya. Ian back yet?'

'No.'

'Oh.' She smiles. 'I was just dropping another of these. I cooked it last night.' She swings a large shepherd's pie under my nose. 'If he's not around, why don't you have it?' I stare at it uncertainly. 'Or maybe freeze it for him if it's not up your street. Guess that kind of thing might be a bit old-fashioned, is it?'

I take the dish hastily, not wanting Anthea to think I'm baulking at accepting it. 'Not at all. Come in.'

'You sure you're not busy? I don't want to disturb you.'

I shake my head and Anthea looks pleased when she skips inside. 'I'll just put it in the fridge for now.' She follows as I walk through the corridor and into the kitchen at the back.

When I turn, she's behind me. 'Cathy, I just wanted to let you know what you did back there was very kind.' I close the fridge door, looking at her blankly. 'Back there in the café. Admitting about your bonfire.'

'Well, I don't know if I'd call it kind exactly, Anthea.'

'Well, honest then. I mean you didn't have to do it. And it's got them off Ian's back so it was very kind to him.'

'Thanks, Anthea.' I look at her, wondering what's really on her mind.

She leans across the marble island then. 'I know Carol was dawdling. What did she say to you? Nothing nasty I hope?'

'She said she knows I'm lying.'

Anthea's face drops. 'What is with Carol? Why would she say something like that?' When I don't reply, her shocked expression morphs into a frown. 'I mean, you wouldn't do that, Cathy?'

I let out a sigh and see her confusion. 'Come and sit down in the living room,' I reply, leading the way and watching behind me as she follows. We move back there, taking our places on one of the big leather couches.

Anthea looks a little stricken when she sits. 'I mean, it's none of my business, Cathy, I shouldn't even be asking you that. If you'd prefer to change the subject just tell me.'

'I don't think Carol likes me.'

Anthea nods, a conflicted frown etching across her brow. 'Well, Carol ...' she says, sounding bemused, 'is Carol. So you won't be the first or the last to feel that way, I'm afraid.' I nod, a little more relaxed as I sense Anthea's understanding. 'I don't think Carol's that awful. Sometimes she just wants us to think she's awful. Her problem is that she can be a little too direct with people.'

I listen, appreciating Anthea's generosity. In this moment I'm merely happy to have her company. I decide to change the conversation. I want this woman to help me understand the things that don't make sense. I need her to do that. She's the only one from the group I've got even remotely close to. 'Anthea, can you tell me about Anna? I know you told me you were friends.'

Sitting up then, she flattens both hands on her knees as she ponders the question. 'Well I'd like to think we were, certainly. I feel I was as close to Anna as anyone in this neck of the woods, but ...' she breaks off, as if confounded by a thought, 'the thing with Anna was that she was very remote. Almost like an island if that makes sense?'

'Distant you mean?'

She waves away the idea. 'No, not deliberately anyway, just harder to fathom. I don't think any of us could really grasp what made her tick. And that bothered people. Made them feel like they weren't on her level or that she didn't care for them.

The Landlord

But she wasn't like that at all.' A look of irritation crosses her face. 'People get the craziest notions sometimes, Cathy, and then just refuse to let them go. So that was how it was I think with a lot of people and Anna. It was clearly unfair.'

'Ian said you were advising her to leave him?' Anthea jolts and immediately I regret telling her this. 'Sorry, maybe I shouldn't have told you that.'

'Ian told you that?' She rubs her throat.

I think about backtracking but decide not to. If I don't probe, I'm not going to learn anything about Anna and Ian. I'm not going to understand what really happened to her. 'Something along those lines. He was drunk, the night of the bonfire, he just spat it out. Probably doesn't even remember.'

'Oh, Cathy.' Anthea winces. 'Ian and Anna had one of those relationships. Just so combustible. Individually each was fine but together it was like watching spiders in a jar, just eating each other alive. Anna sought my advice sometimes, it's true, and all I could honestly tell her was what I think she had already decided.'

'To leave him?'

She shrugs. 'I'm not sure I ever put it like that but it never looked like getting better. Ian was Ian, he wasn't going to change. It's just relationships.' She sighs. 'They're often so …'

'Complicated?'

'Exactly.' She exhales, looking rueful. 'And they were a complicated couple.'

'Did you ever think that Anna could have simply disappeared?'

Anthea leans back, sadness suffusing her face. 'Sometimes. It's a painful thought that Anna would just up and leave, without saying a word to any of us, not even Ian or Jamie. But I guess, in a lot of ways, it's a nicer one than thinking …' her voice trails off.

'That it was Ian?'

She nods glumly, hands pressing her thighs. I don't want to push her further. I don't like to see Anthea's bright bubbly energy diminished like it is now. It looks like an aberration. I change the subject. 'I've never met your husband.'

She brightens. 'Harry? Oh yes, certainly you must.' Becoming herself again, she rolls her eyes playfully. 'Though I dare say you might find Harry very low-key. It's why I love him and very occasionally hate him too.' She lets out a tiny laugh.

'I think you said he works in insurance?'

'Yes.' She throws her hands in the air. 'Don't ask me anything more, Cathy. He gave up long ago explaining it to me and I stopped asking. Although, let's just say between you and me, it seems to pay the bills.' Lighter once more, she jumps to her feet and skips towards the door. 'Anyhow, that's my good deed done, Cathy.' She points to the fridge. 'But it's probably as much for me as anybody if I'm being perfectly honest, because unlike most people I actually like cooking.'

'You do?'

She nods. 'I find it therapeutic. It relaxes me, always has. I don't know why.' She shrugs and smiles as if puzzled by it herself. 'And well done you again, for being brave I mean. We could use more of that round here.'

The darkness has closed in. When I check my phone I see it's gone past midnight. There's no sign of Ian. I go to the window to shut the curtain when I spot the man again. He's on his corner. The same spot once more. But this time he's not looking at me. This time he's looking at Anthea. She is standing at her window with her arms folded but I can't quite make out if she is looking at the man or not.

I step back, my chest tightening. Who is the man? Why has he returned? Why is he staring into Anthea's house? Could she be in danger?

Eventually Anthea drops her hands to her sides, walks to the window and shuts her curtains. I glance back down to the street corner. The man is still there; he gazes at me directly now.

He doesn't look away this time but keeps on staring.

32

Deep within my chest my heart thumps. What does he want? Who is he? Why is he staring at me now and not even caring that I notice? My heart is still drumming as I slip away from the window, retreating from his disturbing gaze. But my breathing won't regulate. The tightness in my chest won't seem to ease up. What if the strange man approaches? Knocks on the door?

My hands tremble when I take out my phone and call JJ.

'Cathy?' He answers immediately.

'JJ, he's there again.'

'Who?'

'The guy,' I whisper, my voice taut. 'The one I told you about. He's on the corner, staring up at me. Like he wants me to know he's looking this time.'

'Fuck.'

'Are you out?'

'No. I'm at home in my flat.' I tap the phone against my forehead. I so desperately want him to come round. 'But I'm still only minutes away. I'm getting on my bike right now, OK?'

'Oh God JJ! Thank you so much.'

'Three minutes tops.'

'You sure?'

'I'm sure, Cathy.' The tension in my body eases a little. 'What do you want me to do when I see him?'

I stall, confused. I hadn't processed this. I try and think. What can I ask JJ to do? I can't put him at risk. This man on the corner could be dangerous. He could be anybody. It's unfair. 'There's no need to confront him,' I say, unsure what else to add.

'Why don't I try and get a picture of him? Discreetly.'

'You think you can?'

'I'll have a go.'

'Please promise me you won't take any risks. He could be ...'

'What?'

'Dangerous.'

'Don't worry. I'll be careful.' He cuts the line.

I swallow hard, the muscles in my back tensing as I crouch in the darkness and wait. Time drags. From my hiding place at the side of the window I crane my neck to spy on the man. With his hands in his pockets, he still stares up at the window, challenging me to come forward. Instantly I pull away, desperate not to get caught spying, hunkering down to the floor and pressing my back against the wall.

The cool plaster is cold beneath my skin and I shiver. I want to move from this room. To get to my bedroom or the kitchen where I can stand up, unwatched and turn on the light. Where I can phone one of my friends. But I won't dare. I won't risk losing sight of this stranger.

The minutes pass, each one feeling like an age as I count them on the screen of my phone, but at last I see a man on a bicycle appear outside. It's JJ. It has to be. My pulse quickens as he draws closer to the stranger who seems to be acknowledging him. The next thing, JJ stops his bike in front of him. I wince, my mouth suddenly bone dry. He wasn't supposed to take any risks but now they look like they're talking? I crouch closer to the window but JJ is back on his bike and pedalling away again. I expect the man to look back up but he doesn't. Instead he turns hastily and paces away up the street at speed. Within seconds, both of them have disappeared. I draw back from the window and hunker back down, my back against the cold wall, exhaling loudly when there's a ping and my phone screen lights up.

It's a WhatsApp message from JJ and when I open it up, I see it's a video clip.

When I play it, I see JJ is asking the man for a light for a cigarette. The man says he doesn't have one. 'Sorry, mistook you for

The Landlord

a mate,' JJ replies and it cuts. But I see the man's face clearly. The camera is perfectly aimed towards him, and even in the darkness he is immediately recognisable. I know it too well; it's my ex-boyfriend Justin.

The phone rings. I startle and the back of my head bangs hard against the wall behind it. But it's only JJ so I answer.

'You get it OK?' he asks, his voice slightly breathless.

'Yes.' I swallow, feeling a little stupid.

'Did he hang about? I didn't want him to catch me checking when I cycled off, so I couldn't see?'

'No, he left. Like he was in a hurry. Thanks so much, JJ.'

'For nothing. Any idea who he is?'

I grit my teeth, pushing myself with effort from the floor and walking over to turn on the living room light. It clicks and my eyes squint at the sudden burst of white light. 'Yes, it's my ex-boyfriend. I'm so sorry but he's the one who's been stalking me.'

'Shit. You OK there by yourself or you need me to come round?'

I go over and snap the curtains shut, gripping the fabric with barely controlled anger. Then I slump down into the big leather couch. I would love JJ to call over, love to talk to him and tell him how bad it is with me right now. All the shit I've had to put up with because of Justin; how the bottom has fallen out of my job; how much I like Ian but how badly I fear I may have him all wrong. And how I don't even know where to start now I've discovered my ex is stalking me. It's too strange. Too surreal.

'Thanks for the offer, JJ, but I'll be fine, honestly.'

'Only if you're sure.'

'I am,' I lie. 'And thanks for doing this for me. I got shit-scared when you stopped close to him on your bike.' A nervous laugh escapes from me. 'Of course at that point I had no idea it was my ridiculous ex, Justin.'

'Well, shout again if anything changes. You've got my number now and I'm only down the road. Yeah?'

'Yeah.'

As soon as JJ hangs up I immediately call Justin.

He picks up.

'Why are you stalking me?'

He snorts. 'Cathy, what are you talking about?'

'Don't lie, Justin. I just saw you.'

'Saw me do what?'

'Justin, stop lying to me. I've spotted you many times. You always go to the same place across the street, and tonight you didn't even try to hide.'

'Cathy, what are you talking about? I was hanging out with some mates and just happened to be in the area, so I popped by. I was hoping you'd come out so maybe we could talk. You're hardly going to answer your phone to me now.'

'How many times, Justin?'

'God, calm down. It's only the second time, OK? And I was only checking in on my ex. What's so strange about that?'

'That's a lie. You've been here a bunch of times.' He doesn't reply. 'And how do you know Anthea?'

'Who?'

'Stop pretending, Justin, the woman across the road who you were staring at. You must know her?'

'You mean the blonde eyeballing me the other side of the street? Fuck's sake, Cathy. How do I know who she is? A nosy cow is all I know.'

I don't believe him but he's shifted into defensive mode. He won't concede anything and I know it. The more I press him the more I know he'll dig his heels in. Make me feel unfair, irrational. But I know there's more to this.

'If I spot you one more time, Justin, I'm calling the police.'

'What? Cathy, get real.'

'I am real and stalking's illegal in case you didn't know.' I hang up on him and switch off my phone. I don't think he'll call me back but just in case. I'm so annoyed by Justin but pissed off with myself too. Why did I never think of him? It's almost always an ex-boyfriend in these stalking situations. But is that what this is now? Stalking. A handful of sightings hardly constitutes a case against him. He'll have to do a lot more before it's anything close to something I can report. And do I really want that? How could I possibly explain it to his mum? She'd never understand. I wouldn't want her to. I wouldn't want her to even have to think about it.

I'll talk with Justin and put him straight, stop this before it becomes a thing. Yet deep down I know there's something else going on. Something about this place that Justin isn't telling me.

I trudge upstairs to bed. I haven't heard from Ian yet but I can't think about that. There's a coiling inside my gut and I roll onto my side, hoping it will die down and let me sleep. It's the feeling I get when something's about to happen and I just can't say what it is.

33

When I get in to work there's a new face.

'Everybody, meet Elaine,' AA announces. 'Elaine's just going to be joining me to observe rehearsals today. I want a little objectivity on how we're doing and Elaine's happy to help.' Elaine waves as we chorus her name. She's almost familiar but I can't say from where. I look over to Malia to see what she thinks but she remains impassive, a blank canvas revealing nothing. She doesn't meet my eye. I fight back the urge to just go over and shake her, to insist we just chat about the incident and get past it, but instead I mirror her, pretending I hardly notice her as I get busy with my warm-up routine.

Rehearsals pass quickly. AA seems to be very pleased with Elaine's 'objectivity' and grabs a private moment with her at every opportunity to do a recap of what we've worked on. Despite being distracted I manage to press on with all my scenes and do a decent job, digging deep to find the relevant emotional pitch in all the right places. It feels as if I've uncovered a little compartmentalisation box and opened it up to unleash its power, as my private world of Ian and Justin and the house on Belleview Road mercifully boxes itself away. The rest of the cast have picked it up too. Malia is exuding effortless perfection, and yet her switch from caring Cordelia to a serious, almost numb expression during breaks is hard to understand. Old John has slipped out of his rut and wrestled himself back to a semblance of respectability and for the first time in days the production is working smoothly.

Evening comes round and AA lets everybody go, but then skips around double quick to whisper a word in the ear of Old John, Malia and myself, telling us to hold back. As the rest of the cast shuffle out they mutter to themselves, staring at us like exhibits in

The Landlord

a wax museum. A portion of them look at Elaine and share some personal remarks. As the room empties, I watch on, registering a sharp change in the ambience. Does AA want to finally address Old John's jokes, as he likes to label them? But why now? Why, after ignoring the elephant in the room for so long? And why bring Elaine in for that discussion?

I look around the room. Elaine smiles. Old John smirks. Malia looks straight ahead, giving nothing away.

Finally, AA clears his throat, and starts to explain.

'Everybody, John, Malia, Cathy,' he begins, his voice reedy and lips twitching. 'I've another announcement to make. It's not an easy one but it's for the best.' Nervously he glances over at me. 'I've decided to replace Cathy with Elaine, beginning tomorrow.' Elaine is nodding repeatedly as if to help with the explanation. Old John rubs his beard, hiding his satisfaction under a gnarled fist, Malia remains impassive. My ribs constrict. 'I'm sorry it's come to this and I'm sorry for the disruption it will cause but it's decided. Any questions?'

Old John shakes his head. I gulp and glance to Malia, but she doesn't budge, instead keeping her attention on AA.

'No,' I hear her say softly.

'Fine,' AA says. 'I'll let you all go.'

Old John marches out, chin held high, silently followed by Malia who refuses to look my way. I stay where I am as Elaine glances at AA.

'Elaine, just give me a minute and I'll be right with you.' Elaine waves, throwing me a pitiful glance before hurrying away. Then AA begins.

'I'm sorry, Cathy, but it's in the best interests of the production.'

'You mean you let me rehearse the whole day just to fire me in the evening?'

Crease lines appear beneath his receding hairline. 'I wanted Elaine to see the production in progress. She's played the part before but it was important she see just how I'm seeking to adapt our version.'

'So you sacrifice me instead of your chauvinist leading man?'

AA makes a dismissive gesture. 'You're the only one calling him a chauvinist, Cathy. I didn't hear Malia complain.'

I step back. I'm hollow inside. AA has trumped me without even trying, because if nobody but me has noticed Old John's slurs or made a complaint then they simply don't exist. It's all just the fantasy of an irrational and difficult woman. Me.

My skin prickles. I think of all the things I could say. All the insults I could hurl at this sly, cowardly excuse of a man. Raw, vicious words bubble up and I feel like a bomb about to explode. But it's too late. We've done that scene already. It's what's brought me to this point. I won't be giving him the satisfaction again. Tears bubble.

Bristling, I squeeze my lips together and march away.

Outside on the street I search for Malia. She's the one person in the group who can understand the injustice of what's happened. But then I remember she witnessed the spectacle herself, watched it unmoved, detached from it like it was somebody else's story and not one she had any part in. And now she's gone. Taking out my phone, I locate my agent's number and press call.

'Cathy, why are you calling me?' Melissa answers. 'You know it's after office hours.' Her voice is sharp.

'I've been fired. From the production.'

The news is greeted with a long, disinterested sigh. 'I know.'

I squeeze my temples which are starting to throb. 'What do you mean, Melissa? Since when?'

Melissa exhales. 'Last week. AA told me. He said he was finding a replacement.'

'Why didn't you tell me?'

'Not my job, Cathy. Andy's the director.'

I squeeze the phone tighter. 'Did he explain why?'

'He said you had insulted the lead for no reason. Failed to apologise and made the whole production awkward to the point of it being unmanageable.'

The Landlord

'It wasn't like that.' I'm about to tell Melissa what really happened when I stop. There's no point. She doesn't want to know.

'Whatever. I thought that was a good opportunity for you, Cathy and now it's gone. Look, we'll talk another time when I'm free. OK?'

Dazed, I stagger back to Belleview Road. A murderous rage courses through my blood, all the way down to my fingertips. AA, Old John, and even Melissa are somehow conspiring against me, allowing me to take the blame where none was ever truly due. Even Malia, the friend I wanted to support some way, has turned a blind eye, letting them all hang me out to dry. Red-faced and hot, I curse at the ceiling as I slam the front door shut behind me. I should be carrying on the job I was hired to do but instead I've been sacrificed in a game of damage limitation, to gratify bruised egos and blow away the sulphureous smell of scandal. I'm the girl who must take the fall and nobody wants to know differently.

I stomp inside and fling myself down on the couch. It dawns on me then that this could be exactly what Ian has experienced. But in truth I know what I'm feeling would pale when compared, because how could I possibly even begin to comprehend how it must feel to be wrongly accused of murdering the person you loved? What he's suffered would be a thousand times worse; and each day that passes he lives it again and again.

I hear myself groan. I so badly want Ian to be innocent, feeling so certain it's the truth, and yet, at every turn, there is something. Some recklessly suspicious act, some impossibly convoluted story which won't add up. My mind strays to Jamie and I recall his anguish as he said the words, *Did he kill Mum? I don't believe so for a minute.*

If it's true what he believes I have to prove it. And now, broke, but free from work, I have the time to do it. Finding out what really happened is the only way this story can end. I resolve that nothing will stop me finding out the truth about Anna.

Not even Ian.

34

It's the humming that wakes me. It's out of tune, some song I've never heard or don't remember. There's the sound of feet too; they're light and quiet but close by, tapping the hard wooden boards gently as they pass. I open my eyes a crack.

Mrs Bastible, Ian's housekeeper, places a vase back on the coffee table in front of me, dusts around it with her long grey duster and moves past me into the adjoining back room, humming tunelessly and not paying me any attention.

When I turn round, she's dusting the large mirror above the second fireplace. The shutters dividing the living and dining rooms are open as usual so I can see her.

I yawn, as I check my phone, shocked to see that I've not only slept on the couch but managed to stay asleep past eleven in the morning. 'Busy?' I say, eager to break the charade of being invisible.

She stops and turns. I brace myself for a rebuke. 'Are you alright?' she says quietly, somewhere near the fringes of sympathy.

'I'm not sure. Don't I look alright?'

She stands stock still, her duster in both hands, studying me. 'You look like something's happened.'

'I got fired. Yesterday.'

She nods, letting the duster hang in front of her and holding her wrist almost solemnly. 'I imagine that must hurt,' she says. Her voice is unexpectedly soft and her eyes, which I remember being almost cruel, peer at me with pity.

'It does. It hurts a lot.' Self pity floods through me and I exhale, trying not to tumble into a perilous sea of dejection. I need a minute to compose myself. This old woman's sympathy has disarmed me, but I can't cry.

The Landlord

Mrs Bastible tucks the duster under her arm. 'I was going to make tea if you'd like a cup?'

I shake my head. 'I'm fine.' With a formal nod she slips away. I hear the noise of cupboards opening and closing in the kitchen, followed by the kettle boiling. Then the noise of a cup on the counter. I don't get up. I don't know where to go.

Moments later I hear footsteps and when I look out to the hall, I see her putting on her coat and picking up a small umbrella.

'Aren't you going to have your tea?' I call out.

'Changed my mind,' she replies, smoothing down her sleeves. She moves to the front door and I think she's about to leave when she turns and walks back inside and stands in front of me. 'You asked me a question the last day I came to the house and I'm not sure I answered it properly.'

I sit up. 'You mean when I asked about Anna?'

She nods, remaining defiantly inscrutable. 'But I don't think you were really asking me about Anna, were you?'

I stare at her, stunned by her sudden openness. 'I think what you really wanted to know was if Mr Fitzsimmons had a part in his wife's disappearance?'

I swallow, hiding my surprise at this question. 'I guess.'

'What if I told you that each of us believes what we'd like to believe. Most people around here are quite certain that Mr Fitzsimmons is guilty as sin. But be careful what you believe, Ms Quinn, because the mind will play tricks on us all. Perhaps you'd do best to remember where original sin began.' Her gaze flits towards the back window.

'It began in a garden?'

'It did.' With a cryptic nod she moves once more to the front door, reaching up and opening the lock. 'I should also let you know that Mr Fitzsimmons advised me he will be returning tomorrow at the earliest, just in case you were unsure.' Our eyes lock together for a second before she looks away. Then quietly, she leaves.

I walk to the window and peer out into the overgrown bushes at the back of the house. The muscle in my neck tightens. Has the housekeeper tried to give me a message? Why? The trees blow gently in the breeze. I feel an invisible tug gently pulling me towards the garden. A reminder of unfinished business.

35

It's late in the night when I get in through the basement and march into the corridor. If Ian is away until tomorrow, I've got plenty of time. I can't quite get my head around the change in the housekeeper. Had I misread her the first time we met? Perhaps she's had a change of heart? There is, of course, a last option – that she's not telling me the truth. But I've put that firmly aside for now. There *is* something in the garden. I just have to find out exactly what.

I use my mobile for a torch and it does the job. It has to, since the batteries on my proper torch have died. I quickly hurry out and past the fox's grave, then the charred remains of Ian's bonfire, and walk straight to his cabin. I'm wondering if I might be able to get in a window but guess it's always worth trying the door first. I give the handle a go and my eyebrows raise as it gives, opening outwards and letting me slip inside. I reach for the switch and when I click it the light comes on.

Though I hadn't expected the front door to be open I'm not surprised I got in. Ian seems like the kind of person who might be relaxed about security. I wouldn't dream of leaving an office open and yet I could imagine him doing exactly that. I find the light works too, despite him telling me that water was short circuiting the fuse.

There's nothing too out of place that I can see. It's your standard wooden garden room. Lots of glass at the front, laminated floor, pine interior painted a gleaming spotless white, a mix of industrial light fixtures to give the whole place a clean, inviting and typically architectural flavour. In one corner he has a reading chair. Beside it a coffee table with a music system. Some bookshelves set back against the wall. Then on the far side a long rectangular desk with a swivel chair on rollers. I see a laptop on the desk and walk over.

I'm intruding. Plain and simple. Peeking where I'm not invited and don't belong. But I'm past caring about all that now. I'm finding out what really happened to Anna Cunningham and how she disappeared that night, and if it involves breaking the rules of respectable behaviour then it's too bad. I sit in the swivel chair and roll towards the desk where I tap the mouse pad on Ian's laptop. The hard drive wakes up and the screen appears just as the switch trips and the light dies.

Luckily the laptop stays on, and Ian hasn't bothered password protecting it. There's a file in the menu bar he has open so I tap on it to bring it up. It's titled *Words for the Departed*.

Dear Anna, I thought of you last night. Imagined that you might pay me a visit. I don't know how, it just seemed something real, like you could undo your disappearance in the quick blink of an eye and magically re-enter my life again. I wanted to tell you how I've found a new girl by the name of Cathy. Sorry, that all sounds a bit confused. She found me really, but it hardly matters, she lives here now. I like her a lot, perhaps more than I'd readily admit, well to anybody that cared to ask. I can tell you, you'd understand, or I'd like to imagine you would anyway. She reminds me of you in many ways. Spirited, strong, kind and pretty, and best of all, I think she might even like me. I'm working hard to convince her of my innocence in your departure. I think I had almost succeeded but I fear I may have fallen short. The ugly truths of the whispering majority may have silently crept into her head and ruined that happy ending. But we're not done yet. Not me, at least. I'm a man who lives in hope, since necessity is the mother of all sorts of mysterious inventions. Anyhow, I just wanted to say it, or write it more accurately, so it's out there, no secrets between us any more, not like before when it seemed there was nothing but. You're still in my mind often and if I can find a way to forgive myself for all the things I got so wrong, I'm hopeful I will forgive you. Who knows, perhaps you could forgive me too in time? But that's all for now. I can see my friend is almost upon me, she's outside sniffing for clues, so I'll have to have a

The Landlord

word. I'm not sure if she should be trying to solve this. I don't want it to end for her the way it had to end for you.

I still, peering at the screen, as my pulse races. I tap the top of the file to shrink it down. I'm not sure what to make of it and yet it's so blatantly clear. If it ends for me how it ended for Anna I will disappear too. Is that what Ian has in store for me? I shudder, the blood in my veins suddenly ice cold.

I flick the torchlight across the walls. There's a bunch of framed photos over near the reading chair. I don't know how I missed them when I walked in but there they are, hanging in a series. Ian and Anna, on holiday somewhere, looking perfectly in love. Ian with Jamie, a happy father and son with fishing rods somewhere with blue skies. And a final one of them all together, Jamie sandwiched in the middle, everybody smiling. Were these moments of perfect bliss or was it a charade Ian was trying to cling to? I can't tell, but the pictures don't look forced. The smiles feel real. The happiness true.

I walk back outside into the garden and shut the door quietly behind me but not before I remember to flick the light switch back off. I must leave no trace. But I'm disturbed by what I've read and it's confusing me. Ian's feelings for Anna seem real and strong and he expresses the same feelings for me. Reading the words initially warmed my heart, but it all fell away so frighteningly towards the end. Why? I don't know because it's all too obscure and it makes me doubtful. I walk back to where he said the fox is buried. I'm looking at it again when my stomach knots.

The blood drains from my face and my mouth goes dry. There's a spade leaning up against the wall. It's the same one I found in the store. It's covered in clay and when I look at the grave, I can see it's been all dug up. There's a mound of soil where there was once grass. *Ian has dug it up.* But why? I grab the spade and start to dig furiously. I don't really know what I'm doing or what I hope to find. The soil comes away easily and I toss it aside. How far must I go I wonder as each shovel tasks me harder and harder? But I'm not about to stop. I carve a small hole at least two feet down reasonably quickly but find nothing. Then I stop. Of course there is nothing, because Ian has removed whatever was in the ground. My stomach heaves at the thought.

I'm panting and hot as I drop to my knees and claw at the soil with my hands. I don't want to find anything and yet I need to. But there's nothing there. I give up and turn my torch back on to scour nearby when I find the chest. It's sitting by the wall, caked with mud. My mouth hangs and I stare. *Fuck. It's been lifted out of the grave.* Now I have to open it. Could Anna's body possibly be inside? Thinking I'm about to retch, I clamp muddy fingers across my mouth and force myself to lift the lid. I shine the torch in and see a blue silk lining. But it's empty.

Nervously I exhale, mopping the sweat from my brow. There's something seriously wrong with this picture. I heave the soil back into position with the spade and put it back against the wall. Then I go over to the remains of the bonfire. It stinks of ash, and a sooty odour rises from it. I see charred bits of wood, the edges of a burnt box, and a melted piece of plastic but that's about it. There's a stick on the ground. It must have been something he used like a poker so I grab hold of it and sift through the debris. There's something not fully burnt and when I pull it free, I see it's a shoe. It's badly melted but I can tell it belongs to a woman and the size is not too far from my own. My only guess is that it has to be Anna's.

Blood pounds in my ears when my phone rings. The shock makes me press accept and instantly I see my mistake. *It's Ian.*

My throat tightens.

'Cathy.' His voice is almost playful. 'What are you doing?'

'Ian,' I eventually manage to gasp. 'Where are you?'

'I'm on my way home. I wasn't sure you were still up.' He sounds a little tipsy. 'Thought we might talk.' I'm breathing hard as I poke the shoe back into the ashes and drop the stick. 'Everything OK?'

'Fine.' The word almost chokes inside my throat. 'Are you far?'

'No. Literally minutes.'

The Landlord

Stifling a shriek, I hang up and start to run. I have to get out of this garden. I can't let Ian know I've been here. I've seen too much. And none of it's good. Frantically I sprint through the grass. A briar snags me and pain sears through me like a knife as it tears the skin on my neck. The blood drips from it but I can't stop. I get to the basement and back out the front and sprint up the steps. Seconds later I'm in the door and sitting in the living room; my chest heaves and I think about running to the bathroom to wash my hands when Ian walks in.

He observes me sitting there in the dark but doesn't move to put on the light. Instead he staggers across to the opposite sofa and collapses onto it. A blend of tobacco and alcohol permeates the space with a heavy stench.

After a minute he pushes himself forward.

'Think we got cut off. Drink?'

I shake my head and immediately regret it. The more drunk Ian is the less chance he will sense my agitation. I try and still my body but it shakes anyway.

'You're dead right, Cathy. I've already overdone it as you can probably tell so we'll just chat.'

'What about?' I ask, my voice struggling to appear calm.

'A confession. One I want to make to you tonight.' My throat tightens.

'What for?'

'My sins, Cathy.' He laughs harshly. 'Sorry, that's not funny. It's about all the *lies* I've been telling.'

'What are you talking about, Ian?' For a second I feel dizzy.

He sways. 'I'm full of *shit*, Cathy and I'd like to come clean.' He tips his chin up, giving me a woozy glance. 'Are you OK? You look a little shaken.' I try to answer but my mouth is clenched shut.

'I got fired,' I finally mumble. 'From my play.'

'Oh fuck. That bloody prick Andy. Why?'

'I stood up for a friend when the lead actor was abusing her. Then he had a go at me, making a show of humiliating me in front of everyone so I told him he was a pig and a pervert.'

He shakes his head ruefully. 'Fuck. I'm very sorry. I had no idea.' He steadies himself. 'I don't want you to argue with me but I'm going to give you something to tide you over for the short term. I'll see to it tomorrow.'

'It's not necessary.'

His hand flies up and he holds it in front of me. 'Allow people to help sometimes, Cathy.' His voice rises. 'We're not all out for something.'

I swallow and eventually he takes his hand down. Now he's looking at my jeans. He can see the mud stains on the knees. His dismay grows when he glances at my hands. Now he notices how they're covered in mud also.

'You've been in the garden again, haven't you?' Mutely I nod. I'm too frightened to speak and yet I know now is the time to push, to question him and force him to give me the explanations I need. 'Oh Cathy,' he whispers, taking a laboured breath. 'We'll have to do this another time now.' He stands up. 'It's OK. Stay where you are.' The words fire from him like darts. 'I'm going to bed. Goodnight.' Seconds later he's gone.

I flatten my hands against my burning cheeks. I know I should leave. Call a taxi and just hurry over to Heather or Babs. It's been so long since I thought about my mum but I wish now that she was still alive, that I could simply call her up and tell her all the mad things that have been happening to me and ask her to share her thoughts which were always so calm and wise. But I can't do that anymore. Mum's been gone for years and so has my brother Desmond, cruelly snatched from me in an accident that never needed to happen. So all I can do is sit there on the couch, my body shivering as I try to figure everything out.

I can't make sense of any of it. There's too much white noise between my ears. Eventually I slump sideways onto the cushions and begin to doze, thinking that's it for the night.

It isn't.

36

I'm woken by the noise of heavy footsteps coming down the stairs and into the hall. It's an undisguised clatter and it can only be Ian. By the time I've roused myself off the couch he has taken his jacket, opened the front door and walked into the night.

I jump up as he furtively paces past the window, head tucked down, clearly going somewhere in a hurry. I don't have time to think. I just grab my keys and jacket and chase straight after him.

I'm tailing him as he beats a quick march down a side street, dipping in and out of shadows from the streetlights while crossing from one side to the next. I choose to stay on the opposite side to him and a distance back. I'm not worried he'll see me as it's dark but I don't want him to hear the sound of my footsteps as I struggle to keep pace.

But he doesn't seem to register my presence at all. When he gets to the junction he veers right and down through the main thoroughfare. All the bars and restaurants which are usually busy and vibrant are completely silent and there's nobody on the streets. I check my watch to see what time it is and find it's 2.45 a.m. Why would anybody go out at this time unless they were up to something?

I spot a humpback bridge ahead. It rises in a small arch straddling the river. Ian marches across it and I just catch a glimpse of him as he sidles down the stone steps which take you to the footpath along the water's edge. It's a wild and overgrown stretch of the waterway. There's a block of flats just across the road backing on to a rough estate and it's not a safe place. At this time of night, it makes no sense at all. I crouch as I follow him over the bridge and down the footpath. On one side of me is water and on the other tall trees and a dense undergrowth of nettles and weeds. It's a popular spot for the homeless and junkies who sometimes sleep rough on the benches which dot the route or take refuge from the rain under the arch of the bridge where it's known some of them shoot up.

There's a reek of stale urine as I inch down the steep steps which run down to the water's edge, and try to stay out of sight. I dodge a lump of dog shit and the remnants of somebody's vomit and know immediately I don't want to be here. Or anywhere even near it. I look down along the gurgling river's edge and see Ian sitting on one of the benches. He's slumped forward, his face resting in his hands, the way somebody does when they're crying. But he's not moving or making any noise.

I get as close as I think is safe and decide not to push it further. Then I slink into the undergrowth where I can watch him.

His phone rings and he picks up.

'Have you got it?' he barks. I don't hear the reply but then he says, 'Good. I'm here … of course I've brought cash.' He sounds annoyed. 'I'm waiting.' Then he hangs up and puts his phone away.

The bushes rustle some yards in front of me and a man steps out. At the same time another man appears from the opposite direction and both run quickly towards Ian. The man nearest to me has a weapon which I think is a stick.

Ian jumps to his feet. 'For God's sake what are you playing at?' he demands, his voice hissing through the darkness. 'Just give me what I came for.'

The man with the stick snorts. 'You'll get what you deserve.'

'Don't!' Ian fires a last warning but they're already on him.

The one with the stick swings it at him but Ian jumps out of the way, charges him and rips it from his hands. He smashes the second man with it in the stomach and flings it away. I think it's finished but the first man comes back, this time lunging for his throat but his movements are too slow and obvious and Ian dodges him, shoving him hard into the water.

The second man sees an opportunity and rushes Ian while his back is turned but he reacts with shocking speed and punches him hard on the jaw. I hear the sound of the bones colliding from where I stand.

'Fuck,' Ian snaps, shaking out his fist. 'Look what you've made me do.' The man staggers and tries to hold him but Ian tosses him into the nettles like a doll. 'I warned you.' He walks over and I fear he's going to kick him but instead he sprints off into the night.

'Shit,' I whisper, instantly wishing I had stayed silent. Deep lines snake across my forehead as I desperately try to still my trembling body. It dawns on me now that I'm all alone. It's pointless screaming because Ian's already fled. The man in the water is dragging himself to the bank as his friend groans and twists on the ground only yards away.

Blood pounds inside my ears as a crippling fear takes hold. I sprint from my hiding spot and clamber back up the steps. I hear the men moving behind me but I race on towards the main road. The yellow roof light of an empty taxi appears and I lunge into the road, throwing myself in front of it.

'What's wrong?' the driver asks, stopping and rolling down his window.

I stare at him, trying to find my voice. 'Nothing. Nothing's wrong.' I'm too terrified to speak. But I can't go home. I give him Babs's address and tell him to take me there. Ten minutes later I'm inside her apartment and quivering like I've caught a fever.

37

'Cathy, what's happened? Why are you trembling?' she asks, looking me up and down, trying to comprehend what's going on.

I start to cry as Babs guides me to her sofa.

When I finally stop trembling, I tell her everything.

The following evening Babs takes me to dinner and we go over everything that's happened again. She wants me to stay with her until I'm OK and I'm so grateful for her generosity. She really is a friend who would do anything for me without even giving it a second thought. After dinner we go to a late-night bar and it's busy because it's Thursday and maybe because it's summer quite a few people have started the weekend early. Heather drops over to join us. Babs already told her the story of what's going on but she wants to see me herself. It's one of the things I love about Heather; as much as she loves myself and Babs to bits, she has her own mind and insists on using it before drawing a conclusion on anything.

Despite the busy crowd we manage to find a table to ourselves where it's not too noisy. I talk through everything again. I'd imagine I'd be tired of relating it but I'm not; somehow explaining everything is helping lift the anxiety which overwhelmed me last night. I've hardly spoken to Heather and she mustn't know what to make of me, especially since the last time we chatted we were doing an over-the-phone personality profile test which I've been trying not to dwell on.

I lay it all out, or almost all of it, because there's still a few pieces I can't quite bring myself to own up to. Like Ian's letter on his laptop for example. I don't know if it's because I'm ashamed

The Landlord

of how far I've gone to find out what really happened to Anna or if there's another reason I'm not admitting this to myself. But it's staying private. For the time being at least.

Heather isn't shocked and she isn't annoyed with me either. I'm relieved because I expected she might be both.

'You've had a really rough time,' she says kindly. 'But you did the right thing getting the taxi to Babs. If you ever feel in danger that's exactly the thing to do.'

'Thanks,' I reply. 'Any thoughts?' I then add sheepishly. I'd gladly pay for Heather's insights, as many already do.

She blows out her cheeks. 'Ian's appetite for violence is alarming.' I nod, knowing it's undeniable. 'You say he hit one attacker with a stick and punched the second.'

'Yes.'

Babs comes in. 'Self-defence though, Heather. I mean you could hardly blame him for that.'

Heather stirs her cocktail, unconvinced. 'And the fox? He had a need to kill that too?'

'Yes.'

Babs raises her drink to her mouth. 'That *is* a bit off.' She takes some and continues. 'But I did meet somebody just the other day who said they had also heard of foxes attacking people.'

'You didn't tell them what Ian had done did you?' I ask, worried.

'God no. It was just a discussion about foxes. Sorry.' Babs makes a guilty face as Heather resumes.

'Then we also know the story Justin put through the letterbox.'

'You mean Ian attacking those guys at the rugby club?'

'I'd nearly pat him on the back for that,' Babs counters.

Frown lines appear on Heather's brow. 'But it's a similar pattern. We know he drinks too much, he's brittle, frighteningly unpredictable and it's very possible he could snap at any moment, that he may have snapped before with his wife Anna.'

The table goes silent. My shoulders sag. Defeat tugs me down like an invisible weight around my neck. 'So you think he killed her?'

'I think he could have killed her, certainly, but only he knows the truth,' Heather concedes, looking back at me sadly. I take a long drink of my cocktail, fearing Heather is right. 'I'm worried too about the grave,' she adds. 'Also, he has an elaborate story about the fox. Then he digs up the grave after you find it. We know there's a chest but now it's empty. And, of course, the fire?'

I'm about to mention Anna's shoe when I decide not to. If I do, I'm not sure there's any way I can cling to the hope of Ian's innocence for much longer.

Babs glances across at me, pity in her kind face. 'Heather, what about Justin?' I'm grateful to her for trying to switch the conversation. She knows I'm sinking, my feeble hopes fading. 'Why do you think he's acting so strange? He's practically stalking Cathy and now sending her all this stuff about Ian?'

'I can't figure that out either,' she agrees with a shrug of her shoulders.

'I've a sense that he knows my neighbour Anthea from the way he was staring at her the other night,' I say.

'Who's Anthea?' Heather asks.

'Her bubbly blonde new friend from across the road,' Babs explains.

'Describe her?'

Bab continues. 'You know the type. Early forties, still fit and trim, down at the hairdresser once a week keeping her blonde highlights just right, stellar nails, does a lot of Zumba, cycling for her cardio, cooks casseroles, organises coffee mornings, loves chairing a committee meeting, and is so nice she makes you feel a little nasty.' Babs tilts her head and bats her lashes at me jokingly.

I smile. For a second I think Babs knows her better than I do. 'That's pretty much Anthea,' I agree. 'But she's nice. Kind, and open. I like her.'

'Would you call her attractive?' Heather asks.

'Very.'

She shoots Babs a look and I catch it. When I glance at Babs, she freezes.

The Landlord

'What?' I ask, suddenly spooked. 'Please don't tell me you think there could be something between them?' I remember Anthea flirting unashamedly with JJ now.

Heather sighs. 'Cathy, I don't know how to say this but from the rumours going round, Justin's not to be trusted.' Her eyebrows pull down. 'But you've seen this yourself with him messing you about with the flat already.'

'He screws around behind my back?' I ask, turning sharply to Babs.

She shrugs. 'Oh Cathy, there's been stories. We don't *know*. But I'd agree with Heather. You just wouldn't know with Justin. He's one of those guys and you're right to steer clear of him.'

Heather gets up. 'I'm sorry, Cathy but I have to get going. I have a meeting in the morning.' She leans across, pulling us both into a warm hug. 'Sorry again about all the stuff with the play too. I know it can't be easy for you right now.'

'Thanks,' I mumble, dizzy with the news that my ex is a cheat. How didn't I know? Why didn't I suspect it?

'But don't for a second think what you did was wrong, OK?' Heather then says, holding both my shoulders and looking at me directly. 'It's the rest of them that have been behaving badly. Your agent Melissa, especially. I've a mind to ring her up myself.'

Babs grins. 'You better go, Heather, before I order another round. Then we'll have to talk about that.'

Heather rubs my cheek and takes her leave. I think Babs might be ready to call it a night too. 'Come on,' she says, seeing I'm still rocked. 'You're going to stay at my place tonight. You'll feel better in the morning.'

38

When I get to the house the next day Ian isn't there so I give him a call but the line is dead. I opt for a message instead.

Just checking when you're back if you can let me know.

I accidentally find myself putting in an X again and have to delete it. But as I do I know how badly I've been bottling up my feelings towards Ian all this time. I know he likes me. I've even read as much in the letter on his laptop and my feelings are the same. So why am I stopping myself telling him? *Because he could be responsible for murdering his wife* the silent voice says. And, despite how much I want to lean to the opposite conclusion, I know there is truth in it. Ian still has a confession I'm waiting to hear. I haven't got any explanation to why he was digging up the fox's grave, or why he unearthed a chest.

I remember the final words of the letter on his laptop. *She's outside sniffing for clues, so I'll have to have a word. I'm not sure if she should be trying to solve this. I don't want it to end for her the way it had to end for you.* The little hairs sprout up on my arms. Could he really have been suggesting he was going to kill me? He's one hundred per cent capable – that was the opinion of his own son Jamie. And Heather, who's too honest to lie, has told me the same thing. And yet I know that Jamie doesn't believe Ian *actually did it*.

I tell myself once more that I have to keep going. That I cannot stop until I find out the truth.

Wearily, I plod up to my bedroom and shake off my clothes. I take a long hot shower and feel instantly better once I've changed. I get a strange sensation as I walk to the back window and look down into the garden. I had expected to be spooked returning

The Landlord

to this giant old house. That all the things that have happened would leave me nervous and stressed. But I don't feel like that. I feel at home; like I'd not rather be anywhere else.

When I check the time, I see it's already gone past twelve so I go out. I decide on Leno's for an early lunch. I want to see JJ, especially as I haven't seen him since he volunteered to come and help me get the picture of Justin prowling on the corner outside that night.

I'm only a couple of seconds out the door when my agent calls.

'Cathy?'

'Speaking, Melissa.'

'I've got something.'

I stop to listen, hope bubbling up. I hadn't expected to hear from her for a while and nor did I want to either. I'm in agreement with Heather, of all the people who've hurt me recently I think Melissa might top the list. I never sensed a shred of sympathy from her and I'm not sure I was even looking for it. Some understanding would have done fine.

'Oh?' I say lightly, praying it isn't more Shakespeare.

'Oranges.'

'What about them?' I hold the phone tighter.

'Well, Club Orange to be more precise.'

'Yes?'

'Want people to dress up as oranges and that's where you come in, love.'

'How do you mean? I don't understand.'

'It's a promo, running alongside Wimbledon. You have to bounce around O'Connell Street in the city centre, engaging people and telling them all about Club Orange. If they enter a draw then they could get a ticket to Wimbledon.'

'Right,' I mumble.

'You don't even have to be able to act,' Melissa says, her impatience surging out of nowhere. 'Just bounce. I'm trying to help you here, Cathy. Surely bouncing isn't beyond you?'

'Are you joking?'

'I'm serious. You made a hash of your last three auditions and you've just got fired by a highly regarded director.'

'He got rid of me because I called out the lead for being a chauvinist asshole but they didn't want to know about it.'

She comes back. 'Well, it was a show which could have opened up all sorts of possibilities. And now you're out of work because you won't keep your mouth shut. So decide, do you want it?'

. 'Melissa …' I force her name out between my clenched teeth.

'Yes?'

'I'm ending our contract today.'

I put the phone in my pocket. I won't cry. Melissa isn't worth tears.

I close my eyes, stand completely still and wait until I calm. I start to count silently but I don't get to ten when something soft touches me on the shin. I look down and see a small dog. It looks like some kind of terrier, small, very curious and intensely cute. He's off his leash and sniffing around my feet.

He pants when I bend down to pat him and his tail wags back and forth.

'Always a good sign when he sniffs your feet.' I look up to see a bright, smiley woman in a flowing summer dress. She has a wide straw hat and a pair of brown retro-styled shades. 'It means you're a good person.' She laughs.

'Really?' I half sob, my mood lifting, as I banish all thoughts of my agent.

'Sure, he's got a nose for good people, this fellow. Walks right up to them and waits for them to stop and say hello. Don't know how he does it but he's never wrong.'

I tickle him under the chin and he pants and whines with pleasure.

'What does he do when he doesn't like somebody?'

'Pees on them and dashes off.'

We both laugh and share a smile. This cheery, red-cheeked woman, with her hippie sandals and booming voice, is the friendliest person I've met in ages. When she extends a hand I take it and we exchange a warm greeting. 'I'm Harriet by the way,' she says. 'And I know you're the beautiful Cathy living over at Ian's place. God this village can talk!'

'Oh,' I say. 'I think I might've heard your name mentioned too.'

'Lord,' Harriet laughs, 'you make me sound notorious, Cathy. What dastardly tales have you heard about me?'

I feel a little silly but just go ahead and tell her. 'Oh, sorry. Nothing really. It was just when I was talking to Anthea about JJ, the Aussie working in Leno's café, she said you had mentioned how he was engaged to be married.'

'Oh, yes, sexy JJ, what an absolutely top bloke.' She nods and beams back. 'But isn't that funny?'

'Why?'

Leaning across she cups her hand to the side of her mouth and whispers, 'Because I don't remember ever mentioning JJ to anybody.' Her two red cheeks dimple then she cracks into laughter, both shoulders lifting as the nest of chestnut curls inside her straw hat bobble. The little dog skips on and she takes a step to follow, patting me gently on the arm as she slips past. 'You want to watch out for our Anthea, a marvellous woman, Cathy, but don't let her get you onto one of her committees or you'll never be free.' Gliding gently, she breezes away to catch up with her dog 'Bye, Cathy, and tell Ian I said hello.'

Heavy-footed, I make my way down Belleview Road. I no longer have an agent. I am unemployed. My ex-boyfriend is acting suspiciously. Ian has vanished and even my new friend in the neighbourhood, Anthea, seems like she's inventing stories about JJ.

When I arrive at Lenos there's a pretty girl I don't recognize behind the counter preparing coffees. She turns and smiles 'Heya,' she says in a friendly melodious voice. I notice her dark glossy hair and trim figure. JJ then appears, almost like I've conjured him.

'Hiya Cathy,' he greets in his sunny Aussie drawl. 'This is Christina. She's just arrived over from Lisbon and started yesterday.'

He turns to her and grins. 'Christina, meet Cathy.' Christina beams and waves as the espresso machine hisses and froths the milk inside the jug she holds.

'Hi,' I return her inviting smile, reining in a weird pang of jealousy that mushrooms from nowhere. How can I possibly resent the over worked JJ from having some extra help, even if she is young and sexy?

'You coming in?' he asks. 'I was just about to call you.'

'Oh?'

'Yeah, cause there's a girl here waiting to see you.' He points to a table and I get a shock when I see Malia, seated way down the corner. She's on her own, staring out the window, a sad look on her pretty face. 'Said she was just going to call you. Guess she won't have to now.' JJ notices me tense and his voice is softer when he speaks again. 'I'm bringing her a coffee. Will I get you one too?'

'That'd be lovely, JJ.'

'Here,' Christina holds out a steaming cup. 'Take this Cathy. I'll make another for my order.'

'Thanks.' I take it in my hands, gratified that I'm instantly warming to her. Then I inhale the rich aroma and make my way off. When I get to the table Malia turns and the edges of her full lips curl nervously to a smile. I return it warily and sit down opposite her.

'I'm sorry I didn't get in touch sooner,' she says.

'Don't be.' My chest heaves. I'm so happy to see her again. The smiling one that used to always greet me each morning before things turned sour.

'How've you been?' she asks in a gentle voice.

I shrug, so many emotions stirring inside me I can only stare back at her in confusion as my throat tightens. 'Up and down.'

'I'm sorry about what happened.' She looks downcast when she says this and I sigh, feeling my heart beating faster. I had no idea Malia's words would mean so much. And yet they do. It's like I've been waiting for them but pretending to myself the whole time that I wasn't.

The Landlord

'You don't need to apologise. You didn't do anything wrong, Malia. If anybody should be apologising it's me.'

Suddenly her hand is out across the table reaching for mine and I grip it. We both share a teary grin. 'Fuck it, Cathy.' She says, frowning. 'You were the only good thing in that production and I know you wanted me to row in behind you.'

I shrug, gripping her fingers tighter. 'I shouldn't ever have expected you to.'

Malia looks down at her coffee, picks up her spoon and stirs it slowly. 'I think it was when you said about the groping, it kind of floored me. I had told you about it in private and then suddenly it was out there ... and ...' She stops, a tear appearing in her eye.

I reach out and wipe it away as it tips onto her cheek. 'It's my fault and I'm sorry. I wasn't thinking. When he had a go at you, I wanted to call out that fucker John for what he is. I felt I needed to support you and ...' I stop, my voice catching inside my throat, 'I had got to a point where I'd had enough. Of everything. All the shit with my ex-boyfriend who's been stalking me, the hostile bloody neighbours from down the road, my landlord Ian wrecking my head day in day out by telling me stories about what happened to his wife which I can't tell if they're truth or bullshit lies.' Malia nods sympathetically. 'So when AA reacted like the spineless wimp he is to Old John being a pig, I—' A tear falls. 'I lost it. I truly fucking lost it, Malia, and I'm sorry.'

We stare at one another. Then after a moment she lets out a teary laugh. 'You know what, Cathy, even though I was so pissed at the time, I'm actually glad you did. I'm glad it's out there. And I don't care now if the rest of them are gossiping about who said it.'

I ease back in my seat noticing her rueful look. 'Did something happen?' I then ask, sensing she wants to tell me more as I watch her drink her coffee.

Malia nods. 'Yes and no.' I hold my cup tensely and wait for her to explain. 'I'm still in the show but I've decided to go public with this. I contacted a journalist friend of mine and she's running a story on it. I also contacted Equity and a really nice woman is helping me put together a case against Old John. Neither him nor AA even know about any of it yet. But they will. Once the production wraps up.'

My eyebrows fork into an arch. 'Smart move.'

'That way I can get the work credit to my name and deal with the issue after.'

'Well, I'm here if you want a witness.'

'Thanks, Cathy. Glad I don't have to ask you so.' She eases back, more relaxed now as she exhales. 'You want to tell me more about all the stuff going on with you then? It sounds like it's been rough.'

My chest rises and I heave out, battling the urge to tell Malia everything that's happened to me since I moved in with Ian. But I know it would be unfair. She's already made a huge gesture by seeking me out and I don't want to distract her from the production which is opening very shortly. 'I dumped my agent,' I offer, a little flicker of pride and large flame of anxiety sparking inside as I say it for the first time out loud.

'Get off?'

'For real. It was coming to a head anyway.'

'God! Big decision.' Malia looks stunned. 'But for what it's worth, I think it's a good one. That woman never seemed to listen to a word you said. And she didn't respect you either.'

'I know.' I didn't feel I needed vindication but now Malia's given it I feel lighter, like I don't have to think about it again. Ever.

'Listen, I if get wind of any hungry ones looking for serious talent, I'm going to put them on to you. Forget AA and the play, Cathy, you've still got loads to offer and deep down you know it.' Malia gets up and throws a ten euro note on the table. 'I've got to split. Don't want to be late back after lunch and give AA and Old John any ammunition.' She grins. 'Make sure you leave the change to that hot Aussie dishing out the coffee. I saw he's got eyes for you, you know?'

'What?' A blush spreads up my neck. 'No.'

'Oh come on now.' Beaming brightly, she winks and leaves.

The Landlord

After our meeting I feel light and free. I'm so pleased that I've patched things up with Malia and moved on and I'm doubly grateful because she didn't have to make the gesture but she did. But as the day wears on my mood begins to slide. Bit by bit all the things that are weighing on me creep a little closer.

It's clear I'm at the centre of a web of lies. Ian's lying. Justin's acting weird. Even Anthea seems like she's making up stories. A terrible image surfaces of a fly trapped and surrounded by hungry spiders. It tugs desperately on the strings of silk which wrap it up tighter each time it tries to escape. The spiders have noted it with interest, now they're just trying to agree which one comes to finish it off. And it occurs to me that I could be the fly, naively wrapping itself in its own web of doom. I remember the words I read down in Ian's cabin at the end of the garden: *I don't want it to end for her the same way it had to end for you.*

A shudder passes through me and I pick up my phone. I need to start making some progress so I can stop worrying, stop tumbling down rabbit holes which all end in disaster. I need to trust my gut and not allow myself to get suffocated with gloomy thoughts.

I ring Ian but again the line is dead. It's like he's completely disappeared. Perhaps he was so angry by my return to the garden he's chosen to stay away. And yet he did say he wanted to confess something, so it doesn't make sense that he would go into hiding. Not if he really meant what he had said. I walk from the huge marble fireplace in the draughty front room of the house to the window and look out on to the street. The darkness is seeping in and it's starting to quieten. I walk back to the brown leather couch and slump down, wrestling the problem I can't seem to solve. Exhausted by all the things I can't make sense of, I doze off, sinking deep into the folds of Ian's old couch. But the thoughts don't stop. Even asleep I keep thinking of strange memories, like the one of Justin and how he looked like he was staring at Anthea out on the street that night. What was he doing? What is he hiding?

I come round a few hours later and find it's after midnight. My eyes are caked with sleep. I yawn and stretch out, rubbing them open, knowing that within the short space of a few days the natural rhythm of my days has upended beyond all recognition. I want to go to bed so I can get a proper night's rest and reset; then I could start tomorrow clear-headed and fresh. With a groan I push to my feet, shuffling across to the window so I can close the curtains for the night. But something outside catches my attention. In the darkness I see a figure on the corner by the lamp post.

My stalker is back and he's staring straight at me.

39

Cautiously I ease back from the window, my movements slow and deliberate, as Justin keeps staring. I can't make him out clearly but I'm sure it's him. After all, who else could it be? I've already caught him in exactly the same place.

Without making a sound I retreat to the hall. Then, very gently, I open the front door, and close it back again, just hard enough so it clicks shut. Justin's still standing there looking over.

It's too risky for me to walk across to him directly. I'm afraid it might seem confrontational and there's a possibility that he might disappear before I get a chance to speak to him. I want him to remain comfortable, like he has absolutely nothing to worry about. He doesn't know what I'm doing yet. But I do.

Tucking my chin down, I hurry over the road to Anthea's, looking straight ahead. The city is quiet and nobody's around. No cars. No noise. Just the wide empty street and us. The lights are out in all the houses with the exception of Anthea's. Everybody's asleep, which isn't unusual since it's gone past midnight. I try to act casual because I want to look like I had forgotten to return something, as if I might be catching Anthea before she turns in for the night. The light is on in the porch of her house and also in the upstairs bedroom which I can tell from the faint glow coming through the closed curtains.

Moving quickly, I slip across the normally busy two-way street and open the small gate to her house. From the corner of my eye I can see Justin is still on the corner. My guess is he's less than forty yards away, probably closer even to thirty.

Once inside Anthea's front garden I use the cover from the hedge that separates her path from the next door neighbour to conceal myself. I stand there, taking a moment to ready myself, breathing long deep breaths. The summer night is still warm and there is a gentle breeze, faintly scented with flowers, but my body is tense, coiled in anticipation, the adrenaline starting to ooze into my bloodstream. I inhale slowly. I know Justin will be trying to figure out what's happening, why he hasn't seen me go up the wide granite steps to Anthea's front door; guessing where or how I could have disappeared. And that's exactly how I need him to be. Because once I make my move I have to run towards him as fast as my legs will take me. The surprise should gain me at least ten yards. Then catching him will be down to my determination.

I take hold of the gate, drawing it back slowly. I let it close gently behind me, craning my neck out to check he's still there. He is and he doesn't see me because he's staring up at the window of Ian's house. I draw back, inhale one final time, then I dip my shoulder, turn into the street, and burst into a sprint.

For a moment Justin hesitates. I gain speed, my feet smacking the pavement hard, my momentum snowballing, propelling me forward. Alerted by the noise he glances across, sees me bearing down on him and jolts. His hands fly from his pockets and he looks left and right, almost in a panic. I run faster as he tries to figure out which road at the junction will help him get away quickly enough. But there's too many choices. It's a four-way crossroads and his hesitation has cost him. In ten strides I'll catch up with him. I'll grab hold of him and not release him until he starts to explain why he's back stalking me alone, in an empty street after midnight.

Finally, Justin springs into action, about-turning with a new-found energy, his coat just a dark fleeting shadow as he belts back up another street and out of view.

But I'm at the corner within a second and I spot him in the darkness. I don't slow down but lean in tight, like a motorbike taking a bend, and hurry straight after him.

'Justin!' My voice is high and shrill in the lonely street. This time he ducks left, suddenly out of view once more. There's a

The Landlord

noise, like branches being pulled and twisted. Then nothing. Almost immediately I find the side street and turn into it. It's a dark narrow back lane, similar to many which run along the border to the long back gardens of the houses. A lot of the buildings are lock-ups where the owners keep cars at night or storage spaces for tools.

'Justin,' I repeat, quieter this time, aware I could wake people or draw them to their windows. Standing still, I listen carefully, certain he's got over one of the garden walls, though I can't figure out how or where. I creep forward. It's a long tunnel of a street, shadowy and dark, but there isn't any clear place to hide. It's the only possibility because I know he can't have got far and if he was still in the lane I'd make out his shape against the walls, even in the darkness. Not making a sound, I inch further down into the shadows, scanning carefully but there's nothing to give me even the slightest clue.

Pausing for a second, I try to think, my eyes straining to make out anything unusual against the walls either side of me. I know Justin. And I know he'd be flapping, trying something hopelessly unlikely. I stare at the big trees either side of the lane as the leaves rustle in the gentle breeze. There's only a few points where the trees even meet the back walls to let somebody climb inside; without using one of the overhanging branches I can't see how the walls could be scaled and even then I don't think I'd manage it. Justin wouldn't have found one of those trees so fast. It would need to be somebody familiar with the area, somebody who knows exactly which wall they can scale.

I stop, a sudden weakness in my knees happening so quickly I freeze. The tiny hairs at the back of my neck are rising up. For a second it feels like my body could give way.

A terrifying realisation is now clear.

It wasn't Justin on the corner.

With a shudder, I retreat out of the alley. Blood pulses in my temples. I don't turn my back, but edge warily away, my ears alert for any sounds. The silence seems to surround me, like something lurking, an animal watching, waiting to pounce. I'm totally vulnerable, out in the open. The stalker could be watching me from a hidden vantage point, plotting the perfect ambush, picking his moment. All I can hear is a deathly hush as I keep creeping backwards. It's exactly the kind of situation where somebody gets murdered and nobody notices. I think of Anna Cunningham. Is this what happened to her? Was she lured to her own death? Did she mistake who she was intending to meet for somebody else and get snared in a trap?

My body quivers as I edge back to the main street. I calculate I'm a hundred yards from my front door, only now that hundred yards feels further than a mile. Do I scream? Will that scare the stalker away? But what if it doesn't? What if it makes him panic? Forces him to quieten me? I'm shivering as I walk, trying to pick up my pace without making a sound. What was I thinking when I ran out? Even though it was only minutes ago it seems so long now. But I know I wasn't thinking, because I had only just woken up. It was a split-second decision.

The kind that gets you killed.

I start to sprint again, hurtling first into the middle of the street where I hope there might be cars, anybody who could see what is going on. But there's nobody. Just the sound of my own footsteps, smacking the road hard with each terrified stride. I don't want to hear another set of footsteps. I know they'll be bigger and faster than my own.

But there aren't any other footsteps. I pant as I reach my front door, my key scratching at the lock as my trembling hand fumbles, finally getting it to turn.

I fall inside, my chest heaving as I slam the door shut, triple-locking it and fastening it with the two extra bolts I've never used before. I pace to the window, scanning the street for any sign of the stalker but it's eerily quiet, like he was never even there, like it never even happened.

Sweating hard I pull the curtains and collapse onto the couch. The adrenaline keeps pumping through me. I don't want to close

The Landlord

my eyes. What if the stalker comes back for me, because he's worried I've seen his face. What if it was Ian?

The thought springs into my mind from nowhere. Yet it can't be Ian. The man wasn't big enough and moved too swiftly. It's impossible that Ian could be so light on his feet. But if it wasn't Ian and it wasn't Justin then who could it be?

I try to recall the image of the man on the corner as I sprinted towards him. I was moving so fast it was hard to take anything in. My mind was too focused on catching up with him, latching on to the person I was sure was my ex-boyfriend, so I scarcely thought at all about what he looked like, how he moved or how he acted. I keep thinking, trying to remember any fleeting clues as I bore down on him in the darkness in the fraction of a second before he made his move to dash away.

Then I remember something. The clothes. Even though indistinct in the darkness they were too dull, too shabby. If it had been Justin, something would have stood out. His sneakers. His jacket. Something. Even when Justin is dressing down, he does it meticulously. It's always a specially printed T-shirt, or torn Calvin Klein jeans. Even if it's a rain jacket, there'll be something about it that says it was selected. I try to picture the man again and again in my mind. The more I repeat the sequence the more certain I become that I glimpsed something..

He had a beard. Not a full one, but something straggly and indistinct. But just as I'm shaping this idea I begin to wonder if I'm fabricating something spurious. I'm high on a toxic mix of adrenaline and anxiety. How can I know if what I'm thinking is clear? Surely I didn't have time to see so much? Is it more likely that in such a state of extreme tension I've concocted a vision of something that never even existed? They say it happens all the time in police investigations and everybody's heard the stories, how if you ask three eyewitnesses what they saw at the scene of an accident it's always three different versions. The problem is I've only got one, but nobody to check it with.

I'm sitting on the couch and starting to get cold when I hear the sound of a door closing. Instantly I jump to my feet, my survival instincts commanding me to act. I rush to the porch and flick on the light. It can't be the front door because I've bolted it so I rush up the stairs to check where it's coming from. The door to Ian's bedroom is ajar and so is the bathroom so it isn't those. I go past the landing up towards my own room but my room also is open as I left it. There's only Jamie's room and the spare room left.

I wait for another noise but don't hear anything. Gritting my teeth I hold still my trembling hand, twist the door latch and pull Jamie's door open. For a second I'm praying it's Jamie, that this is some childish game he's playing; that he can explain everything and I'll try and understand. But the room is empty. Heaving deeply, I back away when I hear a clanking noise in the bowels of the house. I flatten my back against the wall, trying to hush the gasp that spills from my mouth. The sound comes again, like steel on stone. A spade perhaps? I look down the stairs to where it's come from. Sweat prickles on my forehead. There's no mistake, it's coming from the basement.

'*Fuck.*' I curse, hoping nobody hears me. There is a person down there. But how? They couldn't have come in through the front unless they broke the door and I would have heard a noise. The only other possibility is the garden but it's an unlikely way in given the seven-foot wall at the end of the plot. More sounds rise up. I clutch the stairway railing and listen. It sounds like things being moved around, then a door closing, followed by another opening and closing. Panting, I rush downstairs into the living room and grab a poker from beside the fireplace, but as I'm crossing to the window I notice a man come up the basement steps outside.

I hurry to the front door and pull it open, stepping out so I can see him clearly. I keep the poker raised and the heavy door ajar so I can jump back to safety and bolt it fast if I need. We lock eyes and I see it's the same man, the guy from the corner.

The Landlord

He grins nervously as he backs away and out to the foot gate. His clothes are threadbare and shabby. There's a week of rough beard on his cheeks. He stops at the gate, glances at the poker, then tears off up the road, disappearing into the shadows like he was never there.

I understand that not everything Justin told me was a lie. He wasn't the only one stalking me. There is a second man, this unkempt stranger, who was doing the exact same thing, in almost the same spot on the street. I try to make sense of what's happened. The stranger had me right where he wanted me only a short time earlier, bewildered, confused and entirely vulnerable down a back alley. If he had wanted to attack me, he had his opportunity but he didn't take it. Does it mean he was watching me for another reason? Perhaps because he wanted to get into the house but needed to know I wasn't in his way?

But what was in here that would make him so desperate to get inside?

40

At first light I go down into the basement through the front door. There's a text from Ian saying he won't be back till the evening so I decide to take a chance and get in and out quickly while he's still away. There are people walking up and down the street, which is what I've been waiting for, witnesses in case the stalker returns. This morning I know that if I scream, somebody will hear; and I'm also confident he wouldn't be so rash as to try and return. However, I'm not taking chances, so just in case I choose to leave the front door wide open after I go inside. There's a stray bit of fallen branch nearby and I pick it up, wedging it underneath the gap at the base of the door. I test to make it's stiff and secure, and satisfied it's firmly in place, I walk in.

The first thing I check is the garden door but it's locked from inside with a long key and the key is still in the lock which tells me the intruder couldn't have used this route to gain access. I open it up and step into the garden, scanning it to see if there's any signs of somebody being there. There is nothing immediately obvious so I waste no time and shut it again. Then I return to checking the basement.

I start with the back room nearest the garden but when I go inside and run the torch across the floor it feels untouched. Just the same mess I remember from before. Back in the corridor I go the store, grit my teeth and wait for the queasy feeling inside my stomach to ease but it doesn't. Taking a second to compose myself, I pull the door open and again use the torch to search it. To my relief there's no sign of the bloodied spade, or any sign that the man was in there.

The Landlord

I shut it tight and move to the middle bedroom. Again, it's as I remember it from the last time. Hurrying, I move to the final bedroom but, like before, I find it's locked. Stepping back, I decide to ram it. I turn sideways on and bang against it but it doesn't budge. Instead, a piercing pain shoots from my neck down into my arm.

I cry out, grabbing my shoulder, instantly cursing my stupidity. How, in a moment of desperation to get inside this room, had I forgotten about the strain I suffered falling from my bike last year? Now I've aggravated it badly. I wince, rubbing it as I move back out. It's clear I'm either going to have to find the door key or I'm not getting in.

Gingerly holding my arm, I kick away the makeshift doorstop underneath the front door to the basement, and grunt as I squeeze it shut behind me. The search to understand why the intruder broke in has led to nothing. I need to come up with a better plan.

41

I'm surprised Justin texts back so quickly. I read it.

Yeah, I'm around.

Immediately I reply. **Meet me at 2pm.** Another text from him returns.

Fine. Where?

I decide somewhere outside in the open will be best, where it will be busy with people passing by. Just in case things get heated. I pick up the phone and key in my reply to Justin with my thumbs.

The fountain in the park.

The phone pings with a reply. **I'll be there with my dog.**

Surprised, I type back a thumbs-up confirmation and hit send. Justin doesn't have a dog. We talked about getting one many times, even once agreeing on picking one up from the pound, but then, like always, at the last minute something came up, a travel plan he couldn't escape, so we dropped the idea, only to later find out that when he got back the same dog had already been adopted. I sense some deliberate ploy, some game he's playing to get under my skin but I won't take the bait. I remind myself to keep cool. I need him to open up so I must tread carefully.

One hour later I arrive at our meeting point, right next to the bed of blooming hydrangeas in the park. It's a warm day and thankfully there's plenty of people about. Joggers, walkers, people sprawled out on the grass sipping takeaway coffees, friends catching up. I'm taking in the scene when my ex walks into view; hair carefully ruffled, his lean frame wrapped in a striped fitted shirt, skinny jeans and with an incongruous dog leash in his hand.

The Landlord

'Molly,' he scolds, 'get over here, now. What are you doing?' He squeezes the words out through the side of his mouth, trying to conceal his exasperation. Molly, who looks like a black and white collie puppy, is cowering on the grass about twenty feet away from him, ducking low as the bicycles ride by too close to her. 'Get over,' he spits again, 'for fuck's sake? Are you stupid or what?'

A few passers-by hear him and glance across warily. Their faces don't hide their pity, the kind people can't control when they see a dog has the misfortune of getting hitched to an owner it never deserved.

'Jesus,' I gasp, thanking my luck I never convinced Justin to adopt one when we were together. I get to my feet, hurry across and kneel down beside her. After she's sniffed me shyly, I gather her in my arms, stroking her gently to try and help her calm.

Molly shivers and licks my hands nervously. Justin appears by my side patting her roughly on the head, his face balled with contempt.

'When did you get a dog?' I ask.

'I didn't.' He bends down, leaning over her as Molly cowers. 'Because you're not my stupid fucking dog, are you, Molly?' His grin looks menacing as he wraps his fingers around her ear, gripping it in a barely contained pinch. I tense, stepping back.

'Whose is she then?'

'Mum's.' He puts his hands on his hips, no longer interested in appearing to care for her. Molly looks at him warily.

'From where?'

'The pound. Bloody old girl never listens, you know how she is.' I want to tell him that I know his mum well and I know exactly why she might have chosen not to listen to her only son, but I hold my tongue. 'I told her to get herself a cat.' Justin's mum doesn't like cats. She's told us both a hundred times the story of how one killed her pet canary when she was a child and she never got over it. Why's he even suggesting it? He carries on, 'Because old ladies and cats go together like ham and cheese, don't they, Molly? Not like dipshit dogs from the pound.' He steps towards her and Molly springs from my grasp, landing heavily on the ground and peeing near his feet. He jumps away, disgusted. 'Fuck's sake. See what I'm talking about.' Molly scampers to my side, hiding behind my legs.

'For God's sake, Justin.' I strain to control my rising voice. 'Why don't you leave her alone? She's a pound dog. Pound dogs are often traumatised. She needs time to get used to you.'

He juts his chin out, collecting himself, affecting detached disinterest once more. 'Fine. So what do you want to talk about? Have you finally gathered your marbles and figured out that Ian Fitzsimmons is a psychopath who topped his missus?'

'No.'

'What?' He snorts, incredulous. 'Please tell me you're not still planning to go on living there?'

'I haven't decided actually.' I bend down and pick Molly up once more, rubbing her gently, doing my best to reassure her, but she trembles in my hands.

'So what *have* you decided then, Cath?' He wraps the leash around his fist. The steel loops across his knuckles. 'I was hoping you'd at least admit there's still something between us. You've got to concede that much.' He beams a self-satisfied grin, awaiting an affirmation he believes he's due. I swallow hard, struggling to hold in my disdain. I need to keep him onside, to get him to open up, but right now I only want to slap him and call him out for his shameful treatment of this terrified dog.

'You and me were a mistake, Justin,' I say with a pinched voice.

'Oh really?' He puffs himself up as if to make the words bounce off his chest.

'But I'm not interested in talking about us today.'

He folds his arms. 'So what are you interested in?'

Now I drop the bomb. 'I want you to come clean, to tell me why you've been acting weird this past while.'

He freezes, then glances behind him swiftly, before turning back to me. 'What?'

The Landlord

'You know, Justin,' I say slowly, 'since I moved into this house, you've been all strange and I want to know why.'

He bursts out laughing but it sounds hollow, his teeth displaying a wide clownish grin. Eventually it subsides into a thin smile and he checks over his shoulder once more, only this time with worry lines creasing his normally smooth skin. 'Come on, Cath, you aren't being serious?' I pat Molly calmly and wait. 'Aw, fuck's sake, you *are* serious?'

'Just be honest for once, Justin, and give me the truth.'

'The truth?' He snaps, a bewildered look settling on his face. 'The truth is you're away with the fucking birds. Since you shacked up with that killer your brain's gone soft and now you're making shit up and asking me to go along with it. Just get out of that house, Cath, come back to me, and I'll forgive all this nonsense.'

I step clear of him, aware now that the meeting has lurched wildly off course. He's not opening up. He's closing down. The heat is rising to my skin, the muscles in my neck tensing. 'I was at the window that night, Justin, when you were outside. Why were you staring at Anthea? Why have you been lurking around here since I took the room in Ian's house? And why are you so desperately concerned that I get out?' The words seethe from between my teeth as I think about how long I endured this man, blind to his contempt, now so glaring it makes my stomach twist.

'You've lost it, you know that?' he grunts as the muscle in his jaw throbs. He takes a step and inches closer. 'Be *very* fucking careful how you go, Cath. You don't know shit about anything. Not Ian Fitzsimmons. Not me. Not one thing about this whole living, breathing street. Anna Cunningham is gone and you need to wise up and move on.' He takes a hasty, sly peek around before sticking his face into mine. Now his voice comes again, deep and threatening. 'Hang around too long and you might start a fire that burns everybody's house down.' I hold his stare, refusing to be intimidated, but my leg is twitching. I don't know who he is anymore. How didn't I see this person when I spent so many months living with him?

There's something wet on my arm. I realise Molly is peeing again but just then Justin snatches her from me and tosses her to the ground. She yelps as she lands heavily.

'Everything alright, Cathy?' When I look up JJ is hurrying over. Relief floods through me and I stagger backwards, wiping away the wet smudge Molly has left on my arm.

Justin tugs hard on Molly's leash, gives JJ a fake smile which he doesn't return, and hurries away.

'That him?' JJ asks, putting an arm around me and glaring after Justin.

My shoulders are stiff and bunched and I ease them down. 'Yeah.'

'You OK?' I want to hug him, to thank him for appearing so unexpectedly. But I'm frozen to the spot like a rabbit in the headlights. Next thing, both his arms are around me and I'm shaking, a tear rolling from my eye. I flatten my cheek against his chest, inhaling the scent of pastry and cinnamon from his T-shirt. I breathe raggedly as the tension flows away from me and I remember days spent baking with my grandmother in her old house down the country. For a fleeting second I feel like a bit of jigsaw that just found its match. 'You're safe now, Cathy,' he whispers. I let my head fall into the crook of his neck and rest there for a moment. I'm not sure what to do but it doesn't matter because after a few seconds he gently untangles me, wiping the tears from my flushed cheeks. 'Come on, walk me back to the café before the place goes upside down.'

Quietly we stroll, his arm slung round me, my head resting against him. I'd love to open up and tell him everything but now isn't the time. He's got to get back to work. When we get to the front door to Leno's he stops.

'Look, if he gives you any hassle I want you to let me know. Will you do that?' I nod. 'Alright then.' He throws me a pleased smile and I stand an inch taller.

'Thanks, JJ.'

'For nothing,' is all he says.

The Landlord

Back in Belleview Road I struggle to make up my mind on how to move forward. My meeting with Justin didn't go to plan. *Be very fucking careful how you go, Cath … hang around too long and you might start a fire that burns everybody's house down.* I recall the threat, the viciousness of it as he spat the words out; his bristling contempt and how badly he wanted to intimidate me. Could he really do what he insinuated and burn this house down? It seems so extreme and yet there was a venom to him I had never seen before.

I give up thinking about him and shift my attention to the mystery stalker from the other night. I need to find out more about him, to understand fully what he's doing and why. Why would he stalk me if it's not me he's interested in? Is he looking for something or concealing something in the house? Or could it be the garden?

And who is he?

A text pings on my phone. I see it's from Ian.

Sorry. Hope to be back tomorrow. Will explain when I see you.

The muscles at the base of my spine clench as I remember the incident with Ian by the canal. I close my eyes wishing it away but instead I see the shadowy forms of the two men who attacked him, then the harsh crunching sound of bones colliding as Ian smashed one of them across the jaw with his fist. I open my eyes, releasing a gasp at the same time. When he gets back I must make him explain. What was he even doing down there in the middle of the night?

Worry lines spread across my brow as another fresh fear emerges. The big house is going to be empty again. Will Justin try and call? He seems to know exactly when Ian isn't around, almost like he's staking the place out. What will I do if he calls? I don't want to be alone with him inside. I don't trust him anymore. I don't really know who he is.

But as I'm worrying about it, I remember the stalker too. Like Justin, he too has been doubly careful to only make his move when Ian's been absent. There's a chance he could try again tonight, because if he's checking he'll notice Ian isn't here, and he's clearly not afraid of me.

Tensing, I rub the back of my neck where it's grown stiff. I can't stay in the house without any plan. I'm too vulnerable. I think about the basement, recalling how Ian told me there's only a front door key to get inside. But I know that inside the house there's also an internal door down there. It's right at the top of the boarded off staircase next to the entrance to the kitchen at the back of the house. It's locked which means it too must have a key.

Hurrying into the kitchen I start to rummage around. Knowing how little attention Ian paid to securing his garden cabin, I'm confident he won't have gone overboard hiding keys and I'm proven right when I locate a set marked 'basement' inside a mug on a top shelf of one of the cupboards. I pace straight out to the door and give it a try. The first key goes in, twists, and I swallow when I hear the thunk of the lock giving. I try the handle and it eases open cleanly. A heavy stale smell wafts up and I turn away so as not to breathe it in. Then I run down the stairs to try the other two keys on the ring, both of which say 'bedroom'. The keys fit the locks on the second and third bedrooms, but the first room, the one which I hurt myself trying to open, doesn't have a key.

Thick dusty air fills my nostrils and I rush back up, locking the internal door at the top and placing the keys back where I found them.

Now I know I have to visit a certain shop in Capel Street, the one supposed to cater to underground erotic fetishes. There I'm going to find something that can help me make a plan.

42

I'm surprised when I pick them up to find they're real. Or at least to me, they seem real. They're definitely not plastic and the steel feels heavy in my hands. I pull hard with each hand but the cord doesn't yield. Then I slip the little key inside the lock to free myself again and take them off. The handcuffs are going to do the job.

I walk past the display of feather boas, the assortment of brightly coloured dildos, studded black dog collars, chains, skull caps and tubes of lubricant. When I get to the counter the pale, balding man leans forward, away from the rack of hardcore porn titles displayed behind his back. He inspects the cuffs, his grey eyes bulging behind thick-framed spectacles.

He smiles, yellow teeth grinning over thin lips. 'Like a bag?' he asks with a jaded voice.

I nod, feeling a clench in my stomach as the fetid smell of the place rises to meet my nostrils. He slides the cuffs into a brown paper bag, folds it twice and sticks the creased edge with a snipped slice of sellotape. He hands it over to me and I pay him cash. 'Go wild,' he drones dryly. I don't reply. I don't want to waste another second in this squalid hole of a shop.

Back out on the busy city street I take a moment to gather myself, relieved to be free from the cramped space and sticky floor of the sex shop. I steady my nerves, refusing to let the fear which eats at the edge of my mind take over. I can't let Justin intimidate me and I don't want to leave Belleview Road. I want to stay strong and finish the plan I've set in motion. It's laden with risk but I believe it's worth taking. A heady feeling of anticipation lights up inside me and I walk to the bus stop.

When night falls on Belleview Road I've got everything set and ready. It doesn't seem like the corridor light in the basement works but I remove the bulb to be safe. Then I place a steel chain across the grime-streaked floor just two yards inside the front door. I've nailed it into each wall of the corridor using fencing hooks and a hammer I found in Ian's storeroom. It's exactly four inches off the floor and pulled as taut as I could get it. I don't expect it will withstand a huge amount of pressure but in the dark I'm hoping it will snag the shin of anyone who crosses it. After that I will need to use the element of surprise to get the intruder's wrist to the cuffs which are tied to the second last rail of the wooden staircase. I don't know what the condition of the staircase is but I'm hoping the wood is strong enough to hold. I've brought a can of pepper spray, something I picked up on my last holiday in New York two years ago in case I ever needed it. I don't want to use it but it'll give me some small sense of security knowing I have it in case things don't go as intended.

In the living room I sit and watch the light fading slowly outside the front window and finish my second glass of wine. All evening I've been struggling to contain the urge to ring Babs and Heather and let them know what I'm about to do, but I've somehow managed to hold off. If I do, they'll certainly talk me out of it. That means I won't get the answers I need. I thought about calling JJ too but know it would be unfair. I've already dragged him into this, letting him put himself in harm's way, and it wouldn't be fair to do that again. If I want to go ahead with this plan, it has to be my own personal safety I put on the line.

Soon I start to feel drowsy. The courage and excitement which the wine helped take fire has dwindled. In its place now there is uncertainty as doubt mushrooms and the growing darkness erodes my confidence. The house becomes a chamber of distant noises; pipes clanking, taps dripping, rafters creaking. Cool draughts seep through the large bay windows either side of the adjoining rooms. The street outside no longer buzzes and teems with bodies and upbeat conversations. Instead it's desolate and lonely.

The Landlord

I pick up my phone, consider calling Babs to see if I might call over and shelve my carefully devised plan for another night, when suddenly the shadow of the man appears again out on the street. Just like before he's watching me. Staring from his street corner perch, hands stuffed deep inside his coat pockets, his gaze fixed.

I hold still. It's too late to change my mind. He's here. I have to do what I planned. To take things forward some way. Slowly backing away and knocking off the light, I retreat from the front window. Silently, using the internal door at the top of the stairs, I get down to the basement with only the torchlight from my phone for guidance. Once I get to the end of the stairs, I switch it off.

Then I sit alone in the darkness. And wait.

The stranger doesn't enter immediately. I chew my nails, my phone by my side, steadying my breathing so as not to make a sound, trying to adjust to the darkness which remains thick and murky. The minutes slip by. I wrap my arms around my knees, resting the edge of my chin on the bridge formed by my clasped hands, straining my ears to hear the slightest movement.

And then it comes. Footsteps on the granite slabs leading down to the basement entrance. Heavy, tired breaths, the tap of a key as it squeezes through a lock. Then a gentle click and the harsh scrape of heavy wood on the dirty basement floor.

The blood rushes to my head and I rise to my feet, a reflex spurring me to move, despite my intention to stay still. In an instant it dawns on me that the intruder is going to flick on his flashlight and my carefully devised plan will be found to be no plan at all. I tense, unsure if I should flee. The urge to bolt back up the stairs and slam the door at the top, locking it fast, is too strong. Yet I'm so stiff with fear I can't seem to budge.

The man steps inside, breathing out heavily through his nostrils, but he doesn't light up the corridor. Instead he hurries forwards, tripping straight over the chain. There's a shriek as he clatters to the ground and I leap from my hiding place, fumbling in the darkness for his wrist. Groaning, he writhes on the floor, muffled curses coming from his mouth. I find the cuffs, yank his wrist across and twist until I hear the click of steel catching inside steel.

'Hey!' With a snarl he scrabbles to his feet but I jump back to the safety of the stairs, clambering up till I'm high above him. The torchlight beams down on him from the phone as I start the video. 'What the fuck?' He squints, one arm raised like a shield.

'The video is on,' I pant, my chest heaving. 'You're being recorded. Take your hands away from your face or I call the police.' He yanks his shackled wrist against the cuff but it holds tight and he winces. 'I have video identification of you and I'm sending this file to my friend by WhatsApp.'

'Don't,' he snaps, his eyes full of fury. I recognise him immediately. It's the same man. Now I can see him up close I'm shocked that he doesn't resemble Justin at all. I can't believe I ever thought for a second they were the same, even from a distance. Clearly my anxiety has clouded by thinking. This man is tall and athletically built like Justin, but he's unkempt with a ragged growth of beard. His matted hair is dirty and he's dressed in a mismatched collection of old clothes. His eyes are dilated and wild. A mix of anger and possibly fear.

I pretend to tap the keys on my phone as I watch him from the darkness at the top of the stairs. 'Caught this man entering my house,' I say in a rush, the nerves jangling at the end of my fingertips. 'Have agreed to let him go but if you don't hear from me within two hours, report him to the police.' I cease tapping my finger against my knee.

Dots of sweat have sprouted on his pallid skin and he wipes it. 'Fuck are you doing?' he gripes.

I place my phone inside my pocket and fumble for the stairs, gripping the bannister tight to steady my shaking fingers. It's time to act; to use all the skills I learned when training in the youth theatre. To appear the very opposite of what I truly feel, which is numb with fear. 'I want to know who you are,' I begin, affecting a tone of command, 'why you're stalking me, and what you're

The Landlord

doing creeping into this house. If you tell me you're free to go. If you don't, I've no choice but to report you to the police for breaking and entering. Not once, but twice.' I take out my phone again, this time placing the light away from him and pointing it towards the ceiling, a demonstration of my willingness to trade. The reflected light is enough for each of us to see each other in the gloom.

'You won't,' he sneers.

'OK.' I turn immediately and take the steps back up to the house when he replies.

'Hang about. You haven't given me a chance yet.' I turn back and he leans against the railing, noticing the can of pepper spray by my feet on the stairs. He glances back at the chain and thinks for a second. 'You set me up?' The cracked lips inside his beard twitch into a smile, revealing a crooked front tooth. I can't make out what he is, perhaps some strung-out New Age traveller. 'Very clever.' He lifts his manacled wrist. 'Want to get these off me now so we can talk then?'

'Not until you tell me what I need to know.'

With a resigned nod he slouches at the base of the stairs. 'Smart girl. Well then, if I answer your questions, you'll let me get into the room and get my stuff so I can go on my way?'

I swallow, noticing now that he's closer to me than I had anticipated. 'What stuff?'

'Clothes, my shit, all my stuff I don't have the space for now.'

I sense there's more but don't push him. I need his cooperation for now. 'Agreed.'

The reply seems to relax him and he looks up. 'Good. I'm Keith.' His cracked tooth glints as he grins, his hostility momentarily parked. 'I'm an old lodger from a while back. Ian kicked me and the others out some time ago but I've still got my stuff here.'

'Why are you stalking me?'

His eyebrows lift. 'Who said I was stalking you?'

'You've been watching me from your corner like a hawk most nights.'

He leans his long frame back into the railing and stretches out two thin legs. I see holes in the top of his shoes. 'I have to make sure you and Ian are off to bed before I can try and sneak in. If Ian caught me there'd be trouble.'

'Why not ask Ian to let you in? Wouldn't that be easier?'

He shakes his head. 'Not that straightforward.'

'Why?'

He pauses as if weighing up telling me something. 'Because I'm police.'

He waits for my reply but I don't say anything. I'm trying to make sense of what he's revealed. But I can't picture it. 'Rubbish.'

He shrugs his shoulders. 'Alright, I'm not police proper. I'm undercover.'

In the half-light his dark eyes are shining and for a moment I think he might be completely high. I can't fit his story of being a lodger to him being an undercover police officer. It sounds like something he's made up on the spot. It sounds like he's trying to play me for a fool. Why? So I can warm to him? So I'll agree to let him go?

'Why would I believe that?' I ask.

'Because it makes sense.' He scratches his beard. 'The cops are still watching Ian, alright? They contacted me to snoop for them, to see if anything shows up that will help them. I told them I still had keys and access to get in.'

'You're spying on your old landlord?'

'Call it what you will. They were also worried about you after I told them you'd moved in.'

'You're supposed to be protecting me?' I say doubtfully.

'No, merely reporting. Keeping a look out, letting them know if they should be worried.'

'So they're still convinced he murdered Anna?'

He grins. 'Stupid pigs don't know what to think but it's their best guess so if they want to pay me a few quid for reporting every time he takes a crap it's fine by me. Nobody gets hurt and I get some pocket money.'

I can't decide if what he says adds up or he's a confident liar. 'Tell me about this situation you had down here. Why's it such a mess and what was going on?'

He gestures to the other rooms. 'We had a bunch of us. It was sort of an unofficial squat before Ian and Anna got the house so we obtained a legal right to remain in place for a bit. Ian and Anna were totally cool about it and when the time came round to throw us out, they even let us stay on.'

Surprised, I probe more. 'What happened?'

'Ian liked having us about. Sometimes he'd come down and get pissed with us and we'd sort him with a bit of smoke. But then we started making a bit too much noise and it was pissing Anna off. One of the guys, Craig, got busted for possession of ketamine and his case was pending so Anna had enough and insisted we piss off.'

'She threw you out?'

'No. It was all happening when Anna disappeared. Then Ian chucked us out because he knew the cops were going to be in sniffing around and he didn't know what would happen if we were still here, or who might be saying what.'

He recounts the story matter-of-factly, his conviction making me want to know more. 'Tell me more about Anna.'

He stares at the ceiling as he thinks. 'Anna was sweet. She used to even come down and share a drink with us in the beginning but then she hardened up a bit.'

'How?'

'There was some stuff going on between her and Ian. She grew a little cold.' He scratches his scraggly beard. 'She could be quite fierce, some might even say a bit vicious. But I don't think she was bad. It was just stuff going on between them.'

'I don't get you.'

'Sex.' He kicks a scuffed shoe against the wall, crossing one leg over the other. 'She liked it. Only not with Ian. She got a taste for younger blokes. Ian tried to brush it off, thinking it was a phase. But she started rubbing his nose in it. Inviting guys over for a drink that she had an eye on, like she was letting Ian suck it up.'

'What about Jamie? Didn't he notice?'

'Ah, Jamie. Lovely kid. But he was too young and wet behind the ears. Anna had him in her pocket so she could do no wrong. The more ratty Ian got with her, the more Jamie started to hate him.'

The longer Keith talks, the more evident it appears that he knows Ian and his family. I grip the stairs, silently cautioning myself to keep on guard. He could have read all this info online. 'Ian said he'd given the cops plenty of ammunition to hang him out to dry for her disappearance. Was that true?'

'Sure. He was hitting the booze hard and losing his rag with her. Sometimes at home in front of Jamie, sometimes even when they were out. He can lose it a bit when he's drinking.' I tense, remembering the night by the river, the noise of Ian's fist smashing his attacker like somebody cracking a shell. Keith glances at the ceiling as if recalling something. 'There was one night down here with us. One guy, a big bloke called Kevin, made a suggestive joke about Anna and he had him by the throat like he was going to choke him. If we weren't there I don't know how it might have ended.'

I stifle a groan, annoyed at how the story fits too well. Keith taps the bannister.

'Hey,' he says softly.

'What?'

He throws me a sideways glance. 'You want to know if he did it, don't you? You've got a *thing* for him.'

I clear my throat, thankful the dark is hiding the streak of blush fanning across my cheeks. 'What makes you say that?' I throw back defensively.

'It's OK, you're not the first. He's always been a charming bloke but here's the thing ...'

'What?'

'He wasn't the last one with Anna that night she disappeared.'

The Landlord

My chest tightens. 'How do you know this?'

'Because I was there, see, doing a little business outside the club, Mandy's. I saw Anna with another bloke.'

Blood pounds in my temples. 'What bloke? Are you sure?'

His chapped lips grin. 'Don't you worry, love. I'm definitely sure.'

43

My hand slides on the bannister, sweat appearing from nowhere on my palm. I grip it tighter. The thoughts shoot like stray bullets. Is this really true? It could mean so much.

'How do I know if what you're telling me is real?'

'Here.' He reaches into his pocket and pulls out his phone. 'I was a little pissed so I thought I'd have myself some fun by getting a bit of footage of the proceedings that night.' He starts scrolling back through images with his thumb. Rising to the balls of my feet I crane my neck. 'Got it, here we go.' He's about to tap into it when he looks up at me slyly. A silent invitation to come down, to look with him as he shows me what's on his phone. He notices my hesitation. 'You're still scared of me?' He nods knowingly. 'Too right you should be. After all, I could be talking through my arse, couldn't I? I could have made up every last word you heard.' His wild eyes glimmer in the half-light. 'I wouldn't trust me either.' With a flick of his wrist he releases the phone, tossing it up the stairs. I reach out, almost losing my balance, only barely managing to catch it. 'Hit play and you'll see.'

Standing stiffly, I watch as the clip starts. The segment info shows it's only twenty-three seconds long. The camera is focused on the entrance to Mandy's nightclub. There's some drunken chatter and people moving about as the lens wobbles and Keith's slurred voice begins. 'Just a bit of surprise action going on I thought I shouldn't miss.' He sounds drunk. The lens tracks right and stops on a woman who is standing on the pavement kissing a man. Keith zooms in. It's a bit blurry but I recognise the distinctive hairstyle instantly. Anna's glossy black hair shimmers under the streetlights. She's wearing a knee-length stylish coat and black

The Landlord

leather trousers over boots. Suddenly, breaking free, she giggles and faces the camera. Then she strides away, the heels of her boots clacking against the hard ground. 'Naughty Anna,' Keith burbles, tracking the camera out. The man on the pavement, the one she's just been kissing, looks after her longingly.

I know him instantly. How could I not after spending years of my life living with him. It's Justin.

44

My mouth hangs open. I inhale the strong scent of rotten wood and dust, my body momentarily frozen. The clip has stopped but I stare in silence at the phone. Evidence. I want to scream the word as loud as my voice will allow but I say nothing. I merely stare at the phone as if transfixed. *It's a recording of Justin on camera with Ian's disappeared wife the very night she goes missing never to be seen again. If Justin was the last one with Anna on the night she went missing this would make him the chief suspect once the police find out.*

Keith watches, trying to decipher what is going on. I should have said something, a throwaway comment, anything. I heave noisily.

Breathe Cathy.

'Oh *shit*.' Keith finally breaks the silence. 'There's something going on here, right?'

Dazed, I look away from the phone and back at him. 'What?'

'The clip. It's thrown you. You know the guy or what?' I nod. 'Who is he then?'

'A boyfriend.' I clear my throat. 'My *ex*-boyfriend.'

Keith groans, dropping his head against the post at the base of the stairs, butting it softly. 'Shit, shit, shit, that wasn't very smart of me.' He glances up, his wizened features creasing into an apology. 'My mistake, love.'

I tap the phone against my chin, my mind slowly clearing. 'You've done me a favour, Keith.'

He glances up warily. The next second he tries to get to his feet but the chain jerks him off balance. 'Wait. Don't get any ideas about that clip. It's private between me and you.'

The Landlord

'Why haven't you shared this with the police, Keith?'

'That's my fucking business.' The words snarl from his mouth, slicing through the space between us but I don't back down.

'I'm going to need a better explanation.'

'Well, then, how's about the man in question, your ex, happens to be a dealer and it's bad form to grass trade members.'

I rub my temples with my fingertips. The blood pounds beneath the tips. *Justin, the man I lived with side by side for three years, is a drug dealer.* I think of all the designer clothes, the out-of-the-blue concert tickets, the magical cash to pay for flashy restaurants we couldn't afford. And it finally adds up. All those late-night DJing sessions he went to on his own probably never existed. Just another clever front by Justin.

'So you're partners in the drugs business?'

He rubs where the handcuffs have bitten into his wrist. 'Don't be stupid. I'm not a partner of anything. I just throw out a little bit of blow here and there. Your friend's a player. Does quantity, hard shit I don't touch. And he's got his neck in the noose right now since his last consignment got snatched by another gang.'

I think back, marvelling at how easily it makes sense. How Justin was flush with cash one moment and then out of pocket with no explanation. His abrupt need to disappear and lie low, announced to me with no warning, picking his mum's place to hide out so he could live rent-free.

'Why didn't you share this with the police, Keith? This makes Justin a chief suspect.'

Deep lines furrow his pale brow. 'Maybe? What do I know? Or maybe Ian did her in. It's not my business and it shouldn't be yours neither.'

'Sorry, Keith, but it is my business.' I lift his phone up expecting it to be locked but it isn't. The clip comes up and I press down and copy it.

'What are you doing?'

'Sending it to my phone.'

'Don't!' he barks.

'I'm keeping my copy. If that's a problem for you I can always share it with the police instead?'

He slams the railing as the file sends to my WhatsApp. Then I throw him his phone.

'Now what?' he seethes, catching it. I point to the bedroom door behind him. The one I never managed to open.

'Let's get that open. I want to see what's so special you need to hide it inside.' He kneels, his face clouding with despair. Frantically he starts patting his pockets.

'The key. I had it when I came in here.' He keeps rooting. Failing to find it he turns on his phone torch and starts searching the corridor.

'Not in your pocket?'

'Yes,' he fumes. 'Until I was assaulted.' He grits his teeth, the muscles in his neck straining.

I tense. How strong is the railing? What if he breaks free? Not sure what to say I step quietly back up one stair, snatching the pepper spray up. Then he speaks. 'Tomorrow. Same time. I'll come back. I have another key. You release me now and then we'll go inside.'

I hesitate. I need him to leave. I don't know how else this night can finish. And I can't push him too far. I hurry to the top of the stairs. 'Fine,' I say, throwing him the keys to the cuffs. Snatching them, he frees himself immediately and flings them to the floor. I hold the door at the top of the stairs open but keep him in my sight. I need to see him leave. To know he's actually left.

Moving slowly, he backs away from the staircase, steps carefully over the chain and opens the basement front door to the street.

'Watch yourself, girl. Anna's gone, and my guess is you'll be gone before you find her.'

Then he walks into the night and slams the door behind him.

45

The day drags. I go to the park and walk by the water's edge, watching the ducks as they dip their heads under the surface, the heads reappearing a seeming age later to run their bills through the feathers. I desperately want to call up Babs but I know she'll be expecting me to contact the police about Justin and I'm not ready. Why would I trust them with this information when they haven't uncovered anything about Anna? I can't expect her to understand that I'm getting to the end of something, that each day I'm inching closer to the truth about Anna Cunningham's disappearance. It's vital that I confront Justin with this hugely significant find as soon as I possibly can. This new evidence changes everything but I want things to be clear before I make that arrangement.

Last night's meeting with Keith confirmed much of what I believed but it's also opened up fresh possibilities which I hadn't considered until now. Just as Anthea had already informed me, he too confirmed that Anna was no angel. I try to recall his exact words. *She took pleasure in rubbing Ian's nose in her affairs.* Was that what he had said? Was that what Justin was? A pawn in the power game between Ian and Anna? Could Justin have figured this out and got enraged with her? Let his anger get the better of him and hurt her? A shiver passes through me when I recall his fury at our last meeting, the gritted teeth and hissed words as he stepped in close, the dog leash coiled like a weapon around his fist, then his snarled threats. Could he capable of murder? He's not who I thought he was. Not even close.

My thoughts switch to Ian. What would he do if he saw this clip I now have on my phone? I recall the incident by the water in the dead of night, the smell of stale urine, the pitch-black gloom, then shadows coming out of the darkness – and finally the sound of bones crunching. He still hasn't given any explanation for the dug-up grave at the back of his house or the buried chest which I know he unearthed. Why? Why has it taken him so long? The charred remains of what looked like Anna's shoe come back to me and I hasten away from the pond back to a busier part of the park.

As I walk, I put the pieces of Keith's story together yet another time. Ian and Anna were well-disposed to him and the rest of his gang in the beginning, he had told me. Then he said it was Anna who changed – round about the time his friend got arrested on a drugs charge. It all happened at the same time that Ian and Anna's relationship was fraying and Anna was flaunting her infidelity to Ian.

As I tease through it I can see another possibility, one quite different to the story Keith related. Ian didn't want Keith and his friends gone. Ian was incensed with Anna's infidelity. Keith and the others had got on the wrong side of Anna and she was insisting on throwing them out, which meant that Ian and Keith now had a common enemy: Anna. Keith and his friends depended on Ian for their arrangement living in the basement. Is it possible that Ian could have demanded a favour in return? One in which Keith and the others got rid of their common problem, Anna? Is that why they had to leave in a hurry, because now Ian was panicking, knowing if the police spoke with any of them that somebody might reveal something?

Yet Keith claimed to be working undercover, getting paid to keep an eye on Ian, who he said was still under covert police investigation. Could that be true or simply a total fabrication? How would I check?

The possibility that Keith and Ian could have conspired to harm Anna disturbs me. I know it's not impossible; I can see the shared motive. But I also remember Keith talking about Anna fondly as if he genuinely liked her. He even explained how her change towards them was justified given what happened with his friend's drug bust. But I know Keith can't be relied upon. I recall

The Landlord

his wild shining eyes, the unkempt beard, the ragged clothes. He could be anybody; his story a total fantasy. The only clear thing I could say for certain after meeting him was that he was hiding something important inside the locked bedroom. Hiding something he was intent on returning to or protecting. And I'll have to make sure I find out what it is.

I spend the day walking the neighbourhood lost in thought but I'm none the wiser when the evening comes and it starts to get dark. I've done a final loop of the pond inside the park and am making my way out through the main gate when Carol approaches.

'I've been looking for you,' she starts immediately, her finger jabbing directly at my chest.

'Oh?'

'Yes,' she replies in a clipped voice, as if picking up right from where she left off in Leno's café, a vexed scowl on her.

'Something up?'

She folds her arms across her chest. The movement tightens the chain around the little dog's neck and he huddles closer to her feet, a guttural noise coming from his throat. 'Are you in *love* with Ian Fitzsimmons?'

I blush. 'Carol, what are you talking about?'

My clear embarrassment emboldens her. Stepping closer she stares at me directly. 'So why are you lying about making a bonfire in his garden when I know it wasn't you?'

Pausing to gather myself, I try to figure out how I can fend her off without stoking her hostility even further. 'Carol, what is this about? I mean really about?'

She drops her fists onto her hips, her face pinching tighter. 'Anthea may have given you the last word about going to the police on this bonfire, Cathy, but there's a bunch of us who've got your number. We're discussing it again the day after tomorrow and this time I'm sure Anthea's going to see some sense.' She yanks the leash and the dog yelps. Then she bustles away without another word.

I'm deep in thought as I make my way back to the house. There are so many strands in Anna's story and right now they are all knotted. The darkness has fallen quickly and I'm unsettled as I push the through the foot gate. It's half open when I feel something touching my back.

I jump.

Anthea smiles. 'Cathy, my goodness!' She removes her hand, holding it to her chest. 'Are you OK?' I catch my breath, the nervous energy in my body making me jangle, then puff out my cheeks as if I might somehow release it. 'I'm sorry I frightened you.' She looks at me warily. 'Who did you think it was?'

'Shit, Anthea, I don't know,' I snap. 'You just crept up on me.'

She steps back, visibly wounded. 'I said I'm *sorry*, Cathy.'

Instantly I know I've overreacted. 'It's not you, it's—'

'Did something happen?'

I shake my head. What should I tell her? Where would I begin without divulging everything that's going on. 'I'm a little wound-up today, Anthea. That's all.'

'That's OK.' All signs of being offended melt away and she softens. 'I know that happens. Well, I was just coming from having a glass of wine with Lorraine. You remember the lady who spotted the fire in Ian's garden?' I nod and she continues. 'So she's claiming she's certain it was Ian out that night and she's got Carol and one or two others who are agitating again to get the police involved.'

'Yes. Carol accosted me earlier and gave me the story.'

Anthea grips me by the shoulders. 'Don't worry about Carol. I want you to know that I've got your back on this, OK?' She sighs, letting me go. 'Don't get me wrong, I love Carol, I really do. But she's so sure Ian is responsible for Anna's disappearance I think it gets the better of her. I'll do what I can to talk some sense into all of them.'

'Thanks,' I say, wanting her to be gone, my only need to be alone so I can figure out how to move everything forward, so I can try and get some desperately needed rest. I wait, holding the

The Landlord

iron gate open, letting her pick her moment to skip away but she hovers. Her gaze switches from me to the street and she scans it quickly before leaning closer and whispering.

'You haven't seen Ian at all, have you? It's strange for him to be away so much.'

'No.' I'm about to ask her why she is asking when I remember the night of Justin's visit. Justin stood on the corner staring at her as she stood in the front window – almost like they knew each other. How would they know each other? And why would Justin have been looking in her window? Could it really be possible that my ex-boyfriend had an affair with her? And what does he want with her now?

'You know, Anthea ...'

'Yes?'

'There was a man here a short time back ...' I stop, another memory surfacing. It's the day I bumped into Harriet. The day I learned that *Anthea might have a lied about JJ*. Why would she do that? She stares at me expectantly. '... it's nothing, sorry. It's late and I'm tired ... I better run and grab an early night.'

Anthea looks at me, a puzzled expression on her face. 'Of course, Cathy. Come and look in on me when you feel rested.' Squeezing my arm gently she slips away and walks back to her house.

I close the gate and turn, starting my short walk to the granite steps, when I notice something above me in the living room window. Ian stands in the dark, staring down at me coldly. A shiver passes through me as his pallid face retreats into the gloom. I root for my door key in my pocket. But then I look up and see the door is already open.

Warily I make my way up the broad granite steps to the big front door.

'Come in, Cathy,' he whispers in a sombre voice.

The house is in total darkness as I step into the porch. He walks through the living room all the way to the window at the back of the dining room and peers out. Then he returns and stands next to the big couch.

'I'll ask you to close those curtains if you don't mind,' he says rather formally. I do as he asks while he flicks a small side lamp on in the far corner which gives just enough light for us to make each other out. He points to an armchair. 'Please, take a seat.' We both sit. 'I apologise for skulking around in the dark but I just overheard one of the neighbours saying how they're planning to contact the police about my fire in the garden, so I'm trying to get in and out without them knowing I'm here.'

'You're going away?'

'Yes, later tonight. First-class flight to Doha at one o'clock in the morning,' he explains. 'Apparently some Arabian sheikh there likes my work. It'll be a quick in and out but they're making it worth my while.'

'OK?'

'So ...' He sits up, his hands flattened on his knees, unusually businesslike. 'You never got my confession. Would you still like to hear it or have you thrown your lot in with the neighbours already?'

The blood heats beneath my skin but I don't react to the jibe. I can't even understand why Ian would make it. 'I think it's time I hear what you have to say,' I reply, my throat tightening.

Ian leans back into the big armchair, his expression turning serious. 'Well first up, there was no fox buried in the garden, Cathy.'

My stomach twists and I release a gasp. 'Go on,' I say, my voice barely holding steady.

'What I said to you the last time we spoke is true. I'm full of shit, Cathy. I'm not proud of it but it's how it is, so I might as well come clean. I tell far too many lies for my own good, so I think at this point it might be a good idea to wipe the slate clean and try and break the habit.'

'Why did you invent the story about the fox?' I ask, the tension creeping up my back like a vine. 'And if it isn't true, how do you explain your spade covered in blood and hair, Ian?'

The Landlord

Warily I wait for him to answer. He nods, unfazed, and begins. 'The story about the pigeons is true. The fox came in the night to take them. And as a fox does, he finished off every last one of them. I did catch him in the act and I had my spade with me too but it never occurred to me to use it against him. He just eyed me greedily when I shone the torch on him, licked his bloody nose and leaped the side wall with one of the birds in his mouth. And that was that. So now I just had to clean up and I did. I got an old sack out of the store and shovelled the dead birds into it one by one. Then I took the sack and put it in the bin. So, yes,' he stops, nodding at the recollection, 'there was blood on the shovel but what you thought was hair was just the breast feathers of the dead birds.'

I listen, nerves pulsing through every inch of my body. Is he simply telling me more stories or could this really be the truth now? How would I know? What signs would there be? 'What did you have buried in the grave?' As I hear the word 'grave' the darkness seems to close in. I swallow, steeling myself to keep going. 'I already saw the trunk.'

He leans forward, drops his elbows onto his knees and flattens his hands together, almost as if in prayer. He remains like that for a few seconds before sitting back up. 'Incriminating evidence against me, Cathy.'

I shift uneasily. Is he *confessing* now? *Is this it?* I want to get up and run. But these are the answers I've been searching for, begging for. And I have to listen.

'Explain,' I say, my voice strained.

'I kept a journal and various bits of writing on old notepads. Jumbled thoughts and feelings I had towards Anna and our marriage. A lot of them were poisonous. Tracts of hate and resentment for what she had done. Letters full of bile about the pain I'd like to inflict on her while at the same time begging her to come back to me.'

'She cheated on you?'

He waves the suggestion away like a nuisance fly. 'I cheated on *her*, Cathy. I was the one. It was because of me that she looked to others for affection.'

I stare back, confused. 'What happened?'

He slaps his big fist down on the armrest. 'A stupid office fling I had with a young intern who probably just saw me as a stepping stone in her architecture career. It was all over in six weeks when I came to my senses. But it was still too late. The damage was done and Anna decided never to forgive me.'

The image of Anna kissing Justin outside the nightclub rears its ugly head and sticks in my mind. I bid it away but it lingers. How must he have really felt about her affairs? They must have wounded him deeply. *Deeply enough to murder her?* 'You see, Cathy, I was a sitting duck. Everything's lined up to hang me. Clear motive, all my public threats and tantrums, her affairs, and now my written declarations of hatred and lust for vengeance against her.'

'But burying it?'

He's nodding. 'Irrational? Yes, I agree.' He slaps the armrest again and I jump. 'You see, I put it all in a chest at first and gave it to a friend to keep while the police did their investigations. Then when it died down a little I took the chest back. But I couldn't bring myself to rid myself of the stuff entirely. It was like I needed to hold on to what was left of our relationship, even if it was all pain and poison. So I had the daft idea of burying it.'

'So why the bonfire then?'

His dark eyes glitter as he leans forward. 'A moment of *decision*, Cathy. After I met you in the garden that night, I said it was enough now. I could only get closure by burning my own hatred. Letting it disappear in a blaze of light so I could move on. So I ripped every last shred out of that chest and doused it with petrol in one mad moment and watched it disappear. Afterwards I went back to my room and slept.'

I listen as he speaks. I want to believe him. I'm so desperate I'm yearning for his truth. When people feel tortured I know they can do crazy things. Didn't I follow him into the night in the early hours *alone*?

'Ian?'

'Yes?'

The Landlord

'The last night we spoke, you got up in the night and walked to the river to meet two strangers. I know because I followed you.' He shifts uncomfortably and I see his nails gripping the armrests like a cat taking out its claws.

'You *followed* me?' He looks incredulous.

'Yes. You met those men to make a trade but it didn't go to plan. They attacked you and you fought them and fled.'

'Why?' His brows knit together as his voice drops to a whisper. 'Why would you follow me, Cathy?'

Because I think I might love you, I want to roar. Because from the day I walked in the door I've fallen under your spell. Your strange, hypnotic magic, with all its twists and deceptions, which I somehow yet can't resist. But in the eyes of the world you're a *murderer*, Ian. And every little thing you do makes it look more and more likely that it's true. Yet I can't accept it. And your son Jamie doesn't believe it. But we need proof that you didn't harm Anna and that there's another explanation for her disappearance; but you have to help me, Ian. And disappearing into the night to meet two criminals like you did demands an explanation.

But I don't say any of that because I don't feel I can. I don't feel ready. I don't feel safe. 'I have to know the truth, Ian. The truth about what really happened to Anna.'

He lets out an anguished groan. 'It's not what you think, Cathy. I like to smoke a little weed now and then. It helps me cope with all the stress since everything happened. My old supplier is gone and somebody put me on to a new one. I just didn't anticipate how suspect they were until they tried to mug me.' He throws his hands to the ceiling abruptly. 'For God's sake, Cathy, you're putting your life in danger following me in the night like that. What the hell were you thinking?'

'Sometimes I'm irrational too, Ian,' I confess. I suddenly, desperately want to tell him about what I read on his computer in his office; about how I met a haggard oddball called Keith who told me all about their shared history, and how he could have hired him and the others to do away with Anna. But I resist.

'God, Cathy,' he laments softly, showing no signs of noticing my silent turmoil. 'I want to come clean with you now. Lies are so detrimental, for everybody. I know how important it is for you to solve this, and deep down I'm ashamed I haven't solved it myself – because I wanted to simply bury my head in the sand and pray it would all go away. We have to stop keeping secrets you and I.' I nod as his hand reaches out for mine. I let him take it and he holds it gently. 'Cathy, have you discovered anything that could shed light on this?'

My chest constricts. I have discovered that my ex-boyfriend was the last one to see Ian's wife and that he was kissing Anna on the street before she disappeared, the night Ian supposedly left the club with her. I have the evidence on my phone and I could show it to him now. But I can't do that yet. I want to confront Justin first and use it to see what lies he's telling me. If I tell Ian he's certain to confront him immediately, or even go to the police with it. Then I won't get my chance to ever ask him for the answers myself.

'Not yet, but I'm working on it,' I lie. My stomach turns. The lies are so easy I can see now. Is that why Ian has been lying non-stop since I've met him? Because telling the truth is so hard neither of us can bring ourselves to do it? 'You'll help me, Ian, won't you?'

He gets to his feet, presses my hand softly between both of his and lets it go. 'Of course I will, Cathy. But not tonight because I have a flight to the Middle East which is leaving soon and that's my Uber arriving right now outside. We'll talk more when I get back, I promise.' I get to my feet also, unsure how to say goodbye. Without any warning, he folds his arms around me, draws me into a tight hug, and plants a kiss on my lips. Before I can speak, he's grabbed his bag silently, slipped out the front door, and jumped in his waiting car.

I press my fingers to my lips. Anger, surprise, delight all twisting within me.

46

Ian's appearance and departure has happened so fast I'm in a kind of daze when he rushes out the front door and quietly disappears into his taxi for the airport. I plod with tired steps up to my bedroom, feverish thoughts assaulting me. Did I want him to kiss me? I think so, even though the idea still unsettles me. I've been burying my feelings of attraction towards him since I moved in, suffocating them almost. But now it's happened, am I happy? I don't feel it. So much uncertainty is clawing away inside. Why do I still feel like he hasn't told me everything? Is it because I haven't told him everything either? Because I'm concealing possibly the most significant piece of evidence in Anna's disappearance that anybody knows about?

I fall into bed and lay my head down on the pillow. It's a relief to know Ian didn't kill a fox in cold blood with his spade. His explanation about going out in the night to score weed from those dealers could be plausible too, and even though it ended in extreme violence what could I have expected him to do? They attacked him. I saw it myself. He was in grave danger. I'm pleased he's admitted to writing what he did about Anna, accepting how bad he knows it makes him seem. Burying the chest was an act of madness, but he accepted that too and the fire was an act of desperation, because he's admitted he is desperate, hopelessly trying to figure out how to turn a corner that always seems to move further away from him, no matter how hard he tries. He's acknowledged that he's acted irrationally because that's what passion does to people and I know his passion for Anna was real from how he talks about her.

Sadly I also know it's this passion that causes murders all the time.

I want to think only good of Ian. Yet something still nags me. His unswerving ability to sidestep every accusation, to always have an answer to any suggestion that he could be somehow complicit in Anna's disappearance. Is it really possible? Sometimes I know it is.

My thoughts turn to Justin. I move in the bed, recalling my barefaced lie to Ian when he asked me if I had discovered anything significant. What I have discovered is huge. I can't waste time deciding what to do about it. I have to make a plan.

Eventually I sleep, but not for long. A loud roar in the basement rouses me and I bolt upright in the bed.

I jump out, adrenaline coursing through my veins as I put on my hoodie and tracksuit bottoms, snatch my phone and hurry out to the landing. Another sound rises up from deep below. This time a groan, like somebody in pain. The house is in total darkness but I don't turn on the lights. Instead I use the torch from my phone, hurry quietly to the kitchen to get the key to the inside door to the basement. Then I move towards it. Pressing my ear to the frame I listen, adrenaline spiking in my bloodstream. More groans, mixed with curses. I know the voice because I've heard it before. It's Keith.

Twisting the key inside the lock I pull the door open and shine my torch down into the gloom.

'Fuck,' he curses, sitting on the ground and clutching an ankle between two hands. 'You've gone and done it again.' Keith squints and winces as I shine the light on him. I see the glassy eyes, the unkempt beard and tattered clothes. He staggers to his feet and raises an arm like a shield. 'Get that bloody beam off me.'

'I'm sorry,' I say, understanding now what's happened. 'I forgot to remove the chain.'

'Did you forget our arrangement too?' He pats down his pocket, locates something and pulls it out. I can see it's a key.

'No,' I say, waking up quickly. How had I forgotten our agreement? What's inside the room could be crucial to understanding what is going on. Suddenly I'm aware that I am unprepared.

The Landlord

There is no plan this time, no handcuffs, no pepper spray. I have no means of protecting myself from him except running back upstairs to safety.

Cautiously I watch him as he sticks the key inside the lock, trying to decide whether to hurry back into the house. But he isn't presenting any threat. He's almost acting like I'm not even there.

'I need to know what's inside, Keith.' He ignores me and continues twisting the key but it catches and holds. Turning then, he glares over. His eyes are dilated and his mouth looks like a dark crease inside the rough beard.

'No love, you need to mind your own business.' He scratches at his neck, agitated, as he keeps fiddling with the lock which won't give. 'Because I gave you what you wanted and now you need to let me be.'

'That wasn't our deal.'

He butts the door and I hear it thump. 'What's inside here is nothing to do with you and there's a good reason this room is locked.' The exasperation in his voice climbs higher. 'Because coming in here will give you nightmares.'

I grip the railing and wait for the twisting inside my stomach to stop but it doesn't. 'What's in there? Why is it secret? Is it connected with Anna's disappearance?'

Suddenly there's a loud bang when he smacks the door with the palm of his hand. 'What the fuck is going on? Why's it not working?' He wheels on me. 'Were you messing with the lock?'

'I didn't touch the lock. Why would I? You are the only one with a key.'

'Well, somebody did something.'

I rub the back of my shoulder, grinding my teeth as I find the point of pain. In a contrite voice I confess. 'It might be because I rammed it.'

'With what?'

I point to it, wincing. 'It was a couple of days ago, before you came.'

He groans, his hands balling into tight fists. 'Well now it's screwed.' Pacing away he runs his dirty fingers through his matted hair, eyes darting about wildly. I step back on the stairs, unsure if I should run when there's a noise from above. Both of us freeze, our haunted faces looking back at each other as we listen to the big front door swinging open and closed, and the loud heavy footsteps crossing the floorboards above our heads.

Keith glares when he whispers. 'Who is that?'

'I don't know. Ian left to go to the airport. It can't be him, it doesn't make sense.' Pallid and wide-eyed, Keith stares at the ceiling. The footsteps continue, moving slowly to the top of the stairs and I kill the torch.

'Shit.' Frantically he tugs at the key but it's stuck.

The door opens at the top of the stairs. 'Who's down there?' an angry voice asks. *Ian.* He steps onto the stairs and I jump down to the corridor as Keith flashes past me.

'This isn't over,' he spits through clenched teeth, 'and don't get any ideas of going in there.' A second later he's out through the front door and gone. I reach for the key left in the bedroom door lock and stifle a gasp when it comes out cleanly. Hastily, I stuff it inside my pocket, pulling the chain from the corridor wall and tossing it into an abandoned cupboard beneath the front steps. Ian's heavy feet tread slowly down the stairs. 'Cathy?'

'Yes?'

'Would you mind telling me what the hell is going on?'

Minutes later we're upstairs in the living room sitting opposite each other once more on the couches. The air is still, the room quiet. The intimacy we had achieved only a short time ago has vanished without a trace. In its place is a cold feeling of distrust.

'I thought you were supposed to be gone to Doha?'

'That's why you decided to go into the basement?'

I shake my head. 'I heard something.' Ian is clearly livid and I can understand why. He's caught me snooping where he's expressly forbidden me to go. And yet I won't be cowed. I don't understand why he's returned so unexpectedly. Is it really a coincidence? It doesn't feel like it. Did he know Keith was going to turn up? Did he want to catch me down in the basement? 'What happened to Doha, Ian?'

'My sheikh changed his mind and decided to postpone,' he says coldly. 'How did you get the key to the staircase door?'

'I found it in the kitchen. You didn't exactly hide it.'

'I didn't know I had to.'

We both say nothing for a bit. Then Ian speaks. 'What did you hear?'

'A man, breaking in downstairs. Somebody looking for something.'

'So you confronted him?'

'Yes, and he fled. Before you could come down and find him.' I decide to ask a question of my own. 'Do you have any idea who might want to come into the basement? Or what they could be looking for?' He considers for a moment before replying, his expression inscrutable.

'I haven't the faintest idea.' I'm sure he's lying. If what Keith has said is true then he must know exactly who might want to break in and why. 'I can't even figure out how he might have got in.' I understand now, despite our heart to heart, despite the protestations of how things were going to change, despite our kiss, we're somehow back at the beginning. As I'm thinking this it also dawns on me that Keith could have made the whole thing up. Everything he told me could have been a barefaced lie. He even said it himself. It's possible Ian has never met him or doesn't even know who he is.

'Ian?'

'Yes?'

'Is it possible there's something else in this house that could incriminate you? Something somebody might want to use against you?' His eyes narrow and I see his nostrils flare ever so slightly.

Abruptly he stands up. 'Cathy, I'm tired and I think you are too. I say we call it a night. If you want to talk about this more when we're a bit fresher then maybe we can do that. OK?' I don't want to let him go. I want him to sit right where he is and answer my questions. But it is late and I can see he's barely containing his anger. 'I'm sorry if you got a shock by whatever it was you heard and I'm glad they fled into the night. I dread to think what might have happened if I hadn't come home. I hate the thought of you coming to harm.'

I observe him warily. I want to believe what he says but paranoia has taken hold. Did Ian imply a subtle threat by suggesting I might get harmed?

'Sure,' I mumble, squeezing my hands tightly in my lap.

'Goodnight then.' Moments later I hear the door to his bedroom close and he's gone.

I take the key Keith left behind from my pocket and look at it. Ian's unexpected return has helped me get the one thing I needed.

But I remember his warning, the words he hissed as he worked to get the door open … *in here will give you nightmares*. I close my fingers tight around it. Why? What could possibly be in there that's so bad? Things are moving quickly now. I've got to find something before Carol gets the police involved. I know Ian will be watching me closely but there must be a way. My time is running out.

47

The very first thing I do in the morning is to check if Ian's left. His bedroom door is ajar and when I tease it back I see his unmade bed covered with some shirts still on their hangers. I pause, waiting for a sound, but when there's none it's clear he's gone.

I hurry down to retrieve the key to the basement but when I get to the kitchen I find it isn't there. I run back to the hall but find the front door key to the basement which usually hangs there has been removed also. Ian's taken them.

I rub my cheek, letting out a tormented growl. Of course he's taken them after what happened! Which means I can't even get in to try Keith's key to the bedroom.

My head pounds, an ache growing at the front of it. I squeeze my forehead and think about getting paracetamol when I see there's an incoming call on my phone from Heather. With a heavy yawn, I pick up.

'Cathy, how've you been? It's been a while.'

'I'm OK,' I offer meekly, trying to remember the last time we spoke. 'Have you been talking to Babs?'

'I have. She said she hasn't heard from you either and was thinking we should all get together.'

'I know. I guess there's a lot to talk about. Did you have something in mind?' I walk to the kitchen and flip the switch on the kettle.

'I've been thinking, do you remember you were asking me about that test?'

'The personality evaluation?'

'Exactly. So a good friend and academic from New York State University told me about one she's used and she said it's really good.'

'What's it do?'

'It detects psychopathology.'

I stop shuffling around the kitchen. 'OK?'

Heather elaborates. 'It works like a game. You play it with a group so everyone gets questions.'

'And the person doesn't know they're being evaluated?'

'Precisely. We would stack the card deck and figure out the sequence if the dealer is sitting say, to the right of Ian, so he gets the most revealing questions.'

I pause, suddenly understanding what Heather is suggesting. Ian Fitzsimmons may be a psychopath. A psychopath who killed his wife and feels no remorse. A psychopath who I kissed the other night. I can't believe it's even a possibility. Yet if it is I should know. I've asked Heather for this, and now that she's finally responding I can't turn it down.

'I'll check it with Ian. Would coming over here tonight at seven work for you and Babs?'

'We're both free.'

'Perfect.'

'And don't worry about the cards, Cathy. I'll stack them before I arrive and give them to Babs to deal. We'll let her sort out the positions because she'll know how to play it.'

The call ends. I text Ian. **Sorry about last night. My bad.**

I wait a few minutes and hear a ping.

Our bad, he replies. Followed by a smiling emoji.

I heave out and text again. **OK if I bring friends over tonight?**

His text returns. **Of course.**

We're playing a fun card game if you'd like to join. Only if you're not busy.

Love to. I'll bring some food. Can't wait. He signs off with an 'x' and my heart flutters, a weird mix of excitement, surprise and deep-rooted fear all rubbing up against each other inside it. But Ian sounds like he's got over his anger at finding me in the basement. That's the bit that counts, and that he's agreed to join us.

The Landlord

I confirm it back with Heather and Babs who both acknowledge. Then I see another message, from Malia. It's an entrance ticket to a film acting workshop. Below it I see her message which I read.

Cathy. A friend of mine passed this to me but I can't use it so I'm passing it to you. Please go. It's supposed to be amazing. Brilliant directors, agents, contacts. Brilliant workshop sessions. You'll learn loads. But it starts at 11 and runs till evening. Please say yes?!

I think about the basement. I need to get in but I don't know how. I have to figure out a way. I'm about to decline and wish Malia the best when I have a sudden change of heart. My career has flatlined. I need to take any chance I can get. Tapping with my thumbs I send her a big thanks and hurry upstairs to take a shower. I'll do the workshop, then tonight, with the help of my closest friends I'll find out something very important about Ian Fitzsimmons.

48

When I arrive at Belleview Road in the evening I'm late because of the traffic. Heather and Babs have already arrived and Ian has poured the drinks.

'Cathy!' Ian cheers, lifting a wine glass as I walk inside. Babs gives me a warm hug and Heather kisses me on the cheek. The room smells of freshly baked pizza and I see two extra-large boxes from Base sitting on the table. The girls are both dressed in bright summer dresses and Ian looks clean and smart in a white short-sleeve shirt and dark jeans. He plucks a tall glass of white wine off the table and hands it to me. 'Cathy, try this and tell me what you think.'

I taste it. The cool zesty bubbles fizzle on my tongue releasing delicious flavours. 'It's lovely.'

'Well thank God,' Ian says with a gasp of relief and everybody laughs. 'It's an '82 so it's had plenty of time to ferment.'

'You mean it's more than forty years old?' Babs lifts her glass and peers into the golden liquid.

Ian nods. 'But this is a special occasion.' He turns to the table, 'and we have pizza.' Again the girls laugh and I find myself joining in.

'Let's get this game going shall we?' Heather then suggests.

'Yes,' Ian adds, 'Babs has me on tenterhooks since she explained it to me.' He gestures to the dining table. 'Grab a seat.' We shuffle over, taking our glasses with us. I watch the girls carefully as they exchange glances and Babs looks at the seats. Ian sits but surprises me by gripping Babs by the elbow.

'I'll need you right next to me here, Babs,' he jokes. 'So I can pick your brains when mine fail.'

The Landlord

'Of course.' Babs rarely, if ever, gets flustered but I can tell this has thrown her slightly. She grins at him when she moves, then flicks an apologetic glance in my direction.

'How's it work then?' Ian asks, glancing at Heather.

Heather explains it's called *Persona* and involves a dealer giving each player a card. The card is flipped and the recipient must answer the question. The dealer then marks the answer in her ledger with a mark out of ten for its sincerity. Whoever scores the highest overall at the end is the winner. 'But it's really just fun,' she finishes, 'I prefer to call it *Squirm*.'

'Lovely.' Ian beams. 'So who's the dealer?' Nervously I look over to Babs who is still sitting in the wrong seat, cards at the ready. She raises her hand.

'That's me, and there's one bit Heather forgot to add.'

'Oh?' Ian raises an eyebrow.

'The dealer always picks her spot at the table so I'm swapping seats with you, Ian.' She gives him a wide smile, her eyes sparkling.

Ian doesn't budge. It's as if he's waiting for her to say it's a joke. He stares at Babs silently, as if perplexed. Next he arches an eyebrow, beams back at her and jumps up.

'All yours, Babs, my pleasure.'

With the seats exchanged, I breathe again, and the game begins.

Babs deals. 'First question for Ian.' She flips the card. 'Are you more or less intelligent than you appear to the outside world?'

'Easy,' he replies calmly. 'Less.' We all giggle and Ian joins in. 'You did say to be honest?' Babs makes a sly note in her ledger.

'Heather, have you ever cheated on your partner?'

'Yes.' Babs and I gasp as Heather shrugs and smiles.

'Beautifully candid,' Ian says playfully.

'Cathy.' Babs switches her attention to me with a dramatic flourish. 'Have you ever had a crush on an older man?'

Instantly I redden. 'No.'

'Noted,' Ian quips.

Heather grabs the next card. 'Now Babs.' Babs bites her knuckles as if terrified. 'Have you ever had sex in a public place?'

I expect her to recoil but she smiles, unfazed. 'Certainly.' Once again I'm gasping but Heather merely throws her a knowing glance as she marks it in the ledger.

Ian taps her on the elbow gently. 'Very bold, Babs.' Both my friends throw their heads back laughing and it dawns on me that they're acting the game out to perfection. A little late, I try to join in but feel stiff and awkward. *You're a professional actress*, I remind myself. *This is what you do. Get into character before it's too late.* Babs taps the cards and the game sets off again.

Silently I think about the game. Is everybody telling the truth or are we all lying? Of course everybody could be. I mask my nerves with a broad smile as I glance across to Heather. She's watching us all in between sips of wine and mouthfuls of pizza but it's Ian she's really studying. She's glued to him, scanning his features, noting his movements, observing every twitch and crack of his smile.

The questions come fast and thick and Heather and Babs act out the party atmosphere but as each round goes by the questions for Ian become darker. 'Would you kill your boss if you thought you could get away with it?' 'Certainly.' 'Have you ever harmed an animal?' 'Several times.' 'Did you ever dream of killing your mother?' 'Yes.' 'Have you told a lie in the last twenty-four hours?' This time he frowns, swirling the wine in his glass before putting it down slowly. 'Definitely *not*.'

Instinctively I open my mouth to disagree but snap it shut when I remember it's a game. A game I have to pretend to enjoy because my friends are here for a reason. *To help me.*

Babs keeps flicking the cards coyly, teasing us all into coughing up the truth with each round of probing questions. Babs is playing the part of the provocative dealer, like some kind of villainous croupier from a billionaire's luxury yacht, Heather is playful and light but also hawk-eyed beneath the girlish smiles and fun revelations. Ian appears thoroughly pleased, fully engaged in the game's spirit and the best I can do is mask my confusion and fear with a nervous smile and claps of hands in between gulps of wine.

The Landlord

Eventually the game concludes.

'Time for the score count,' Babs declares, tucking the last of the cards away. Heather does a finger tap drum roll on the edge of the dining table as her phone beeps.

'Oh, you better hurry that up, Babs, our Uber's just arrived.'

'Well,' she announces. 'There's one clear winner. And it's *Ian*. He's head and shoulders more sincere than all the rest of us put together.'

Ian roars laughing. 'I can't believe it.' He looks genuinely shocked. 'Maybe we should check the maths.' Heather claps and gets up. She hugs me quickly, makes room for Babs who does the same and they both wave to Ian, thanking him profusely as they hurry out the door to the hallway.

'Pleasure's all mine,' he replies, as we all stand there huddled together. 'But I confess that once again I've drunk way too much and have to get to bed. I've a breakfast meeting first thing and I already feel a sore head coming on.' He turns to face me squarely. 'Cathy, thanks so much for organising this beautiful evening.'

He looks into my eyes, and I sense he might want to say something else, but he moves away, quickly walking up the stairs to his bedroom. I see him close the door to his room as the taxi beeps outside. When I look round Heather and Babs are already out the door. I dash after them and catch up with them by the front gate.

'Tell me what you found out,' I whisper urgently.

Babs winces as Heather frowns. 'Oh shit, Cathy. I'm so sorry but I'm almost certain Ian Fitzsimmons is a psychopath.'

49

'Come with us,' Babs whispers. 'You don't have to stay.'

'Do,' Heather agrees. 'It's probably the best idea, Cathy.'

But already I'm retreating. 'I'm fine. I'm sure.'

'Cathy,' Heather repeats quietly, 'you know it's for the best.' But I'm higher up the steps again now and almost at the top.

'Oh God.' Babs groans, her cheer evaporating, 'Cathy, at least please lock your door and keep your phone on. In the morning we can decide what to do.'

'Sure,' I say, my voice faint. Is it my pride compelling me to stay? My determination to prove Ian innocent; my desperation for Heather to be wrong?

Heather opens the door to the cab. 'Cathy, promise me you'll do what Babs said?'

I don't reply but wave goodbye and watch as they get inside the car and leave.

When I wake in the morning I realise I've been completely stupid. The whole point of last night was to get Heather's professional evaluation of Ian. And once she gave it to me, I threw it back, because I didn't like it. *Because you didn't believe it* the silent voice answers.

Ian's gone. I can see from the open door to his bedroom and I remember he said he had a breakfast meeting. But there's no time to be lost anymore, not even a second. My friends won't let it go. They'll insist on talking sense into me eventually and won't let me stay here much longer. Then there's Carol. I remember her plans to resurrect the police inquiry because of Ian's fire. The meeting must be soon.

A *psychopath* Heather had called Ian. The word sends a chill through me. I rub my neck. I can't believe it's true. The more likely

The Landlord

psychopath is Justin. I'd been living with him for years and he had concealed his true nature the whole time. Surely that's more clearly the sign of a true psycho? Heather and Babs haven't seen the hard evidence showing Justin with Anna on the very night she disappeared. What would they say if I showed them that?

Once I'm dressed I drop over to Leno's to see JJ. I want him to come with me when I confront Justin. When Justin gets this clip from me everything's going to change. I can't predict how he'll react.

'Hey, Cathy.' Christina, JJ's new Portuguese assistant, greets me warmly. 'Coffee?' I look around in search of JJ but I can't see him.

'Actually I was hoping to catch JJ.'

'He said he's going to be in a bit late because he's fixing his bike.'

'I'll just sit down for five minutes and have a juice then.'

'Be with you in a minute.'

When I find a seat I take out my phone and call JJ but his phone rings out. Christina brings the juice and I gulp it thirstily. Then I pull up the clip of Justin with Anna. My heartbeat quickens as I paste it into a WhatsApp message and start to type.

I have concrete evidence that you were the last person to see Anna Cunningham alive. Meet me at the same place. I hit send, jolting as adrenaline shoots into my blood. His reply is instant.

When?

I type back. **Now.**

Another reply. **Fine.**

There's a tingling in my fingertips when I pick up the glass and finish the juice. I place it down and compose a new message to JJ.

Meeting my ex now in the park. Same place. Worried it might get ugly. Please come if you can. I hit send, rise to my feet and leave some change on the table. As I leave, I bite my lower lip and try to quell my rising fear.

This morning the sky is grey with heavy clouds and the park is quiet. Justin is standing there waiting when I arrive, arms folded across his chest, no hint of a smile, no trace of humour.

'Well,' he spits.

'So you're a drug dealer.'

He sticks his chin out. 'Very good, Cath, you've finally woken up.'

'I don't give a shit about your business, Justin. I want to know about Anna Cunningham.'

He sneers. 'What you waiting for then?'

'How long were you seeing her?'

'Couple of months.' His voice is flat and disinterested.

'Why?'

'Well, let's see now …' He taps his chin smugly. 'She was easy on the eye, had bags of cash she liked to throw at me and,' he grips his crotch lewdly, 'knew what I needed. Perhaps she was everything I didn't have at home?'

My stomach knots. I grit my teeth, straining not to take the bait and snap back. I need the truth. 'Did you kill her Justin?' I ask calmly.

He grimaces. 'Don't be stupid.'

'Then why didn't you tell the police you saw her on the night she disappeared?'

'Because they mightn't have believed me,' he snarls. 'They might have got ideas about running the ruler over me, you fool. Busted my hard-won operations.'

'And you decided to let Ian take the rap?'

He smacks the palm of his hand against his forehead. 'You don't get it, you stupid bitch. It's him that's made her disappear.'

I step back, the speed of his flaring temper surprising me. My body tenses. 'How do you know?'

'Because it's obvious. He knew she was dating someone and got mad.'

'Did he know it was you?'

He waves his hands furiously. 'No, but it doesn't matter. He knew there was somebody and he's a violent alco who'd been threatening her for years. So even you, Cath, if you weren't such a sad, love-struck puppy, could see he's the one. Not to mention the pile of cash he stood to gain.' He spits on the grass. 'All I did was let the police do their job and not get in their way.'

The Landlord

He folds his arms as if the conclusion is obvious and proven. But he hasn't properly answered my questions. 'What about Anthea? What's going on between you?'

He laughs harshly. 'Nothing. She was just her bitchy mate who liked to tag along on occasion.' He rolls to the balls of his feet, momentarily less assured.

'There's more.'

Sneering now, he looks off into the distance. 'Fine. I snogged her once or twice.'

'You slept with her too?'

'No.' He tips his head back, amused. 'It was just a joke between me and Anna to see if she would. I could see she was another desperate cougar so we just had some fun with it.'

'Why was she staring at you the night you came to Ian's house then?' He unfolds his arms with a look of surprise. I know this look. It's the one Justin puts on when he's afraid he's going to put a foot wrong.

'Very good, Cath, seems like you've been paying attention finally.' He drops his hands into his pockets and I see the knuckles flexing inside his denims. 'I hadn't seen her since that night with Anna.'

'She was out that night with Anna?'

'I didn't say she was with her. I said I saw her sometime during that night,' he corrects me. 'So, anyway, last week when she saw me on the street she invited me in. I thought she wanted to pick up where we left off but she came out with a whole other plan.'

'What?'

'To pay me to get you out of the house and away from Ian.'

My mouth opens as my brain races. 'Why?'

'Fuck do I know,' he snorts. 'Because, like the rest of the world who are wide awake, Cathy, she knows he's a wife killer who's topped her mate and knows she's doing you a favour even if you can't see it for yourself. And anyway, it's all her husband's money, so why would she give a shit?'

'I don't believe you, Justin. She told you something. What did she say?'

He shrugs, throwing me a pitiful smile. 'She said you were naive and wouldn't listen to her advice but at least there was a chance you'd listen to mine.'

I rock back on my heels. Could it really be true or is he getting under my skin, knowing she's the one person in the neighbourhood who's reached out to me, who's made an effort to be friendly.

'Sorry, Justin, but it looks to me like you killed Anna because deep down you knew she didn't really care for you. Because she had Ian, a better man in every way that matters. She was probably tired of you and decided it was time to go back so you chose to seek revenge and I'm guessing Anthea might know something about it.'

He explodes furiously. 'She went in a car, you fool, just minutes after I snogged her on the street.'

'Went in a car with who?'

'I didn't see but clearly it was him, wasn't it?'

'You're lying, Justin.' He glances away furtively. I'm sure I've caught him out now. Justin is many things but brave isn't one of them. 'There's no way you'd have risked kissing Anna if Ian was on the street.'

'I didn't say he was on the street. He was still in the club.'

'So you saw him in the club?'

'No, but Anna said she had seen him earlier.'

'In the club?'

'She didn't specify. Who bloody cares?'

'I do. Because an eyewitness told the police that Ian was in the club. Was that eyewitness you, Justin?'

'Yes,' he yells. 'Because I was helping the police do their job you stupid cow.' His lips pull back over his teeth as he lunges towards me hissing fiercely. 'Because after that she disappeared, for good. And that's what's going to happen to you too. Because no matter how long you live, you'll never see the wood from the trees.'

'I think she can see it just fine,' somebody says. I turn and see JJ walking over slowly. 'Get out of here, Justin.' I reel away from

The Landlord

Justin so fast JJ has to catch me. He places an arm gently across my shoulders, leaning towards my ex. He's taller and a lot more well-built than Justin, who is already shrinking back. 'Is that alright with you, or do we need to settle this another way mate?'

Justin slinks further away to safety. 'It's not finished, Cathy,' he spits. 'Don't get any ideas about that clip.' Turning, he hurries away and out of sight.

JJ walks me back safely as far as the café. When we get to the door he stops.

'That got pretty heated.'

I nod. 'Shit, JJ. I so badly want to figure out Anna Cunningham's disappearance but I need more time.'

'And you don't have it?'

I shake my head, dread rising. 'Carol's going to get the police to pull Ian in any day now.'

He listens calmly, running his thumb against the gold stubble on his chin. 'Cathy,' he then says kindly, 'I know you've got a bit of a soft spot for Ian and I can see why, but are you thinking now he's responsible?'

'That's the thing,' I whisper. 'I can't say. I've caught him lying to me; quite a few times now. And my friend Heather, who's a lecturing psychologist, told me she firmly believes he's a psychopath.'

JJ rubs a finger along his jaw, appearing unconvinced. 'Doubt it, Cathy.'

'Why?'

'A hunch.' There's something about JJ's easy confidence that gives me fledgling hope. 'What do *you* feel?' I shrug, not knowing what to say. 'What about Justin? It sounded like you know he's somehow involved.'

I nod. 'I just learned there was something between him and Anthea.'

JJ sighs. 'I see.' His face tells me this isn't a shock.

'Really?' My naivete hits me like a punch. 'You already knew?'

'Sorry, Cathy,' he concedes, his eyes softening, 'guess you accidentally overhear the whispers sometimes in the café.' His shoulders shrug lightly. 'Anthea's got her good points but I wouldn't be surprised if she might be open to the idea of someone like Justin. But that's just my feeling. Call it a weakness. But people have all kinds of unexplained pieces to them. I mean she's close with Carol, and you know Carol.' JJ's generosity is almost boundless. I've seen how these customers walk right in like they own the place, clicking their fingers, gabbing too loudly, poking fun at the display on his wall like ignorant idiots, but JJ doesn't have a harsh word for any of them. My heart bleeds for him a little as I turn towards him.

'Yeah,' I agree. 'I know her.'

'Was it because you told him you knew about Anthea that it got so heated with Justin?' he then asks, steering the conversation back.

'Anthea was only a small part of it. The big surprise was that he was having a relationship with Anna.'

JJ steps back. 'He was?'

'And I've got video evidence showing he was the last one to see Anna the night she disappeared.'

He whistles. 'Christ, Cathy.' He sounds alarmed. 'What are you going to do with it?'

'I don't know yet. I'm making my mind up tonight.' Suddenly there's butterflies in my stomach. Justin and Ian have both lied to me repeatedly. Even Anthea hasn't been honest. And Carol is openly plotting against me. 'Say, you wouldn't like to come over tonight. I'm …' I hesitate, my voice shaky, 'a bit lonely at the moment.'

He touches my arm gently, his mouth turning down. 'Oh man, I'd love to, but we've got a birthday booked in for the evening.' The energy fizzes out of me and JJ notices. 'Would it work if I swung up to you after? Maybe before midnight if it dies early?'

'Thanks, JJ. You've no idea how grateful I am.'

Smiling again, he disappears inside.

50

As soon as I'm in the door I find the note from Ian.

Jamie's home so we've gone to a hotel in Wicklow. A surprise treat for him! Back tomorrow probably. Thanks again for last night. Talk soon.

Ian

The upbeat tone of his message is jarring. Last night was no game for me. It was a nerve-shredding test; and one that Ian's failed. 'A psychopath,' I whisper, the word almost like a sting on my lips. I read the message again, but this time have a fresh idea. There's a chance to get back to the basement, if I can figure out a way in.

Immediately I hurry upstairs and open the door to Ian's room. My shoulders tense as I step inside but I know I have to do this. I scan the space, the big double bed, two bedside lockers with lamps, his wardrobe against the back wall. A mahogany chest of drawers. Then an old antique desk with a chair in front of the window facing into the back garden. And lastly, the ensuite bathroom.

I start with the bedside cabinets, opening them and glancing inside but see nothing but books and notepads alongside some architectural magazines. I go to his wardrobe and open that. It's crammed with shirts and casual jackets. I stand on my tiptoes and check the top shelf. There's a washbag, a razor and brush, ear plugs, AirPods, aftershave but no keys. I shut it and the smell of aftershave wafts out. I drop to my knees and open the first drawer of the old mahogany chest. It squeaks and sticks but eventually yields. There are socks and boxer shorts stuffed inside and I lift them aside rummaging beneath, seeking out the bottom and the corners but find nothing.

I force it back with clenched teeth. Without the internal or external access keys to the basement I can't get into the bedroom where Keith has something hidden. I have to find one of them. But if it's not in his bedroom, where has Ian put it?

I try the next drawer of folded T-shirts but again find nothing. I pull out the last drawer, blowing the hair which is sticking to the sweat on my forehead, then I see it. A glass jam jar, with two keys inside. I know them instantly as I've seen them before. The key to the front door to the basement and the key to the internal door. I take the one for the internal door out, snap the drawer shut and jump to my feet.

Down in the basement, I go straight to the bedroom door and stick the key Keith left behind into the lock. I try and twist it but there's no movement. I keep working it, gently easing it back and forth, waiting for it to give a little more each time. I think I'm getting somewhere when it sticks fast, refusing to budge. 'Oh come on,' I groan, my voice low and hushed, a nervous chill passing through my body as the smell of earth and damp rises. The memory of my last visit resurfaces. Keith's agitation, Ian's footsteps, then his voice and lastly his appearance out of the darkness on the stairs. I try once again but get nothing. Now I recall Keith pounding it with his fist in frustration before fleeing into the night.

I lean on it but pain shoots up into my shoulder.

'Fuck,' I curse, swapping my hands around, this time using my good arm to try and press the door and the weaker one to twist the lock. But it isn't helping, so I go back to tinkering and twisting the knob. Bit by bit my patience wanes. I've been more than half an hour at it and my frustration has peaked. I try and think of what else I could use to smash it clear. I no longer care if I break it. It has to be opened.

In a rush I hurry upstairs and search around for something heavy that I can use but find nothing, only the heavy house furniture which won't work. I consider going back down and kicking it but fear I may only jam it more.

The Landlord

I slump onto the couch. Weariness is taking hold. I will myself to calm, to slow down so I can let myself think. But I don't think of anything and start to sleep.

When I come round, I wake with a start. Outside the daylight has disappeared. The trees outside on the street melt into the shadows. Jumping to my feet, I hurry back down the stairs to try the key again. It's still inside the lock where I left it. I give it a gentle twist.

This time it turns.

Blood stains the filthy worn carpet. Giant dark circles of it, then jagged lines connecting to smaller dried pools. Nearby smashed bits of glass, beer cans, empty wine bottles, a cracked pint glass with a jagged rim. It too is covered in what appears to be blood. Something dark has congealed inside it at the base and streaks of it cling to the edges like melted candle wax. The place reeks of stale ash, sweat and fermenting alcohol. There's trash everywhere, upturned chairs, filthy bedclothes thrown on the floor, even a plate with chips spewing out of a torn brown bag with giant whiskers of mould sprouting from it.

I stand still, my arms out by my sides, my back stiff, the fear that I might touch something by accident almost paralysing. The hair on my arms raises in dozens of tiny lumps, my skin suddenly cold. I want to run. To forget I've ever seen it. But I can't. I'm here. I've got where I wanted to go and I have to try and understand every detail.

Wallpaper the colour of faded cream is spattered with patterns of blood. Big sprawling arcs of dark, dried blood. It's almost as if somebody sprayed it on or used a brush to flick it everywhere. I wrap my arms around my body, retreating towards the door. Is this where Anna was murdered? My glance returns to the cracked beer glass on the floor and my stomach heaves.

I cover my mouth and stay still, waiting for it to pass, when I spot the bag. It's a large black sports bag wedged into a corner. I walk over and unfasten the zip. There's a sharp noise followed by a powerful scent. I pull the opening wider and the stuffed plastic bags bulge wider releasing their grassy fragrance.

It's marijuana. Dozens of bags of it crammed inside this huge sports bag.

Dropping to my knees, I flatten the bags and squeeze the zipper together, peeling it back shut. The blood pounds in my temples when I stand back up and lift it. Then I hurry out into the corridor and close the door behind me. Quickly I move to the storage room under the staircase where Ian keeps the garden tools, unbolt it and push the bag inside. Then I close it and make my way back to the living room.

I move to the window, sweat bubbling on my brow, clueless as to what to do next. But there's somebody outside. Somebody down on the street near the corner, hands in his pockets. The ragged coat familiar, the unkempt beard.

Keith has returned.

51

A thousand thoughts pulse through my brain as I stand there looking out, an endless stream of pictures of what might have happened downstairs. Was it Keith and the other squatters who murdered Anna at Ian's request? Was it something Ian did after he got them all out but Keith found out about? Why didn't the police have enough evidence to convict Ian if they found this?

I can't think clearly and I see Keith is already approaching the house, his attention focused on me. I turn away but I'm sure he knows I've seen him. Do I call the police now? Show them what I've found? But surely they've found it already? And if Keith really was involved, would he have ever let me get that close to the room? I can't understand it.

I glance back out the window, but only in time to see the trailing edge of Keith's coat as he marches down to the basement.

My skin prickles when I hurry out of the living room and over to the internal door to the staircase.

I get down the first two steps, my phone torch on and out in front of me illuminating the gloom.

The door pushes in and Keith enters. Immediately he sees the bedroom door ajar and deep lines furrow his pale brow. 'What have you done?' he asks darkly.

'I got inside.'

'Fuck.' He smacks the wall. 'Why? Why did you bloody do that?'

'Because I had to know the truth.' I remember now why he's come. What he needs to recover but won't find because I've hidden it. I have to use it to get him to talk, to tell me whatever it is he really knows. A shiver passes through me as the torchlight glints in Keith's manic stare. 'Was it you and your friends who murdered Anna?'

He runs a hand through his oily hair, pulling at it wildly. 'It's not what you think.'

'You need to explain.'

'Anna was never there.' He approaches the bottom of the staircase.

I grip the bannister. 'Then who was?'

'It's the night I was telling you about. When we all got out of hand. We were roaring pissed and one of the lads, Larry, was mucking about when he landed on a beer glass with his foot.'

'Why would I believe that?'

'Because it's what happened. Then he went berserk and started kicking his leg everywhere because he was high on special K. The blood went all over. Ian freaked when he saw it and chucked us all out. Then he locked it up because he got paranoid about the cops seeing it.'

'So why's he keeping it a secret?'

'I guess he just couldn't deal with it after Anna went missing. He didn't know I still had keys which is why I was able to use it to stash my stuff and sneak back in without him knowing.'

'Did the police see it?'

'No.'

'How come?' I stare at him in disbelief, refusing to buy what he's telling me.

'Ian lawyered up. He's a smart guy, you know. And a good friend of his is a high court judge so he's connected too. Don't mind what you've read online, the cops had nothing to tie him to Anna's disappearance so they couldn't force a search of his house. It was only after the night when we all lost it here in the basement that he started getting paranoid and sent us packing.' He seems to start calming down. 'Look I warned you not to go in. I knew you'd start jumping to the wrong conclusions. It looks like a fucking death chamber in there.' He grips the large wooden ball at the base of the bannister and leans against it, his dark eyes

The Landlord

peering into mine suspiciously. I wait, wondering what he intends to do next. 'I need to go in,' he then announces lurching away.

Seconds later he's out again, glowering, his arms held out rigidly from his sides. Tension bristles from him.

'Don't come closer,' I say, my voice barely holding steady. 'It's still the same deal, Keith. My friend has your image and knows what to do with it if she doesn't hear from me.'

'You slippery fucking bitch,' he spits.

'You'll get your drugs. But you need to know that I've photographed them also and unless you tell me what I need, they get uncovered too.'

'I've told you what I know,' he growls.

I shake my head. 'I confronted Justin who told me that Anna left in a car the night they were at the club.'

'Oh Christ.' He clenches his fist and I think he's going to punch the wall but he slaps it instead. 'You don't listen. So what if she did? How does that change things. I've even got a clip of her in the car but what does it matter?'

I pause, taking a second to register the importance of what he's just told me. 'Send it to me now and you'll get your drugs.'

He leans against the door frame, his suspicion clear, then he takes out his phone and starts to scroll. Seconds later my phone pings. 'Fine. There,' he says.

I open the video file cautiously, keeping one eye on him. Then I press play and see Anna once again. She's dressed as I remember in her fashionable coat, black leather trousers, exquisite hair and grabbing the back door to a grey saloon car. Somebody else is getting in the other side and one foot sticks out. Seconds later both doors shut and it takes off.

'Was Ian in the car with her?'

He shrugs. 'My drugs. Now.'

I point below me. 'There, in the store. It's not locked.' Instantly he marches away and retrieves his bag. Scowling, he storms across to the exit door.

'One last thing. Was Ian in the club with Anna?'

256

'No.' He turns, hoisting the bag over his shoulder. 'He stopped going to Mandy's because he reckoned she'd be there. He was in Corks across the road.'

'Did you see him leave?'

'No. He wasn't on the street when Anna left.'

'You don't think there's a chance he was in the car with Anna?'

'None.' He taps the door frame. 'Somebody knows what happened to Anna but let it go now. You pull the dog's tail long enough it'll rip out your throat.'

52

I sit on the stairs in silence. The walls of the house reverberate from the slamming of the basement door. There is a beep on my phone and the battery dies, killing the torch light with it.

The darkness envelops me as the musty smell of earth rises from the basement floor. Somebody left the nightclub with Anna the night she disappeared. Keith has given me the evidence. If I can find out who it could mean everything. There must be a way.

I remember Keith's warning. *Pull the dog's tail long enough it'll rip out your throat.* Was it a warning, or maybe even a threat? I glance down into the gloom noticing the open door to the front bedroom and my stomach knots. There was so much blood; almost everywhere. Can I really believe Keith's explanation? It reminds me of Ian's explanations; too easy, too convenient.

The doorbell rings, the noise shattering the eerie silence and I jump from my sitting position so fast that I bang against the wall. I wipe where my arm has brushed against it. A smear of grime coats my fingers and I shudder. Again the doorbell rings and I hurry up the steps, shutting the internal door to the basement behind me. It can't be Ian. He has his own door key. But then who could be calling at this time of night? Cautiously I tread with light steps through the porch area to the front door. I don't turn on the light but look out through the spyhole into the eerie darkness.

The spyhole is covered.

The bell rings a third time making me jump. 'Who is it?' I call out with as much confidence as I can muster, but I hear my voice straining.

'Cathy, I just wrapped up the birthday party,' a man's voice outside comes back, 'and decided to check in on you?' The muscles along my spine uncoil as I recognise the friendly Australian accent. 'You OK?'

'JJ!' I gasp, pulling the door open. His cheer turns to concern when he sees me. I beckon him inside and he enters. Then I shut the door and guide him to the living room where I flick on one of the side lamps.

'Did something happen, Cathy?'

We both sit opposite each other in the living room. 'Oh god, JJ,' I say, no longer able to hold it in anymore. 'I don't know how much longer I can take this.' My voice cracks. 'I think it's too much now.'

He leans forward. 'Why? What's changed?'

And then I tell him. Everything. About all the things that happened with Ian since I moved in; about what happened with Justin and then later with Keith. What I've discovered about Anna's disappearance. The new evidence Keith's given me.

He listens attentively and calmly, a picture of patience, nodding his understanding, letting me know that he understands. 'It's beautiful that somebody still cares about her at least,' he then says quietly.

A lump forms inside my throat. It's exactly what JJ would say. I remember Gerald and his sarcastic sidekick Stewie, the day their cycling club had all convened in Leno's, commandeering the venue like it was their own living room, and how the only thing they seemed to care about when discussing Anna's disappearance was the diminishing value of their properties, or the inconvenience of having Ian still living next door to them – almost talking about her like she wasn't a living, real person, somebody they knew, somebody Anthea was even good friends with. 'Thanks so much, JJ. It means a lot to have somebody listen.' I have a sudden urge to stand up, walk over and sit down beside him; to rest my head against his chest; because this kindness means everything to me in this moment. We hold each other's gaze and I open my mouth to speak but close it again when I see he's already started talking.

'I could go down and have a look at the bedroom in the basement for you, if you like. Maybe I'll see something or notice

The Landlord

something that might help.' He waits, sensing my reluctance. 'You don't have to come. I'll be fine on my own.'

'There's no light.'

He flicks on his phone torch. 'Don't worry, Cathy. Got one here.' He gets to his feet. 'It might be a good idea for a second person to witness this just in case.' He hesitates.

'Something happens?' I swallow, a new fear rising. 'Like you mean to me, JJ?'

He walks over and rubs my arm gently. 'Nothing's going to happen to you, Cathy, alright?' I nod, blinking back a tear. 'I was thinking in case somebody got in there; somebody who's connected to what really happened and cleaned it up somehow. Do you see what I'm saying?'

'OK,' I say, gathering myself with a small sniffle. 'It's the first room to the front.' I get to my feet and take his hand. 'Come on.' I lead him to the top of the staircase. A waft of damp, stale air whooshes up from the gloom. I watch him descend, the small light from his torch illuminating each step as his feet tap one after the other. As he disappears into the dark I tense. *He's going to be fine* I tell myself and yet my leg is trembling.

'JJ?' I whisper. There's no reply and my body stiffens. 'JJ!' I say, louder this time. My stomach lurches. I open my mouth to scream his name when he suddenly reappears. With slow steps he makes his way up the stairs.

'You didn't exaggerate.' He blows his cheeks as he reaches me and shuts the door behind him. 'That is shocking. What do you want to do now?'

I clutch the back of my neck and give myself a second until the momentary panic subsides. JJ is back. JJ is fine.

'Everything OK, Cathy?'

'Yeah,' I whisper, a flush of red spreading across my cheeks. 'I guess I'm still working out what to do with this information Keith has given me. I haven't fully processed it. No sooner had he slammed the door warning me away than you arrived.'

'So Keith said he was sure Ian wasn't in the club and almost certain he was in Corks across the road. Is that right?' he asks, not seeming to notice my hot face in the faint light.

'Yes.'

'I know the manager to Corks. She's an Aussie. We bumped into each other at a mate's barbecue a couple of weeks back. I'll call her tomorrow and see if I can get hold of the CCTV footage. Would that help?'

'JJ, that'd be huge.'

He shrugs. 'What other ideas have you got?'

I regain my composure. 'I need to figure out who was in the car with Anna. That's crucial.'

He gets up, moves across and sits down beside me. 'Let me have a look.' I give him the phone and he clicks on the clip. We both watch as it plays. When Anna gets into the car he pauses it. 'We have a blurred shoe from the other passenger but nothing more?'

'Yeah.'

'OK.' He hands the phone back and I inhale his spicy aftershave. His long lashes blink as he sits there thinking. 'What about downstairs?'

I nod. 'I'm going to get a sample of the blood. Then somehow I have to get hold of Anna's medical records and find if it matches.'

'Good. If I can think of some way to help I'll call you tomorrow.' He rises to his feet. We pause, looking into each other's faces, and then I break away, leading him to the front door. 'I should have something from the footage from Corks.' He stands patiently by the door and I open it for him, my heart sinking a little as he steps out into the night. 'I'd love to stay but I can see you need your sleep, Cathy.'

'Yeah,' I say, not really meaning it, hoping he somehow knows.

He stands there looking across the street. I think he's about to leave when he turns towards me. 'Listen I know you want to find what really happened to Anna because you can't believe Ian could be responsible and I think that's really admirable. But if you even

The Landlord

get a flicker of doubt that you're in danger you have to promise to come look for me. Will you do that?'

I nod as a question that's been at the back of my mind comes to me. I don't want to offend him; he's been so kind. But I want to know the answer. 'Why JJ? Why are you doing this for me?'

His stubbled cheeks fold into a grin. 'Because from the moment you walked into Leno's café I've thought about you every day.' He steps forward and gives me a soft kiss on the cheek. Before I can react he runs down the steps and climbs onto his bike. I hold my hand to where his lips were seconds ago. The night feels suddenly electrically charged. I want to say something but I can't find the words. I watch him wave and cycle into the night.

53

I stand in the basement bedroom with the kitchen knife gripped tight. Even in this early summer morning the place has the feeling of a graveyard; dark, rotting and forgotten; blood seeping into the earth, stories of death almost whispering from the walls which surround me. I think of going to the window and teasing the curtain open an inch, just enough to let in a crack of light, but I don't.

I must pass through this place unnoticed. I must get in and get out as fast as I can. I don't want to be down here. Keith was right. It *is* starting to give me nightmares, like last night, when I twisted and turned inside my bed, certain in my dream that somehow I was trapped down here, the filthy bloodstained carpet wrapped around me, binding me tight, imprisoning me so I couldn't move; couldn't breathe.

I swallow, reluctantly ingesting the dank air and move across to the wall.

I stare at the patterns of spatter ingrained on the wallpaper, a knot tightening in my stomach, then carefully I start to scrape, watching the flecks of dark, dried dust drop onto the perfectly white sheet of A4 paper I've brought along with me. When I'm satisfied I've got enough I stop, folding the paper to secure it and placing it in my pocket. I blow the dark residue from the edge of the knife, wincing as the flakes drop to the carpet, when there's a noise.

'Cathy?' My body jolts. 'Cathy?' the voice calls again.

It's coming from outside but I can tell it's close. 'Jesus,' I sputter, my heart galloping as I hurry to the window so I can look out through the curtain. Immediately I see the powder blue jeans and

The Landlord

fresh white trainers, then the pretty blonde hair. It's Anthea. She comes down another step towards the basement door and I drop the curtain, hurrying back into the corridor. 'Coming,' I say.

'You're in the basement?' She tries the front door but it holds firm. 'Everything OK in there, Cathy?'

I open the door and step out, instantly shutting it firm behind me. 'Hey, Anthea.' I brush past her awkwardly.

'Has Ian cleared out the basement then?' she asks, glancing at the basement door.

I pace up the steps towards the ground level and wait as she follows me very slowly. 'No, I just dropped a key down there the last time I sat out with Ian in the garden.' I pull a strained smile. 'But I found it.' I hold it out so she can see it. 'So all good.'

'In the garden?' Her eyebrows raise. 'The last time I suggested to Ian we sit in the garden to enjoy a bottle of wine he was adamant it was a no-go area. "It would put me to shame walking you through there" I remember him saying.' Her bright eyes search my face.

'It's not that bad,' I lie, boldly kicking into my full acting mode, 'but yes it's definitely not somewhere he'd be keen to show I guess.'

'Mm,' Anthea agrees, the suspicion in her voice still evident.

'And how are things with you?' I say, steering the conversation back to safety as I point to the front door at the top of the granite steps. 'Can I invite you in for a coffee?'

'That would be lovely, Cathy, but I won't impose.' She brightens at the suggestion. 'I was just checking if you might like to join me for dinner tonight. Harry and the boys are off doing some male bonding over tents in the mountains so it would be lovely to have company.'

'Erm ... sure.'

'Eight OK?'

Suddenly I remember the text I got from JJ earlier. The manager of Corks nightclub has invited me to go in and scan their CCTV footage at seven. 'Yes,' I say, deciding I won't disappoint her, 'but I might be a little late.'

'Fab.' She beams a smile, rubbing my arm. 'See you then.'

As soon as she turns to leave, I hurry up the front steps but when I get to the front door I find that I have forgotten the key. 'Shit,' I mutter, running back down and hurrying behind Anthea to the foot gate. 'Forgot I have to get milk.'

'Catch you later, Cathy.' Anthea bounces across the road.

I wave, wait for her to cross safely before checking my pocket. Nervously I swallow. It's still there. The folded paper with the blood sample. My stomach squirms. I have to get moving, to find a way to get it tested. But I'm locked out of the house with no phone and no keys. I walk to the corner, my brain struggling to think of what to do next or where I might go. I pause to look back at the house.

Out of nowhere Ian has appeared and he's walking in the front door.

Immediately I hurry back, jogging up the broad granite steps. I press the doorbell and wait there when I notice Anthea. She's standing by her window watching me but retreats from view. In the same moment the door opens. 'Cathy. Lovely to see you.' Ian's dressed in new clothes. He's clean-shaven, his hair is combed neatly. He gives me a relaxed smile. 'Come in. Were you jogging?'

'Yes, but I … forgot my keys so thank God you came back.'

'Lucky,' he says. Suddenly I remember the inside door to the basement is still open. *No.* The blood-spattered bedroom in the basement is *unlocked*. My mouth gapes as I expect to see him march his way down to the kitchen. 'Well then,' he turns, skipping lightly up the stairs, 'I just stopped by to pick up my phone charger and power bank, this bloody old phone of mine can't last even for a day now.'

I hurtle to the door at the top of the stairs which leads to the basement, grab it in my hands and snap it shut without a sound. Then I hurry back to the porch. Seconds later Ian returns.

'Myself and Jamie decided to stay down in Wicklow for another night,' he says casually.

'He's back for a few days then?' I try not to pant.

The Landlord

'Yeah. Oh, it's a long story, Cathy. Father and son stuff. We're talking about a lot of things we should have got through long ago but it's great. Progress, at last.' He opens the front door. 'Sorry I'm rushing but I've got a business lunch with a client. Don't worry I know you and I need to talk and we will. Soon.'

My fingers tighten around the folded paper inside my pocket. There are so many questions I want to throw at him. About the bloody mess in the room he's had under lock and key beneath our feet, about Keith and his friends and all the little details that won't add up. I want to tell him too about how Justin was kissing Anna the very night she disappeared and I have the footage on my phone. 'Ian?'

He waits, holding the door, smiling. 'Yes?'

'The night Anna disappeared …' I watch his smile fade at the mention of her name. 'What time do you think you got home?'

He shuts the door quietly. 'Just before half one. As usual I had drunk too much. I walked home but that's about as much as I remember.'

'You weren't in Mandy's nightclub?'

'I don't believe so. Although an eyewitness claims I was.' He sighs, touching my arm lightly. 'We'll get to the bottom of all this soon, Cathy, I promise. Only right now, I've got to dash.'

I nod but notice his mouth turn down. 'Fuck,' he snaps and I flinch.

'What?'

He clutches his head, squeezing his eyes shut. Then his smile returns like nothing happened. 'Just remembered I was supposed to bring drawings from my office but I've forgotten.'

With a shrug he opens the door and leaves.

54

Not wasting a second I get busy on my computer, searching Google, desperately trying to figure out what ways I can get the blood analysed. But there's too much information. I find myself diverting down cul de sacs as the links keep taking me to true life murder cases in the USA, serial killers, psychopaths who chopped up their victims, and some who even ate the bodies. My stomach lurches and I snap my laptop shut. I don't have time to lose doing research. I need to think on my feet, to figure out who can help me right now! But the harder I strain, the less clearly I think and a headache comes on.

I'm about to go looking for a painkiller when, out of nowhere, the breakthrough comes. Ben Chedworth, my old boyfriend from years back. He was probably the kindest and most obliging boyfriend I ever had; I had spent months lamenting the fact that I never really fancied him until I finally conceded defeat, admitting bitterly to myself that if there wasn't any chemistry I couldn't blame myself, but I'd have to be brave and pass Ben the bad news. He had cried and suggested we stay friends and I had agreed readily. But then the friendship had fizzled out and life moved on.

I never felt either of us were to blame, now I hope he just feels the same. If I can get hold of him, he could be the one to help me.

'Yeah, it should be doable,' he explains, popping the top button open on his white lab coat. 'It's a basic ABO test and it will pull up the type. Of course genetic testing would yield something more detailed and specific but I wouldn't have access to that kind of tech at this lab since it's not what we do.'

The Landlord

'That's OK,' I tell him. 'If you can even get the type it's brilliant.' Calmly he takes the paper off me and opens it carefully to look inside.

'You scraped this?'

I nod. 'Off a wall.'

He pops his lips. Is he curious, suspicious? I can't be sure. 'I have to be honest, Cathy, it wouldn't really be in line with how we do it here, to be doing a test like this with no records or explanations. Do you get what I'm saying?'

I frown, my heart sinking. I blush. Perhaps I was crazy to think Ben would want to help me. I don't even really understand what he does for a living, except that it's a lab-based research role with a huge pharmaceutical multinational. 'I know, Ben. I know this is unfair of me, popping up here out of the blue, since we haven't been in touch. And ...' my voice falters. I need him to understand how important this is, how desperately I want his help. I draw on the skills I've honed over years on stage and in front of cameras, giving in to the emotion which swells inside me. I tip my chin down and a tear tracks my cheek.

'I'm sorry,' he interjects. 'Look, maybe there's something I can sort out.' His voice drops to a whisper and he clears his throat. 'It would have to be strictly in confidence, only between us, if you get me?' I nod rapidly. 'No paperwork, no records. Just a verbal from me, is that OK?'

'God, Ben, it would mean a lot.'

He inhales deeply, his frown easing away. 'How old do you think it is?'

'More than a year but less than two. That's probably as much as I know.' He gets to his feet and I stand up too. I don't want to detain him. I don't want him to have even a second to change his mind. He was a good boyfriend and I'm still sorry we didn't work out, but we can't go back there now. This isn't the place or the time.

I rub where the tears have spilled onto my cheeks and sniff quietly.

Ben looks at me. He's still the unassuming guy I remember from before. 'I've missed you, Cathy,' he says, sighing. 'And listen don't worry now, OK. Hopefully I'll get you a result this evening and I can text it to you. Will that work?'

I nod, gratitude almost bursting through my skin.

He folds the paper carefully and slips it into the pocket of his white lab coat. 'It's a nice surprise, really, just to see you again,' he says, turning and walking back the way he came out. I watch my old boyfriend pass out of the reception area and through the special security doors back into his high-tech facility and wonder how I graduated from Ben to Justin over the years. I can't answer that right now because I have to focus my mind on the tasks in hand. Only when I find Anna's medical file will the whole point of going to Ben with the dried blood make any sense.

I shudder as a new thought enters my mind. What if I get a positive ID of Anna's blood type? What then? It will mean the story Keith was spinning me about what happened in that room was a plain fabrication. The proof will be concrete: Ian Fitzsimmons is exactly what Justin first said he was, *a murderer*.

The thought sticks with me during my journey back to the house and I'm queasy with anxiety when I get to Belleview Road. As I reach the gate I stop and look up at the huge old Georgian facade.

For the first time I can remember the house feels threatening, almost like something alive, watching me, waiting for me to enter. I change my mind and decide not to go inside. Instead I walk down to Leno's.

Christina's there again, clearing tables.

'Alright, Cathy?'

'Hi Christina, just looking for JJ again.' She gathers up some cups and plates from an empty table and breezes over.

'Give us a sec.' She takes the tray off to the kitchen and hands it to the KP before coming back. Now she's pointing to the artwork on the wall. 'Anthea was in with a few friends for lunch.' I see a

The Landlord

couple of new sculptures and a series of three boomerangs with extravagant paint work on them. Only the middle one is gone from its holding. 'She managed to damage a piece so he's bringing it over to a mate to get it patched up.' She looks unimpressed.

'She broke the boomerang?'

'Nah.' She curls her hair behind her ear revealing three studs and a gold hoop. 'She just fucked it up is all.' She gives me a wink and whispers conspiratorially. 'Pricking about with it and telling him how her sons used to love them as toys and JJ was explaining that they were actually weapons.' I get the picture instantly, imagining Anthea, probably meaning well but blundering along with compliments so gauche only JJ could stomach them. She points to the pair remaining, 'These two are for making birds fly towards hunters, and the middle one is for taking them down with a direct hit.'

'They're beautiful,' I say.

'I wouldn't mind if she apologised but she just thought it was funny and JJ was too kind to tell her off.'

'That's JJ,' I agree.

'I'd have stuck it up her arse with the repair bill attached,' she says, grinning. Some customers appear. Christina covers her mouth and rolls her eyes to the ceiling when we see it's Anthea and Carol. 'Better get back here.' She sweeps away, bringing a tray of used glasses back inside the kitchen.

If Anthea has heard something she doesn't let on.

'Hey,' I say.

Carol marches up to me and stops suddenly, fixing on me with a fake smile. 'So Anthea tells me you're snooping around in Ian Fitzsimmons's basement now?' Anthea, who has moved over to the kitchen entrance, wheels round, her mouth forming a circle.

'I'm sorry, Carol?' I reply.

'Oh come on, Cathy.' She steps closer, arms folded across her chest, her eyes narrowing. 'Even you've now figured out that he killed Anna.' She sticks out her chin. 'So what did you find? Anything you'd like to tell us about?'

'Carol,' Anthea snaps angrily before I can say anything, 'I really think that's *enough*.'

Carol raises her hands as if surrendering as she turns towards her. 'Sorry, Anthea but some things are just better off said up front.' She looks back to me. 'You did notice how she didn't have an answer though, didn't you?'

Anthea glares at her frostily. She's so cross she's almost unrecognisable. 'Carol, I want to have a private word with Cathy. Could you be really good and wait for me outside for a second?' Carol doesn't reply. Instead she eyeballs me coldly and slips away without a sound.

When Anthea sees she's out of earshot she gives me a contrite glance and shrugs. 'I'm sorry, Cathy. I was just nipping in to collect a bracelet I left here earlier, and I know I shouldn't have told her but …' She stalls as if reluctant to continue.

'But what?'

She sighs apologetically. 'But I *do* feel you were overstepping this morning. Ian has a right to privacy, Cathy. And if we're trying to help him get over Anna's disappearance, you're hardly helping by digging around his basement where he's expressly told you not to go.'

I grit my teeth, bewildered that Anthea could even suggest it was OK to gossip with Carol. For a second I imagine letting her know that I found out she tells lies since I met Harriet. That I discovered she was dating my ex-boyfriend, despite her happy marriage, despite the fact he was still going out with me. But I hold back. Because when I see her tonight I'm going to be looking for answers and if I spit all that out now, there won't be a tonight. 'You're right. I'm sorry,' I say in a soft voice.

'Oh Cathy,' she replies sympathetically. 'It's nothing. In fact I should be apologising for gossiping.' She slips past me. 'But listen I need to get back out to Carol. She rang me earlier about going down to the police today so I have to drum some sense into her. But don't worry, I will.'

Immediately I feel silly for getting so irate with her. 'Thanks,' I reply, masking the guilt that bubbles inside me.

On my way back to Belleview Road I think about calling JJ but change my mind and choose to text him instead. Last night's kiss feels too recent. I don't know how I feel about it. I was so pleased when he did it, so grateful for his honesty in telling me how he feels about me. But my feelings towards him are still mixed up. I haven't even allowed the possibility of JJ as a romantic interest in my life. I've been too focused on Ian.

Going to look for Anna's medical file in the house. Will have the blood analysis by tonight. Thanks again for last night. Call me when you can. XX

The two kisses go in accidentally. I'm about to delete them when I think better of it and leave them.

As I walk up the steps of the house and open the door, a shiver passes through my body. I need to find Anna's medical records. I don't know when or if Ian is coming home and I have to work fast.

I rule out the basement and focus on the house, starting with Ian's room. My heart rate quickens when I tease the door open but I find it's empty. Like before, the bed's unmade and there's a shirt on a hanger draped over the duvet which is rolled back from the bedsheets. Pacing inside, I begin with the bedside cabinets, lifting out what I find inside. I move to the big wardrobe and scan it quickly but see no sign of papers so I close it and hurry back out to the landing.

Taking the key to the internal door to the basement from my pocket, I run down and open it up. Then I go down the stairs and through the corridor until I get out through the back door to the garden. My body tenses as I look down the wild overgrown mass of tangled green. I unclench my fists and move quickly to Ian's office. When I get there I stop. Panting, I try the door, biting my lip when it gives and opens inwards.

Grey clouds drift across a darkening sky overhead threatening a downpour. I go inside and move quickly to the corner desk. When I pull out the small drawers I find papers. There are lots of them, all jumbled together with clips of old news articles as well as family photos. I take them out, placing them on the floor. Then I begin sifting through them, hands jangling, as I place each piece aside one after the other.

But the papers don't give me what I'm looking for. I can't find anything that belongs to Anna. Only old bills, rough work sketches, tax forms. Picking them all up I put them back, my teeth grinding in frustration as I shut the drawers tight. A line of sweat has broken out on my forehead and heat rises beneath my shirt. I move to the door and let myself out. I don't want to spend any more time in here. I don't want to stay longer in the garden.

My feet break into a run. Silently I curse myself for my stupidity. I couldn't find anything in Ian's garden room because he's already told me *he burnt every last shred of evidence against him.*

My head pounds when I get back inside the main house and lock the door which leads down to the basement. I turn, leaning against it, straining to think of another plan when an idea occurs. A place I haven't checked. Under Ian's bed.

Dashing again I bound up the stairs until I'm back inside his room. I drop to my knees pulling away the tangle of old shoes and press my cheek flat against the carpet. There's a cardboard box so I reach in and pull it out. On it is written one word: Anna. I swallow as my body stills, then I reach for the lid, tensing as I open it up. Inside there are handwritten pages. I pick them up, scanning them as I read. It's Ian's work. It's the poems he spoke about, and the fragmented diary entries. It seems he hasn't destroyed every last thing as he claimed. Scattered among them are more pictures. They're mostly of holidays, group shots of all of them – Ian, Anna and Jamie – posing together, smiling and looking genuinely happy. I place the pictures down, my shoulders sagging, a groan of dismay rising from the back of my throat.

But then I see it. The wide brown paper file. I reach for it, brushing off the layer of dust. It's Anna's medical file. My hands tremble as I flip paper after paper, desperately scanning each, hoping my eye will catch something. Sweat prickles my scalp and

The Landlord

I keep thumbing faster and faster. Then I see it clearly. Blood group *AB*.

Instantly I stuff the contents back inside the box but stop when I hear a noise. It's the sound of a key twisting in the front door.

My body freezes and I stare at the door. But I know I can't stay like this. Without making a sound I press the lid back on the box and rise to my feet. Then I kick it under the bed, sweeping the cluster of shoes in after it, before ducking out and scurrying up the stairs to my own bedroom. The sound of the front door closing against the latch rises up through the hall.

'Anybody home?' Ian's voice reverberates through the house. 'Cathy?' Panicking I leap to my bedroom wardrobe, stumble inside and pull the door. Why is Ian back? And has he seen me leaving his bedroom?

Desperately I try to calm my breathing but it's coming thick and fast, the noise of it beating against the closed door of the wardrobe and back to my flushed face.

'Why do I get the feeling she's been snooping?' I hear him say, his voice rising with anger as the noise of his footsteps moves in the direction of the kitchen.

Muffled sounds of doors opening and closing can be heard below. Then the clatter of feet retreating deeper into the house. Into what I am certain must be the basement. A door slams and I hold still. 'Fuck!' I hear the word roar up from deep below. 'How did she get into that room? It was locked. I'm sure of it.'

Sweat drips down my neck. Ian must have found the door open to the bedroom in the basement, which means he knows I've seen the blood-spattered walls. Footsteps pound the stairs, growing closer with each second. I grip my hands together but still they shake.

'Cathy?' A knock sounds on the door as he barks my name. I don't reply. I peek through the gap in the wardrobe doors as Ian steps inside the bedroom. His eyes flash as he scans the room. 'Cathy?' he snarls, moving to the bed, reaching for the duvet and whipping it away. 'For God's sake.' Snatching up a pillow, he hurls it at the wall. Next he rounds and begins walking back towards the wardrobe. 'You silly, silly girl.' Through the tiny gap I see him raising his hand. I brace myself, not daring to close my eyes. 'Enough,' he roars, pulling back at the last second and slapping his forehead furiously. 'This has gone too far. Now it has to end.' My chest rises and falls and I watch as he storms out and down the stairs. Seconds later the front door opens. The last sound I hear is it slamming hard behind him.

My hands won't stay still as I order the Uber on my phone. I'm sweating and my chest heaves so hard it could burst when it arrives outside. I hurtle from the wardrobe and don't look back till I'm safely inside the car.

I'm not sure there's really a point in going to Corks nightclub anymore now but I give the driver the address, wiping hot tears, and we drive away.

55

'It's not locked,' the girl called Susan says, leading me through to the private basement office at the back of Corks nightclub. It's dark. Black walls, black ceiling, even black leather-backed chairs. 'Caro said you can work away, the file's open.' She flicks on a light switch and a dim bulb hanging from the middle of the ceiling slowly comes to life. She points towards the open laptop on the desk, shuts the door and leaves.

Quickly I sit. The footage is listed in files by date. I find the night of August twelfth, the night Anna disappeared never to be seen again, and open it up. The footage starts at ten in the evening so I speed forward to one a.m. I already know from the clip I got from Keith that Anna was out on the street around two a.m. so if Ian claims he left the club early then my guess is that one hour before is a good place to start.

I tap the mouse pad, the muscles along my spine coiling as the hard drive drones. The voice inside my head is kicking off again. It's screaming at me to stop. *Why? Why am I doing this?* It's clear Ian killed Anna Cunningham. I found her blood in his basement, the very basement he's been hiding. Only an hour ago he looked ready to kill me too.

You don't know that for certain, I hear myself counter. *And Ben Chedworth hasn't come back with the analysis of the blood I found yet.*

My lips fold together as I press play and the pictures begin, showing images of the bouncers moving around at the club entrance. I understand now that if I don't find Ian on this footage it's quite possible that nothing of what Keith was saying is true and perhaps he was, like Justin claims, inside Mandy's nightclub all along. I swallow and keep my eyes glued to the screen as the minutes tick away. The images keep flowing, mostly gangs of people still coming into the club and the odd few going out again. There's no sign of Ian.

I keep thinking, working through the information he gave me already. He claimed he left the club early. But he also claimed he had drunk too much so he couldn't be certain. The footage rolls on. More revellers shuffling in and out. The bouncers pacing back and forth making small talk. A brief period of inaction.

And eventually a lone figure emerges.

I see the wide shoulders, the thick dark hair, the familiar angle of his chin as he turns to the bouncer outside.

Ian Fitzsimmons.

'Shit.' I tap the pad, stopping the video and hitting rewind. Ian is wearing a light navy casual jacket. He uses the rail to steady himself at the top of the stairs, says something to the bouncers, and they both laugh. Then he stumbles away and up the road. I check the clock. The time is 1.37 a.m. I pull out my phone and check the clip I have of Anna departing in the car. It's 2.05 a.m.

Ian is walking home twenty-eight minutes ahead of his wife. The video footage is right in front of me telling me what's happened. *He wasn't there. He wasn't with her. He isn't on the road.*

Instantly I screenshot the footage and email it to my inbox. 'Christ,' I gasp, dropping back into the chair, my whole body on fire. I'm staring into space when my phone pings.

There are two new messages. The first from JJ, the second from Ben Chedworth. I grip the back of my neck. That's the one I've been dreading ever since the idea even entered my mind. But I have to know if the blood in Ian's basement matches the profile on Anna's medical file.

I tap the phone, almost afraid to read, but knowing I have to. And I see it then.

Blood type AB.

It matches Anna's blood. It's the same type.

My stomach heaves and I gasp. Seconds ago I was certain there was hope but what now? With this evidence it's almost certain that Anna Cunningham was murdered, and the person who murdered her was her own husband, Ian Fitzsimmons.

My phone rings. *Ian.* I flinch, dropping the phone. It bangs loudly against the desk.

I reach for it, my back stiffening when I pick it up. Can I really speak to him now? What do I say? Shouldn't I simply cut the call and phone the police? Finally I press accept.

'Cathy?' The voice is angry but contained. 'Where are you?'

'I can't tell you, Ian. I think you know why.'

There's an exasperated sound, like teeth sucking. 'We need to talk.'

'We're talking.' My voice is hoarse, the words barely more than a whisper.

'You shouldn't have gone into that room, Cathy.'

'I had no choice, Ian. I had to find out the truth about Anna. Now I have.'

'What have you found?' he demands urgently.

'The blood on your walls matches Anna's blood group. It's her blood, Ian. She was murdered in that room.'

'For God's sake, Cathy don't say that,' he seethes. 'It's not the truth.'

'Then what is?'

'It was our lodgers having a party that got out of hand. I was there when the accident happened.'

'Keith and his friends? Yeah,' I whisper, 'I met him and he fed me the same story, Ian. But I don't believe it. You and Keith both wanted Anna gone and I think together you made that happen.'

'For Christ's sake, think about what you are saying.' He pauses, breathing heavily down the line. 'How do you even know about Keith?'

'Because I met him, in the basement, the place you kept me away from. I discovered him, the same way I discovered the other secrets you kept.'

'Cathy, it's not true,' he pleads. 'I was protecting you. I didn't want this poison to enter your soul the way it's entered into mine. I had to keep secrets. And don't you dare tell me you didn't keep yours from me too.'

'What secrets?'

'You think I didn't know about your game? The one you invited your friends to play that night. Was it to uncover a liar? Or a psychopath maybe? You think I didn't see what was going on?' Stunned I keep listening, trying to figure out how he hid the truth from me so well. 'And what about your boyfriend, Cathy? The one you told me was your ex. You think I don't know it was Justin who was seeing Anna.'

My eyes widen. 'What? How did you know he was my ex?'

'I saw him the very day you arrived, Cathy.'

'And you knew about him and Anna?'

'Yes,' he replies, his voice heavy with exasperation.

'Did you know it was Justin who last saw her after she left Mandy's nightclub that night?'

The line goes silent. My head pounds. I hear Ian clear his throat and then the sound of his deep sombre voice. 'Why haven't you told me this? Why only now?'

I squeeze my eyes. *Why I am I suddenly doubting the truth?* Doubting that Ian is anything other than a murderer? And yet the sound of his anguished voice feels so at odds with that being possible. 'Ian,' I plead. 'You left Corks nightclub at 1.37 the same night. I've already found this evidence but you need to tell me more about that night. What can you remember? There must be something?'

I hear a tired groan. 'I met her earlier.'

'Anna?'

'Yes. She was with Anthea and Carol in a bar and it was around ten or so. She went off to the restroom with Anthea and left me with Carol. They were gone for an age and I hadn't much to say to Carol since she's always despised me so I went out for a fag. When I came back I finished my drink and made plans to meet

The Landlord

with friends later but then everything goes hazy. I'm almost certain that Carol spiked my drink although I have no proof. As soon as I got up and left it was like I'd been hit by a train.'

'So Anna was out with both of them? Is it possible they went to Mandy's nightclub with her?'

'That's what I assumed but both of them said they never saw her again after the pub because they went for a drink together while Anna went and did her own thing.'

I swallow. *Carol and Anthea.*

'I want to meet you tonight, Cathy,' he whispers, his voice low and deep. 'I want to get closure, Cathy. It's time.'

A beep sounds on my phone. *JJ.* 'I'm calling you right back.' I hang up. I hit the answer button but instantly my phone powers down and dies. The battery is dead.

'*Shit.*' I drop it on the desk, cursing as I remember my arrangement to call in to Anthea. I get to my feet, snatch the phone and hurry out of the nightclub. On the street I hail a taxi and direct him to Belleview Road.

The car snakes through the Dublin city traffic. It's not far and soon we draw close. But my legs are starting to shake. Anthea and Carol must know something. They were with Anna too that night. Why did they leave her to go off by themselves? And why would Carol spike Ian's drink? Could it have been one of them that got in the car with Anna?

I watch my phone carefully. It's hooked to my portable charger pack now and finally the first flicker of a charge is showing with a green light. Almost immediately I see JJ's name light up the dial. I hit answer and his voice comes down the line.

'You see the pic I sent you?'

'No?' Quickly I scroll the phone as his voice comes back over the speaker.

'Have a look, Cathy,' he replies excitedly. 'I got a friend who specialises in aerial photography to check out the image of Anna getting into the car with the friend. He suggested running it through a photo app he uses, so I did and this is what I found.'

I pull up the picture. He's zoomed in tight on the shoe. It's a white sneaker and it's clearly a woman's leg. I can make out the brand because the resolution is so good.

'It's a white Skechers tennis shoe,' I say as the taxi stops outside Ian's house.

'It is, Cathy. And I've seen one of the women wearing that same shoe at the café but I just can't remember which.'

I tap to pay for the taxi and turn to look out the window. It's the little dog I see first. He's squatting on the front patch of grass and squeezing out a shit. A blonde woman with a dry, tight face watches on indifferently with no intention of cleaning it up.

My eyes flick to her feet.

She wears white Skechers tennis shoes.

'It's Carol,' I whisper, stepping out of the car and putting away my phone. 'It's *fucking* Carol.'

56

Blood surges to my cheeks as my fingers curl. I want to grab her by the throat and ram her against the railings. I want to take her by the hair and stuff her face in the shit her little dog is squeezing out onto Ian's grass. I want to tell her that she's a lying, conniving bitch and I've got the evidence to prove it. I move towards her, a murderous rage pulsing through my veins, overwhelming me.

She sees me and crinkles her nose. 'I'd pick it up but I forgot the bags.' She looks back at the dog as it squirms and squeezes its spindly body. She's in no rush to interrupt it. She's hardly bothered by my appearance at all.

I command myself to smile. I still have to get her to talk, to learn more. If I attack her she'll close down. 'That's OK, Carol,' I tell her, glancing admiringly at her feet. 'You know I was thinking of buying myself a pair of the exact same tennis shoes?'

Carol peers down with practiced disinterest. Then she looks back up at me, baffled. 'You're a funny one, aren't you, Cathy?' She turns and stands closer to me. 'My dog is taking a shit right on your doorstep and you just want to talk to me about shoes.'

I shrug, refusing to let my smile fall. 'Well, it's nature's call, isn't it, Carol?' I point down at the shoes. 'Can you tell me, are they as comfortable as everybody says?' I try and get a closer look to make sure it's the exact match to the pair in the clip. I'm certain it's them.

She rolls her foot over and studies it for a second. 'They're nothing special. I only picked them up last month and had always worn Adidas until then. I can't see what all the fuss is about, but Anthea never stops going on about them.'

Last month? I reel backwards, clutching the back of my neck. This doesn't make sense. 'Anthea?' I say like I've just been punched.

The dog finishes up and trots back over. 'Yes. She's been wearing them for years. Even wears them out when she's dressing up can you believe?' Carol curls her lip. 'I mean, who wears bloody tennis shoes going out to dress up? Only Anthea would have the nerve to get away with it.' She shortens the leash and the dog yelps as she yanks it closer. 'But I guess that's why we're all in awe of her, now that she's replaced Anna Cunningham as Belleview Road's queen bee.'

She cocks her head, glancing at the steaming lump of shit on the grass, and struts off down the street.

I turn, my attention switching instantly to the house across the road. Anthea is at the window watching us but retreats stealthily into the shadows.

It was *Anthea*, I realise. *She* was the last one to see Anna alive.

Dodging the oncoming cars I sprint across the street. Anthea has the door open before I can even knock.

'Come in, come in,' she greets keenly, her voice bright and inviting. She's freshly showered, in a white shirt, and made-up. Her blonde hair is bouncing and a peach-tinged waft trails in her wake as she leads me inside. 'Welcome, *finally*, to our humble home.' We walk further into the house as she sashays past a giant, spotless dining table with a gleaming bowl of fruit in its centre.

The house is the polar opposite of Ian's. Everything original is gone. In its place I note a mix of expensive upgrades. Pristine cream leather sofas, white plastered walls, buffed chrome coffee tables with smoked polished glass, two cinema-sized, pancake-thin television screens on the walls. The artwork is a collection of generic framed prints, and there's a scattering of family portraits hung at odd angles which were clearly done in a studio. But there's no warmth in any of the faces. Anthea, her husband and three sprouting sons look like mannequins more than a living family.

Anthea is twirling around pointing at different things and, I sense, waiting for my awe to find some words. When no words are forthcoming she stops and stares at me. Puzzled lines criss-cross her brow as she asks, 'Is everything alright, Cathy?'

I remain still, my legs planted firmly on the floor, my arms folded across my chest. 'You were the last one to see Anna Cunningham alive, Anthea. Why didn't you tell the police?'

For a moment she freezes, open-mouthed and staring, like I've gone completely mad. Next she's tutting and walking away to the light switch on the wall. 'Oh Cathy,' she sighs, dimming down the harsh glare from the rack of gaudy lights above us. 'What on earth gave you that idea?'

I study her as she glides to the opposite side of the dining table and grips the top of a chair in her hands. 'It's pointless lying, Anthea. I've got footage of you getting into the car with Anna on the last night she went out to Mandy's nightclub. And JJ has it too.'

There's a tiny twitch in the corner of her painted red mouth as she glances towards the kitchen. 'I have a couple of minutes before I have to turn off the oven so perhaps we should sit,' she replies gently, easing herself into the chair. I take my seat opposite her on the other end of the long table. 'How did you find it?' Crestfallen, she drops her elbows down, slumps forward, holding her face with her hands.

'I looked, Anthea, because just like you, I never believed Ian was guilty of murdering his wife as the police thought.' She nods as if in pain. 'But unlike you I wasn't the last one to disappear with her on the night she vanished into thin air.'

The sinews in her throat pull taut as her gaze moves to the ceiling and I notice her tears glistening. 'I couldn't say anything, Cathy. Anna didn't want me to.'

'Why?'

'Because she was *disappearing*.' She gives me an anguished look as she lays her hands out on the table and studies her collection of rings. 'She told me everything that evening. I even arranged it that Carol would spike Ian's drink so he would lose all memory of the night. The poor guy couldn't even remember if he had come to the club with us or not.'

Blood pounds in my temples. I'm floored by what I hear. I had never properly considered the possibility that Anna could arrange her own disappearance. But of course, it happens. 'Why? Why did she want to disappear, Anthea?'

She makes a fist, gnawing her knuckles. A tear tracks her cheek and she wipes it away. 'Anna was afraid. You've seen how Ian is? She knew he had found out about Justin.'

The mention of Justin pricks me. 'Yes, Justin. My boyfriend, who you shared.'

She shakes her head. 'I'm so sorry, Cathy. For Anna it was all a game. And she was so strong and independent. She had this power over all of us. To get us to do things we wouldn't even dream of ...' Her voice breaks off.

'Like Justin?'

Anthea groans, her face stricken. 'Yes.'

'So what did you *do* exactly?'

When she looks up at me she is frowning. 'Oh, it was nothing. Just stupid mucking about. I really don't know what came over me. I'm ashamed even talking about it now. How could I have even dreamt of being so foolish?' She glances down at the table sadly. 'You'd have to have known Anna to understand the effect she could have on people.' Her downtrodden eyes cast over to me, pleading. 'I never meant for any of it to happen, Cathy. I really hope you can believe me.'

'Where did Anna go, Anthea?'

The frown lines on her brow deepen, like each word is causing her fresh torture. 'Oh, God, Cathy. That was the thing. Anna was far too clever to confide in any of us. She knew we were too gossipy. She merely told me when she was leaving my house that it was the last I would see of her. That any of us would see of her.'

'She was here? This was where you went to in the car?'

She shifts, straightening a little in her seat. 'Yes, for a final farewell drink. Anna said that was what she wanted.' Another tear falls to the table. 'You see,' she swallows noisily before continuing, 'she told me she knew the police would suspect Ian was involved and wanted him to get the blame.'

My mouth hangs. 'Why?'

With both hands she clasps either side of her face, staring wildly at me. For a second all I can see is a terrified, wounded animal. I worry she's clamping up, but then she speaks, her voice strained and high as she chokes back more tears. 'Because their love had turned to hatred and Anna wanted revenge. She even told me about a room in their house, in the basement, where one of their lodgers had cut himself. She said it was covered in blood and that she would plant her own blood down there too and make it look like the perfect crime scene. It was …' she stops and gulps. 'It was *savagely* cruel.' There's a pinging noise inside the kitchen. The chair screeches on the floor as she stands. 'Sorry, Cathy, my timer for the oven.' She gestures apologetically. 'Let me run and switch it off and I'll fetch us both some drinks.'

I watch as she hurries past me, and I grapple with this new information. Anna disappeared. Anna framed Ian. Anthea collaborated. Was this the reason all along that she was so worried about looking after Ian? That she found the neighbourhood witch-hunt so offensive? Because she herself helped frame Ian for a murder that never happened? I grit my teeth, stunned at the cruelty, yet understanding how it could happen too. Seconds later Anthea reappears.

'I'm so sorry, Cathy,' she says, sniffling. In both hands she holds fluted glasses of what looks like sparkling wine. She offers me one and I take it. 'Champagne, a fifty-year-old bottle Harry was given by one of his clients, but Harry doesn't drink.' She raises a quivering smile. 'I had wanted it to be a surprise since I had been waiting so long for you to drop over.' I look at the glass and she shrugs. 'I guess I didn't really see the night going like this.' She doesn't toast but sheepishly raises her own to her lips and sips. I've never witnessed Anthea so sad. My head hurts. I don't know how I can apologise; I never meant to distress her but I'm angry with her and she isn't blameless. I'm about to speak when her doorbell rings and we both jolt, swapping a look of surprise.

'Are you expecting someone?' I ask, placing my untouched glass on the table.

Anthea glances at the front door. 'Give me two seconds, Cathy.' She slips away, returning almost instantly. 'It's Carol. I could see her through the keyhole.' Her voice is a whisper. 'I'll make some excuses so she doesn't stay but maybe hide in the kitchen or something for a minute. If she sees you it mightn't be so smooth.'

I nod, watch her hurry back out and pick up my wine glass, but notice its colour under the light. It looks different to the perfect gold of Anthea's glass, darker somehow. I smell it but there's nothing off.

I keep twisting it in my fingers, agitated by a growing paranoia. Quickly I switch the glasses around, taking Anthea's instead. There's a modern floor-to-ceiling glass sliding door all along the back room wall which leads out to a raised deck facing the garden. I heave it open with a grunt and hurry out, sliding it back into place. Then I run lightly across the deck and down into the darkness where I'm hopeful I can't be seen.

Like at Ian's house, the garden layout is wide and deep. I walk past a neat lawn until I come to a break. On the either side are big trellis frames covered in creepers partitioning the space. I walk through the gap to where there is a small patio with a table and then another expanse of grass. I empty the champagne onto the grass and place the glass back on the table.

Walking further down into the garden, my mind reels with what Anthea has revealed. To think that she had concealed this information all this time! That she had hidden it from the police! And yet I understand she had no choice if she was helping Anna disappear. She was helping a friend by doing what she was asked. If somebody was really at fault, wasn't it Anna? Hasn't everybody said how special Anna was? How she could sway people to doing whatever she demanded? Ian even told me the same himself.

The Landlord

The trees down at the end of the garden whistle and twist with the gentle breeze and my chest constricts. The noise reminds me of that night in the lane, when I chased Keith and found I had put myself in grave danger. Something isn't right that I can't explain. I think of Justin. How did Anthea manage to keep her relationship with him secret for so long? Did she know he was my ex-boyfriend? She could have. And is it true that Anna disappeared without a trace with the deliberate wish of framing Ian? It seems too cruel, even though I know it happens all the time.

I keep moving. Despite the darkness I can see the garden is perfectly laid out and tidy. It's cared for and organised, except for a paved segment off to one side which looks strangely uneven. I move across to it, shining the feeble light from my phone torch at it. The battery light flickers and I curse, realising I've left the power bank in the taxi. I glance back up at the house, but seeing no sign of Anthea or Carol, I drop down to my knees to inspect it closer.

There's a corner of black plastic sticking out a few feet away near the edge of the small rectangle of lumpy paving bricks where it rises up between the slabs. I get hold of it, tugging it gently, but it doesn't give. Then, not making a sound, I grip it tighter, pulling until some soil comes out and the paving slabs buckle and lift away.

It's clear the paving is badly laid and unlikely to be a professional job, certainly not the kind of landscaper that Anthea would hire. I keep tugging at it, sensing now that it's not a small piece of rubbish as I had thought, but something larger and deeper beneath the ground.

I grunt with the effort, gritting my teeth as I check over my shoulder. But still there's no sign of Anthea or Carol. My heart is already racing. *What is this?* Looking around I notice a shovel against the wall nearby so I get to my feet, rush across and grab it. Without wasting a second, I run back and start digging.

I jab the spade into the soil, kicking its edge so hard it hurts my foot and I cry out. But I don't stop, knowing Anthea could appear any second. I shove the spade in deep, bend my back and lift the bricks and soil clear.

Frantically I keep working, stabbing, lifting, tossing, as the soil and bricks tumble away. Sweat bubbles on my forehead, wets my scalp and slides down my back as my arms labour with each swing and thrust of the shovel. I soon see there's a roll of plastic.

Why would there be a roll of plastic barely contained beneath the soil in Anthea's house. Unless ... unless?

I wheeze, my muscles straining for more oxygen. The loose soil is coming away freely, effortlessly now.

'*Come on, Cathy.*' Lungs heaving, I pant, certain that any moment Anthea must come looking for me. I have to get to the bottom. I have to find what really is buried here.

Once more I stab the spade into the soil, grunting as it wedges it deeper, when it unexpectedly stops. I tap the handle, feeling the tip push into something soft.

My stomach lurches but I won't give up. I throw the spade aside, drop to my knees and scrabble with my hands. The soil is sweeping away almost like sand. The end of a rolled tube of faded white plastic eventually appears; and sticking out of it is a mud caked boot.

Next I see the leg. A human leg, wrapped in decomposed black leather.

It's a body. *It's got to be the body of Anna Cunningham.*

The convulsion in my stomach is so sharp I almost fall over. I choke down the rush of food that rises. Scrabbling to my feet I mop my brow and it leaves a muddy smear. I can no longer see properly because of the tears which have started to stream.

'Anna ...?' I whisper. When I draw away the garden spins around me. She's been murdered by Anthea and buried in a shallow grave all this time. Right across the road from Ian. So close, and yet all this time perfectly concealed. 'No.'

I gulp but the air doesn't seem to reach my lungs.

Turning round I look up at the house.

The cold steel hits me so hard in the face it clangs in my ears.

57

There's blood everywhere. Spouting out of my nose, streaming down my forehead, getting into my eyes. I'm gasping and trying to get my balance when the second blow of the shovel lands. This time it's not the sharp steel but the wooden butt of the handle. There's a loud crack as it connects with my jaw.

I stagger backwards, winded, a searing ripple of pain slicing through me.

Behind me somebody grunts and when I turn towards it, my neck distended as I struggle to balance, Anthea is swinging the shovel again. It thumps me in the stomach, doubling me over. My body collapses to the earth, my eyes rolling to the back of my head, already closing.

I'm not sure how much time passes before I revive. When I awake the first thing I hear is the sound of Anthea breathing. She leans on the shovel, peering down at me. There are flecks of blood around her mouth and chin and more on her white shirt.

'You're still with us?' Her lips twist with a sinister grin. 'My, you *are* tough, Cathy.' I try to move but my body doesn't respond. The message isn't transferring from my brain to my limbs. I fear it's shutting down as some kind of survival mechanism. She hunches down, placing her shovel aside. 'But *I* knew that the first day I met you. I said, Anthea, *that* girl's a survivor. It's such a pity Anna isn't with us to see this. She would have liked you a lot, Cathy.'

I move my mouth to speak but blood oozes inside it. I choke for a second before spitting it out. There is a throbbing along the length of my jaw and my tongue feels heavy and thick. Anthea reaches her hand to my face. I flinch when she sweeps the hair from my forehead. 'There, now, that's better,' she says.

When she lifts her fingers away I see they're covered in blood. 'Anthea ...' I whisper, the word lisping from my mouth.

She leans close, twisting to bring her ear closer to my lips. 'I'm sorry, I can't hear you, Cathy. Save your energy. You can't have long left.'

I turn away from her, waiting for the blood to drain from my mouth. Wincing, I speak again. 'What are you doing Anthea?'

'Nothing,' she says, sitting back up. She sounds surprised I've asked. 'The poison you drank should be doing everything.' Calmly she curls a blonde lock behind her ear. 'I saw you finished it all so that's good because it will speed things up. I'm amazed you're still here given how fast-acting it's supposed to be.'

My stomach knots. She *had* tried to poison me. A glimmer of hope pulses through me but I don't let it show. Anthea must not see it. I haven't drunk the poison. She doesn't know I swapped my glass with her.

'Don't worry, Cathy, I never gave you the champagne. That was a cheap sparkling wine from Tesco. The fifty-year champagne was what I was having, because I really wanted to celebrate wrapping up loose ends.'

Blood drips from my nose as I exhale. If Anthea has drunk her glass she may not last long. My jaw clenches as I try to move my toes ever so slightly and my heart lifts when they respond. 'But the basement?' I whisper. 'Anna's blood? How?'

'Ah,' she laughs, her eyes full of a manic energy I don't recognise. 'So you want to know everything before it's over.' She reaches out and for a moment I fear she's going to cover my mouth, but she takes hold of a knotted clump of hair and tidies it back from my forehead. 'I might as well indulge you, Cathy. Yes, you're right. It's the details that matter.'

Stock-still I blink as she grows animated. 'Of course I knew you were in the basement and had found the room. You were so eager, desperate really to understand Anna's mystery. That was a nice touch, wasn't it? You see, by complete fluke, Anna discovered, the night that bunch of thugs got high, that Kevin, who almost managed to slice his own foot off, had the same blood type that she had, because it was Anna who drove him to A & E. When she learned he was AB she was worried because he had a lost a lot of blood and it's the rarest type, so she volunteered to donate, since hers was AB too.'

'The blood on the wall wasn't Anna's?'

'No, but ...' she breaks off, as if momentarily lost in thought, 'that was the thing with Anna, you see. It was what I loved so much about her but what enraged me too. She was so amazing. So kind and surprising. And such a cruel and heartless bitch. All at the same time.' Her face darkens.

'I don't understand.'

'No. How could you?' She turns on me, her voice heavy with accusation. 'Because you never saw how she treated Ian. How she could look at me like I was a piece of dirt on her shoe and the next minute laugh with me and make me feel like the smartest, prettiest girl in the room.'

'But you were friends?'

Her mouth turns down. 'Yes, good friends, because I wanted to be most like *her*. But I never could, Cathy, because I never had what Anna had.' She looks away, her head shaking side to side. 'Because she had it all you see. Oh, I had done alright. Married a provider, got the nice house. But I didn't matter, Cathy. I didn't rule in any boardrooms. I never could bring people to heel like Anna. And, I never had Ian.'

'Ian?'

Her pretty face suffuses with sadness. She takes a second as if pushing down a burst of pain. What is it? Grief? Sorrow? Or is the poison working?

'Yes, Ian, Cathy.' She chokes down a sob. 'I saw the way you longed for him from the moment you met him. Well, you weren't alone. But I *loved* him, Cathy.' She picks up a piece of clay and flings it at the wall and I watch the muscle in her jaw tense. 'Ian is what a man should be.' She glares down at me. 'Oh I had Harry, yes. Sensible, useful Harry. And our arrangement worked. I bred while dull Harry stocked our accounts. But that's not what I wanted, Cathy. I wanted passion and I knew Ian could give it. I knew I could be kind to him, could look after him and allow for the wildness which made him so impossibly beautiful. I didn't care if he shouted and got drunk and blew the roof off the house. I *wanted* that. And I would never treat him with the disdain that Anna did, belittling his talents, throwing herself around, forcing him to find solace at the end of a bottle.'

I turn to glance at Anna's dug-up grave. 'So why this?'

We both stare at Anna's broken leg. A putrid smell of decomposed flesh rises and I grit my teeth, clawing the soil with my nails.

'It wasn't meant to be, Cathy,' she seethes. 'I told her she could just disappear. Take Jamie and start afresh. She didn't have to carry on destroying Ian. They could be free of each other and happy. I was Ian's chance of happiness and Anna knew it.'

'What did she say?'

'She laughed. Harsh, cruel laughter, the kind that only Anna could do so well. She said I was a deluded fool to think I ever had a chance with Ian. That I was lucky I even managed to find Harry.' Her teeth grind together making the muscle in her jaw quiver. 'She said she'd drive over my dead body sooner than disappear with Jamie.' She starts to twitch suddenly. Little spasms around her mouth, the muscles misfiring. Then her head jerks back and I stare on as her whole body goes stiff. She raises her arms in the air and I think she might be having a fit but then she smashes them down to the ground inches from my face. 'So I *struck* her, Cathy.' She glowers at me wild-eyed. 'Struck that vicious, horrible bitch with everything I had.' Her arms wrap around her body and she rocks back and forth, mouth hanging open like a wound, bitter tears staining her cheeks. Then her voice drops to a whisper. 'And the spade went clean through her skull.'

After a moment she stills. I exhale as she stares vacantly into empty space. I think she might have passed out when a sharp ring breaks the silence. Anthea wakes from her trance, snatching the phone from her pocket, answering before stopping to think. But the phone slips from her grasp, landing close to me.

'Anthea?' Ian's voice calls out.

Her horrified gaze meets mine.

'*Ian*,' I scream, heaving on to my side. I need to get to my feet, to run, but my body won't move properly. I'm still too weak.

When I look up Anthea has the spade held high once more.

58

I lunge for the phone. The spade crashes down, missing my skull, but clattering hard on my back. I scrunch my eyes and cry out but don't hear any sound. My body spasms, shooting sparks of pain in every direction.

'Cathy?' Ian calls, his voice alarmed. I reach out but Anthea's foot lands hard on my wrist. I grunt, tugging at her ankle with my free hand but she stamps it down harder as she sweeps up the phone. When she releases my wrist I clutch it to my chest and try to sit but she kicks me forcefully in the ribs. There's a loud thump and I bite down hard.

'Ian?' Anthea replies with a strained voice.

'Anthea? I thought I heard Cathy, what's going on? Is she with you?'

'Oh?' She mops the sweat from her forehead. I think about the poison, trying to understand how it cannot have affected her yet. 'No.'

'Well where are you?'

'At the house.' She affects a light tone, rubbing the dirt off her knees, watching me like a hawk. I lie where I am, holding my side. 'Why?'

'I'm here at the front door and it's open so I wasn't sure if you had just popped out. I'm actually walking inside right now.'

'I didn't know it was open …' I watch the fear catch like fire in her eyes, '… well OK.' She tugs at her clothes, frantically rubbing them down. 'There's champagne in the kitchen, grab yourself a glass.'

'Where are you?' He sounds suspicious.

'Coming. I'm just at the end of the garden.' Her eyes bore into me, her agitation making her almost unrecognisable. 'I'm on my way right now.'

With a snort she stomps away, kicking out at Anna's leg. There's a snapping sound and it falls. She stops then, clutching her stomach. I try to sit up. Has the poison finally kicked in? Could she finally be fading right in front of me? I cling to the fledgling hope.

Anthea spins, tensing when she sees me push myself into a sitting position. In a hurry she runs to pick up the spade and I see the crazed look on her face in the darkness. I fumble awkwardly, trying to get to my feet but failing to get my balance. Then I hear the sound of the sliding door opening on to the deck.

With a muffled curse Anthea flings the spade down and hurries towards him but Ian is already outside. In one hand he holds a glass of champagne and in the other the bottle. He places the bottle on the outside table and drinks his glass thirstily.

'Where's your glass, Anthea?' he calls over.

'In the kitchen,' she replies, moving towards him warily.

'Right.' I'm about to scream when Ian runs inside. 'Back in a second.' Anthea stops, turning to check I haven't moved. When she sees I'm still sitting she stays where she is but Ian reappears almost immediately. 'Sorry,' he says topping up her glass from the bottle, 'I took the one you left on the dining table, so this one's for you.' He extends the glass towards her but Anthea stalls.

The glass on the dining table was the one Anthea set aside for me!

'Ian!' I scream but my voice only rasps his name. I watch hopelessly as he drinks down the remainder of his glass. Ian has taken the poison, *not Anthea*.

I see him wince and stare at the empty glass but instantly his attention switches to Anthea. 'What on earth happened to you?' Anthea doesn't reply. 'Anthea! What have you done?' he demands.

'Ian,' I roar, my voice finally returning.

'Cathy?' His gaze darts from Anthea out to the garden beyond her. 'Cathy's here, isn't she? And you're covered in blood. Oh Christ, Anthea?'

'Don't, Ian,' she begs.

Ian ignores her, dashing down from the deck, running towards me. He's gaining speed when suddenly he stops, dropping to his knees and grabbing his stomach.

Anthea runs to him. 'Ian? Ian, are you OK?' Her voice sounds high and shrill.

He lumbers to his feet, tries to walk, but stumbles.

'I'm here, Ian,' I call, my legs still not able to move.

'Cathy?' With a grunt he heaves himself back to his feet and keeps going. But now he can only stagger off balance.

Anthea tries to put her arms around him. 'Ian, you're sick. I need to help you. I have to get you to a hospital immediately.' He pushes past her.

'It's poison,' I scream, 'she meant it for me, Ian.'

'Poison?' He looks back at Anthea who stands there motionless. Then he turns, noticing Anna's broken leg lying on the ground yards from where he stands. 'Oh Jesus, *no*.' He falls to his knees, reaching out to touch the decayed remains of Anna's boot. 'It was *you*, Anthea?' He lifts a handful of soil and drops it through his fingers. 'You *murdered* Anna? Why?'

Anthea unfreezes and claws at her hair in a wild frantic movement. 'I love you, Ian. I always loved you. Anna didn't care about you. She wanted to destroy you. To make your life a living nightmare.'

Ian lies down next to Anna's grave, a choking noise coming from his throat. 'Anna, forgive me,' he pleads. His voice drops down into a guttural howl. Then his head yanks back and his body begins to convulse.

Anthea screams, running to him. Blood streams from his open mouth. 'Ian, listen to me,' she pleads, 'I have to get you to hospital, please. You're dying.' He holds up his hand, as if warning her to stay back, writhing as his body fights the poison. 'It was all figured out,' she whispers, manic now. 'Everything had been forgotten and moved on. But then,' she wheels around to point a finger at me, '*she* had to come along. To dig it all up. To unearth the nightmare we had all buried.'

'No, Anthea, Cathy wanted the truth. And you're …' His voice fades away for a moment, but eventually returns. '… You're a cold-blooded murderer.'

Anthea clenches her teeth, then runs to pick up the spade.

'You,' she rages, the whites of her eyes flaring as she points accusingly at me. '*You* made this happen, Cathy. Because you couldn't leave it alone. I tried to put you off, God knows how many times, I tried.' She brushes away the unwanted tears. 'Well, Cathy Quinn, now I'm making you *pay*.'

59

'Don't, Anthea.' The words come out in a scream. But she's long past hearing what I say. The skin stretches in a cruel grimace across her cheeks. Now her bloodied face is set like stone, the spade swinging high.

Then she breaks into a run.

I heave myself up but only manage to get into a sitting position with my arm held out like a human shield. I know it's useless against the weight and power of the spade, a last hopeless plea to Anthea rather than any form of defence. But it's all in vain. Anthea isn't stopping. She's finishing it this time and I watch her body coil like a snake about to pounce, when suddenly Ian scrambles to his feet and tackles her to the ground.

Anthea drops the shovel, winded by the force of the blow. She's rolling back and forth on the ground, groaning noisily, and I think the strength has finally gone from her but I'm wrong. She recovers and reaches for the spade. This time Ian throws himself on top of her to pin her down. I'm sure she's finished, yet next she lets out a guttural shriek, writhing free from his grip and scrabbling on top of him.

Helpless, I can only watch as she holds the spade crossways above his neck, spittle foaming at the corner of her mouth as she flattens it down. Ian's legs kick as she crushes his throat, severing the supply of oxygen to his brain.

'Anthea,' I beg, dragging myself up, 'don't.'

Somehow Ian gets his hands underneath the shovel to push it back but his strength is fading.

'Stop it, Ian,' Anthea whimpers. 'She's the only thing that's come between us. And she knows too much now. This is the only way.'

The Landlord

Ian grunts as the spade presses deeper into his neck. I try and get to my feet but still my legs won't respond.

Then I hear a voice.

'Cathy? It's JJ.' And it's coming from my phone. It's trapped under my hip but I can still hear him clearly. 'I'm outside your house. Is everything OK? Where are you?'

'Anthea's garden,' I yell. 'Call the police.'

The phone beeps as the battery gives up and JJ disappears like he was never there. But the sound of his voice has distracted Anthea. Ian seizes the opportunity to give a final push and turns her over.

In a second the situation has changed. Now Ian holds the spade across her neck, sweat dripping from him as he speaks. 'You murdered my wife, Anthea.' A tear rolls from his eye, dropping onto Anthea's cheek as he presses harder.

'Ian,' I scream. 'Let her *go*.' But he doesn't flinch. Instead he keeps pressing, harder now. In a daze I drag myself across to them.

'You destroyed my family,' he says, his face so close to Anthea's they are almost touching, 'killed every good thing.'

I shove him but there's no strength in my arms and he doesn't move. 'Stop Ian,' I plead.

Anthea chokes, her feet smacking frantically against the earth, the fight in her snuffing out. Her breathing rattles as the oxygen to her brain fades.

'For *you*,' she gasps, terrified. 'It was all for *you*, Ian.'

Her tears fall as she stops wriggling and goes limp. Ian's body sags and he falls off her to the ground. He touches Anthea's hair but she remains still.

I take his hand and he grips it like a drowning man. 'Hang on, Ian. Please.'

Suddenly he reaches out and pulls me towards him. 'Thank you, Cathy,' he whispers, his eyes startled and bloodshot, 'you never gave up.'

I wrap my arms around him, my heart splintering. 'I still haven't, Ian. I'm getting you help now.'

He nods but his body spasms. Then his brow furrows and his focus switches to something behind me.

I turn to see Anthea rising to her feet. With a new strength I can't explain she marches across, grabs the spade and strides back to where I lie next to Ian. 'Goodbye, Cathy,' she says, hoisting the spade high above her head. I need to react but I'm closing down, frozen and unable to move, my only chance to save myself evaporating. I shut my eyes and wait for the final stab of pain, for the sharp edge of Anthea's spade to slice through my skull, just as it did to Anna.

Yet it doesn't happen. Instead I hear a deafening crack and when my eyes open I see only Ian. He has jumped between us and the spade has caught him hard across the face.

His legs buckle sending him crashing to the ground with a thud.

60

Blood. It bubbles from his nose. Thick, dark and steaming in the night air. I want to scream. To hide. But I can't take my eyes from his face. Now the blood spouts from his ear, a long arc splashing across the grass.

Christ. How did it come to this?

I look at the shovel. It's red and dripping. This was not how it was supposed to end. But it isn't over. Before night turns to day there will be more blood.

Lots more blood.

I see the shovel in Anthea's hand, red and dripping. I feel my heart imploding as the terror in her eyes detonates in a violent scream. She clutches at Ian's head, trying to stop the spray of blood but it isn't working. Ian's blood hoses onto her clothes as the life disappears from his body.

I lunge for the shovel but Anthea punches me hard and I feel a sting of pain as the rock from her ring finger pierces my cheek. With a grunt she yanks me by the hair and drags me past Ian across to the patch of grass in front of Anna's corpse. I claw at her, digging my nails into her wrist, but Anthea's strength is too much. Snarling, she flings me to the earth like a doll and grunts.

A second later she kneels down and grabs my neck so hard that her fingernails break the skin. Pulling me towards her, she shoves her anguished face up to mine. 'You've lived too long, Cathy,' she whispers, 'it's time to die.' Releasing me from her grasp she hauls herself back to a standing position.

She lifts the spade, her fingers flexing as she adjusts her grip along the shaft. I look into her eyes, praying that I might see some recognition, some connection that will allow her to pause but she stares straight through me. I am something dead to her already. Something that must be buried.

Sweat drips down my face. I cough out blood, clenching my teeth, bracing for the final blow when there's a noise.

'*Stop*, Anthea.' It's JJ's voice. He roars the words from where he stands on the garden deck.

Anthea doesn't flinch. She doesn't even turn to look at him. The edges of her mouth twist and she whips the spade up and away from her body in a clean arc. Her eyes shimmer and I hear a venomous roar as she swings the spade over her back and coils. Then she moves to strike.

But the boomerang blade is already crunching through her shoulder, splitting her flesh and tearing a hole through her body.

There's a shrill cry. The shovel drops from her hands and she collapses to her knees. Blood pours from her mouth as she stares listlessly into space.

I rush to help her but the light is already fading as my vision blurs.

The last thing I see is JJ's kind eyes peering down at me. 'Stay still, Cathy,' he says, 'the police are coming.' Then everything goes dark.

61

Ian was dead by the time the paramedics arrived. They told me I was lucky to survive Anthea's frenzied attack. The report listed two broken ribs, a fractured jaw, a chipped cheekbone, and eleven stitches at the top of my scalp where the spade had lacerated my skin.

Anthea wasn't so lucky. JJ's boomerang didn't break any bones but she bit down on her tongue so hard when it went through her shoulder blade that it almost severed. JJ had to rush to her aid immediately, which prevented her from suffocating, but she still suffered a minor stroke due to lack of oxygen to the brain. After a long spell in intensive care she recovered without any brain damage but her coordination didn't return properly and her speech is permanently affected.

The police interviewed me on the second day of my stay in hospital. I told them everything I knew and JJ helped, backing me up on all the details I had shared with him. Babs and Heather also came forward to corroborate any pieces of the story that they could.

Ian's old lodger Keith disappeared without a trace. The police neither confirmed nor denied that he was working on their behalf and just said they would follow it up internally.

Carol was brought in for questioning in relation to her drugging of Ian and obstructing justice by withholding evidence. Because the police didn't have proof they didn't press any charges but it didn't matter. Shortly afterwards her dog was run over and she got involved in a road-rage incident with a random stranger. She attacked the man's jeep in broad daylight with a golf club and then attacked the driver who suffered a burst eardrum. The same day she was arrested and charged with GBH.

Justin was arrested and charged with obstructing justice. His mother pleaded with me to whitewash him out of the story and I agreed to downplay his threats against me but it turned out to be a lost cause. He got sentenced for misdirecting the original police inquiry and also for drugs which they found in his mother's mews house. They're giving him four years in Mountjoy.

After three months of recuperation, Anthea was deemed fit to proceed with the police prosecution. Her good friend Gerald stepped in to represent her, after her husband Harry got a barring order against her. Gerald also agreed to defend Carol for her GBH charge.

Ian was cremated in a very private ceremony organised by his son Jamie and attended by a select bunch of his friends and family, myself included. Afterwards Jamie invited me for lunch.

The inside of Flaubert's Michelin-starred restaurant is a little different to what I had expected. The furnishings are softer, the ambience more relaxed, the staff younger and less affected. But the food is everything I hoped it would be.

'You know how Dad liked his food,' Jamie says, a kind smile banishing his sadness for a moment. 'I thought it would only make sense if we did a farewell lunch to him in the kind of style he would have approved of.' The pretty Croatian waitress called Magda sweeps across to our table, lifts the fifty-year-old white wine bottle from its cooler, and sees it's finished.

'Another?' she asks politely.

I indicate I'm good with a gesture and Jamie thanks her but declines. She leaves us and takes the empty bottle with her, bowing gracefully.

'Think Ian might have liked the wine too,' I reply, fondly remembering the evenings I spent with him enjoying a little too much of his carefully selected favourites. This makes Jamie smile and he raises the remainder of his glass for a toast. 'To your dad,' I say and we clink gently. 'To Ian's generosity and all the good memories he left us.'

The Landlord

'To Dad,' Jamie echoes. I hold his sad gaze, trying not to let the pain of knowing Ian's gone overwhelm me. I want to be OK for Jamie, to let him know that I'm always there for him, whenever he needs me. We both sip and when the last of it goes down my throat I see how Ian's discerning taste has transferred with perfect faithfulness to his son. My glance shifts to our empty dessert plates. It's been the perfect meal and I almost don't want it to end, but I know JJ is waiting for me and I can't be late.

'So will you at least consider the offer?' Jamie pleads, circling back to what we discussed earlier. 'I know it's a lot to digest but it would really mean so much to me if you agreed Cathy. It's what I want, and I'm certain Mum and Dad would have approved.'

I twist the stem of the glass and give him my most appreciative smile. I don't want to disappoint Jamie, not today of all days, but just like Ian, his generosity knows no bounds and I'm a little thrown.

'I've spoken with Dad's solicitor and his estate, coupled with Mum's, is too vast already, Cathy, trust me. I don't need our old house anymore but it holds too many memories for me to pass it to a stranger. Knowing it was yours would make me sleep much better at night.'

I lean closer to him. 'Jamie, you know I'm going away for a spell so what I'd like to propose is that you keep thinking about it. When I'm back in six months' time, if you still think this is for the best, then I'll be happy to consider it. I don't want you making any hasty decisions. It's an emotional time for all of us. Your happiness is what matters now.'

Jamie rises from his seat, steps across and hugs me in a warm embrace. 'That makes me happy Cathy,' he says, letting me go. Then gently he places his hands on my shoulders. 'In six months' time then.'

JJ took care of me every day in hospital and helped nurse me back to health. When I got out he insisted I come stay with him in his small loft apartment. He made no assumptions that we would be together and only wanted to help. But it didn't matter. Ian was gone. I had successfully cleared his name, and though I was devastated that I couldn't save him, I knew I had to let it go. To move forward it was important I accept that he was gone. Then I could be a valuable support to Jamie who was going to need me.

I didn't shy away from my growing feelings for JJ. He was a comfort to me in this darkest time, just as he had been in the weeks before Ian's death, and without any effort or awkwardness, the most natural love grew between us.

I helped him in the café for a month until his friend returned to take it back and we handed it over. It was bliss to be busy with stuff to do so I didn't have time to get caught up inside my own head, and working with JJ was like a dream. The more I got to see him, the more I learned to appreciate the beautiful soul that he is.

I followed my old Shakespeare production to see how it fared with the critics. Unsurprisingly it took a mauling in the press. Andy was panned as 'imaginatively lacking', Old John was sledgehammered as 'hammy and out of date'. Only Malia was rightfully celebrated as 'the one joyous spark of light in this thoroughly pointless production'. It didn't run long and when it closed, Malia's article appeared in the papers and online, whipping up a storm of protest and outrage on her behalf. Within a fortnight both Andy and Old John were dragged before a misconduct enquiry by Actors' Equity and suspended from the union indefinitely. An outpouring of sympathy for Malia flowed, with many posting online of similar experiences, and she was stunned yet happy to find herself an unexpected figurehead for many in the same boat.

Within a month of me terminating my contract with Melissa, five of her most prominent clients deserted and moved to other agencies. One of them posted online about breaches of trust, unfair treatment and also mishandling of payments. At first Melissa came out denying all allegations, until two more clients posted the same and she came clean. One week later her agency went into liquidation.

The Landlord

The last I heard she had quit town, declared bankruptcy, and gone to live in rural Wales. I had no bad feelings towards her. It just sounded sad.

I expected my own career would go on hold for a while. After Ian's death I merely wanted to recover from the trauma of that terrible night in Anthea's house. But in a surprise move, one of the agents from the workshop that Malia had gifted me made contact out of the blue. Two weeks later, LA-based Mia Goldberg from International Artists signed me up, helping me land the lead part in a major TV series.

Shooting starts in nine months' time.

It's nine in the morning. In exactly twenty minutes' time the plane is leaving for Sydney in Australia. JJ's convinced me to come and live with him there for a while. Just till the series in LA goes into production. His intellectual property for his design work finally came good and his company has taken off. I know from reading about it in the papers that he's done extraordinarily well but when I ask him about it he just tells me modestly in his perfect Aussie drawl, 'Aw, you know, Cathy. We did alright.'

With the checks all out of the way, and the baggage stored in the overhead lockers, the plane takes off and soon begins to inch above the clouds. It's a nice feeling to be up in the sky, floating away to somewhere new, and it makes me think about my friends Babs and Heather. I can't wait till they come and visit us next month. I pick up the in-flight magazine. I'm about to browse through it when I notice the model on the front reminds of someone and I put it back hastily. He's a lookalike of my old ex-boyfriend, Justin.

Next thing I'm remembering the conversation I had with him way back before he dumped me out of the flat.

'What are you thinking about?' JJ asks, his blue eyes fixing me like kind, shining stars.

'I'm just remembering when I was doing that personality course with the employment agency and it was bugging me something terrible when I was chatting to Justin about it.'

'Why?'

'Because the test told me that my strongest trait was my judgement of character.'

'So?' JJ throws me one of his surprised faces.

'Well there were all these times he mentioned when I'd got it so terribly wrong.'

JJ leans over, planting his lips on mine, giving me a familiar, caring kiss. Slowly he eases away and sighs. 'Think about it again, Cathy. Had you really got it wrong?'

I tap my chin, piecing it together slowly. Justin mentioned Kieran who I invited to my Debs and turned out to be gay. But I hadn't got it wrong because I really liked Kieran and always knew he was. It wasn't an issue for me and I didn't want to go picking some random guy that I'd have to end up snogging even when I didn't want to. Then he mentioned the guy in Italy who had pretended to get us discount ferry tickets but conned us. Only what Justin didn't know is that the guy never conned us, he just came back late with the tickets and I saw him waving them furiously at us from the quay as we sailed away. I never said anything because I knew Justin would get mad when he found out we had bought new tickets for no reason. Then, I remember the flatmate. She was a girl called Tanya who I invited to share a flat with myself and another friend, Kate. I knew she had a habit of stealing things but I wanted to try and help her because her mother had been recently admitted to hospital with a chronic kidney disease. It was only when she robbed Kate's wallet that I had to reluctantly agree to asking her to move on. She was actually a lovely person who was a bit traumatised, but I knew Justin would never have understood that, no matter which way I explained it to him.

Lastly, I think of Anthea, the one neighbour in Belleview Road who I actually believed was a nice person. Did I really think she was bad now? Not really. She fell prey to an obsession with a man who had so much to offer, and that obsession ultimately destroyed her, taking her to a place she never belonged, turning her into somebody she wasn't deep down. 'No,' I finally reply. 'I don't think I had.'

'Maybe it could have been something you had but didn't always pay attention to?'

I remember Justin and all the times I tried to overlook his faults. The lies, the deception. The cheating.

I nod. 'Yeah, I think maybe that's it.'

'All in the past now, anyhow. I can feel it.' JJ flashes a grin.

I drape my arm around his warm neck, drawing him closer and kissing him softly. 'Thanks, JJ. I guess in time we'll see.'

ACKNOWLEDGEMENTS

Huge thanks to my editor Cara Chimirri who has been so full of enthusiasm and excitement for this book from the get go. Thanks for all your willing help, pithy insights and astute guidance – all of which were invaluable in shaping this into the final story. It has been a pleasure and I'm looking forward to working on many more together. Thanks to Hodder UK and Ireland and the teams in London and Dublin for working hard on my behalf and to Jo Dickinson for her help and support. Well done to Cari Rosen for some eagle-eyed copy editing and more also.

Big thanks to my family, Pam, for all your belief and sacrifices, and for facilitating me with the time and space to stay creative. To the wonderful Zo for your infectious enthusiasm and whip smart suggestions, and the bright shining star Lar, for all your thoughts and opinions which help me so much. Thanks to my good friends (you know who you are!) for all the support and constant encouragement with my writing. It's great to have you, and support means a lot, so keep it coming! During sticky patches where sticking and clicking seems so impossibly elusive, it's a comfort to know you're there in the wings.

I'd also like to say a special thanks to the many amazing authors who I've been lucky enough to meet and get to know a little. They have been so unbelievably generous with their time, reading my work and volunteering assessments. So Chris Ewan, Liv Matthews, Andrea Mara, Kim Slater, Catherine Kirwan, Jane Corry, Tim Logan, Leah Pitt, Heather Critchlow, Edel Coffey, Callie Kazumi, Tim Weaver – please all take a bow because I believe you deserve it! I know how ridiculously busy schedules get in between writing and other professional and personal commitments so I take my hat off

Acknowledgements

to you all and would like to let you know how much I appreciate your kindness and encouragement.

My sincere thanks to Darley Anderson and the hard working team there who do so much on my behalf, especially my impossibly talented agent Camilla Bolton (may you be in my corner forever!), Jade, Georgia and all the rest of the team who help in every way behind the scenes.

And of course, may I never forget – to all you wonderful readers out there, enjoying a little down time to pick up one of my books. Please keep reading, and I'll keep writing.

Would you commit a crime to save your family?

Don't miss *One Perfect Stranger*, the completely gripping psychological thriller by R.B. Egan.

'I devoured it in one weekend'
Andrea Mara
'Brilliant... never lets up'
T.M. Logan
'I raced through al the unexpected twists and turns'
K.L. Slater

HODDER & STOUGHTON